DISSONANCE

B O O K   O N E

IMAGE COMICS, INC.

Robert Kirkman — Chief Operating Officer
Erik Larsen — Chief Financial Officer
Todd McFarlane — President
Marc Silvestri — Chief Executive Officer
Jim Valentino — Vice President
Eric Stephenson — Publisher / Chief Creative Officer
Corey Hart — Director of Sales
Jeff Boison — Director of Publishing Planning & Book Trade Sales
Chris Ross — Director of Digital Sales
Jeff Stang — Director of Specialty Sales
Kat Salazar — Director of PR & Marketing
Drew Gill — Art Director
Heather Doornink — Production Director
Nicole Lapalme — Controller

IMAGECOMICS.COM

For Top Cow Productions, Inc.
For Top Cow Productions, Inc.
Marc Silvestri - CEO
Matt Hawkins - President & COO
Elena Salcedo - Vice President of Operations
Henry Barajas - Director of Operations
Vincent Valentine - Production Manager
Dylan Gray - Marketing Director

To find the comic
shop nearest you, call:
1-888-COMICBOOK

Want more info? Check out:
www.topcow.com
for news & exclusive Top Cow merchandise!

DISSONANCE

——— BOOK ONE ———

CREATED BY
MELITA CURPHY

WRITER
SINGGIH NUGROHO

RYAN CADY

ARTIST
SAMI BASRI

COLORIST
SUNNY GHO

KANAYA GABRIEL

COVER ARTIST
VARSAM KURNIA

LETTERER
JAKA ADY

GRAPHICS
COMOLO

PRODUCER
SUNNY GHO

EDITOR
ELENA SALCEDO

CHAPTER 1

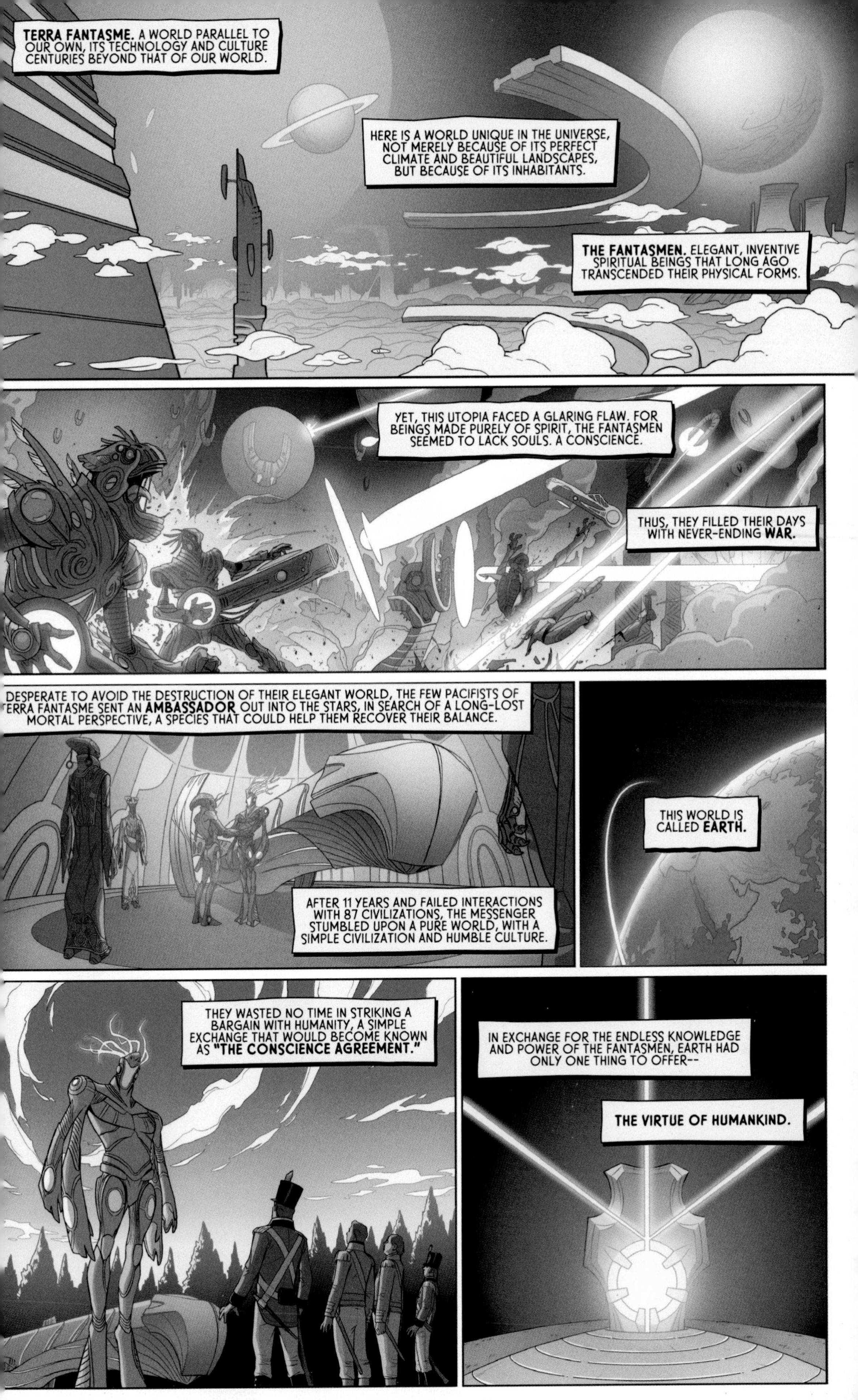
TERRA FANTASME. A WORLD PARALLEL TO OUR OWN, ITS TECHNOLOGY AND CULTURE CENTURIES BEYOND THAT OF OUR WORLD.
HERE IS A WORLD UNIQUE IN THE UNIVERSE, NOT MERELY BECAUSE OF ITS PERFECT CLIMATE AND BEAUTIFUL LANDSCAPES, BUT BECAUSE OF ITS INHABITANTS.
THE FANTASMEN. ELEGANT, INVENTIVE SPIRITUAL BEINGS THAT LONG AGO TRANSCENDED THEIR PHYSICAL FORMS.
YET, THIS UTOPIA FACED A GLARING FLAW. FOR BEINGS MADE PURELY OF SPIRIT, THE FANTASMEN SEEMED TO LACK SOULS. A CONSCIENCE.
THUS, THEY FILLED THEIR DAYS WITH NEVER-ENDING WAR.
DESPERATE TO AVOID THE DESTRUCTION OF THEIR ELEGANT WORLD, THE FEW PACIFISTS OF TERRA FANTASME SENT AN AMBASSADOR OUT INTO THE STARS, IN SEARCH OF A LONG-LOST MORTAL PERSPECTIVE, A SPECIES THAT COULD HELP THEM RECOVER THEIR BALANCE.
AFTER 11 YEARS AND FAILED INTERACTIONS WITH 87 CIVILIZATIONS, THE MESSENGER STUMBLED UPON A PURE WORLD, WITH A SIMPLE CIVILIZATION AND HUMBLE CULTURE.
THIS WORLD IS CALLED EARTH.
THEY WASTED NO TIME IN STRIKING A BARGAIN WITH HUMANITY, A SIMPLE EXCHANGE THAT WOULD BECOME KNOWN AS "THE CONSCIENCE AGREEMENT."
IN EXCHANGE FOR THE ENDLESS KNOWLEDGE AND POWER OF THE FANTASMEN, EARTH HAD ONLY ONE THING TO OFFER--
THE VIRTUE OF HUMANKIND.

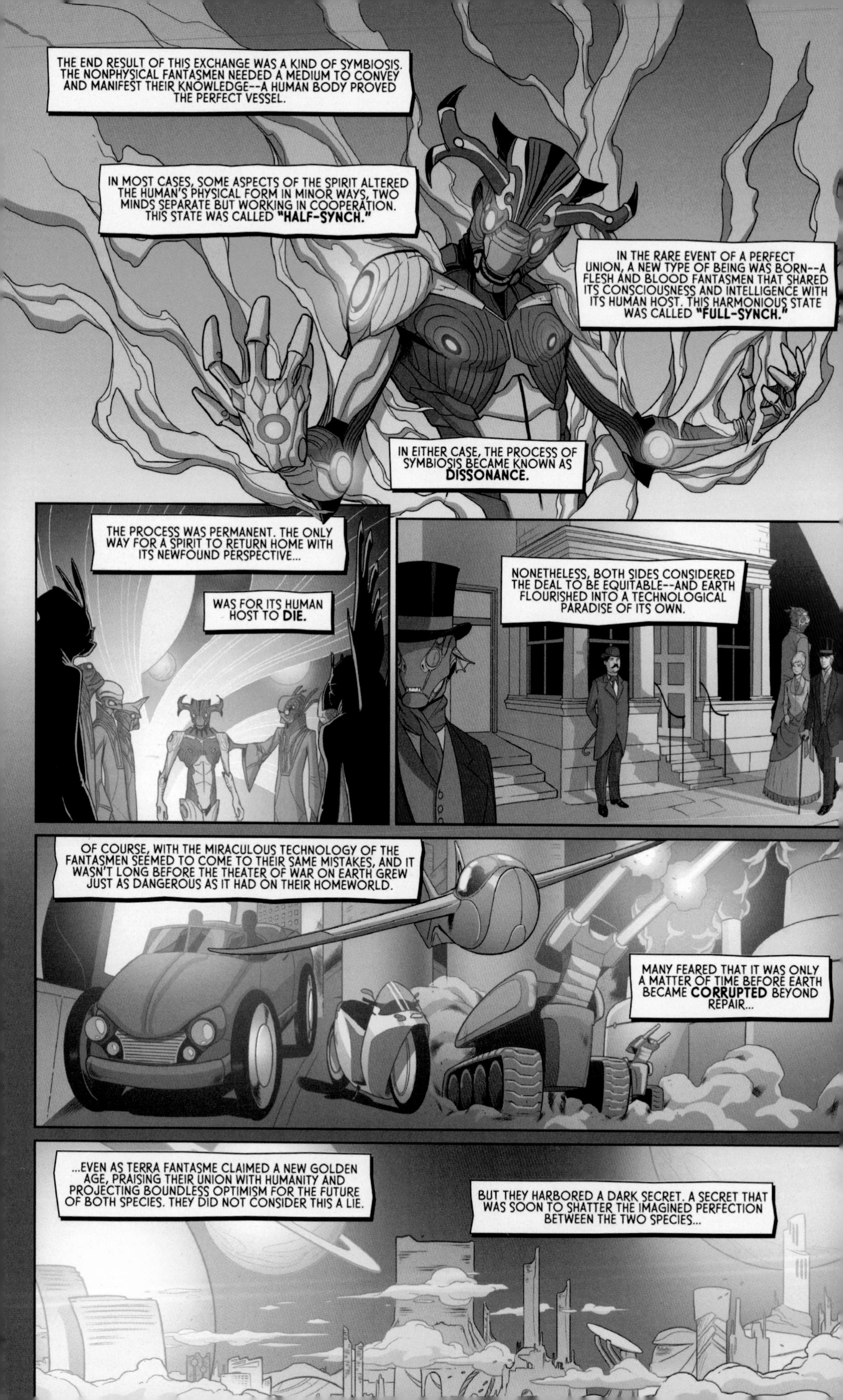
THE END RESULT OF THIS EXCHANGE WAS A KIND OF SYMBIOSIS. THE NONPHYSICAL FANTASMEN NEEDED A MEDIUM TO CONVEY AND MANIFEST THEIR KNOWLEDGE--A HUMAN BODY PROVED THE PERFECT VESSEL.
IN MOST CASES, SOME ASPECTS OF THE SPIRIT ALTERED THE HUMAN'S PHYSICAL FORM IN MINOR WAYS, TWO MINDS SEPARATE BUT WORKING IN COOPERATION. THIS STATE WAS CALLED **"HALF-SYNCH."**
IN THE RARE EVENT OF A PERFECT UNION, A NEW TYPE OF BEING WAS BORN--A FLESH AND BLOOD FANTASMEN THAT SHARED ITS CONSCIOUSNESS AND INTELLIGENCE WITH ITS HUMAN HOST. THIS HARMONIOUS STATE WAS CALLED **"FULL-SYNCH."**
IN EITHER CASE, THE PROCESS OF SYMBIOSIS BECAME KNOWN AS **DISSONANCE.**
THE PROCESS WAS PERMANENT. THE ONLY WAY FOR A SPIRIT TO RETURN HOME WITH ITS NEWFOUND PERSPECTIVE...
WAS FOR ITS HUMAN HOST TO **DIE.**
NONETHELESS, BOTH SIDES CONSIDERED THE DEAL TO BE EQUITABLE--AND EARTH FLOURISHED INTO A TECHNOLOGICAL PARADISE OF ITS OWN.
OF COURSE, WITH THE MIRACULOUS TECHNOLOGY OF THE FANTASMEN SEEMED TO COME TO THEIR SAME MISTAKES, AND IT WASN'T LONG BEFORE THE THEATER OF WAR ON EARTH GREW JUST AS DANGEROUS AS IT HAD ON THEIR HOMEWORLD.
MANY FEARED THAT IT WAS ONLY A MATTER OF TIME BEFORE EARTH BECAME **CORRUPTED** BEYOND REPAIR...
...EVEN AS TERRA FANTASME CLAIMED A NEW GOLDEN AGE, PRAISING THEIR UNION WITH HUMANITY AND PROJECTING BOUNDLESS OPTIMISM FOR THE FUTURE OF BOTH SPECIES. THEY DID NOT CONSIDER THIS A LIE.
BUT THEY HARBORED A DARK SECRET. A SECRET THAT WAS SOON TO SHATTER THE IMAGINED PERFECTION BETWEEN THE TWO SPECIES...

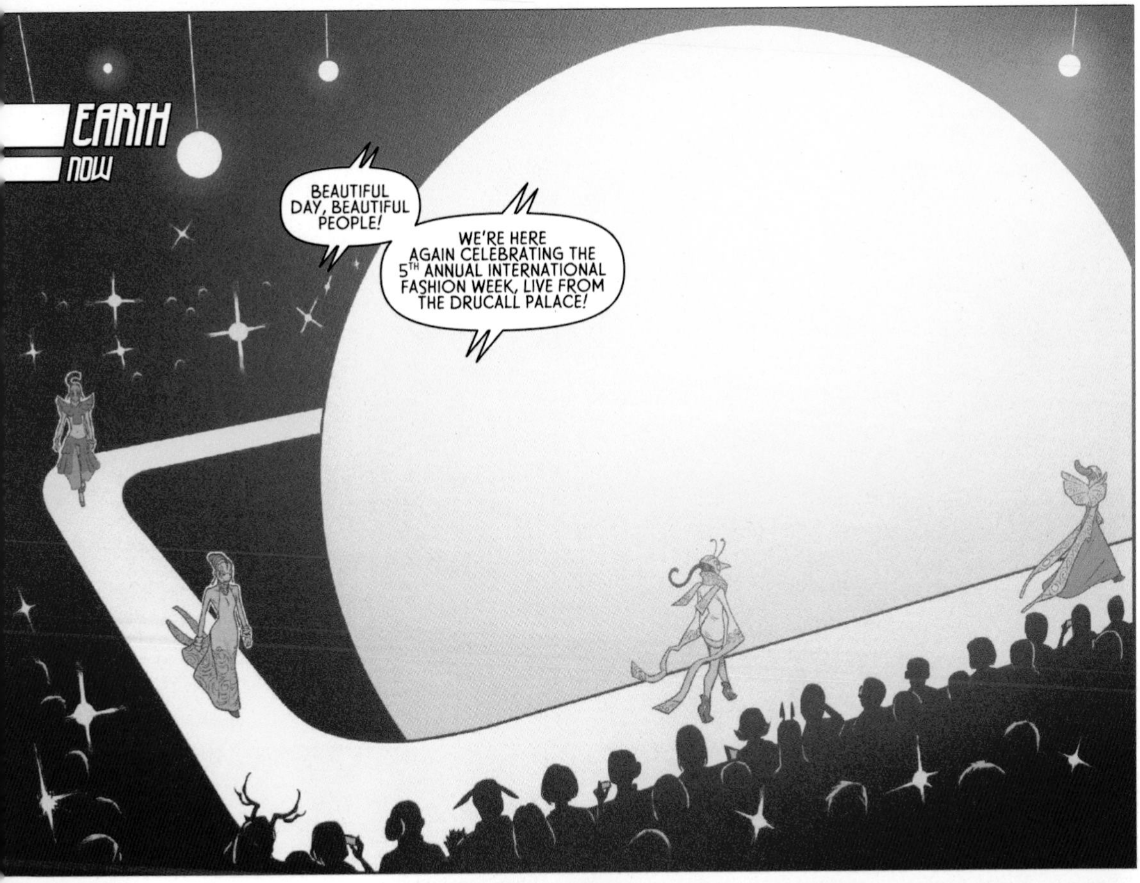
EARTH
NOW
BEAUTIFUL DAY, BEAUTIFUL PEOPLE!
WE'RE HERE AGAIN CELEBRATING THE 5TH ANNUAL INTERNATIONAL FASHION WEEK, LIVE FROM THE DRUCALL PALACE!

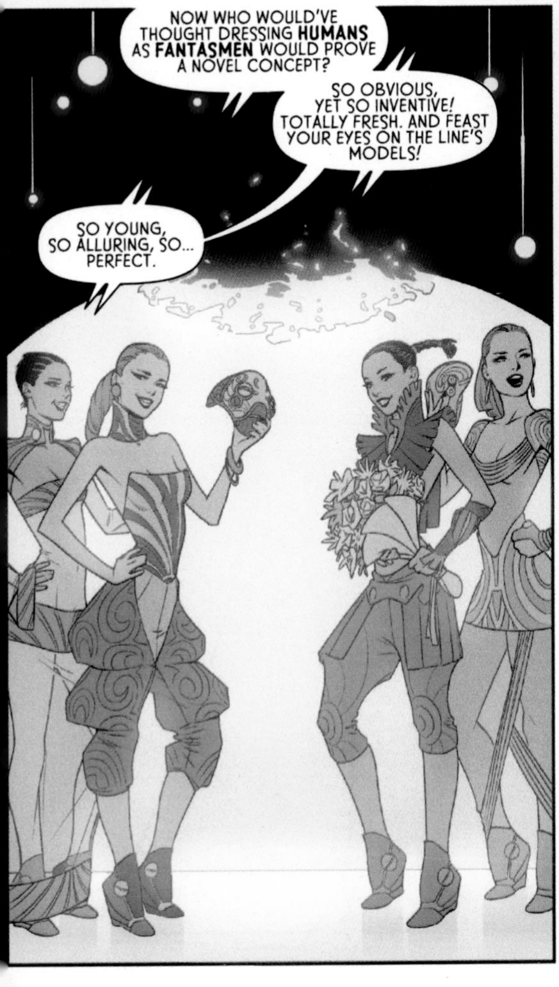
NOW WHO WOULD'VE THOUGHT DRESSING **HUMANS** AS **FANTASMEN** WOULD PROVE A NOVEL CONCEPT?
SO OBVIOUS, YET SO INVENTIVE! TOTALLY FRESH. AND FEAST YOUR EYES ON THE LINE'S MODELS!
SO YOUNG, SO ALLURING, SO... PERFECT.

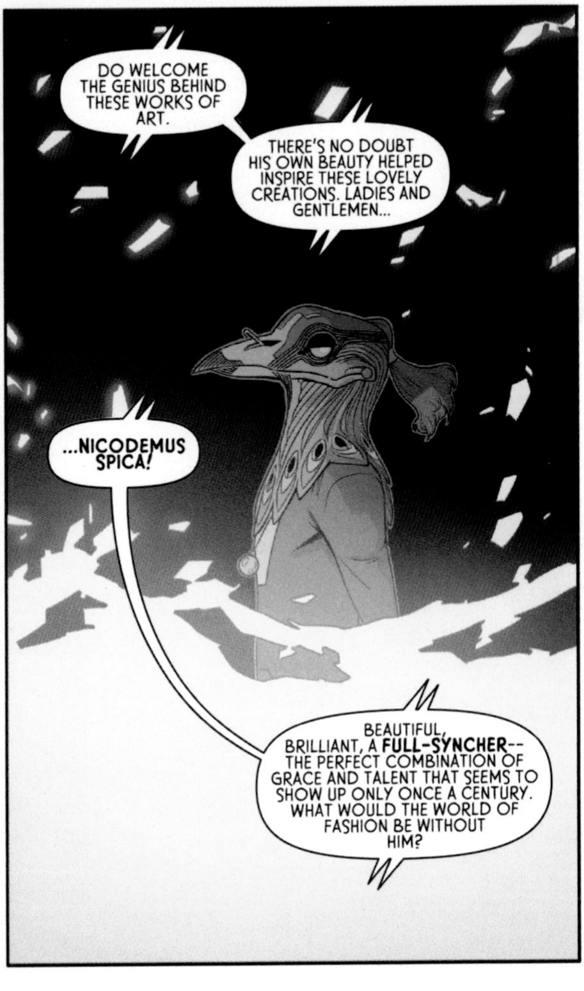
DO WELCOME THE GENIUS BEHIND THESE WORKS OF ART.
THERE'S NO DOUBT HIS OWN BEAUTY HELPED INSPIRE THESE LOVELY CREATIONS. LADIES AND GENTLEMEN...
...NICODEMUS SPICA!
BEAUTIFUL, BRILLIANT, A **FULL-SYNCHER**-- THE PERFECT COMBINATION OF GRACE AND TALENT THAT SEEMS TO SHOW UP ONLY ONCE A CENTURY. WHAT WOULD THE WORLD OF FASHION BE WITHOUT HIM?

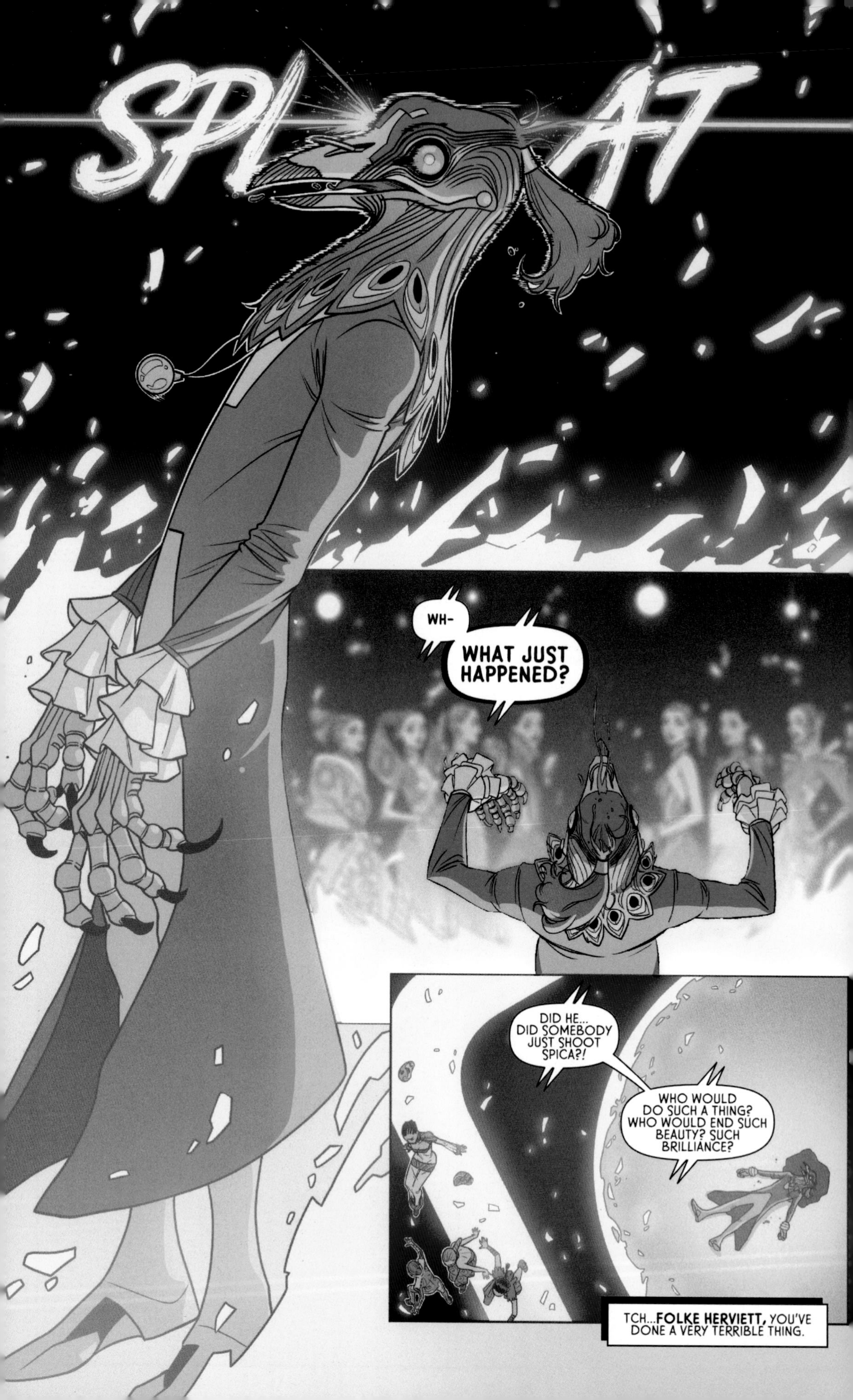
SPL AT
WH-
WHAT JUST HAPPENED?
DID HE... DID SOMEBODY JUST SHOOT SPICA?!
WHO WOULD DO SUCH A THING? WHO WOULD END SUCH BEAUTY? SUCH BRILLIANCE?
TCH...FOLKE HERVIETT, YOU'VE DONE A VERY TERRIBLE THING.

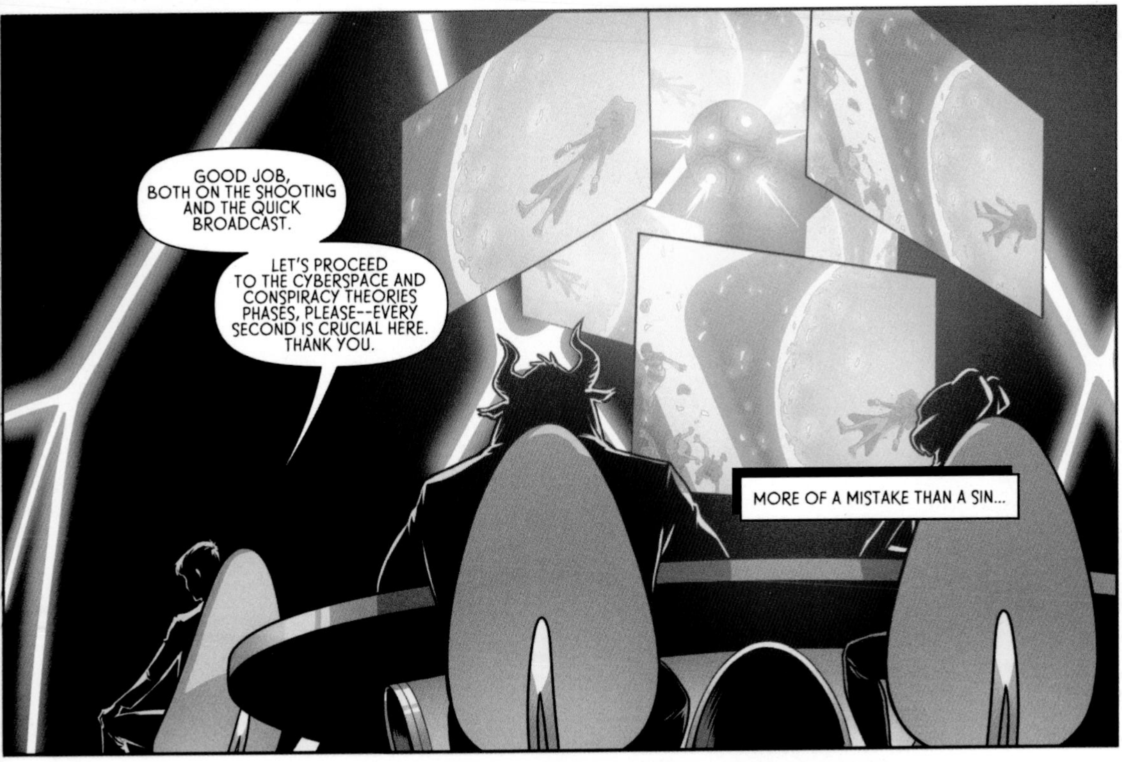
GOOD JOB, BOTH ON THE SHOOTING AND THE QUICK BROADCAST.
LET'S PROCEED TO THE CYBERSPACE AND CONSPIRACY THEORIES PHASES, PLEASE--EVERY SECOND IS CRUCIAL HERE. THANK YOU.
MORE OF A MISTAKE THAN A SIN...

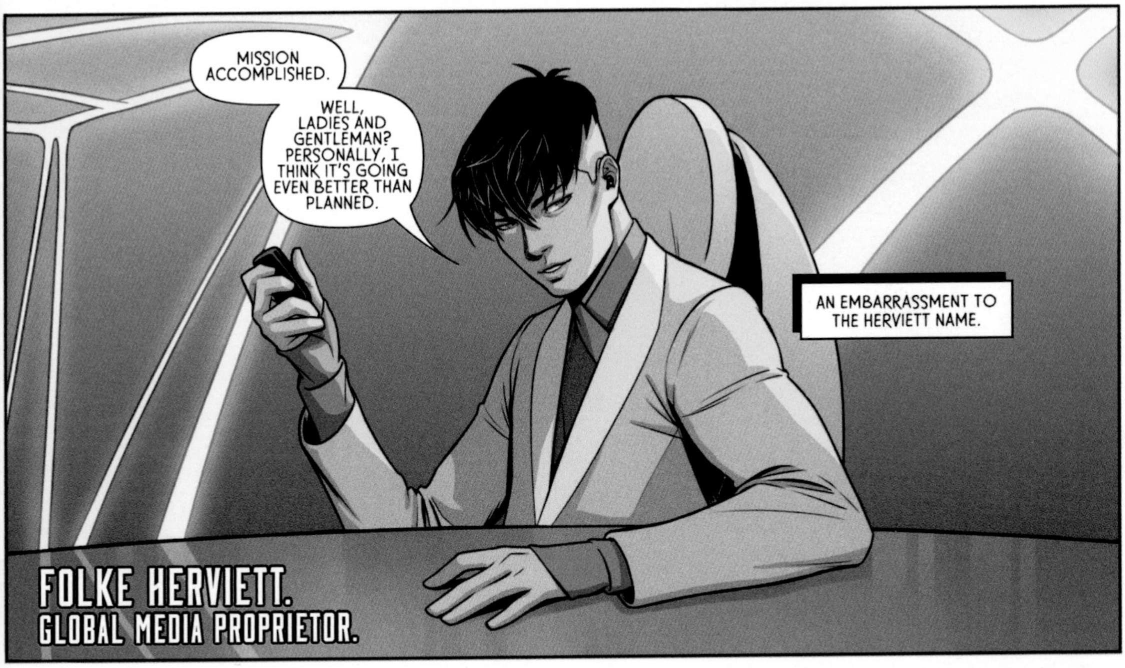
MISSION ACCOMPLISHED.
WELL, LADIES AND GENTLEMAN? PERSONALLY, I THINK IT'S GOING EVEN BETTER THAN PLANNED.
AN EMBARRASSMENT TO THE HERVIETT NAME.
FOLKE HERVIETT.
GLOBAL MEDIA PROPRIETOR.

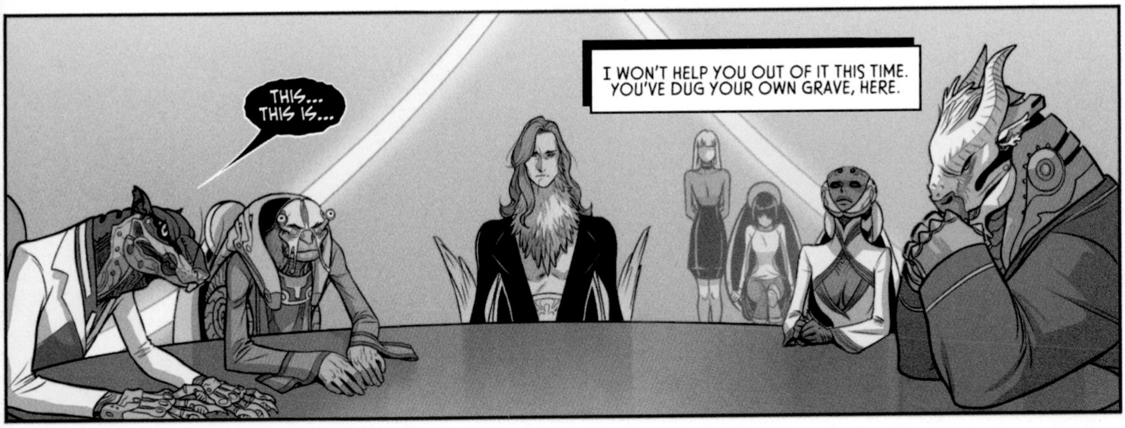
I WON'T HELP YOU OUT OF IT THIS TIME. YOU'VE DUG YOUR OWN GRAVE, HERE.
THIS... THIS IS...

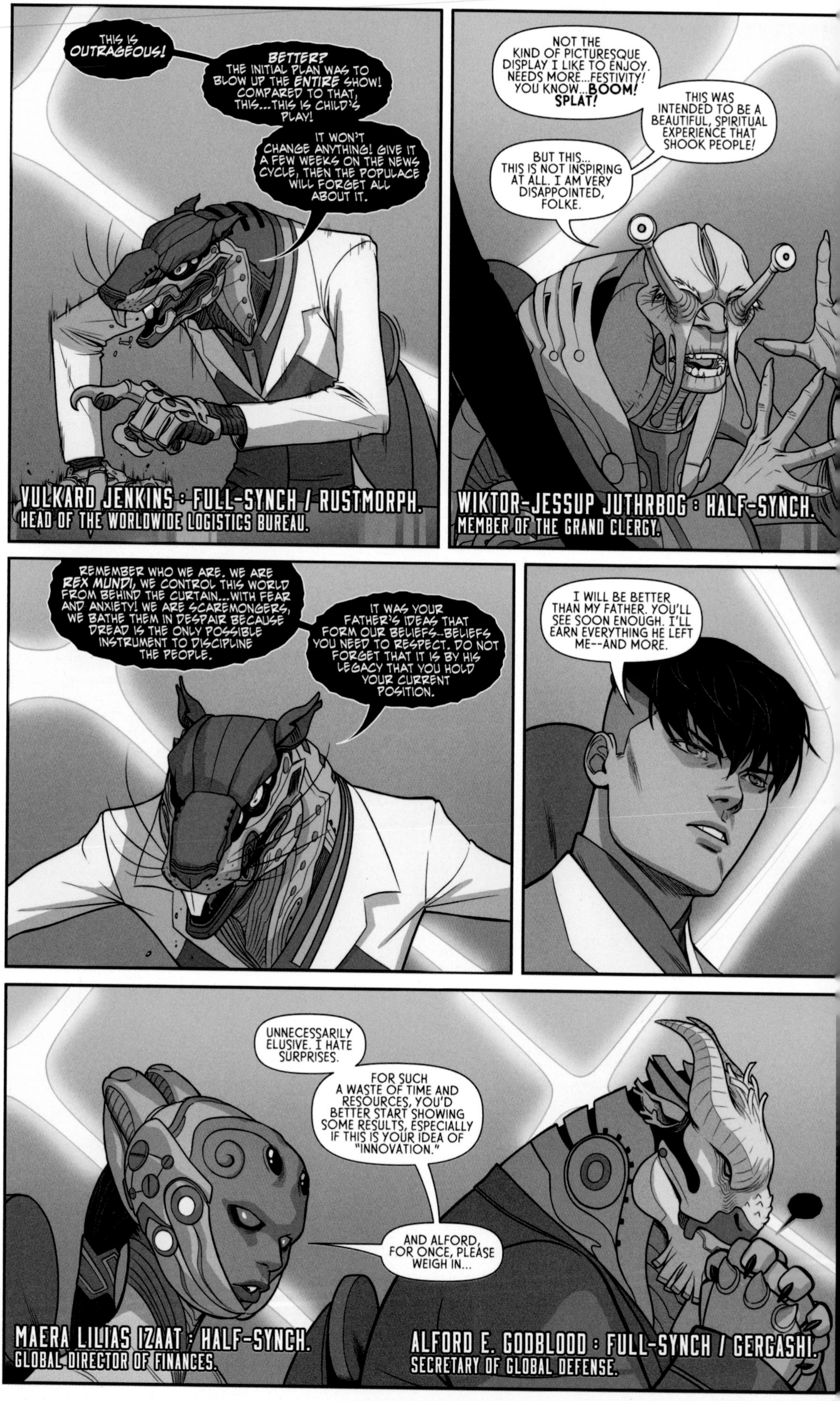
THIS IS OUTRAGEOUS!
BETTER? THE INITIAL PLAN WAS TO BLOW UP THE ENTIRE SHOW! COMPARED TO THAT, THIS...THIS IS CHILD'S PLAY!
IT WON'T CHANGE ANYTHING! GIVE IT A FEW WEEKS ON THE NEWS CYCLE, THEN THE POPULACE WILL FORGET ALL ABOUT IT.
VULKARD JENKINS : FULL-SYNCH / RUSTMORPH.
HEAD OF THE WORLDWIDE LOGISTICS BUREAU.
NOT THE KIND OF PICTURESQUE DISPLAY I LIKE TO ENJOY. NEEDS MORE...FESTIVITY! YOU KNOW...BOOM! SPLÄT!
THIS WAS INTENDED TO BE A BEAUTIFUL, SPIRITUAL EXPERIENCE THAT SHOOK PEOPLE!
BUT THIS... THIS IS NOT INSPIRING AT ALL. I AM VERY DISAPPOINTED, FOLKE.
WIKTOR-JESSUP JUTHRBOG : HALF-SYNCH.
MEMBER OF THE GRAND CLERGY.
REMEMBER WHO WE ARE. WE ARE REX MUNDI, WE CONTROL THIS WORLD FROM BEHIND THE CURTAIN...WITH FEAR AND ANXIETY! WE ARE SCAREMONGERS, WE BATHE THEM IN DESPAIR BECAUSE DREAD IS THE ONLY POSSIBLE INSTRUMENT TO DISCIPLINE THE PEOPLE.
IT WAS YOUR FATHER'S IDEAS THAT FORM OUR BELIEFS--BELIEFS YOU NEED TO RESPECT. DO NOT FORGET THAT IT IS BY HIS LEGACY THAT YOU HOLD YOUR CURRENT POSITION.
I WILL BE BETTER THAN MY FATHER. YOU'LL SEE SOON ENOUGH. I'LL EARN EVERYTHING HE LEFT ME--AND MORE.
UNNECESSARILY ELUSIVE. I HATE SURPRISES.
FOR SUCH A WASTE OF TIME AND RESOURCES, YOU'D BETTER START SHOWING SOME RESULTS, ESPECIALLY IF THIS IS YOUR IDEA OF "INNOVATION."
AND ALFORD, FOR ONCE, PLEASE WEIGH IN...
MAERA LILIAS IZAAT : HALF-SYNCH.
GLOBAL DIRECTOR OF FINANCES.
ALFORD E. GODBLOOD : FULL-SYNCH / GERGASHI.
SECRETARY OF GLOBAL DEFENSE.

COME ON, WE ALL KNOW ALFORD WILL JUST KEEP UP HIS SILENT ACT.

LET'S JUST LET THIS ONE SLIDE, EH? THE SCHEME IS NOT EVEN THAT CRUCIAL. CONSIDER IT A...**TEST** FOR HOW FAR WE CAN TRUST OUR NEWLY APPOINTED HERVIETT.

REMFREY MILDEHR : HALF-SYNCH.
HEAD OF GLOBAL PHARMACEUTICAL INDUSTRY.

A TEST HE'S ALREADY FAILED.

PLEASE NOT YOU TOO, REMFREY. LET'S KEEP THE STRAIGHT AND NARROW. ALL THIS "INNOVATION" IS JUST ANOTHER WORD FOR ERROR.

BELIEVE ME, MAERA, I UNDERSTAND.

BUT LET ME POINT OUT THE REAL ISSUE HERE. FOLKE HERE FAILED, BUT THE **FAMILY** HERVIETT HASN'T COMPLETELY LET US DOWN.

BOY, THUS FAR, WE'VE BEEN QUITE HAPPY WITH YOU AND **YOUR SISTER'S** PERFORMANCE. IT'S BEEN BRUTAL BEYOND OUR EXPECTATION. SO WHY ACT ALONE, WITHOUT HER INPUT? WHAT ARE YOU TRYING TO PROVE?

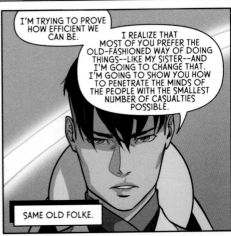

I'M TRYING TO PROVE HOW EFFICIENT WE CAN BE.

I REALIZE THAT MOST OF YOU PREFER THE OLD-FASHIONED WAY OF DOING THINGS--LIKE MY SISTER--AND I'M GOING TO CHANGE THAT. I'M GOING TO SHOW YOU HOW TO PENETRATE THE MINDS OF THE PEOPLE WITH THE SMALLEST NUMBER OF CASUALTIES POSSIBLE.

SAME OLD FOLKE.

THE ONLY THING THAT NEEDS FIXING AROUND HERE, DEAR BROTHER, IS YOU.

IF IT WAS REALLY ABOUT MAXIMUM EFFICIENCY, YOU'D LET ME EXPLAIN IT TO THE REX MUNDI. EASE THEIR MINDS. BUT HERE'S YOUR EGO, DESTROYING YOU.

ENJOY THE SPOTLIGHT--I'LL BE ENJOYING YOUR DOWNFALL.

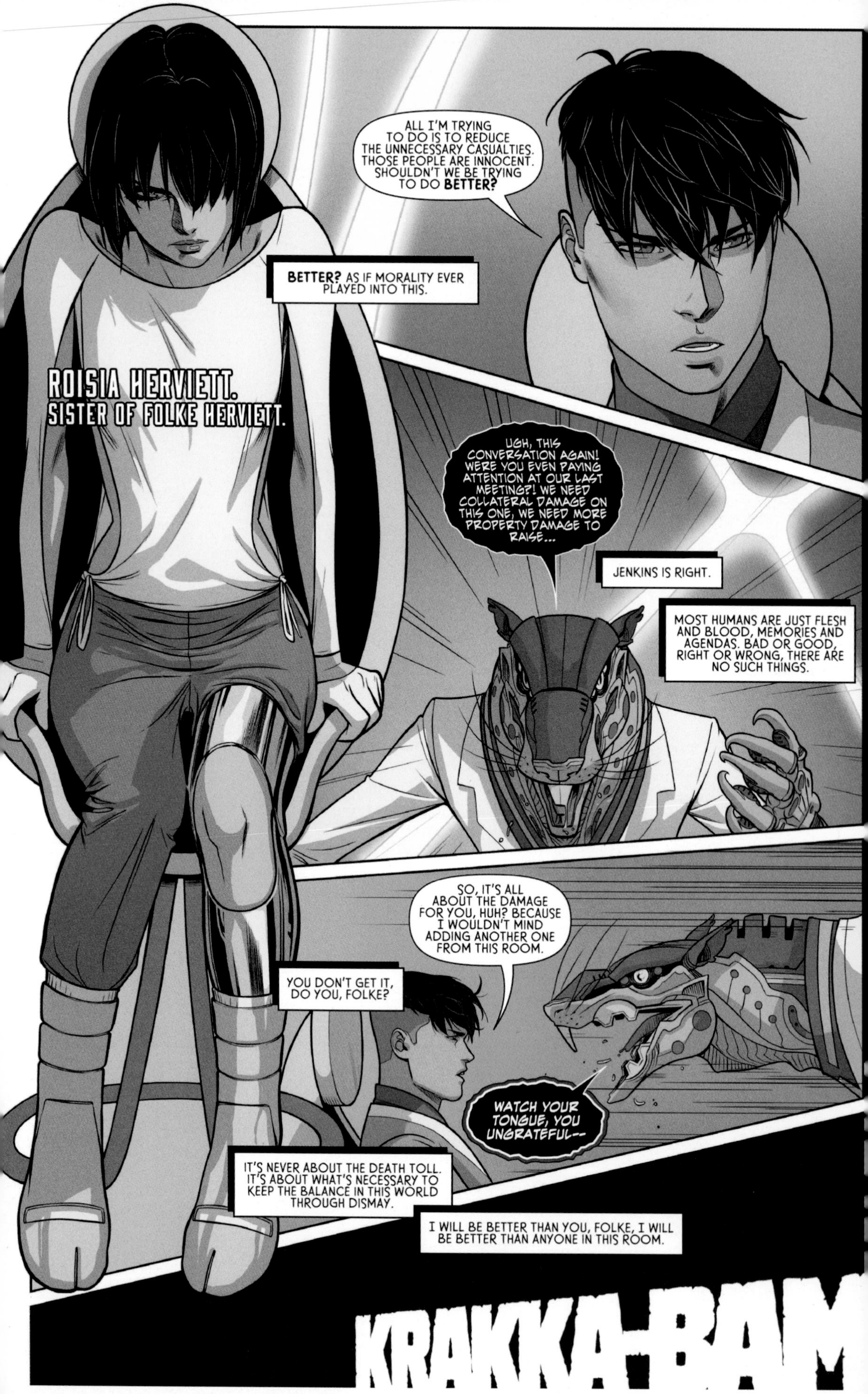

ALL I'M TRYING TO DO IS TO REDUCE THE UNNECESSARY CASUALTIES. THOSE PEOPLE ARE INNOCENT. SHOULDN'T WE BE TRYING TO DO BETTER?
BETTER? AS IF MORALITY EVER PLAYED INTO THIS.
ROISIA HERVIETT. SISTER OF FOLKE HERVIETT.
UGH, THIS CONVERSATION AGAIN! WERE YOU EVEN PAYING ATTENTION AT OUR LAST MEETING?! WE NEED COLLATERAL DAMAGE ON THIS ONE, WE NEED MORE PROPERTY DAMAGE TO RAISE...
JENKINS IS RIGHT.
MOST HUMANS ARE JUST FLESH AND BLOOD, MEMORIES AND AGENDAS. BAD OR GOOD, RIGHT OR WRONG, THERE ARE NO SUCH THINGS.
SO, IT'S ALL ABOUT THE DAMAGE FOR YOU, HUH? BECAUSE I WOULDN'T MIND ADDING ANOTHER ONE FROM THIS ROOM.
YOU DON'T GET IT, DO YOU, FOLKE?
WATCH YOUR TONGUE, YOU UNGRATEFUL--
IT'S NEVER ABOUT THE DEATH TOLL. IT'S ABOUT WHAT'S NECESSARY TO KEEP THE BALANCE IN THIS WORLD THROUGH DISMAY.
I WILL BE BETTER THAN YOU, FOLKE, I WILL BE BETTER THAN ANYONE IN THIS ROOM.
KRAKKA-BAM

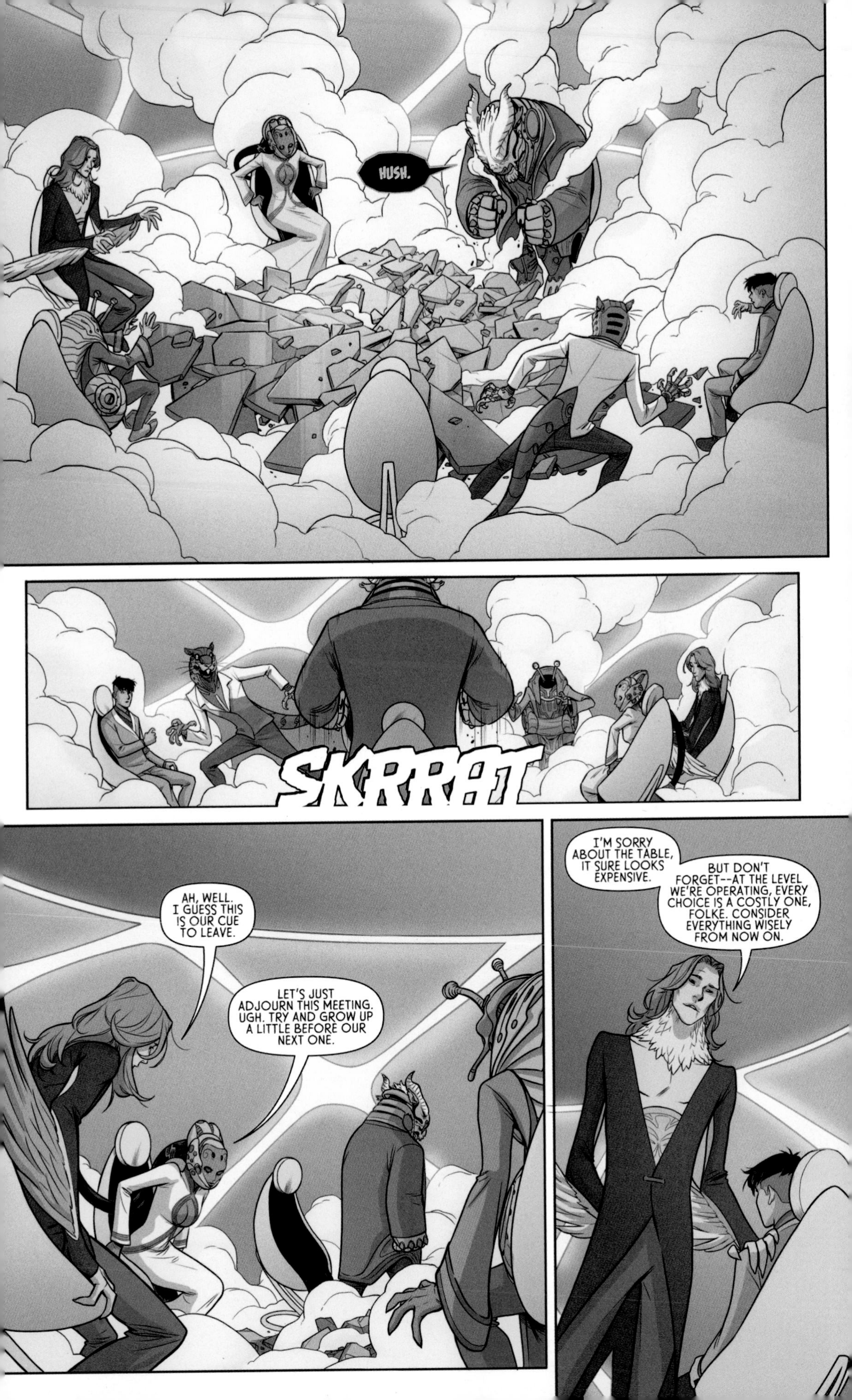
HUSH.
SKRRAT
AH, WELL. I GUESS THIS IS OUR CUE TO LEAVE.
LET'S JUST ADJOURN THIS MEETING. UGH. TRY AND GROW UP A LITTLE BEFORE OUR NEXT ONE.
I'M SORRY ABOUT THE TABLE, IT SURE LOOKS EXPENSIVE.
BUT DON'T FORGET--AT THE LEVEL WE'RE OPERATING, EVERY CHOICE IS A COSTLY ONE, FOLKE. CONSIDER EVERYTHING WISELY FROM NOW ON.

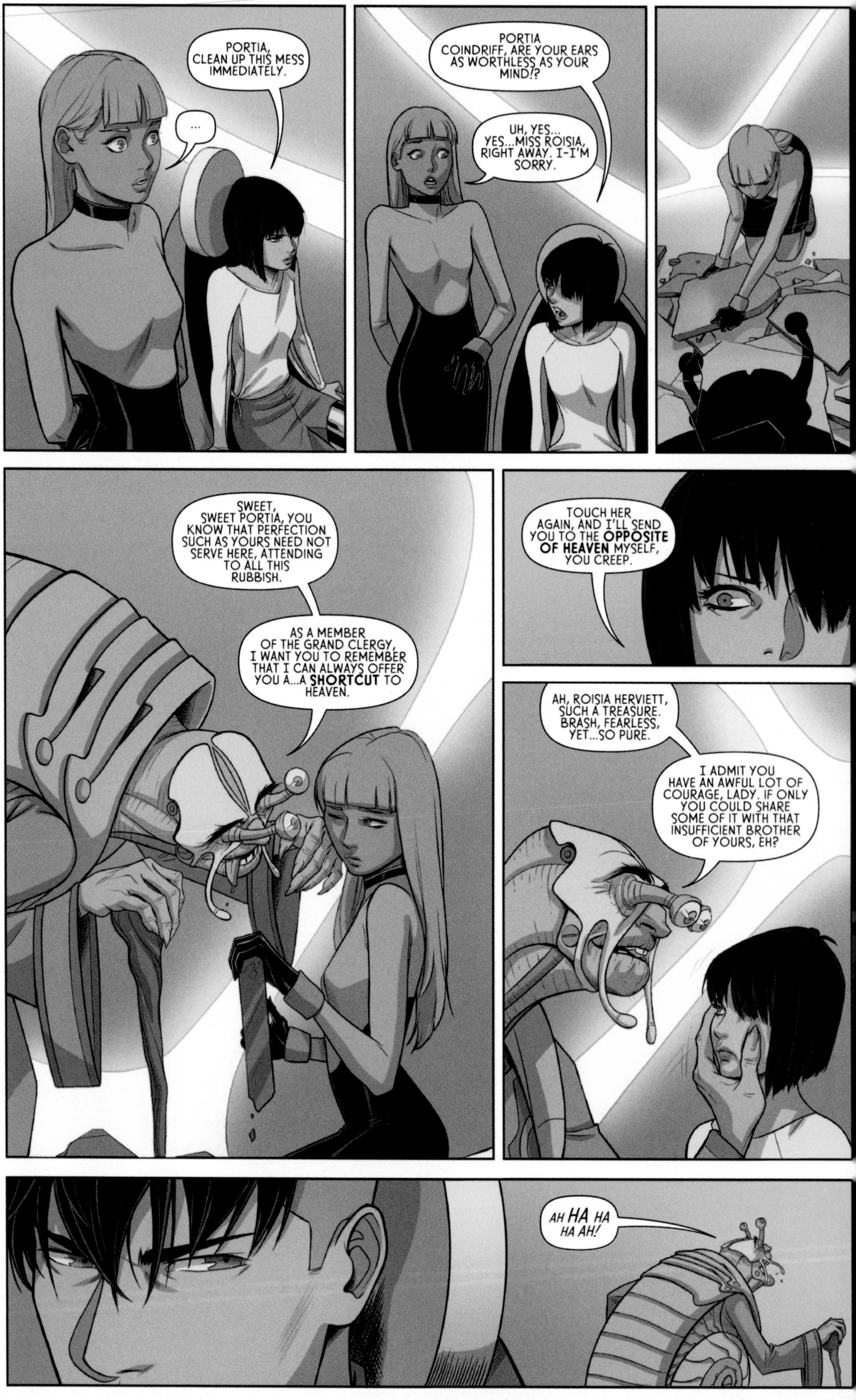
PORTIA, CLEAN UP THIS MESS IMMEDIATELY.
...
PORTIA COINDRIFF, ARE YOUR EARS AS WORTHLESS AS YOUR MIND!?
UH, YES... YES...MISS ROISIA, RIGHT AWAY. I-I'M SORRY.
SWEET, SWEET PORTIA, YOU KNOW THAT PERFECTION SUCH AS YOURS NEED NOT SERVE HERE, ATTENDING TO ALL THIS RUBBISH.
AS A MEMBER OF THE GRAND CLERGY, I WANT YOU TO REMEMBER THAT I CAN ALWAYS OFFER YOU A...A SHORTCUT TO HEAVEN.
TOUCH HER AGAIN, AND I'LL SEND YOU TO THE OPPOSITE OF HEAVEN MYSELF, YOU CREEP.
AH, ROISIA HERVIETT, SUCH A TREASURE. BRASH, FEARLESS, YET...SO PURE.
I ADMIT YOU HAVE AN AWFUL LOT OF COURAGE, LADY. IF ONLY YOU COULD SHARE SOME OF IT WITH THAT INSUFFICIENT BROTHER OF YOURS, EH?
AH HA HA HA AH!

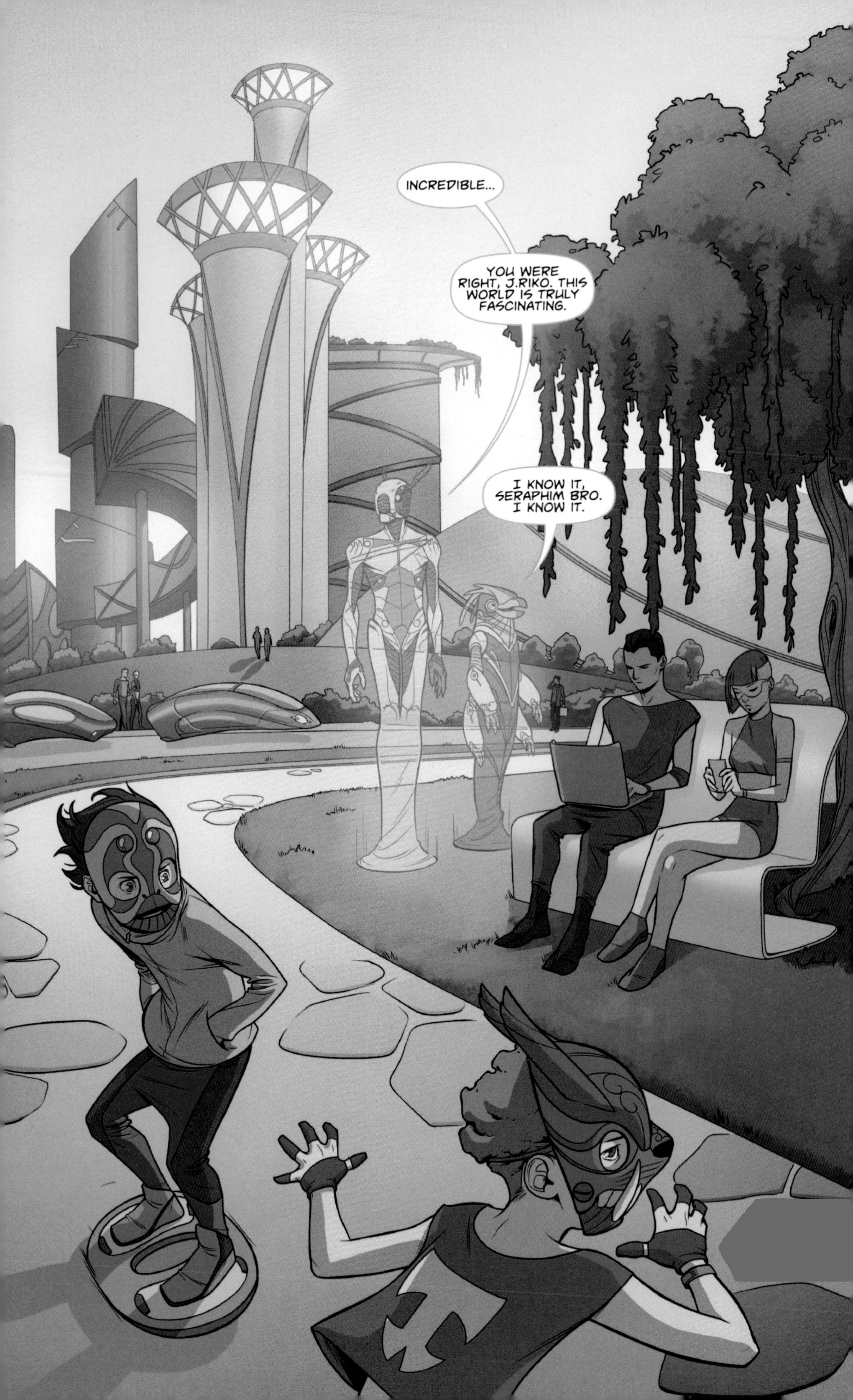
INCREDIBLE...
YOU WERE RIGHT, J.RIKO. THIS WORLD IS TRULY FASCINATING.
I KNOW IT, SERAPHIM BRO. I KNOW IT.

THEY'VE BENEFITTED SO MUCH SINCE THE AGREEMENT.
KINDA THE POINT, MAN.
SO... HOW'S OUR BELOVED HOME? IT'S BEEN TOO LONG SINCE I HEARD NEWS FROM TERRA FANTASME.
WE'RE BENEFITTING, TOO. EVERY DAY, THINGS GROW MORE... CIVILIZED.
BUT ENOUGH ABOUT HOME. WHY ARE YOU STILL IN YOUR SPIRIT FORM? YOU'VE BEEN HERE LONG ENOUGH--WHY HAVEN'T YOU UNDERGONE THE DISSONANCE?
TROUBLE FINDING A PERFECT HUMAN TO PAIR?
WHOA, SLOW DOWN, COMPADRE!
I ACTUALLY HAVE FOUND THE PERFECT PAIR, BRO, BUT...SHE'S A 68-YEAR-OLD WIDOW WHO LIVES WITH HER 12 CATS. UGH, I DON'T WANNA BE STUCK IN THAT BODY FOREVER...NOT FOREVER, BUT...YOU KNOW WHAT I MEAN.
I JUST WANT TO EXPLORE HUMAN CULTURE FIRST, PIM. THEY ARE REALLY INTERESTING! HAVE YOU HEARD OF SEX? VIDEO GAMES? GUMBALL MACHINES? PHILATELY? BUZKASHI? EVERYTHING EACH OF THEM DOES IS CRAZY INTERESTING, AND I HAVE TO STICK WITH SYNCHING TO JUST ONE OF THEM?
AND BESIDES....

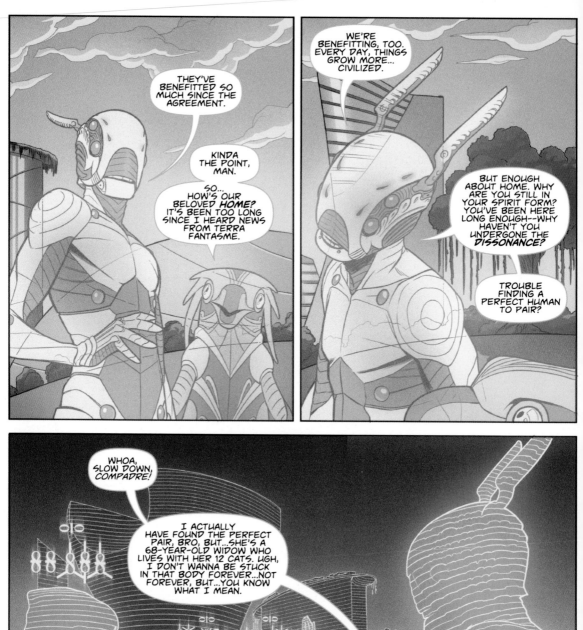

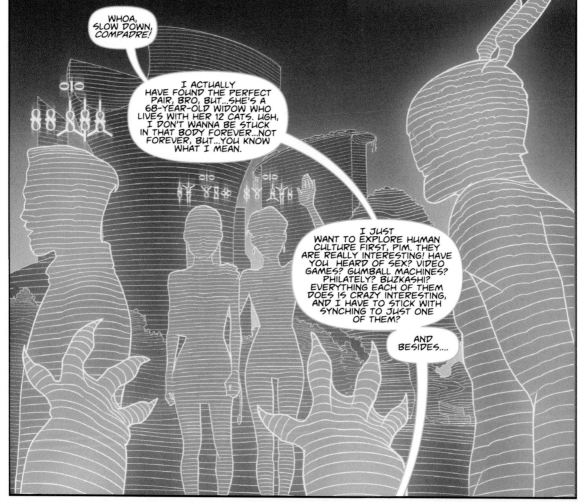

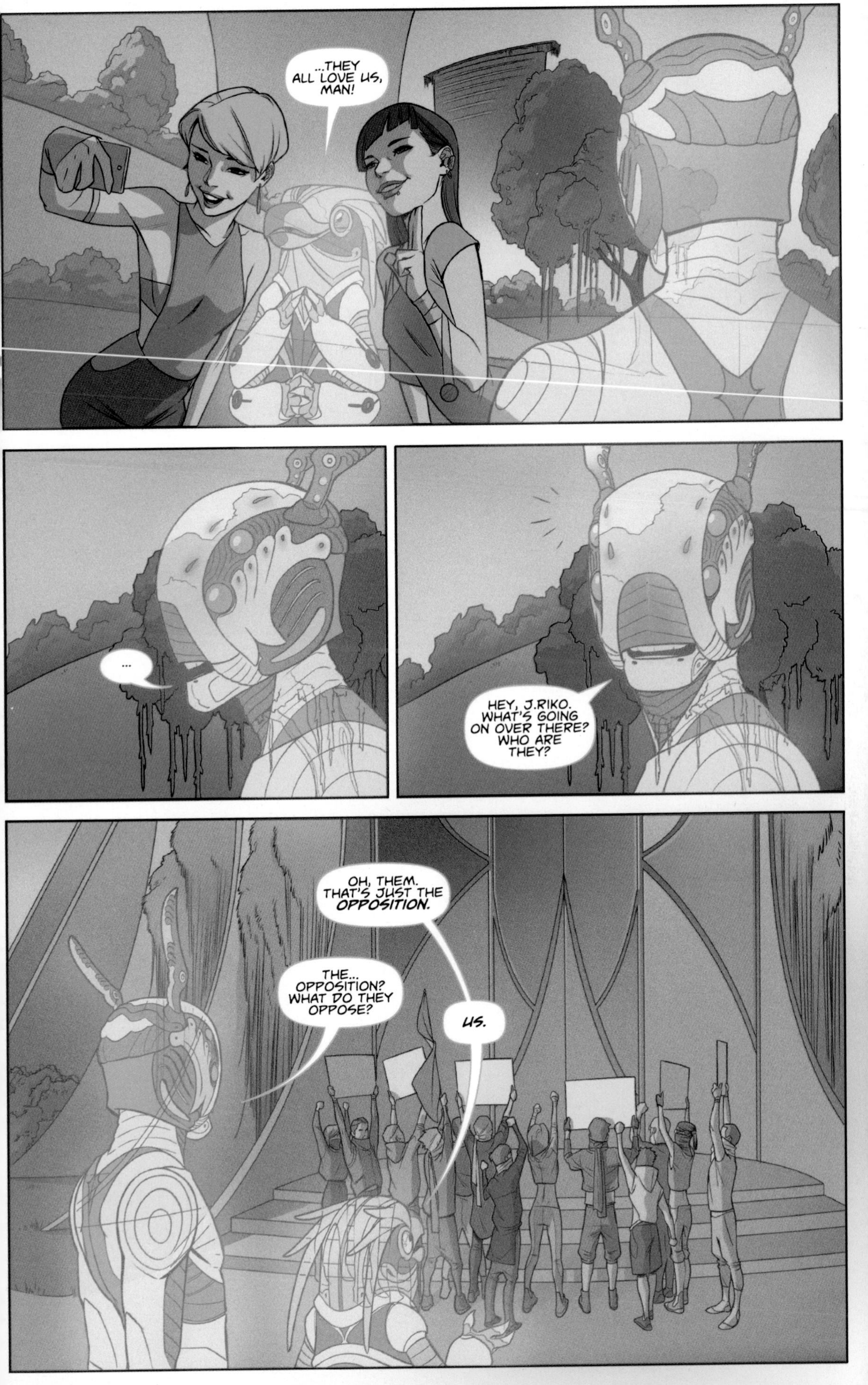
...THEY ALL LOVE US, MAN!
...
HEY, J.RIKO. WHAT'S GOING ON OVER THERE? WHO ARE THEY?
OH, THEM. THAT'S JUST THE *OPPOSITION.*
THE... OPPOSITION? WHAT DO THEY OPPOSE?
US.

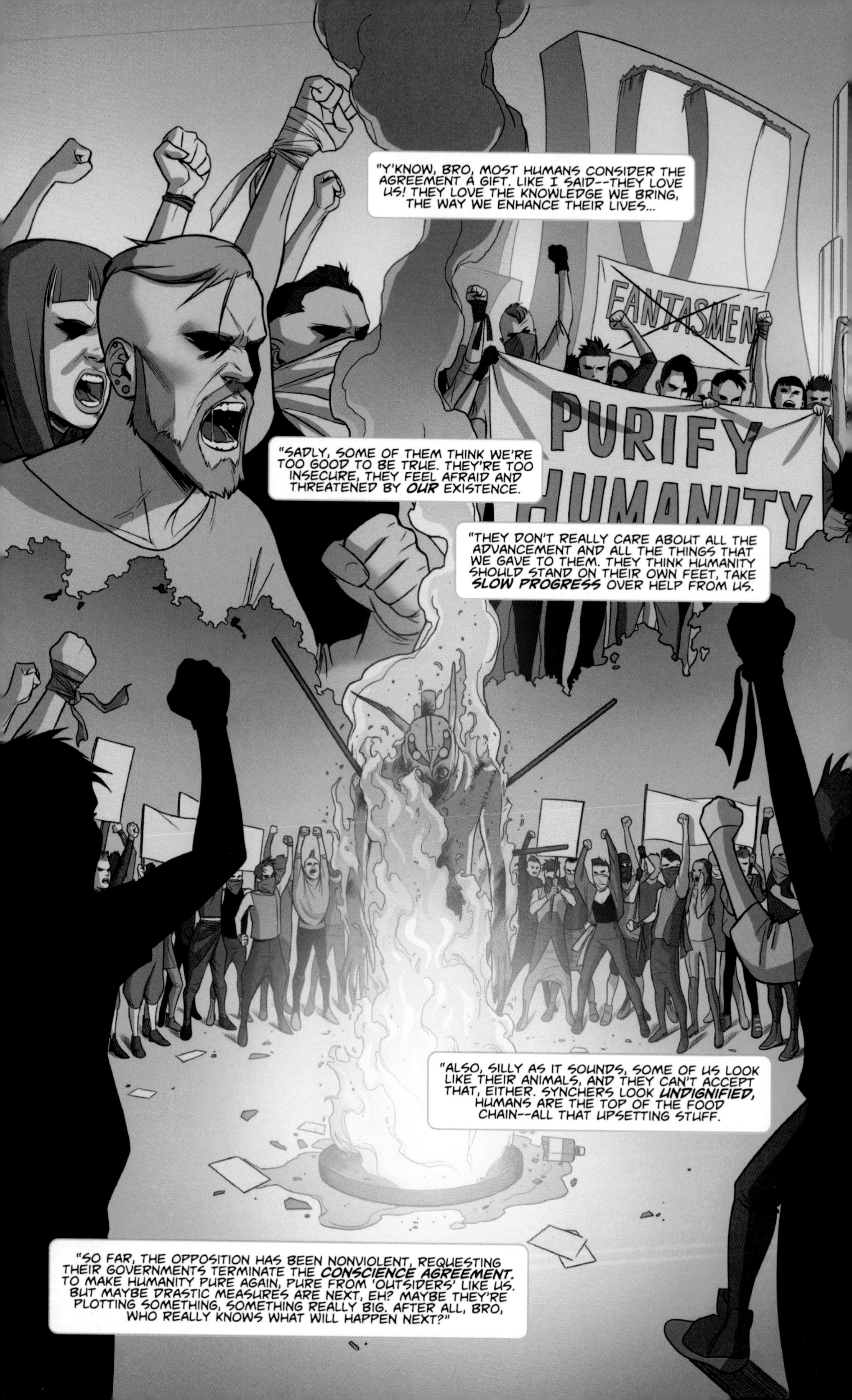
"Y'KNOW, BRO, MOST HUMANS CONSIDER THE AGREEMENT A GIFT. LIKE I SAID--THEY LOVE US! THEY LOVE THE KNOWLEDGE WE BRING, THE WAY WE ENHANCE THEIR LIVES...
FANTASMEN
PURIFY HUMANITY
"SADLY, SOME OF THEM THINK WE'RE TOO GOOD TO BE TRUE. THEY'RE TOO INSECURE, THEY FEEL AFRAID AND THREATENED BY OUR EXISTENCE.
"THEY DON'T REALLY CARE ABOUT ALL THE ADVANCEMENT AND ALL THE THINGS THAT WE GAVE TO THEM. THEY THINK HUMANITY SHOULD STAND ON THEIR OWN FEET, TAKE SLOW PROGRESS OVER HELP FROM US.
"ALSO, SILLY AS IT SOUNDS, SOME OF US LOOK LIKE THEIR ANIMALS, AND THEY CAN'T ACCEPT THAT, EITHER. SYNCHERS LOOK UNDIGNIFIED, HUMANS ARE THE TOP OF THE FOOD CHAIN--ALL THAT UPSETTING STUFF.
"SO FAR, THE OPPOSITION HAS BEEN NONVIOLENT, REQUESTING THEIR GOVERNMENTS TERMINATE THE CONSCIENCE AGREEMENT. TO MAKE HUMANITY PURE AGAIN, PURE FROM 'OUTSIDERS' LIKE US. BUT MAYBE DRASTIC MEASURES ARE NEXT, EH? MAYBE THEY'RE PLOTTING SOMETHING, SOMETHING REALLY BIG. AFTER ALL, BRO, WHO REALLY KNOWS WHAT WILL HAPPEN NEXT?"

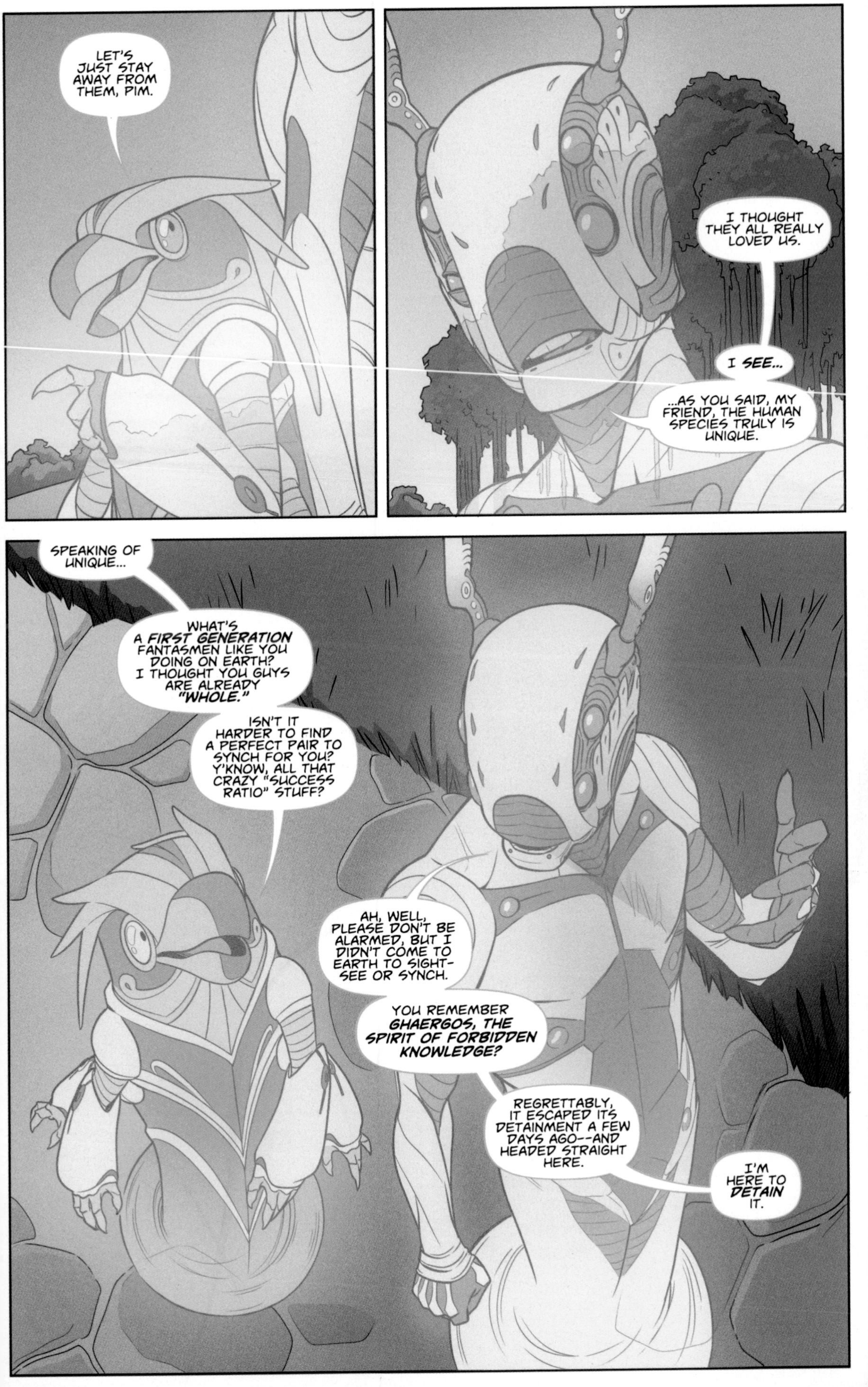
LET'S JUST STAY AWAY FROM THEM, PIM.
I THOUGHT THEY ALL REALLY LOVED US.
I SEE...
...AS YOU SAID, MY FRIEND, THE HUMAN SPECIES TRULY IS UNIQUE.
SPEAKING OF UNIQUE...
WHAT'S A FIRST GENERATION FANTASMEN LIKE YOU DOING ON EARTH? I THOUGHT YOU GUYS ARE ALREADY "WHOLE."
ISN'T IT HARDER TO FIND A PERFECT PAIR TO SYNCH FOR YOU? Y'KNOW, ALL THAT CRAZY "SUCCESS RATIO" STUFF?
AH, WELL, PLEASE DON'T BE ALARMED, BUT I DIDN'T COME TO EARTH TO SIGHT-SEE OR SYNCH.
YOU REMEMBER GHAERGOS, THE SPIRIT OF FORBIDDEN KNOWLEDGE?
REGRETTABLY, IT ESCAPED ITS DETAINMENT A FEW DAYS AGO--AND HEADED STRAIGHT HERE.
I'M HERE TO DETAIN IT.

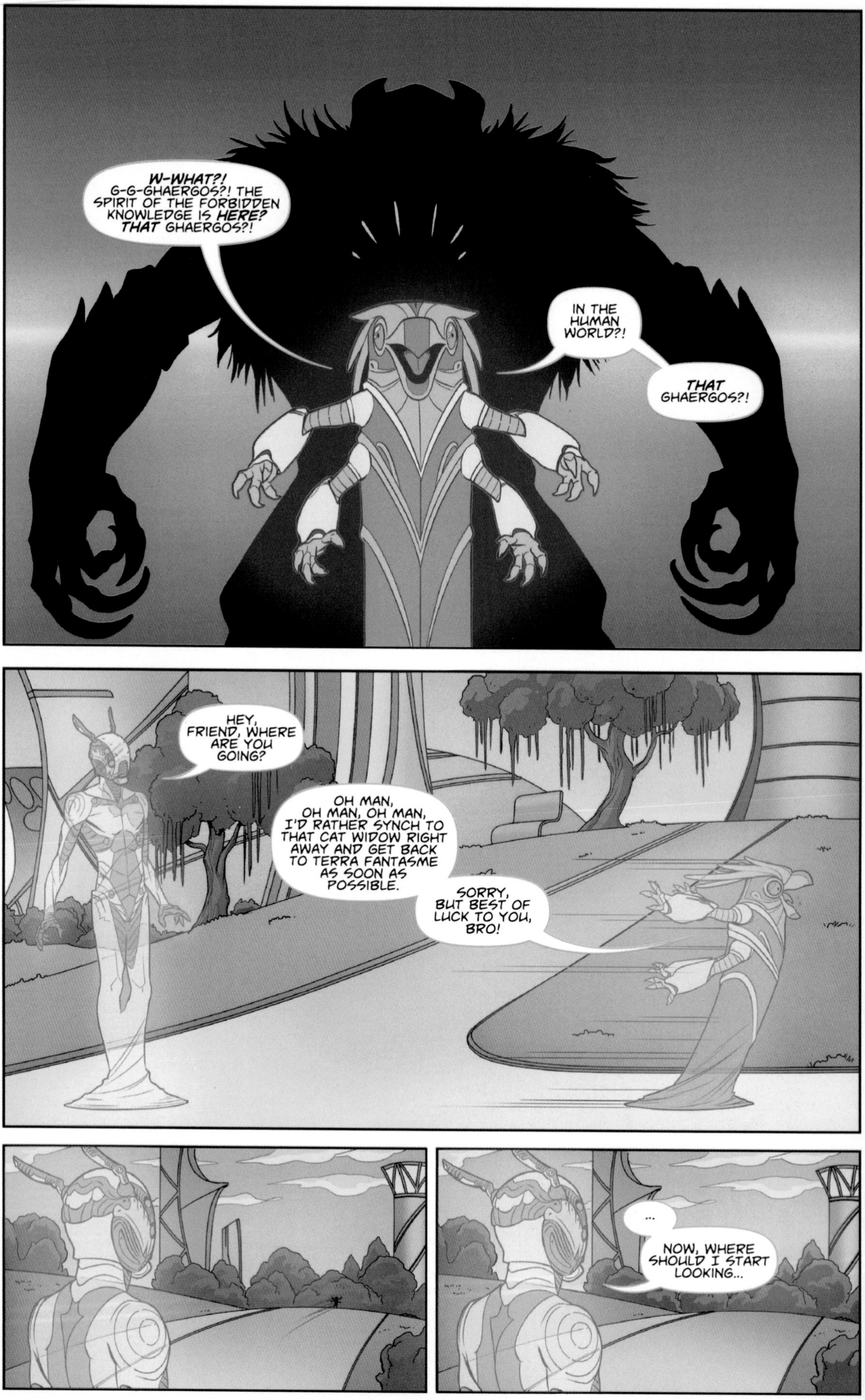
W-WHAT?! G-G-GHAERGOS?! THE SPIRIT OF THE FORBIDDEN KNOWLEDGE IS HERE? THAT GHAERGOS?!
IN THE HUMAN WORLD?!
THAT GHAERGOS?!
HEY, FRIEND, WHERE ARE YOU GOING?
OH MAN, OH MAN, OH MAN, I'D RATHER SYNCH TO THAT CAT WIDOW RIGHT AWAY AND GET BACK TO TERRA FANTASME AS SOON AS POSSIBLE.
SORRY, BUT BEST OF LUCK TO YOU, BRO!
...
NOW, WHERE SHOULD I START LOOKING...

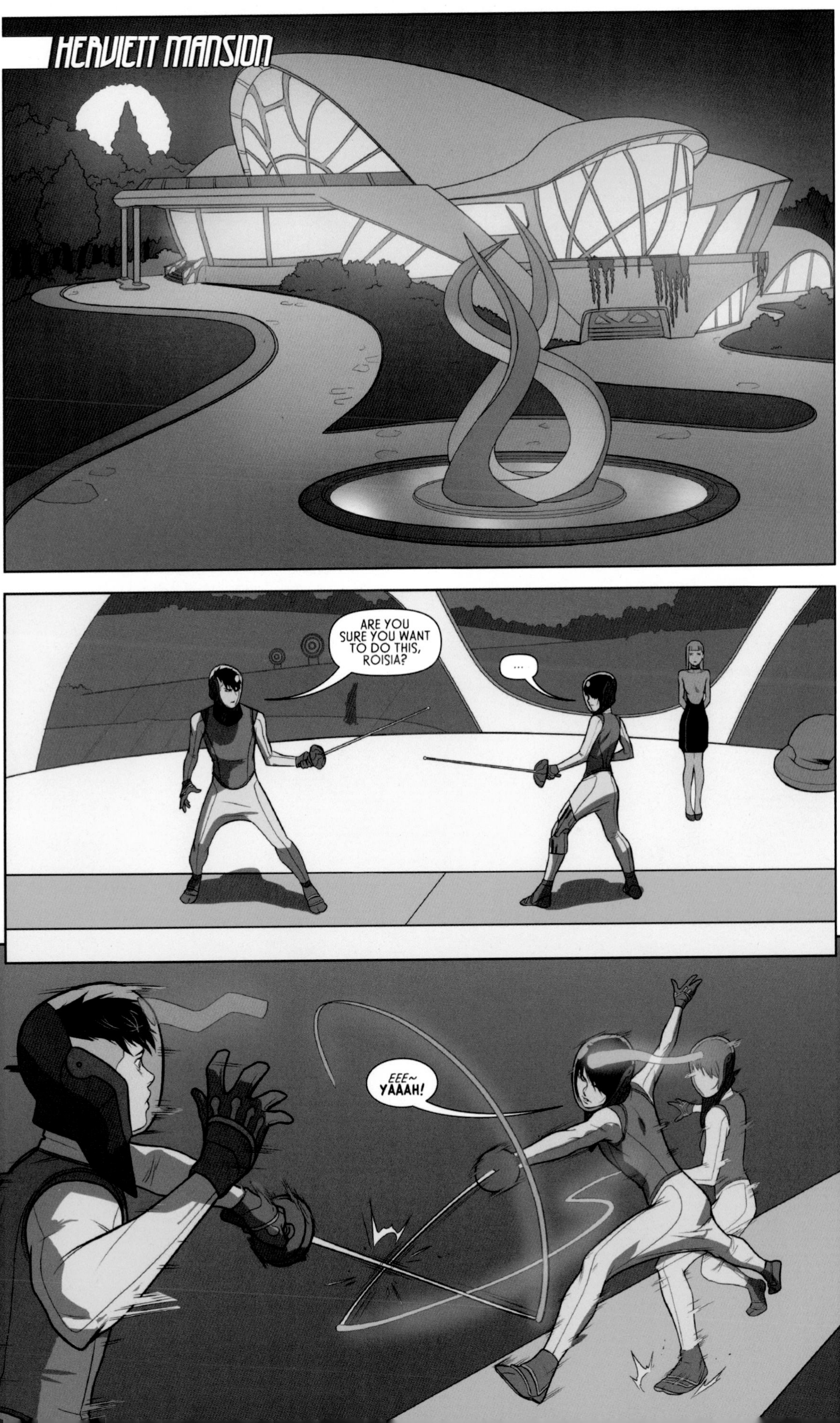
HERVIETT MANSION
ARE YOU SURE YOU WANT TO DO THIS, ROISIA?
...
EEE~ YAAAH!

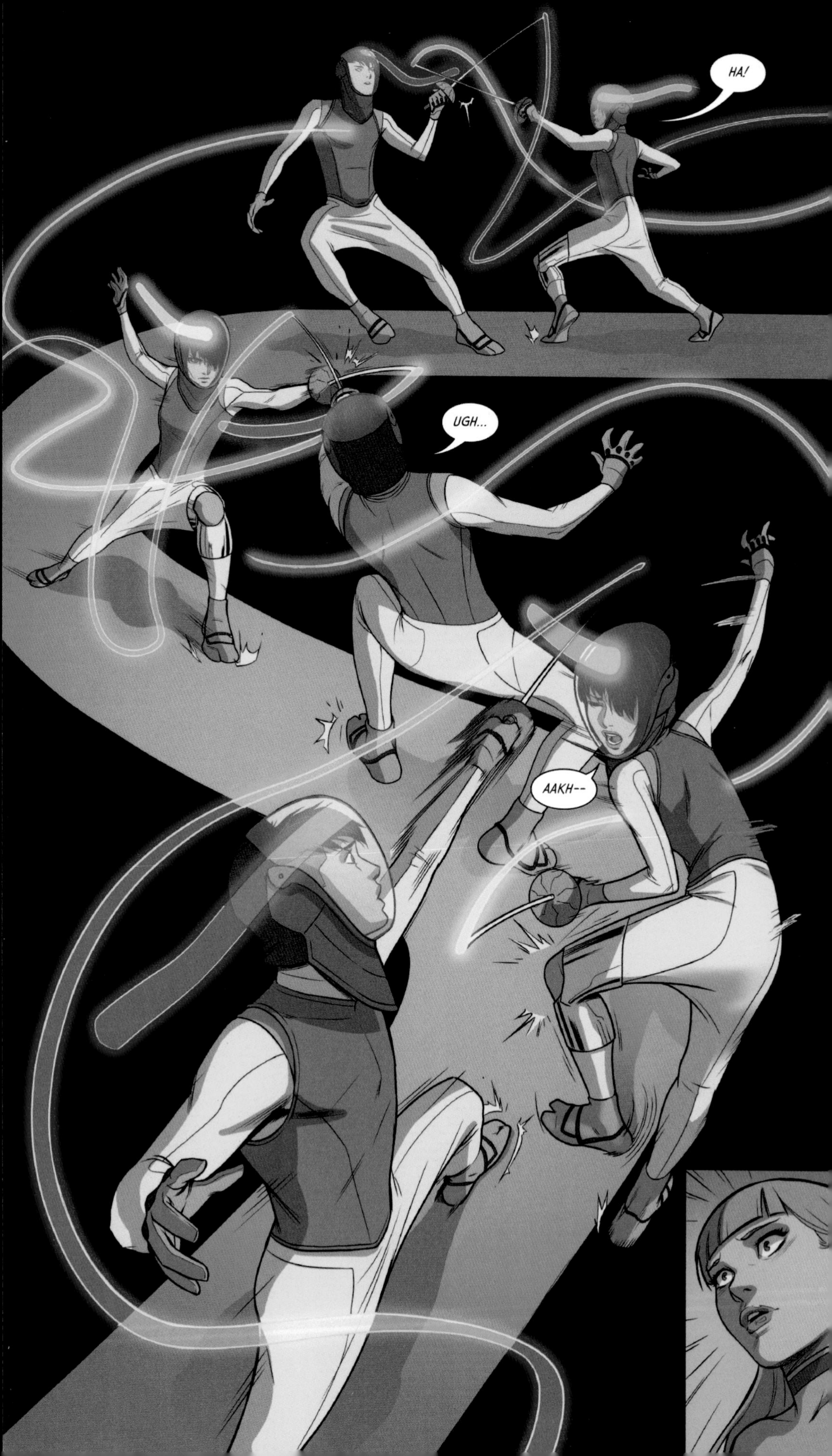
HA!
UGH...
AAKH--

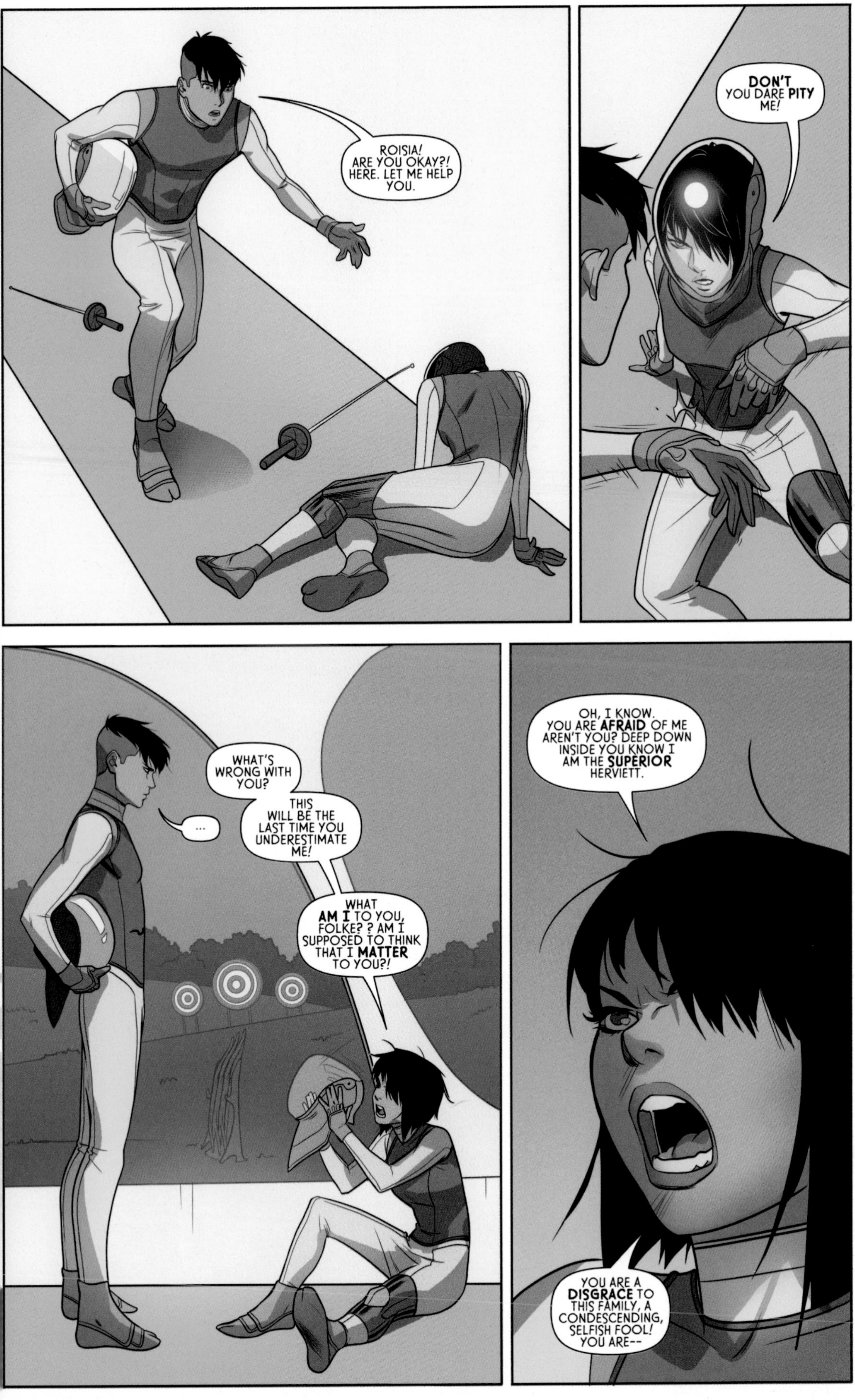
ROISIA! ARE YOU OKAY?! HERE. LET ME HELP YOU.
DON'T YOU DARE PITY ME!
WHAT'S WRONG WITH YOU?
...
THIS WILL BE THE LAST TIME YOU UNDERESTIMATE ME!
WHAT AM I TO YOU, FOLKE? ? AM I SUPPOSED TO THINK THAT I MATTER TO YOU?!
OH, I KNOW. YOU ARE AFRAID OF ME AREN'T YOU? DEEP DOWN INSIDE YOU KNOW I AM THE SUPERIOR HERVIETT.
YOU ARE A DISGRACE TO THIS FAMILY, A CONDESCENDING, SELFISH FOOL! YOU ARE--

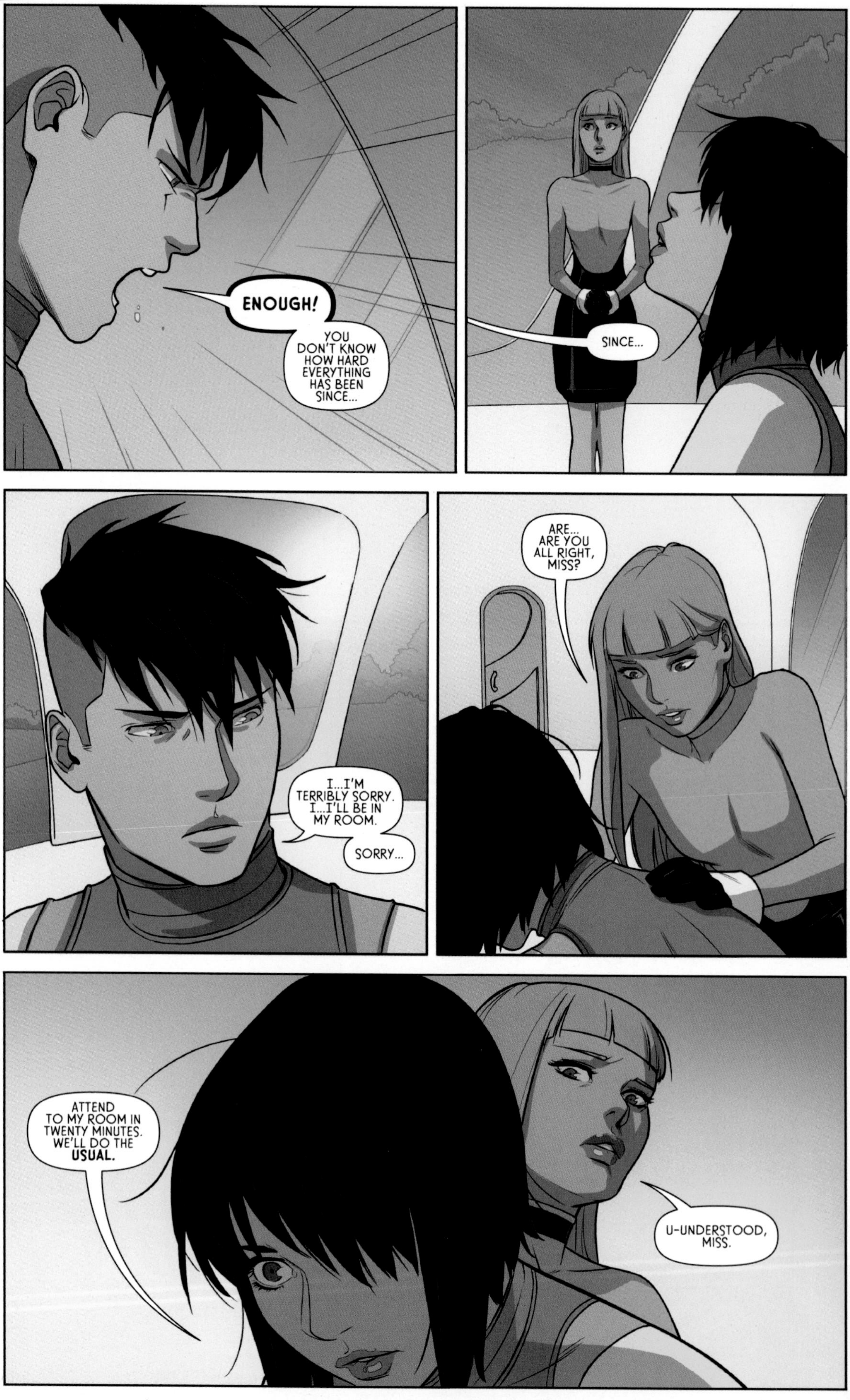
ENOUGH!
YOU DON'T KNOW HOW HARD EVERYTHING HAS BEEN SINCE...
SINCE...
I...I'M TERRIBLY SORRY. I...I'LL BE IN MY ROOM.
SORRY...
ARE... ARE YOU ALL RIGHT, MISS?
ATTEND TO MY ROOM IN TWENTY MINUTES. WE'LL DO THE **USUAL.**
U-UNDERSTOOD, MISS.

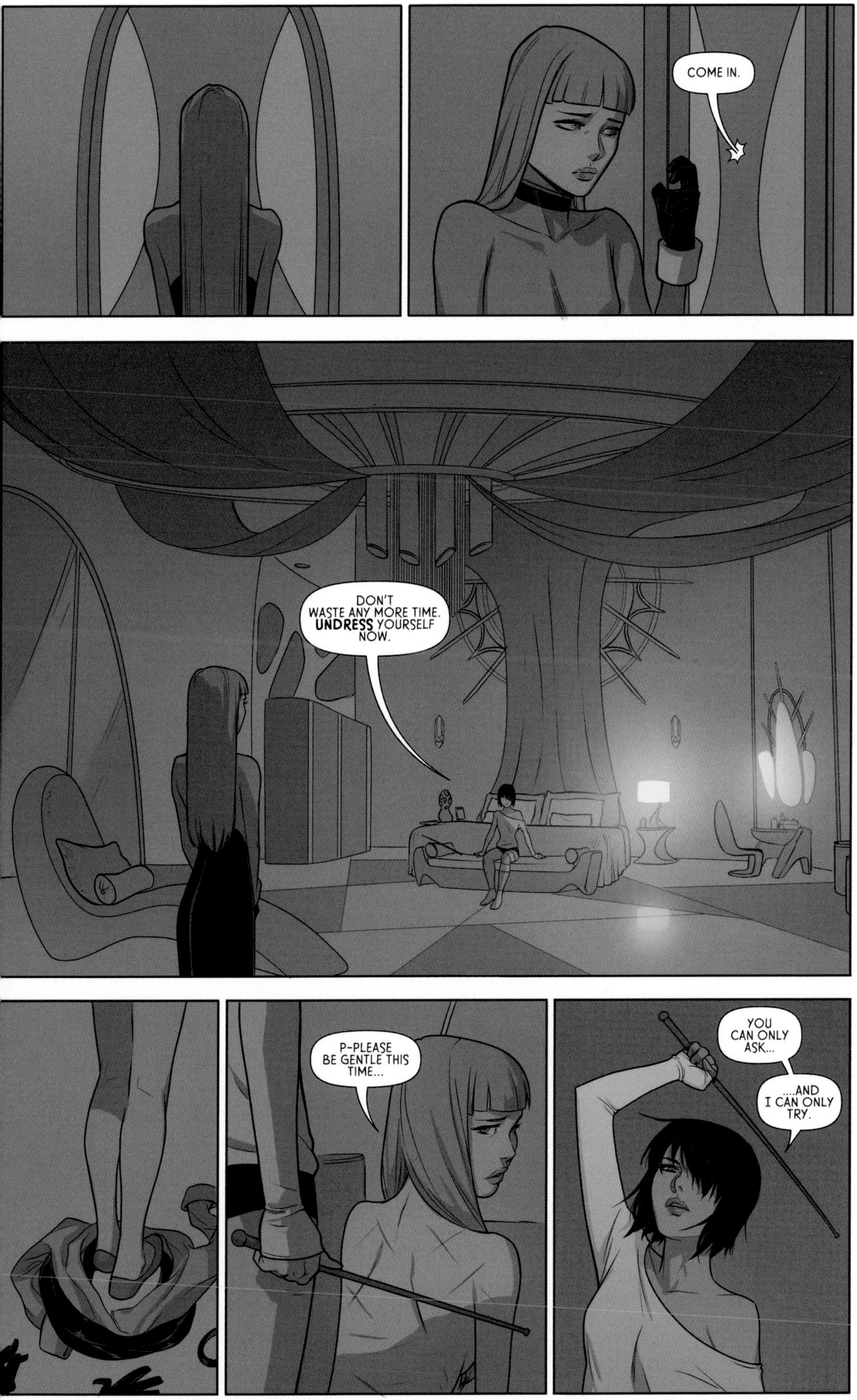
COME IN.
DON'T WASTE ANY MORE TIME. **UNDRESS** YOURSELF NOW.
P-PLEASE BE GENTLE THIS TIME...
YOU CAN ONLY ASK...
....AND I CAN ONLY TRY.

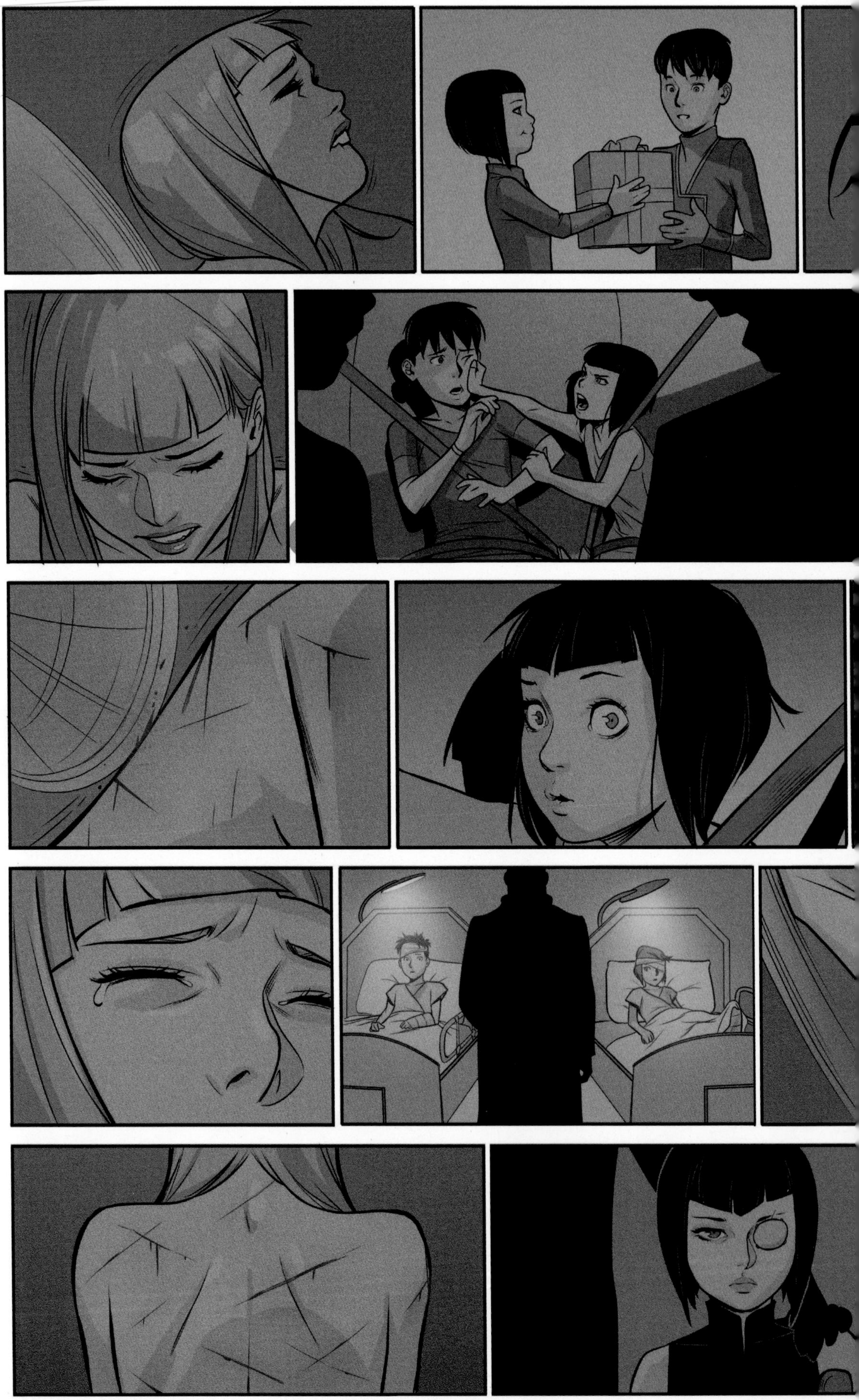

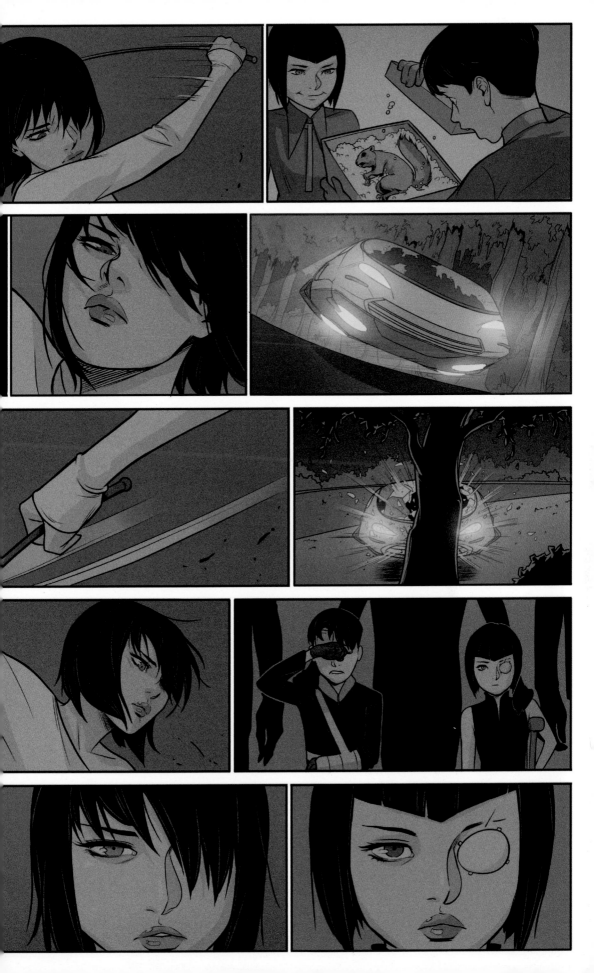

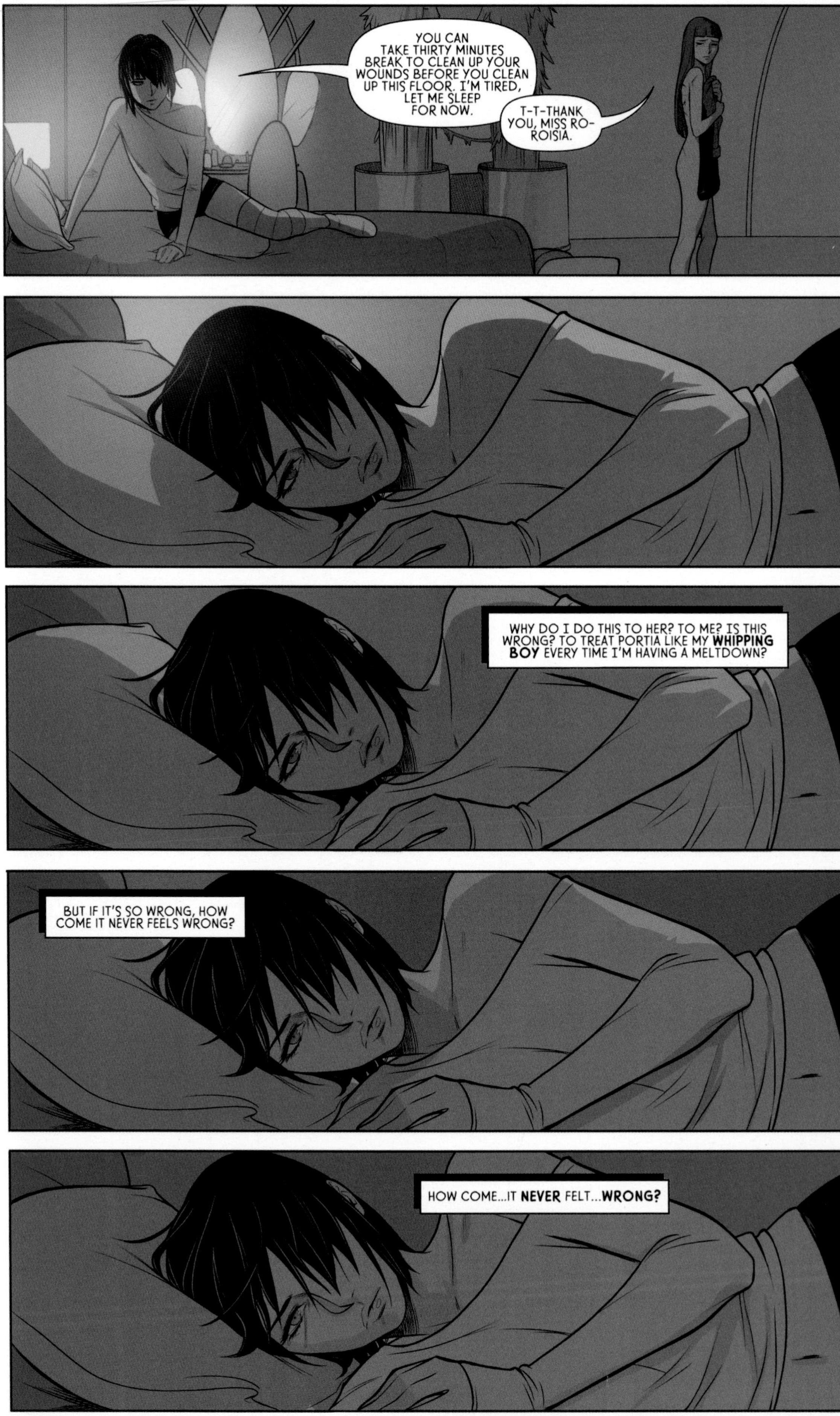
YOU CAN TAKE THIRTY MINUTES BREAK TO CLEAN UP YOUR WOUNDS BEFORE YOU CLEAN UP THIS FLOOR. I'M TIRED, LET ME SLEEP FOR NOW.
T-T-THANK YOU, MISS RO-ROISIA.
WHY DO I DO THIS TO HER? TO ME? IS THIS WRONG? TO TREAT PORTIA LIKE MY **WHIPPING BOY** EVERY TIME I'M HAVING A MELTDOWN?
BUT IF IT'S SO WRONG, HOW COME IT NEVER FEELS WRONG?
HOW COME...IT **NEVER** FELT...**WRONG?**

CHAPTER 2

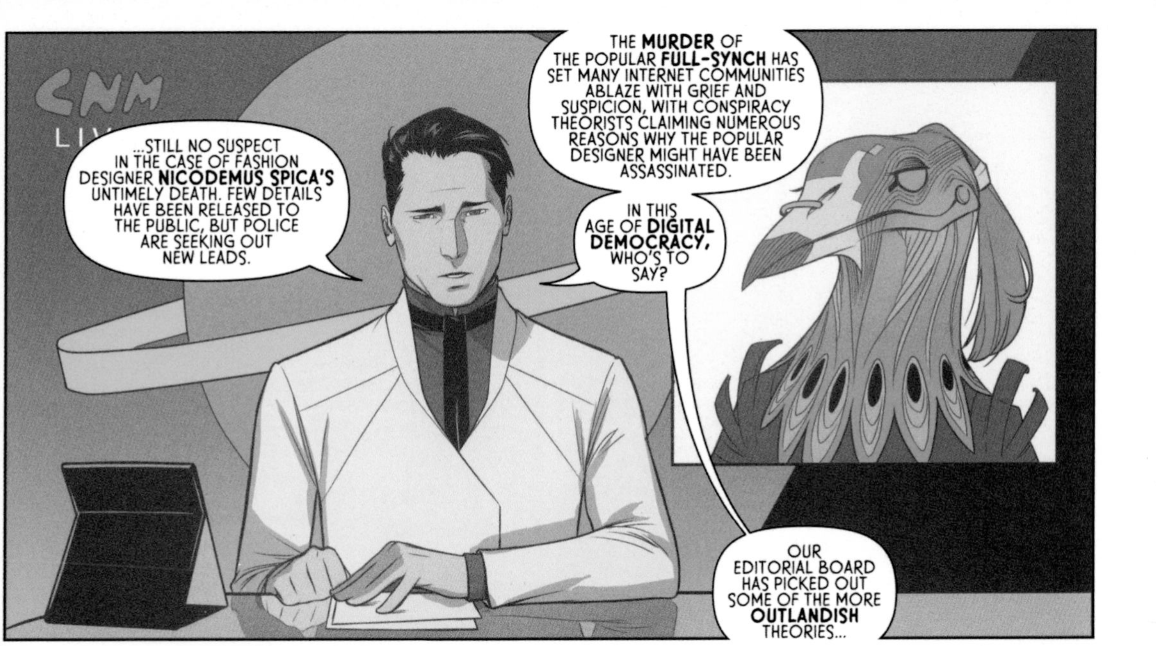
CNM
LIV
...STILL NO SUSPECT IN THE CASE OF FASHION DESIGNER NICODEMUS SPICA'S UNTIMELY DEATH. FEW DETAILS HAVE BEEN RELEASED TO THE PUBLIC, BUT POLICE ARE SEEKING OUT NEW LEADS.
THE MURDER OF THE POPULAR FULL-SYNCH HAS SET MANY INTERNET COMMUNITIES ABLAZE WITH GRIEF AND SUSPICION, WITH CONSPIRACY THEORISTS CLAIMING NUMEROUS REASONS WHY THE POPULAR DESIGNER MIGHT HAVE BEEN ASSASSINATED.
IN THIS AGE OF DIGITAL DEMOCRACY, WHO'S TO SAY?
OUR EDITORIAL BOARD HAS PICKED OUT SOME OF THE MORE OUTLANDISH THEORIES...

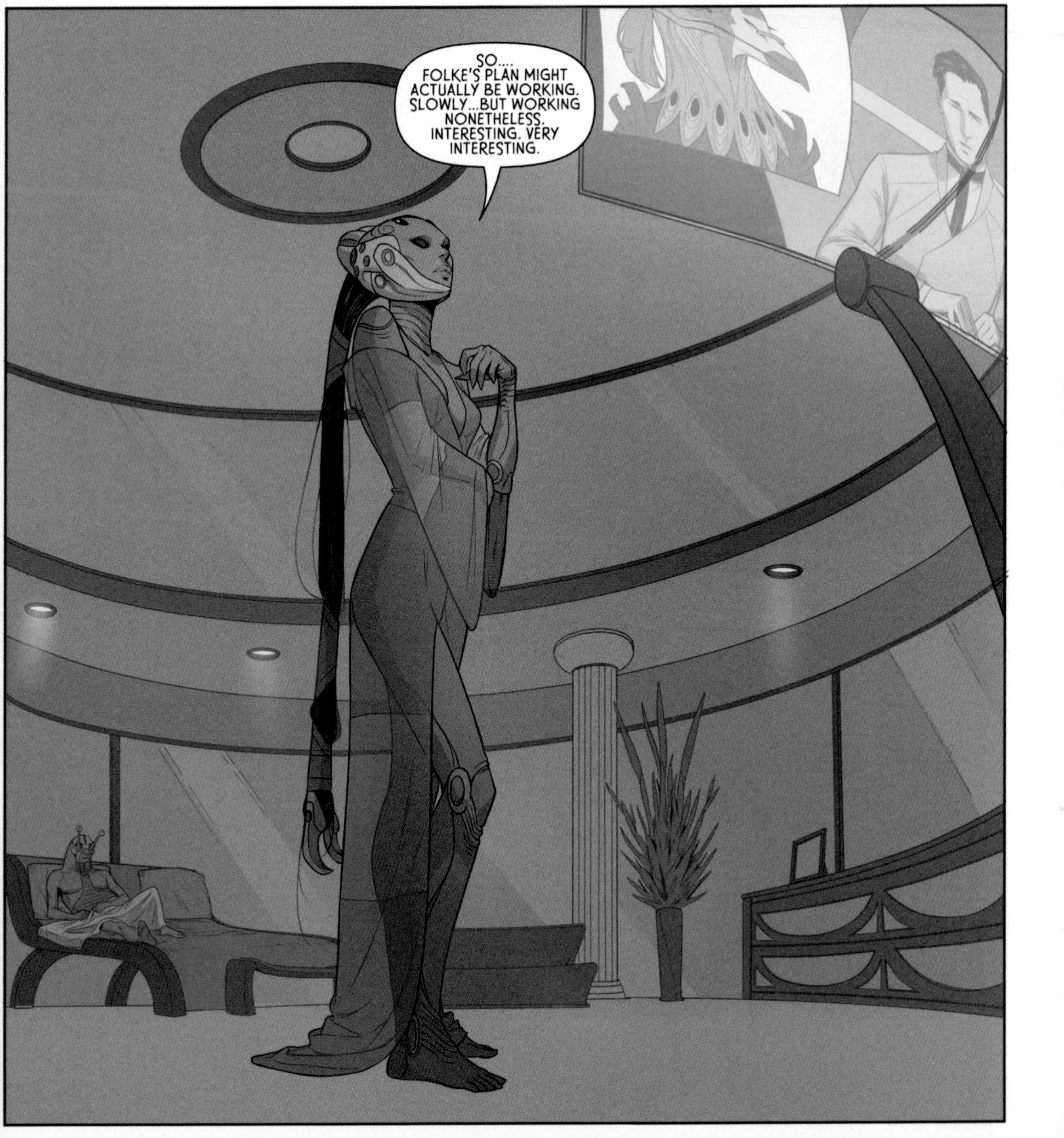
SO.... FOLKE'S PLAN MIGHT ACTUALLY BE WORKING. SLOWLY...BUT WORKING NONETHELESS. INTERESTING. VERY INTERESTING.

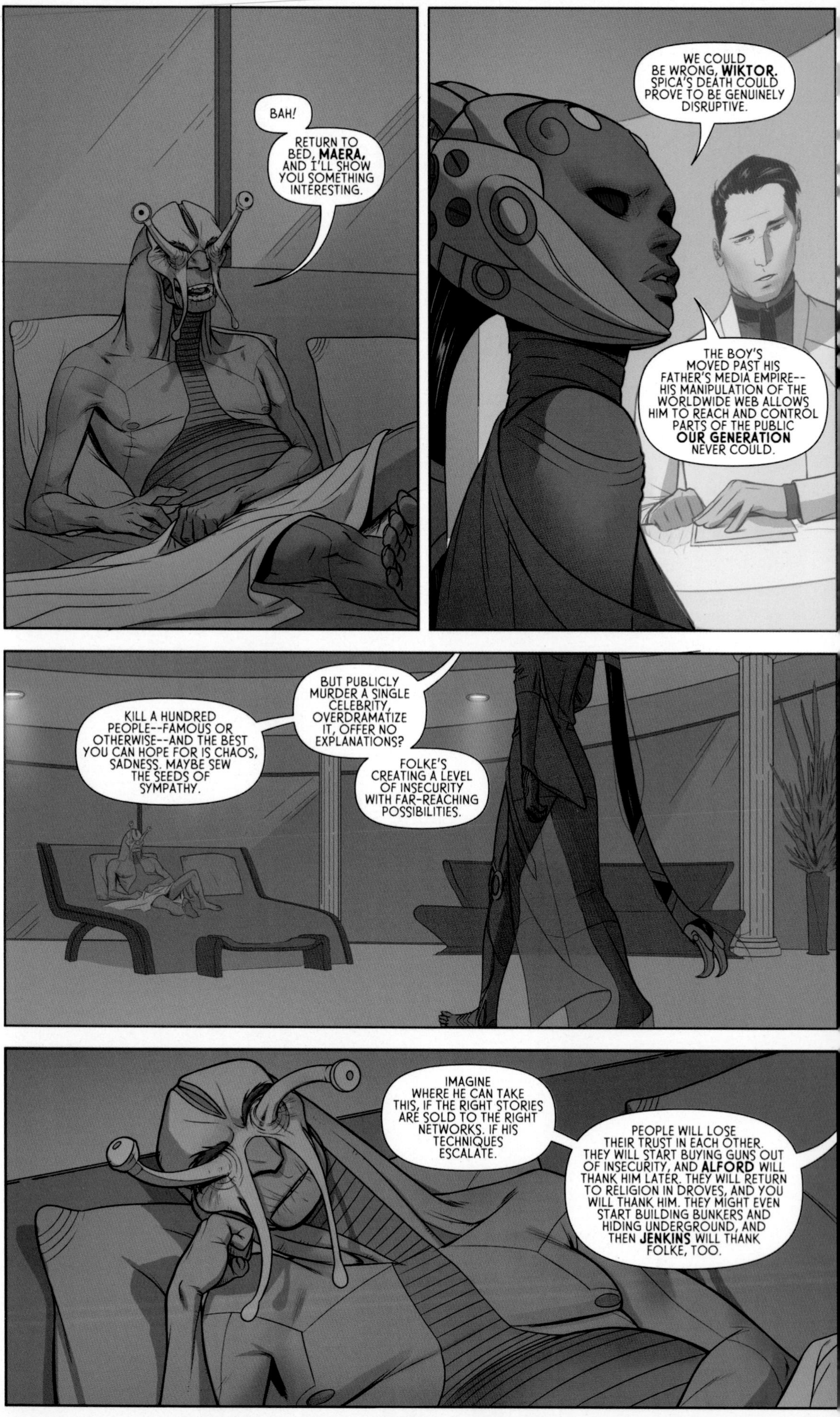
BAH!
RETURN TO BED, MAERA, AND I'LL SHOW YOU SOMETHING INTERESTING.
WE COULD BE WRONG, WIKTOR. SPICA'S DEATH COULD PROVE TO BE GENUINELY DISRUPTIVE.
THE BOY'S MOVED PAST HIS FATHER'S MEDIA EMPIRE--HIS MANIPULATION OF THE WORLDWIDE WEB ALLOWS HIM TO REACH AND CONTROL PARTS OF THE PUBLIC OUR GENERATION NEVER COULD.
KILL A HUNDRED PEOPLE--FAMOUS OR OTHERWISE--AND THE BEST YOU CAN HOPE FOR IS CHAOS, SADNESS. MAYBE SEW THE SEEDS OF SYMPATHY.
BUT PUBLICLY MURDER A SINGLE CELEBRITY, OVERDRAMATIZE IT, OFFER NO EXPLANATIONS?
FOLKE'S CREATING A LEVEL OF INSECURITY WITH FAR-REACHING POSSIBILITIES.
IMAGINE WHERE HE CAN TAKE THIS, IF THE RIGHT STORIES ARE SOLD TO THE RIGHT NETWORKS. IF HIS TECHNIQUES ESCALATE.
PEOPLE WILL LOSE THEIR TRUST IN EACH OTHER. THEY WILL START BUYING GUNS OUT OF INSECURITY, AND ALFORD WILL THANK HIM LATER. THEY WILL RETURN TO RELIGION IN DROVES, AND YOU WILL THANK HIM. THEY MIGHT EVEN START BUILDING BUNKERS AND HIDING UNDERGROUND, AND THEN JENKINS WILL THANK FOLKE, TOO.

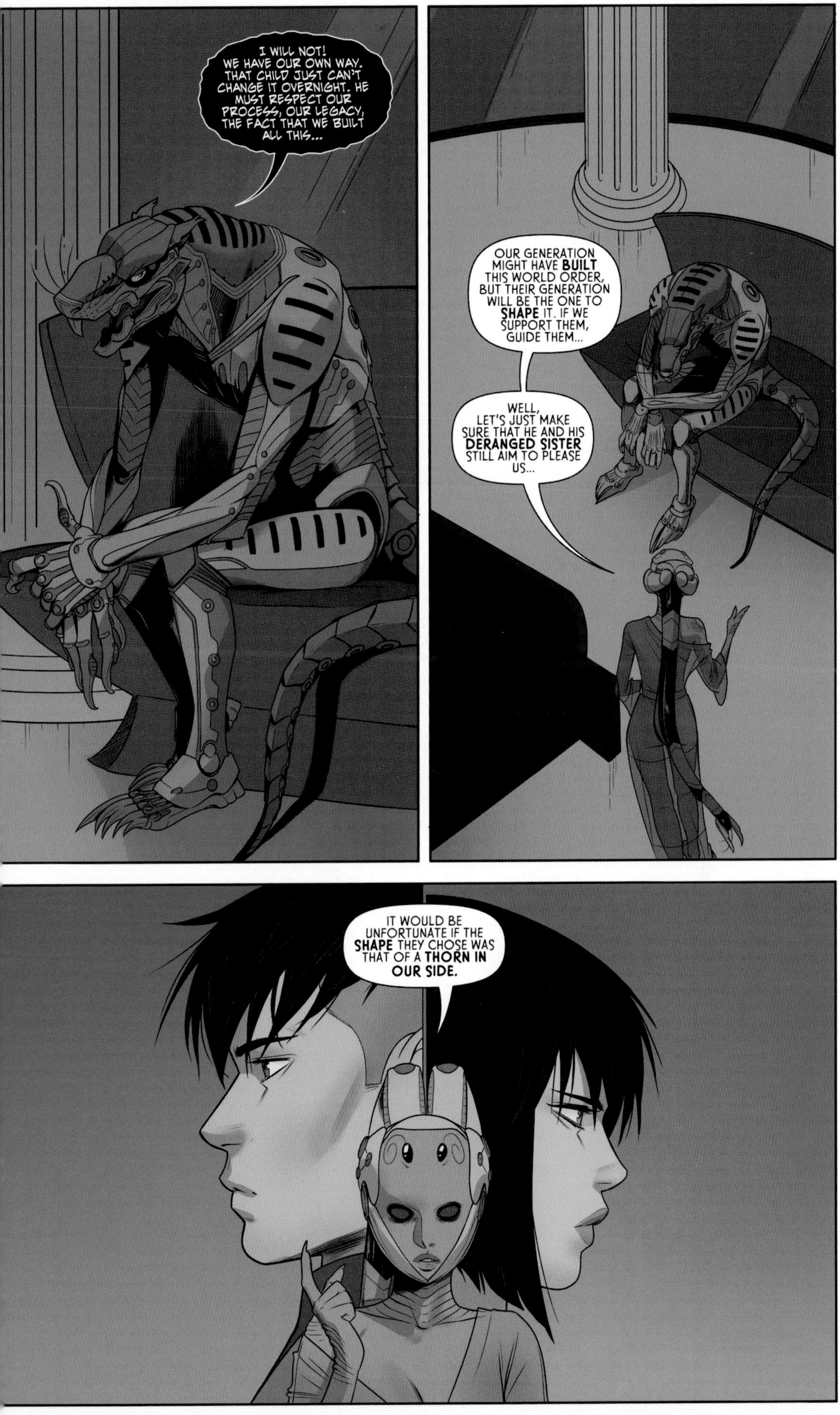
I WILL NOT! WE HAVE OUR OWN WAY. THAT CHILD JUST CAN'T CHANGE IT OVERNIGHT. HE MUST RESPECT OUR PROCESS, OUR LEGACY, THE FACT THAT WE BUILT ALL THIS...
OUR GENERATION MIGHT HAVE BUILT THIS WORLD ORDER, BUT THEIR GENERATION WILL BE THE ONE TO SHAPE IT. IF WE SUPPORT THEM, GUIDE THEM...
WELL, LET'S JUST MAKE SURE THAT HE AND HIS DERANGED SISTER STILL AIM TO PLEASE US...
IT WOULD BE UNFORTUNATE IF THE SHAPE THEY CHOSE WAS THAT OF A THORN IN OUR SIDE.

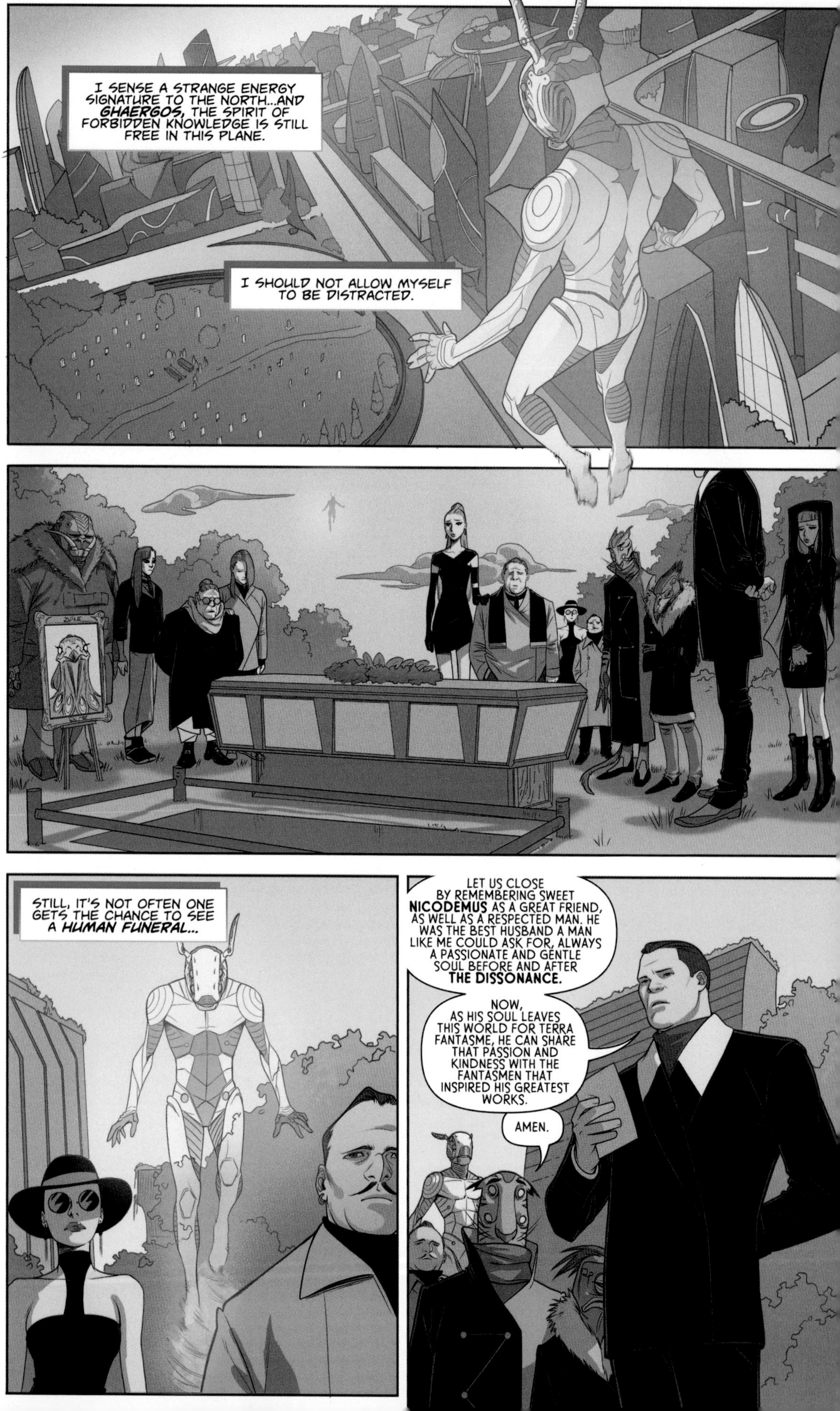
I SENSE A STRANGE ENERGY SIGNATURE TO THE NORTH...AND ***GHAERGOS***, THE SPIRIT OF FORBIDDEN KNOWLEDGE IS STILL FREE IN THIS PLANE.
I SHOULD NOT ALLOW MYSELF TO BE DISTRACTED.
STILL, IT'S NOT OFTEN ONE GETS THE CHANCE TO SEE A ***HUMAN FUNERAL***...
LET US CLOSE BY REMEMBERING SWEET **NICODEMUS** AS A GREAT FRIEND, AS WELL AS A RESPECTED MAN. HE WAS THE BEST HUSBAND A MAN LIKE ME COULD ASK FOR, ALWAYS A PASSIONATE AND GENTLE SOUL BEFORE AND AFTER **THE DISSONANCE.**
NOW, AS HIS SOUL LEAVES THIS WORLD FOR TERRA FANTASME, HE CAN SHARE THAT PASSION AND KINDNESS WITH THE FANTASMEN THAT INSPIRED HIS GREATEST WORKS.
AMEN.

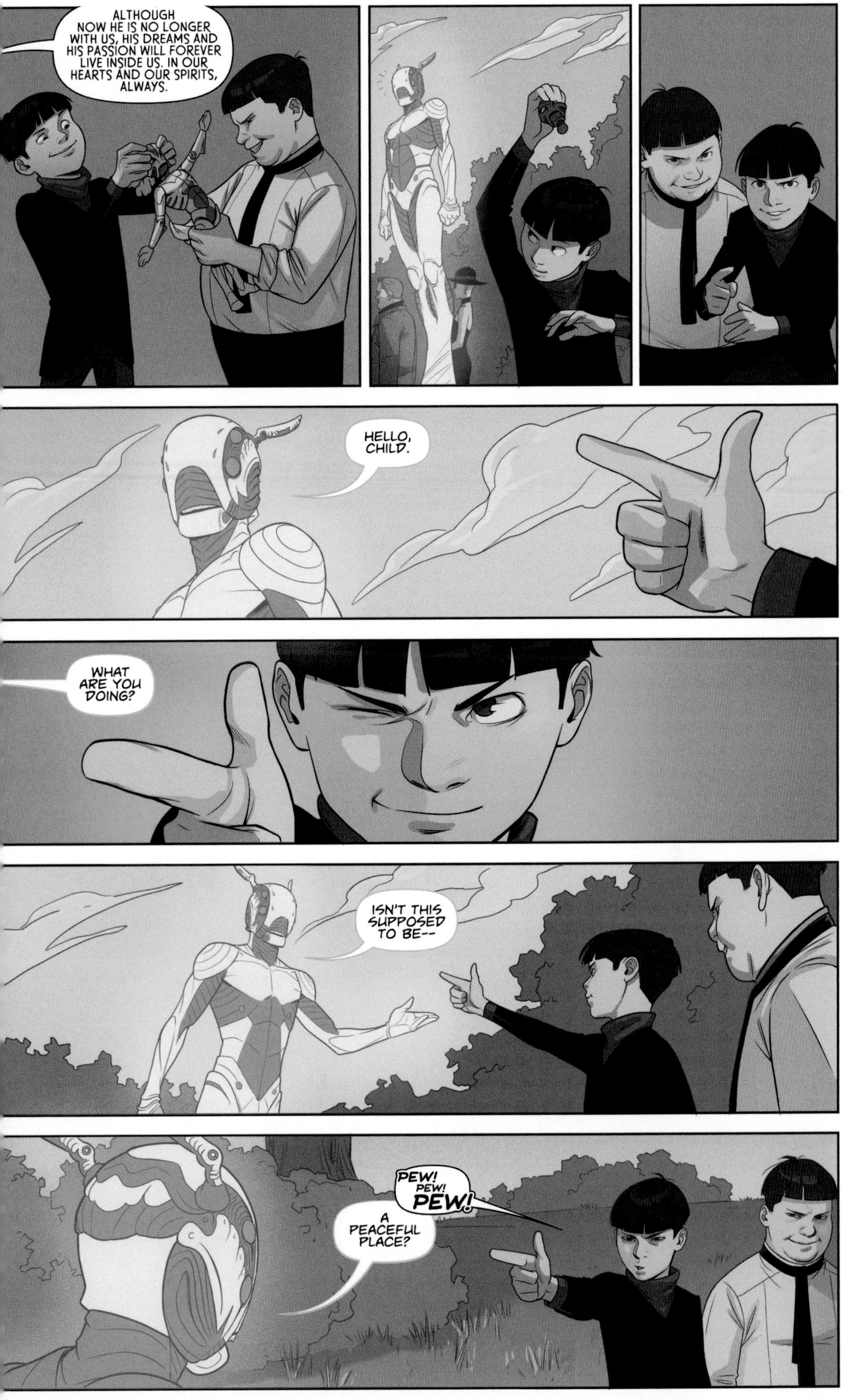
ALTHOUGH NOW HE IS NO LONGER WITH US, HIS DREAMS AND HIS PASSION WILL FOREVER LIVE INSIDE US. IN OUR HEARTS AND OUR SPIRITS, ALWAYS.
HELLO, CHILD.
WHAT ARE YOU DOING?
ISN'T THIS SUPPOSED TO BE--
PEW! PEW! PEW!
A PEACEFUL PLACE?

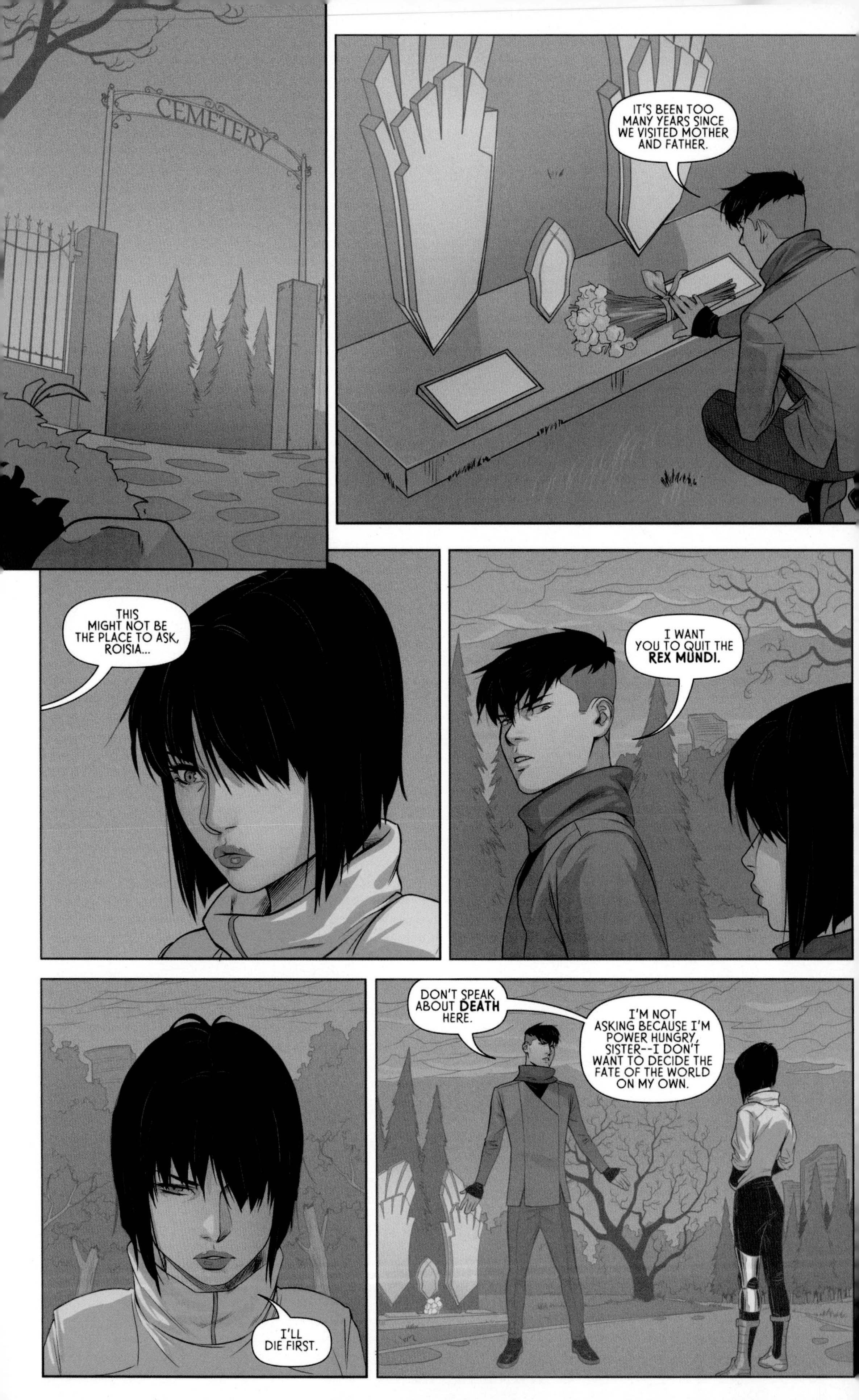
CEMETERY
IT'S BEEN TOO MANY YEARS SINCE WE VISITED MOTHER AND FATHER.
THIS MIGHT NOT BE THE PLACE TO ASK, ROISIA...
I WANT YOU TO QUIT THE **REX MUNDI.**
I'LL DIE FIRST.
DON'T SPEAK ABOUT **DEATH** HERE.
I'M NOT ASKING BECAUSE I'M POWER HUNGRY, SISTER--I DON'T WANT TO DECIDE THE FATE OF THE WORLD ON MY OWN.

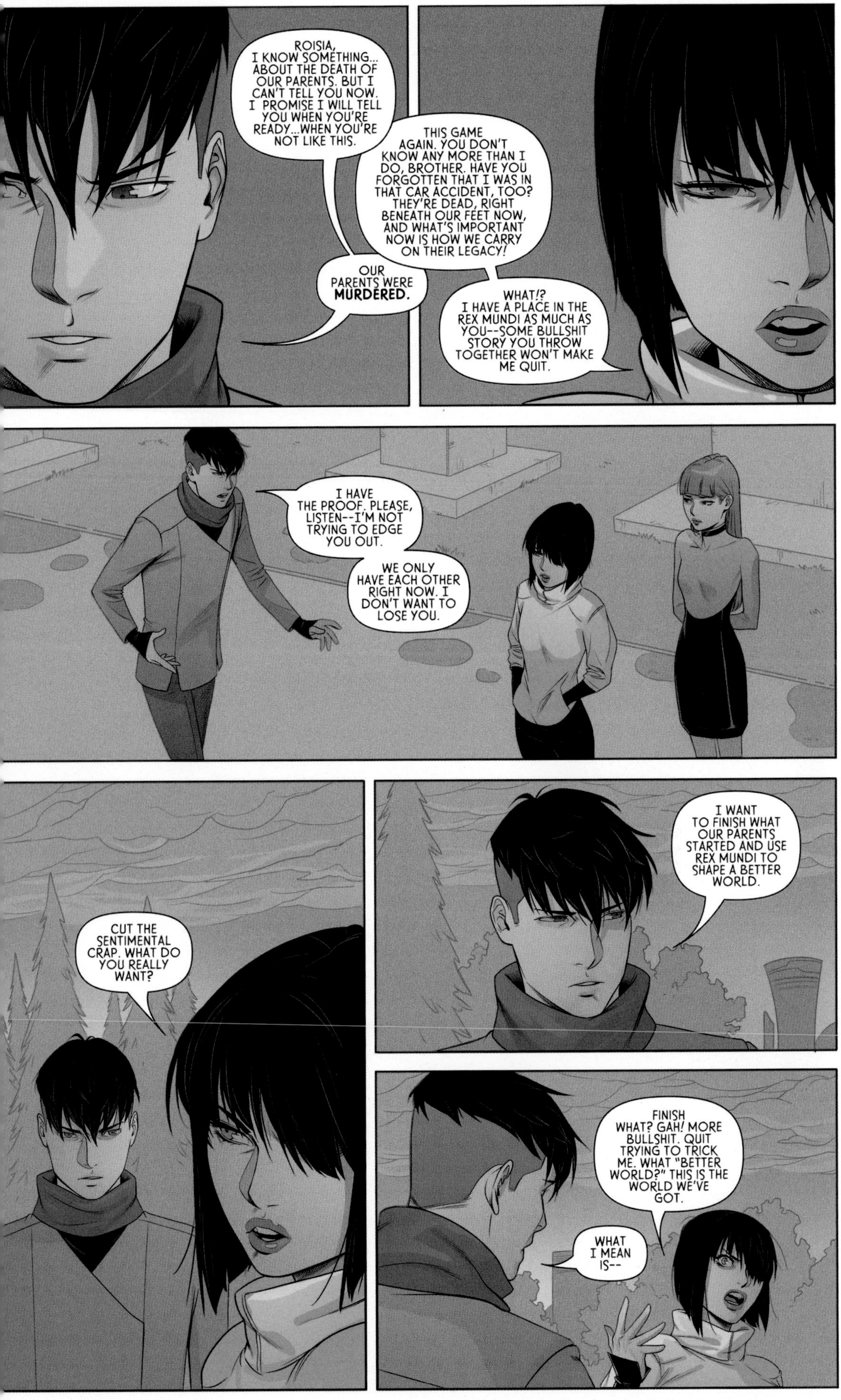
ROISIA, I KNOW SOMETHING... ABOUT THE DEATH OF OUR PARENTS. BUT I CAN'T TELL YOU NOW. I PROMISE I WILL TELL YOU WHEN YOU'RE READY...WHEN YOU'RE NOT LIKE THIS.
THIS GAME AGAIN. YOU DON'T KNOW ANY MORE THAN I DO, BROTHER. HAVE YOU FORGOTTEN THAT I WAS IN THAT CAR ACCIDENT, TOO? THEY'RE DEAD, RIGHT BENEATH OUR FEET NOW, AND WHAT'S IMPORTANT NOW IS HOW WE CARRY ON THEIR LEGACY!
OUR PARENTS WERE **MURDERED.**
WHAT!? I HAVE A PLACE IN THE REX MUNDI AS MUCH AS YOU--SOME BULLSHIT STORY YOU THROW TOGETHER WON'T MAKE ME QUIT.
I HAVE THE PROOF. PLEASE, LISTEN--I'M NOT TRYING TO EDGE YOU OUT.
WE ONLY HAVE EACH OTHER RIGHT NOW. I DON'T WANT TO LOSE YOU.
CUT THE SENTIMENTAL CRAP. WHAT DO YOU REALLY WANT?
I WANT TO FINISH WHAT OUR PARENTS STARTED AND USE REX MUNDI TO SHAPE A BETTER WORLD.
FINISH WHAT? GAH! MORE BULLSHIT. QUIT TRYING TO TRICK ME. WHAT "BETTER WORLD?" THIS IS THE WORLD WE'VE GOT.
WHAT I MEAN IS--

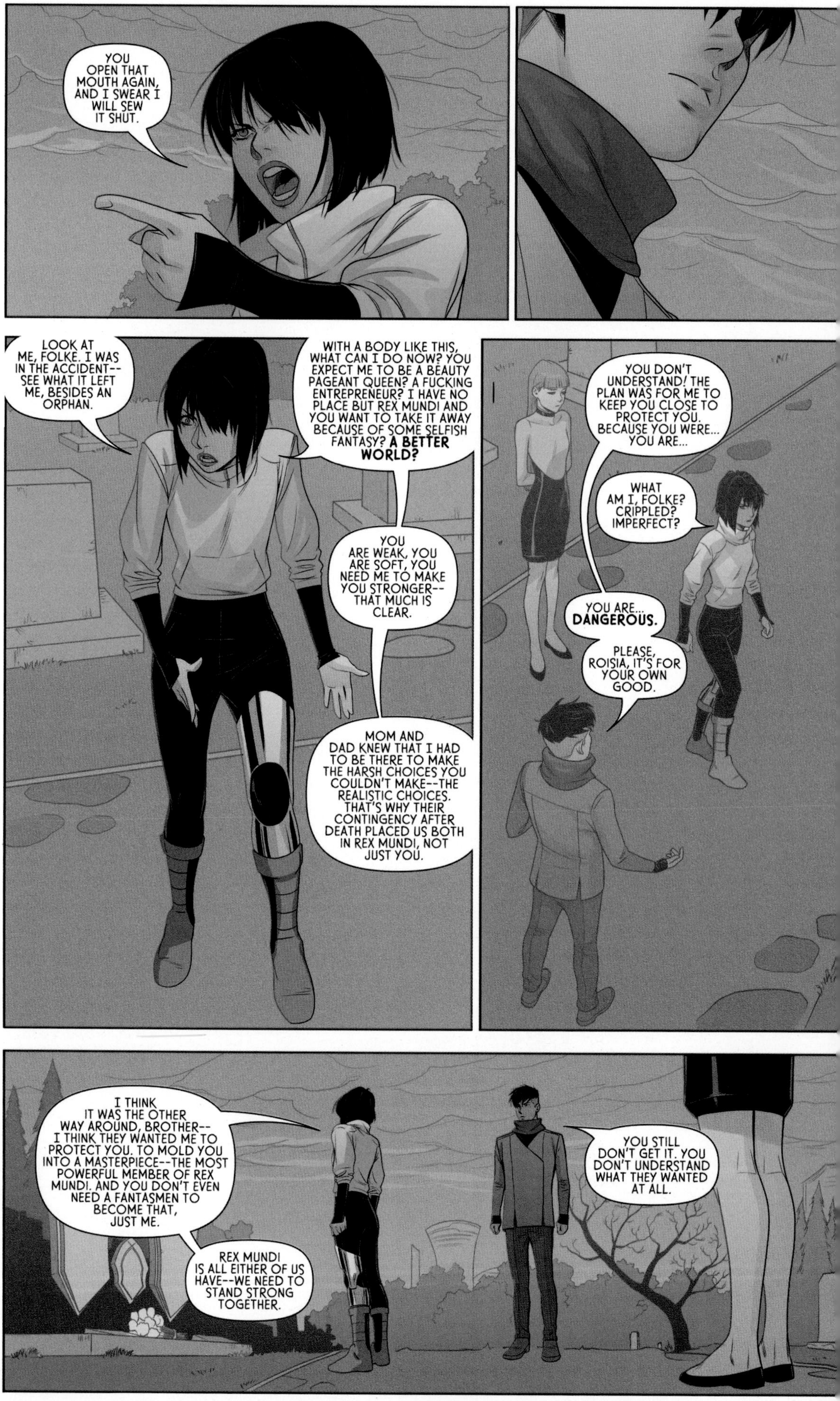

YOU OPEN THAT MOUTH AGAIN, AND I SWEAR I WILL SEW IT SHUT.
LOOK AT ME, FOLKE. I WAS IN THE ACCIDENT-- SEE WHAT IT LEFT ME, BESIDES AN ORPHAN.
WITH A BODY LIKE THIS, WHAT CAN I DO NOW? YOU EXPECT ME TO BE A BEAUTY PAGEANT QUEEN? A FUCKING ENTREPRENEUR? I HAVE NO PLACE BUT REX MUNDI AND YOU WANT TO TAKE IT AWAY BECAUSE OF SOME SELFISH FANTASY? **A BETTER WORLD?**
YOU ARE WEAK, YOU ARE SOFT, YOU NEED ME TO MAKE YOU STRONGER-- THAT MUCH IS CLEAR.
MOM AND DAD KNEW THAT I HAD TO BE THERE TO MAKE THE HARSH CHOICES YOU COULDN'T MAKE--THE REALISTIC CHOICES. THAT'S WHY THEIR CONTINGENCY AFTER DEATH PLACED US BOTH IN REX MUNDI, NOT JUST YOU.
YOU DON'T UNDERSTAND! THE PLAN WAS FOR ME TO KEEP YOU CLOSE TO PROTECT YOU. BECAUSE YOU WERE... YOU ARE...
WHAT AM I, FOLKE? CRIPPLED? IMPERFECT?
YOU ARE... **DANGEROUS.**
PLEASE, ROISIA, IT'S FOR YOUR OWN GOOD.
I THINK IT WAS THE OTHER WAY AROUND, BROTHER-- I THINK THEY WANTED ME TO PROTECT YOU. TO MOLD YOU INTO A MASTERPIECE--THE MOST POWERFUL MEMBER OF REX MUNDI. AND YOU DON'T EVEN NEED A FANTASMEN TO BECOME THAT, JUST ME.
REX MUNDI IS ALL EITHER OF US HAVE--WE NEED TO STAND STRONG TOGETHER.
YOU STILL DON'T GET IT. YOU DON'T UNDERSTAND WHAT THEY WANTED AT ALL.

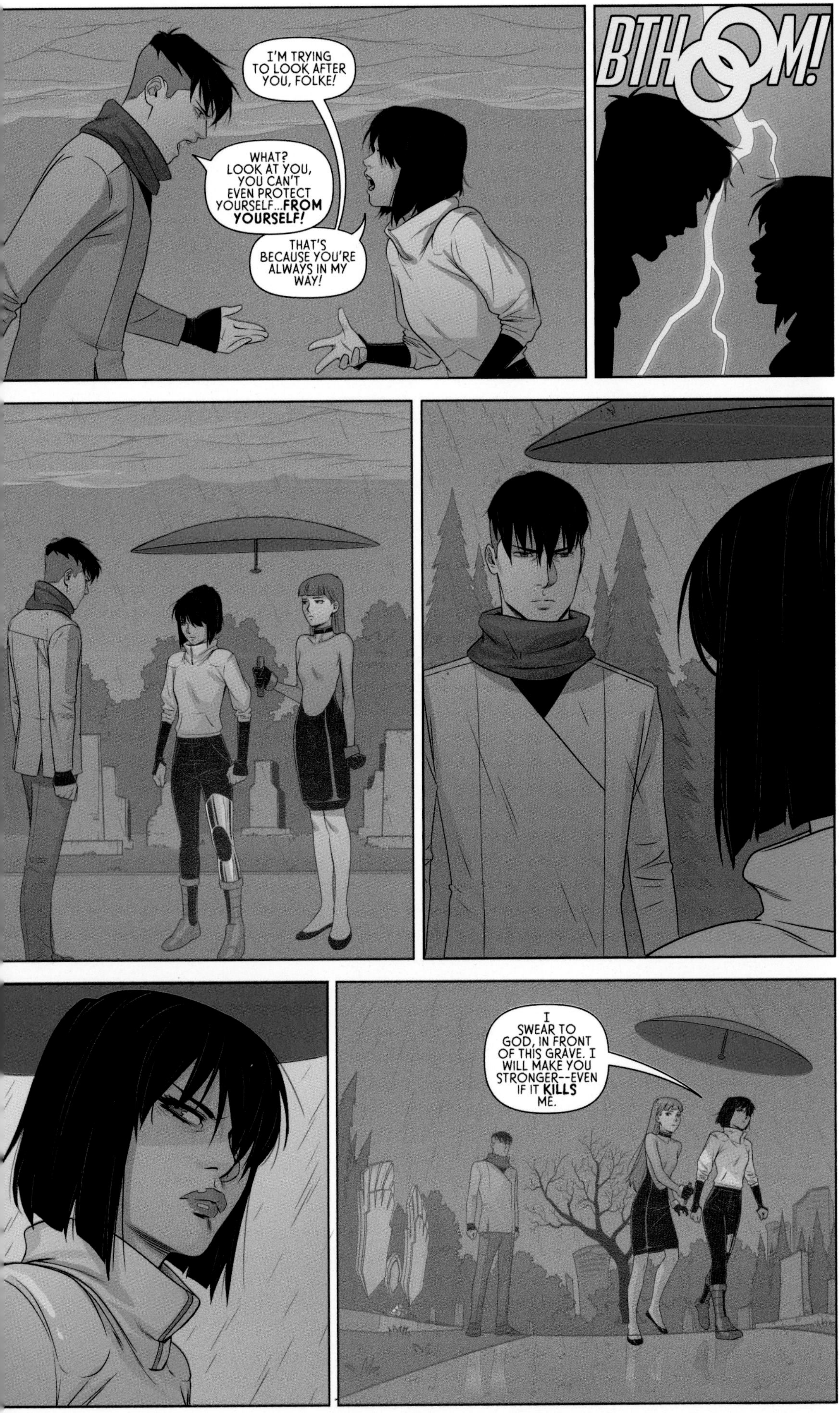
I'M TRYING TO LOOK AFTER YOU, FOLKE!
WHAT? LOOK AT YOU, YOU CAN'T EVEN PROTECT YOURSELF...**FROM YOURSELF!**
THAT'S BECAUSE YOU'RE ALWAYS IN MY WAY!
BTHOOM!
I SWEAR TO GOD, IN FRONT OF THIS GRAVE. I WILL MAKE YOU STRONGER--EVEN IF IT **KILLS** ME.

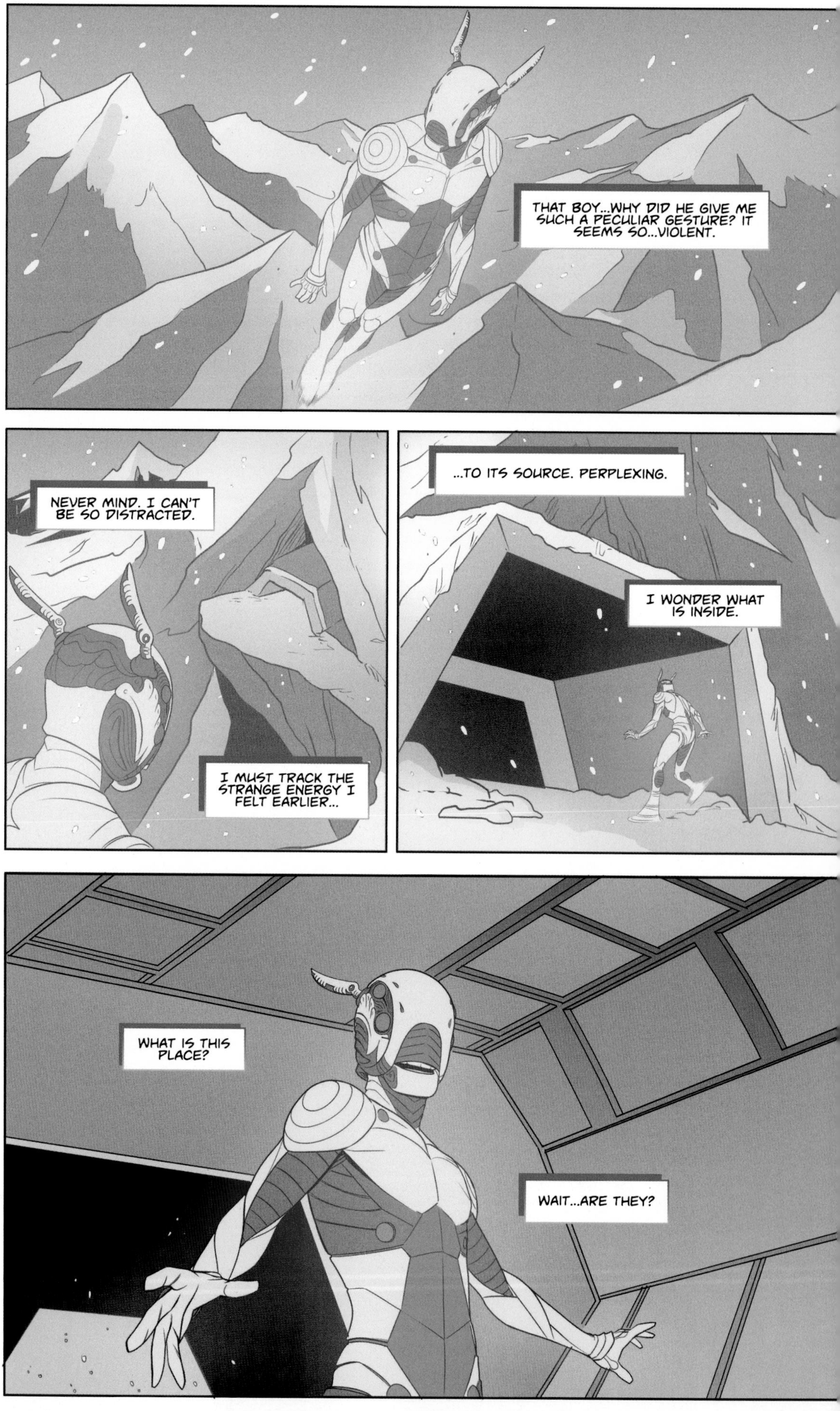

THAT BOY...WHY DID HE GIVE ME SUCH A PECULIAR GESTURE? IT SEEMS SO...VIOLENT.
NEVER MIND. I CAN'T BE SO DISTRACTED.
I MUST TRACK THE STRANGE ENERGY I FELT EARLIER...
...TO ITS SOURCE. PERPLEXING.
I WONDER WHAT IS INSIDE.
WHAT IS THIS PLACE?
WAIT...ARE THEY?

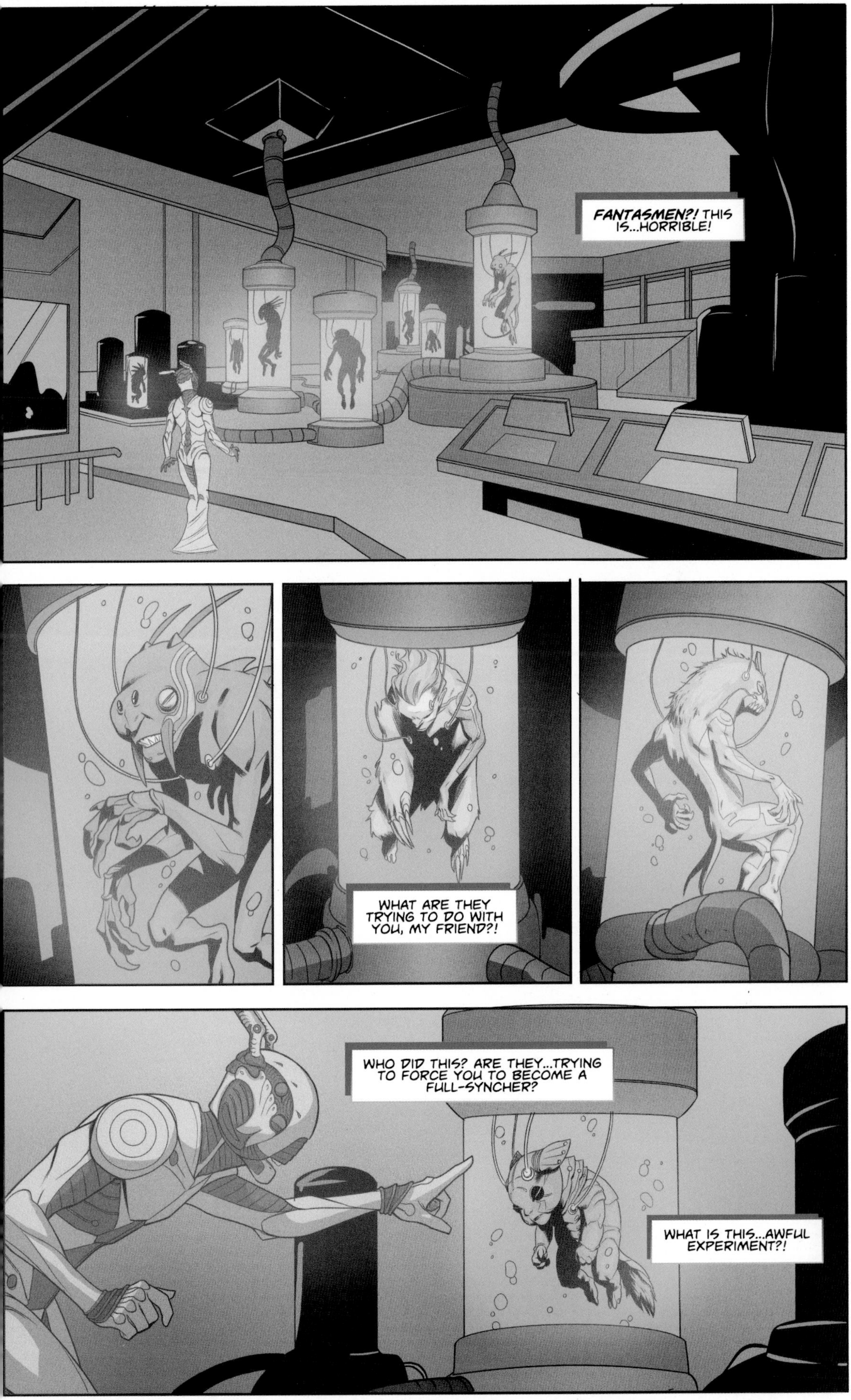
FANTASMEN?! THIS IS...HORRIBLE!
WHAT ARE THEY TRYING TO DO WITH YOU, MY FRIEND?!
WHO DID THIS? ARE THEY...TRYING TO FORCE YOU TO BECOME A FULL-SYNCHER?
WHAT IS THIS...AWFUL EXPERIMENT?!

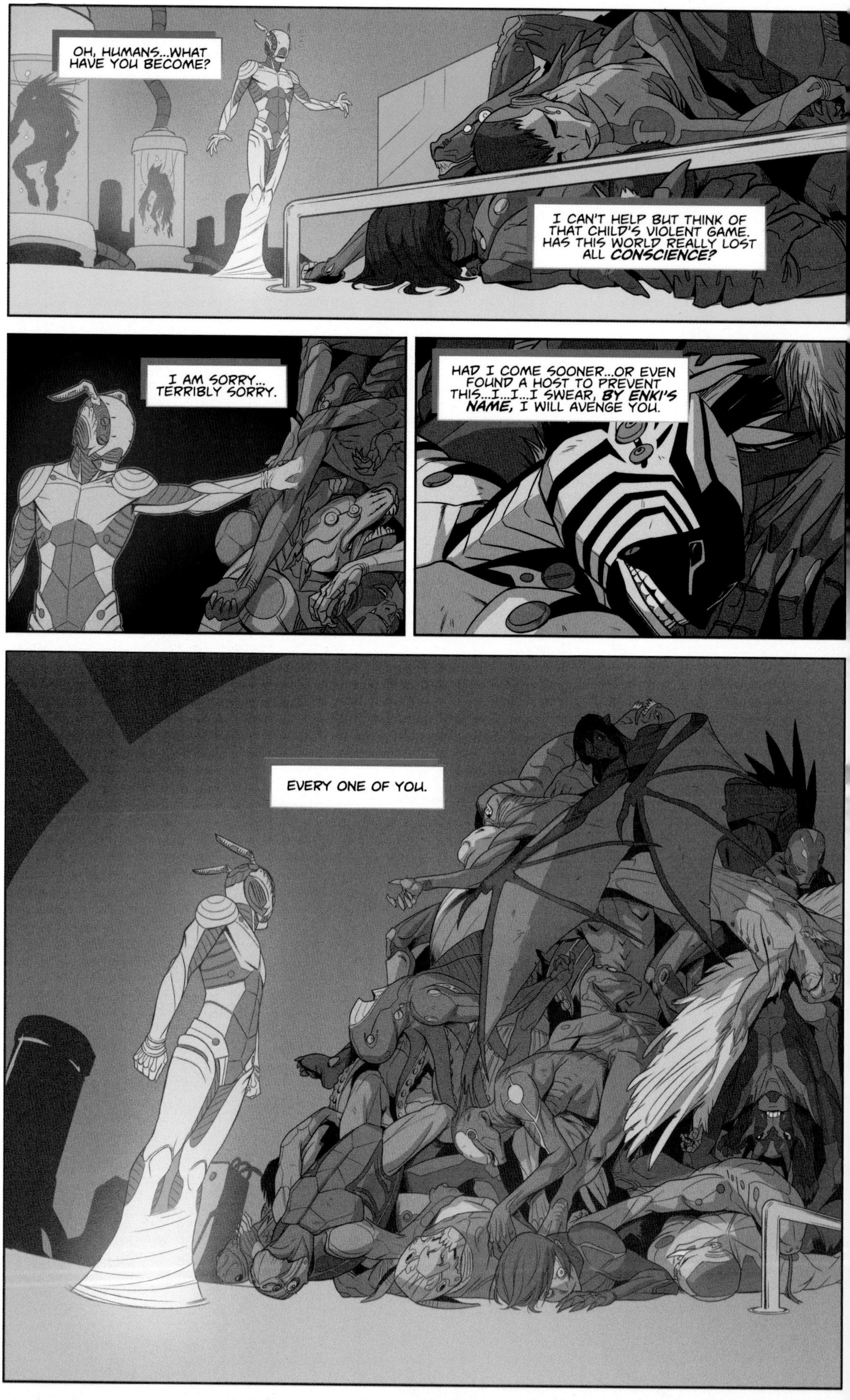
OH, HUMANS...WHAT HAVE YOU BECOME?
I CAN'T HELP BUT THINK OF THAT CHILD'S VIOLENT GAME. HAS THIS WORLD REALLY LOST ALL CONSCIENCE?
I AM SORRY... TERRIBLY SORRY.
HAD I COME SOONER...OR EVEN FOUND A HOST TO PREVENT THIS...I...I...I SWEAR, BY ENKI'S NAME, I WILL AVENGE YOU.
EVERY ONE OF YOU.

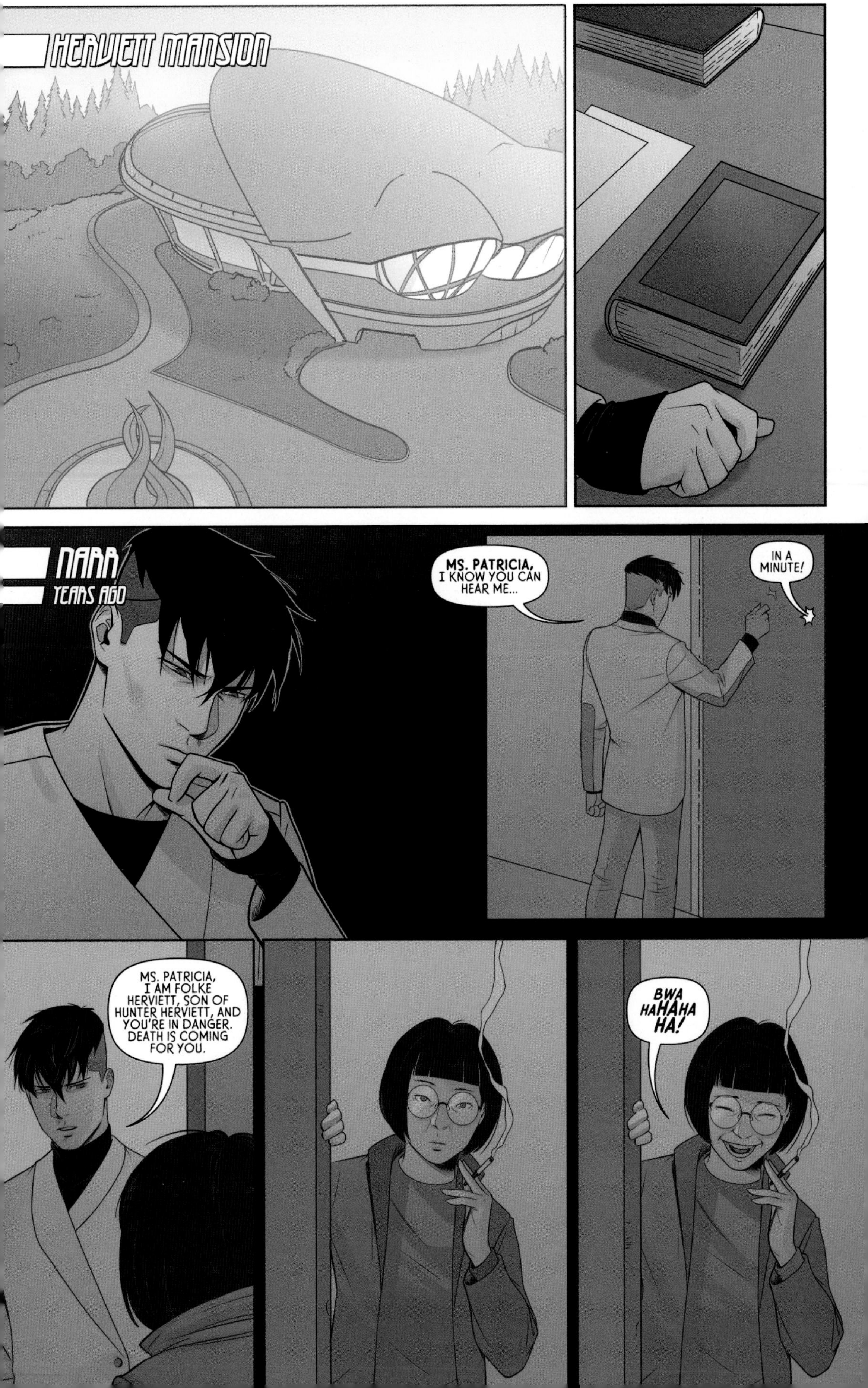
HERVIETT MANSION
NARR
YEARS AGO
MS. PATRICIA, I KNOW YOU CAN HEAR ME...
IN A MINUTE!
MS. PATRICIA, I AM FOLKE HERVIETT, SON OF HUNTER HERVIETT, AND YOU'RE IN DANGER. DEATH IS COMING FOR YOU.
BWA HAHAHA HA!

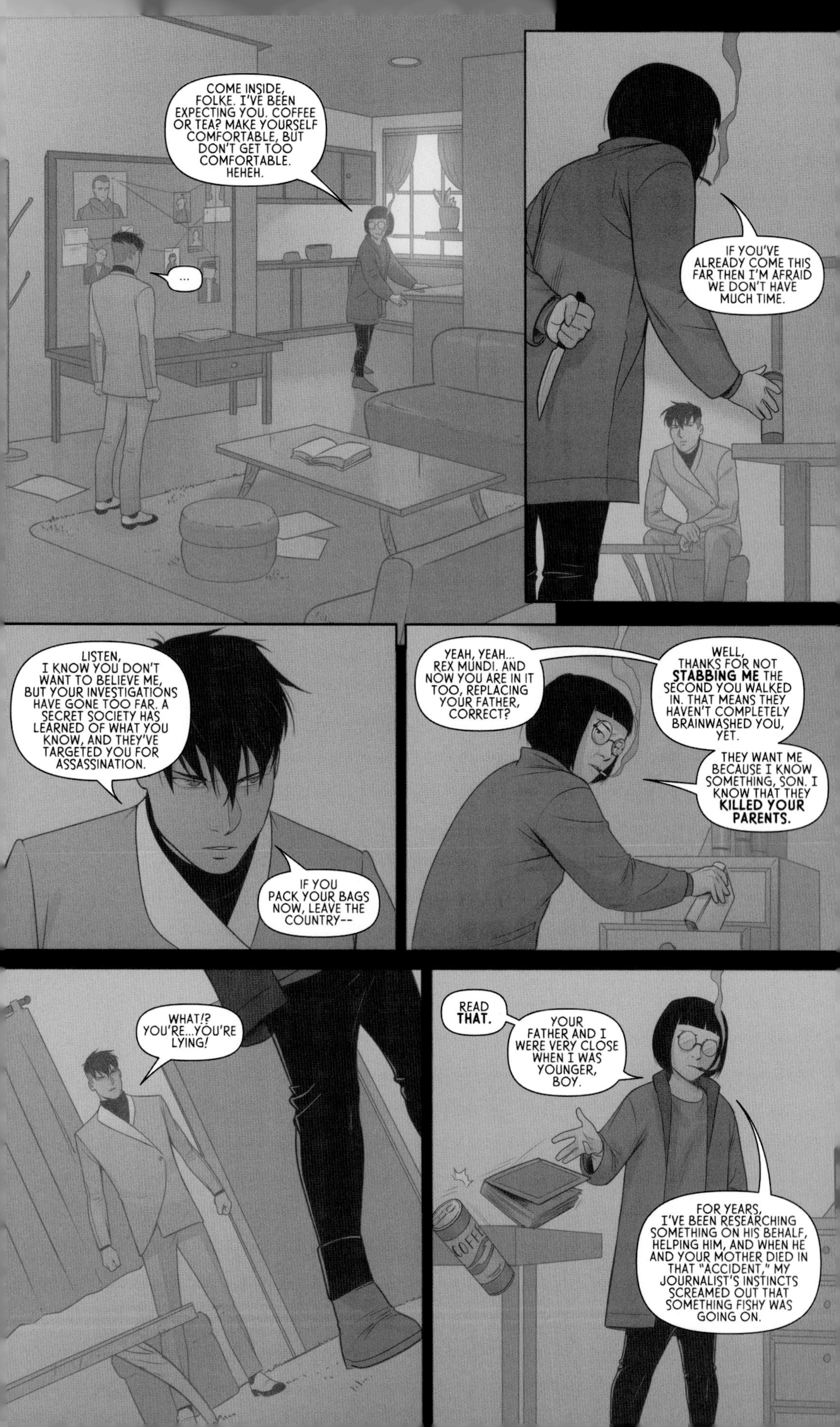
COME INSIDE, FOLKE. I'VE BEEN EXPECTING YOU. COFFEE OR TEA? MAKE YOURSELF COMFORTABLE, BUT DON'T GET TOO COMFORTABLE. HEHEH.
...
IF YOU'VE ALREADY COME THIS FAR THEN I'M AFRAID WE DON'T HAVE MUCH TIME.
LISTEN, I KNOW YOU DON'T WANT TO BELIEVE ME, BUT YOUR INVESTIGATIONS HAVE GONE TOO FAR. A SECRET SOCIETY HAS LEARNED OF WHAT YOU KNOW, AND THEY'VE TARGETED YOU FOR ASSASSINATION.
IF YOU PACK YOUR BAGS NOW, LEAVE THE COUNTRY--
YEAH, YEAH... REX MUNDI. AND NOW YOU ARE IN IT TOO, REPLACING YOUR FATHER, CORRECT?
WELL, THANKS FOR NOT **STABBING ME** THE SECOND YOU WALKED IN. THAT MEANS THEY HAVEN'T COMPLETELY BRAINWASHED YOU, YET.
THEY WANT ME BECAUSE I KNOW SOMETHING, SON. I KNOW THAT THEY **KILLED YOUR PARENTS.**
WHAT!? YOU'RE...YOU'RE LYING!
READ **THAT.**
YOUR FATHER AND I WERE VERY CLOSE WHEN I WAS YOUNGER, BOY.
FOR YEARS, I'VE BEEN RESEARCHING SOMETHING ON HIS BEHALF, HELPING HIM, AND WHEN HE AND YOUR MOTHER DIED IN THAT "ACCIDENT," MY JOURNALIST'S INSTINCTS SCREAMED OUT THAT SOMETHING FISHY WAS GOING ON.

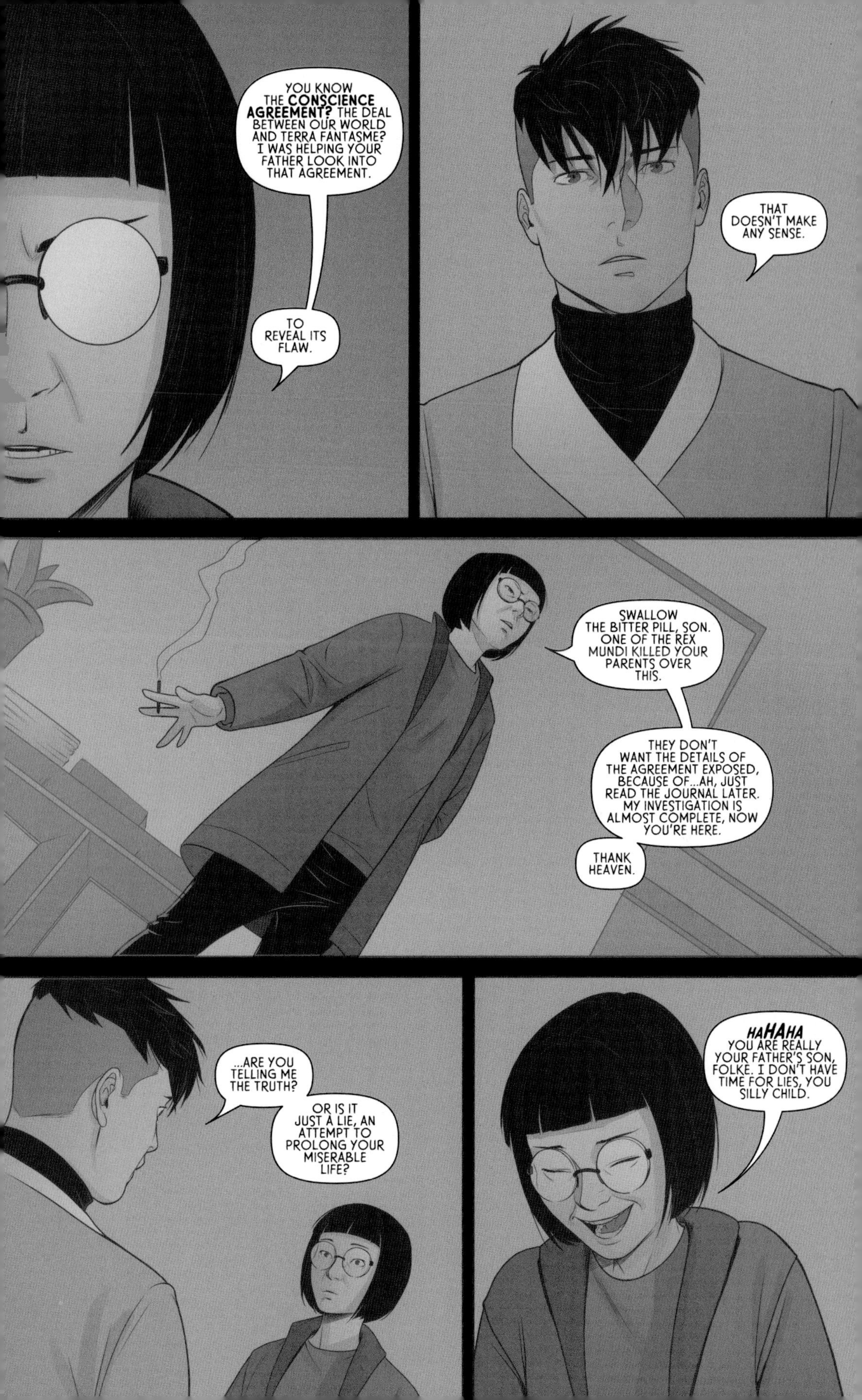
YOU KNOW THE **CONSCIENCE AGREEMENT?** THE DEAL BETWEEN OUR WORLD AND TERRA FANTASME? I WAS HELPING YOUR FATHER LOOK INTO THAT AGREEMENT.
TO REVEAL ITS FLAW.
THAT DOESN'T MAKE ANY SENSE.
SWALLOW THE BITTER PILL, SON. ONE OF THE REX MUNDI KILLED YOUR PARENTS OVER THIS.
THEY DON'T WANT THE DETAILS OF THE AGREEMENT EXPOSED, BECAUSE OF...AH, JUST READ THE JOURNAL LATER. MY INVESTIGATION IS ALMOST COMPLETE, NOW YOU'RE HERE.
THANK HEAVEN.
...ARE YOU TELLING ME THE TRUTH?
OR IS IT JUST A LIE, AN ATTEMPT TO PROLONG YOUR MISERABLE LIFE?
HAHAHA YOU ARE REALLY YOUR FATHER'S SON, FOLKE. I DON'T HAVE TIME FOR LIES, YOU SILLY CHILD.

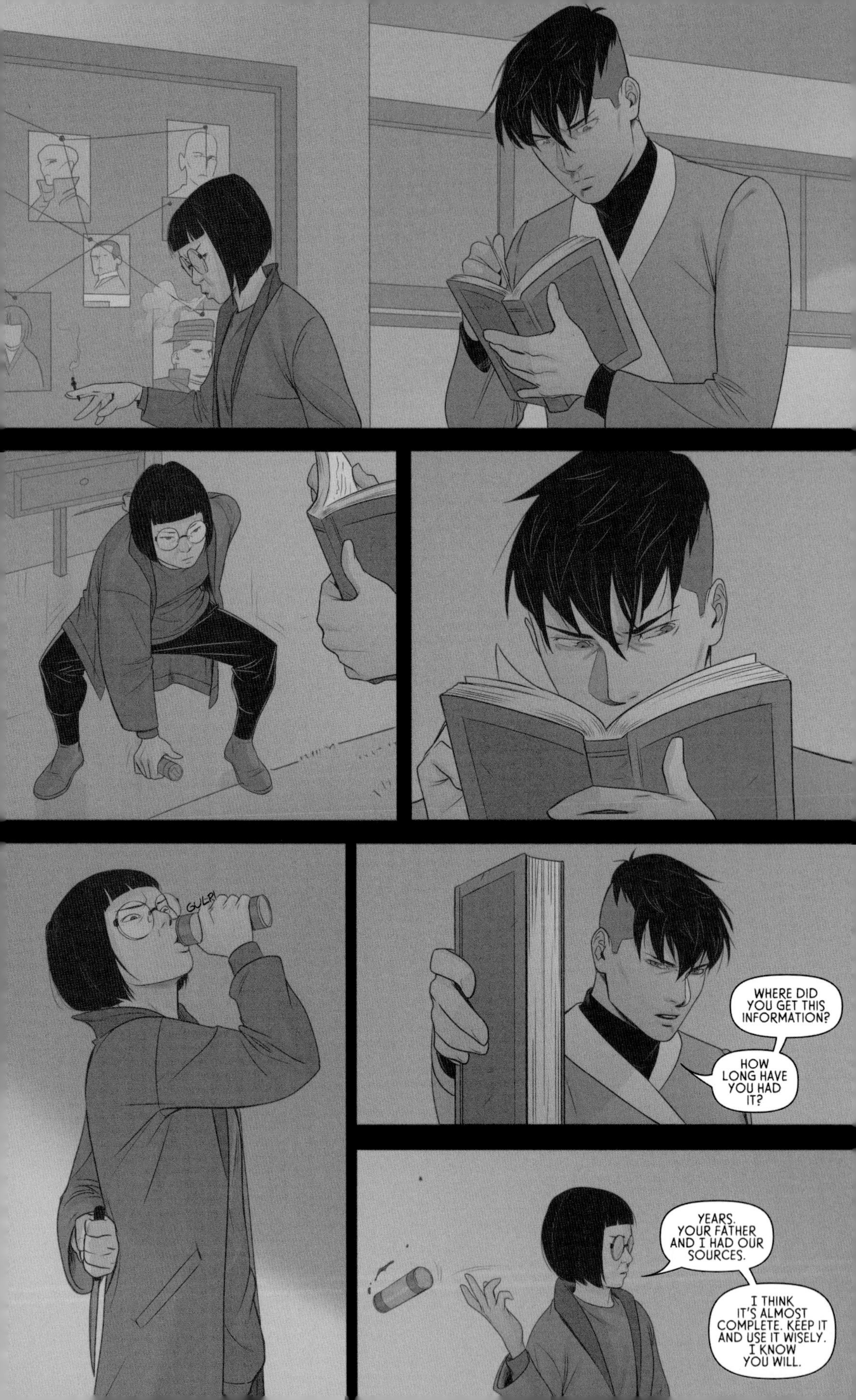
GULP!
WHERE DID YOU GET THIS INFORMATION?
HOW LONG HAVE YOU HAD IT?
YEARS. YOUR FATHER AND I HAD OUR SOURCES.
I THINK IT'S ALMOST COMPLETE. KEEP IT AND USE IT WISELY. I KNOW YOU WILL.

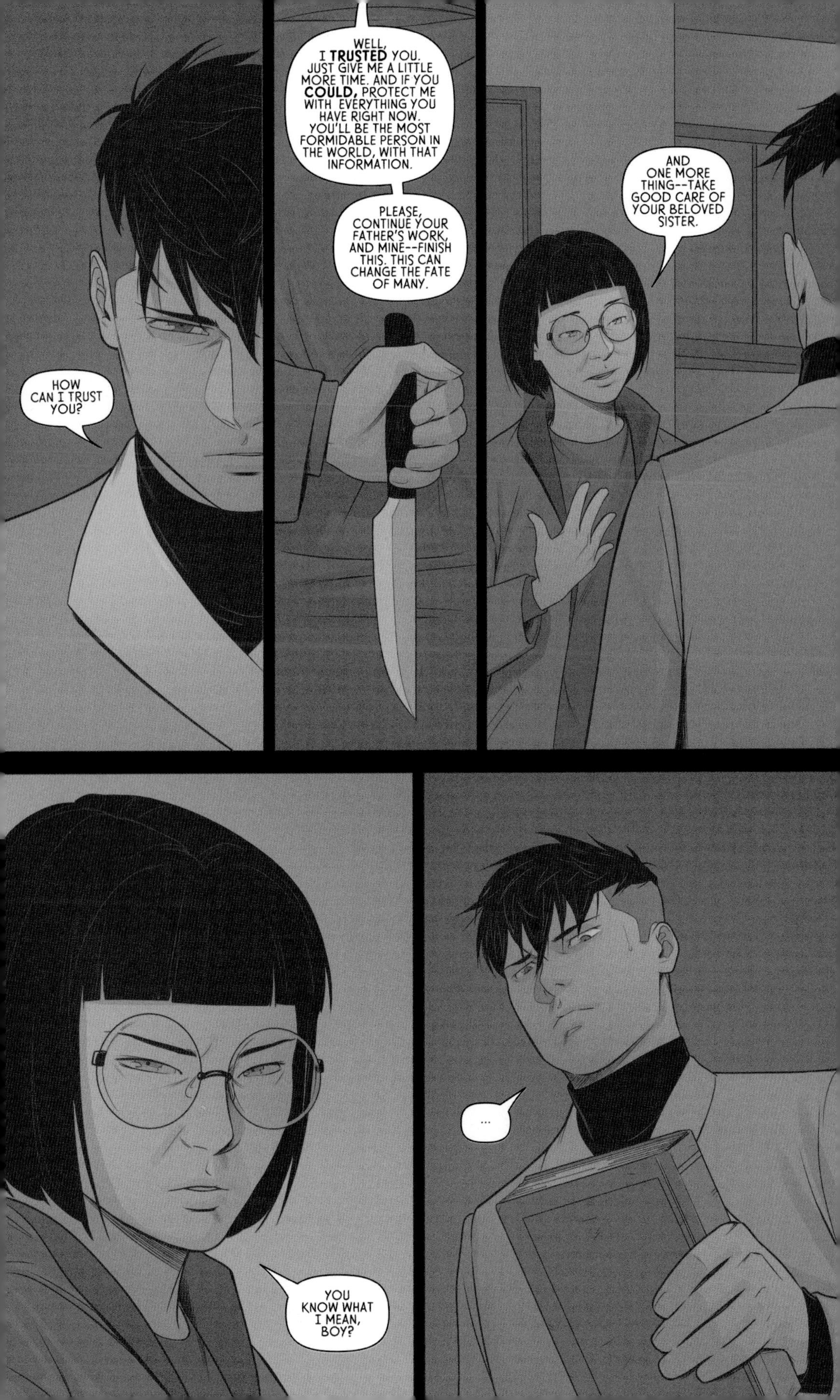
HOW CAN I TRUST YOU?
WELL, I **TRUSTED** YOU. JUST GIVE ME A LITTLE MORE TIME. AND IF YOU **COULD,** PROTECT ME WITH EVERYTHING YOU HAVE RIGHT NOW. YOU'LL BE THE MOST FORMIDABLE PERSON IN THE WORLD, WITH THAT INFORMATION.
PLEASE, CONTINUE YOUR FATHER'S WORK, AND MINE--FINISH THIS. THIS CAN CHANGE THE FATE OF MANY.
AND ONE MORE THING--TAKE GOOD CARE OF YOUR BELOVED SISTER.
YOU KNOW WHAT I MEAN, BOY?
...

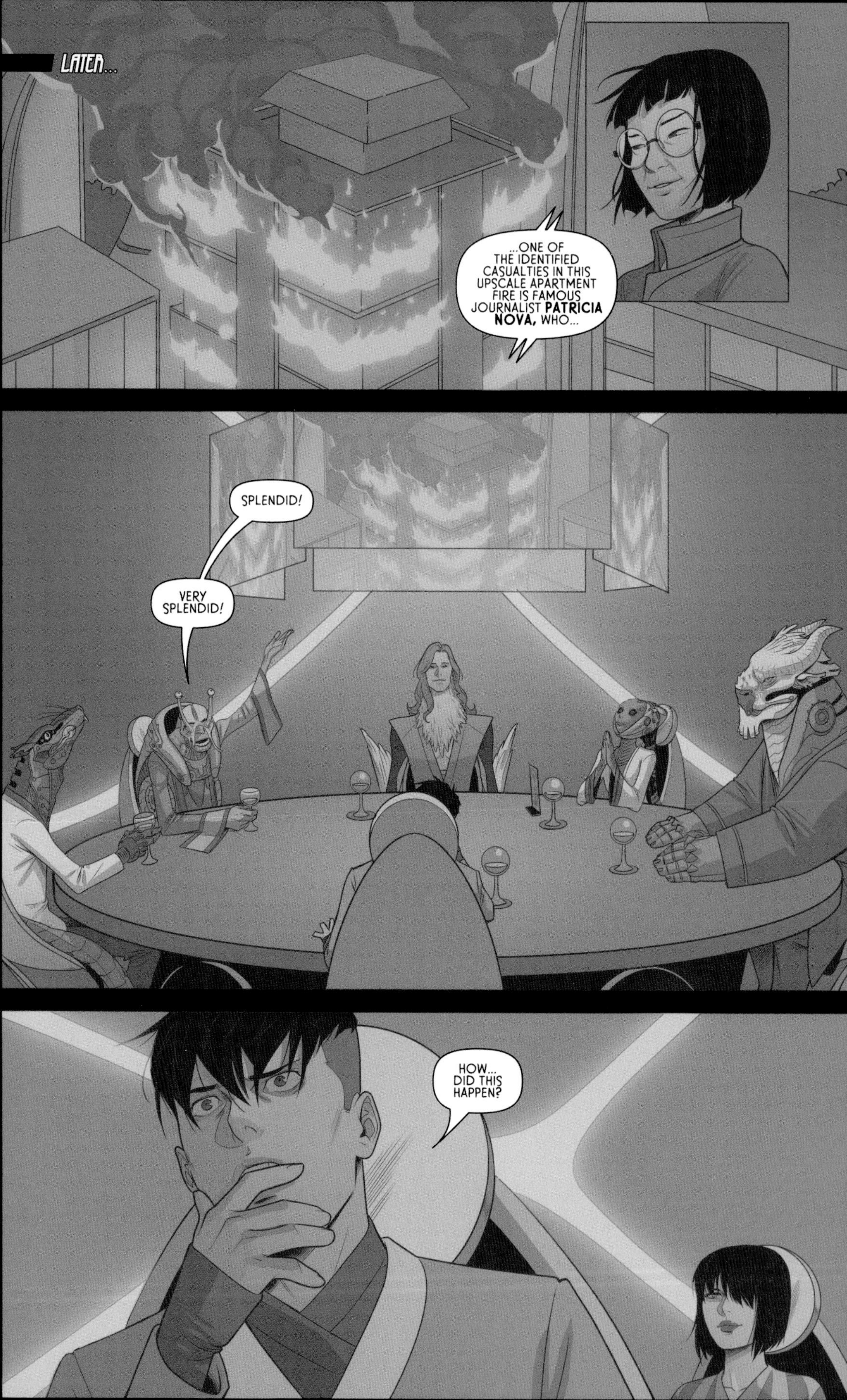
LATER...
...ONE OF THE IDENTIFIED CASUALTIES IN THIS UPSCALE APARTMENT FIRE IS FAMOUS JOURNALIST PATRICIA NOVA, WHO...
SPLENDID!
VERY SPLENDID!
HOW... DID THIS HAPPEN?

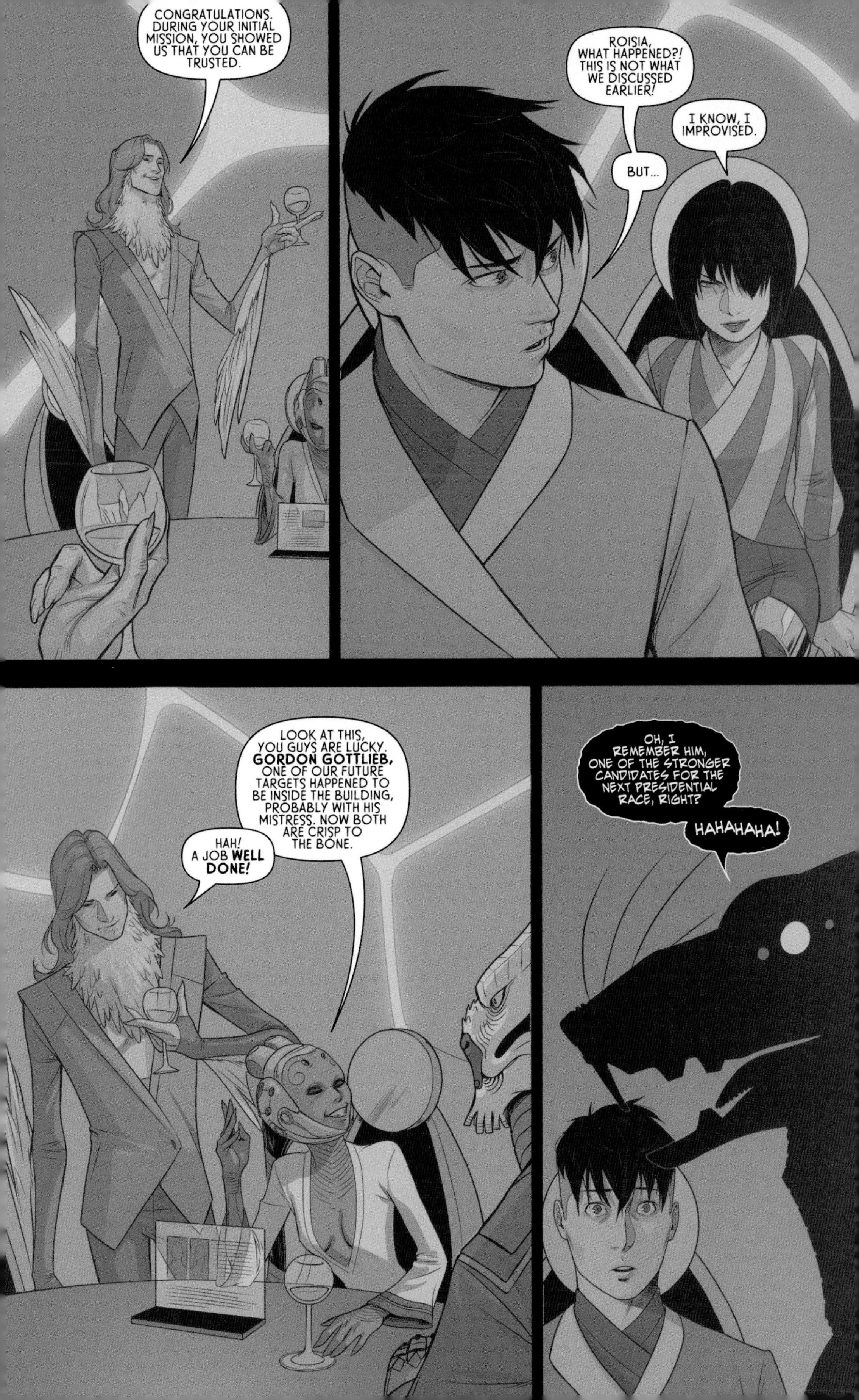
CONGRATULATIONS. DURING YOUR INITIAL MISSION, YOU SHOWED US THAT YOU CAN BE TRUSTED.
ROISIA, WHAT HAPPENED?! THIS IS NOT WHAT WE DISCUSSED EARLIER!
BUT...
I KNOW, I IMPROVISED.
LOOK AT THIS, YOU GUYS ARE LUCKY. GORDON GOTTLIEB, ONE OF OUR FUTURE TARGETS HAPPENED TO BE INSIDE THE BUILDING, PROBABLY WITH HIS MISTRESS. NOW BOTH ARE CRISP TO THE BONE.
HAH! A JOB WELL DONE!
OH, I REMEMBER HIM, ONE OF THE STRONGER CANDIDATES FOR THE NEXT PRESIDENTIAL RACE, RIGHT?
HAHAHAHA!

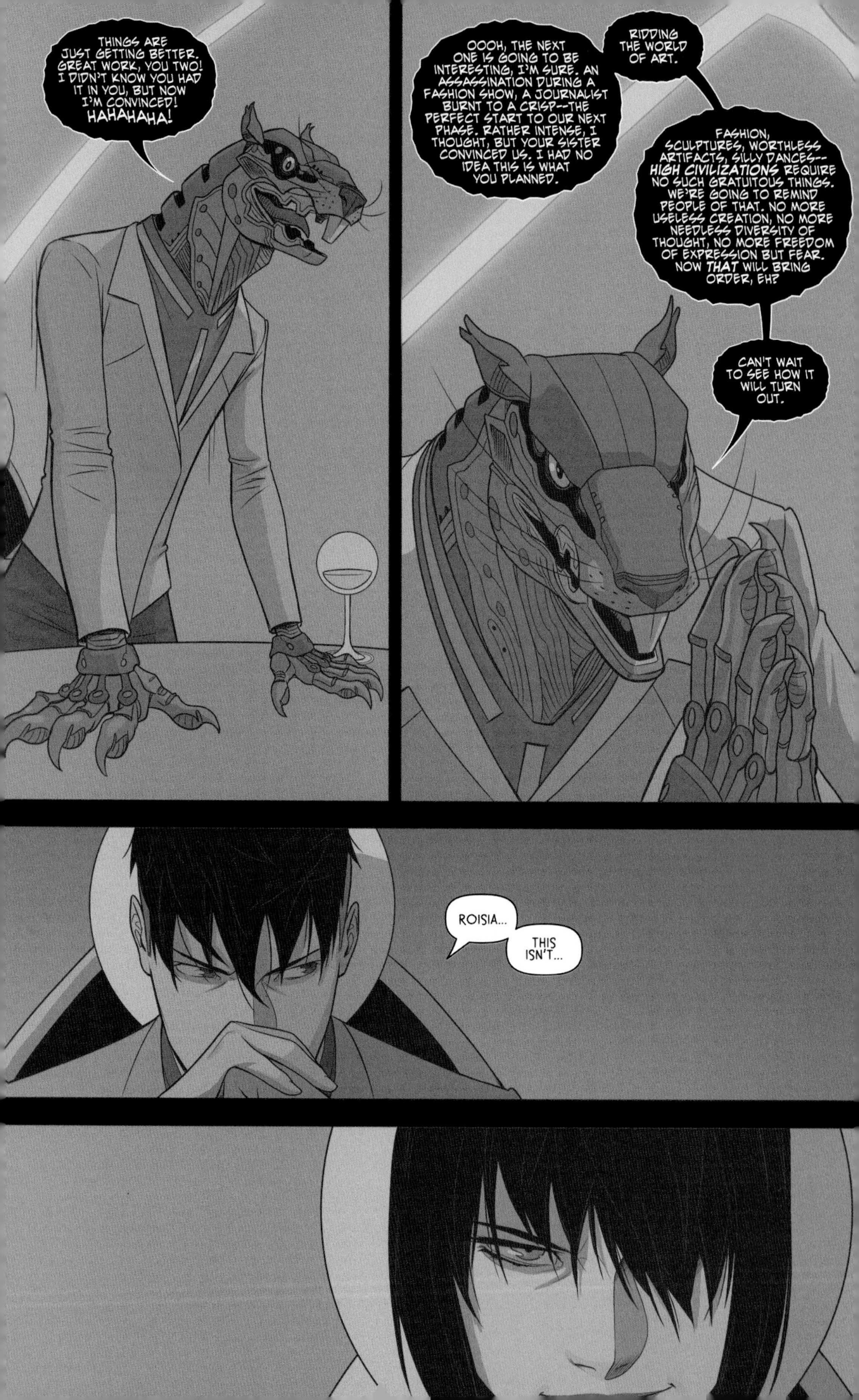
THINGS ARE JUST GETTING BETTER. GREAT WORK, YOU TWO! I DIDN'T KNOW YOU HAD IT IN YOU, BUT NOW I'M CONVINCED! HAHAHAHA!
OOOH, THE NEXT ONE IS GOING TO BE INTERESTING, I'M SURE. AN ASSASSINATION DURING A FASHION SHOW, A JOURNALIST BURNT TO A CRISP--THE PERFECT START TO OUR NEXT PHASE. RATHER INTENSE, I THOUGHT, BUT YOUR SISTER CONVINCED US. I HAD NO IDEA THIS IS WHAT YOU PLANNED.
RIDDING THE WORLD OF ART.
FASHION, SCULPTURES, WORTHLESS ARTIFACTS, SILLY DANCES-- HIGH CIVILIZATIONS REQUIRE NO SUCH GRATUITOUS THINGS. WE'RE GOING TO REMIND PEOPLE OF THAT. NO MORE USELESS CREATION, NO MORE NEEDLESS DIVERSITY OF THOUGHT, NO MORE FREEDOM OF EXPRESSION BUT FEAR. NOW THAT WILL BRING ORDER, EH?
CAN'T WAIT TO SEE HOW IT WILL TURN OUT.
ROISIA...
THIS ISN'T...

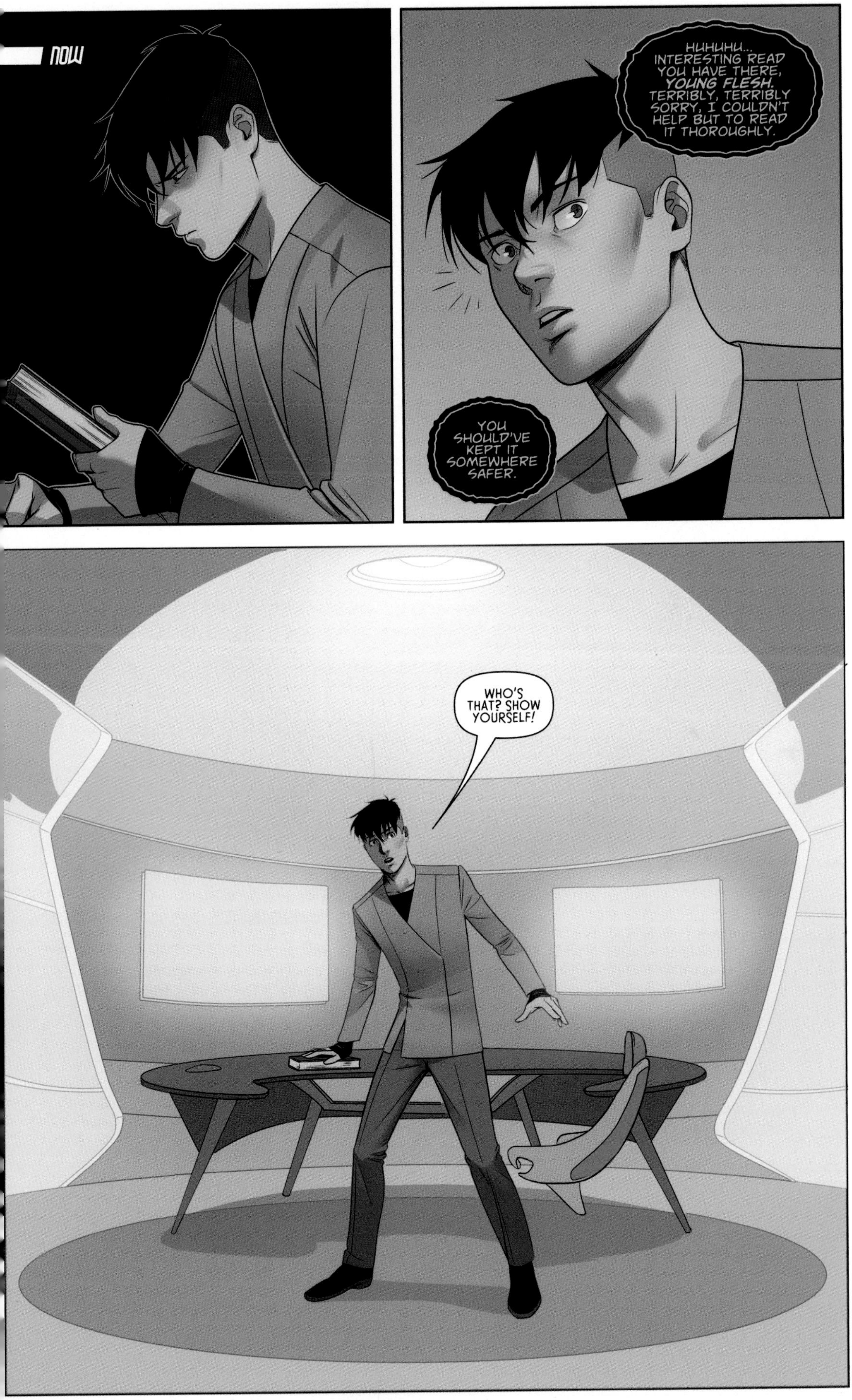
NOW
HUHUHU... INTERESTING READ YOU HAVE THERE, YOUNG FLESH. TERRIBLY, TERRIBLY SORRY, I COULDN'T HELP BUT TO READ IT THOROUGHLY.
YOU SHOULD'VE KEPT IT SOMEWHERE SAFER.
WHO'S THAT? SHOW YOURSELF!

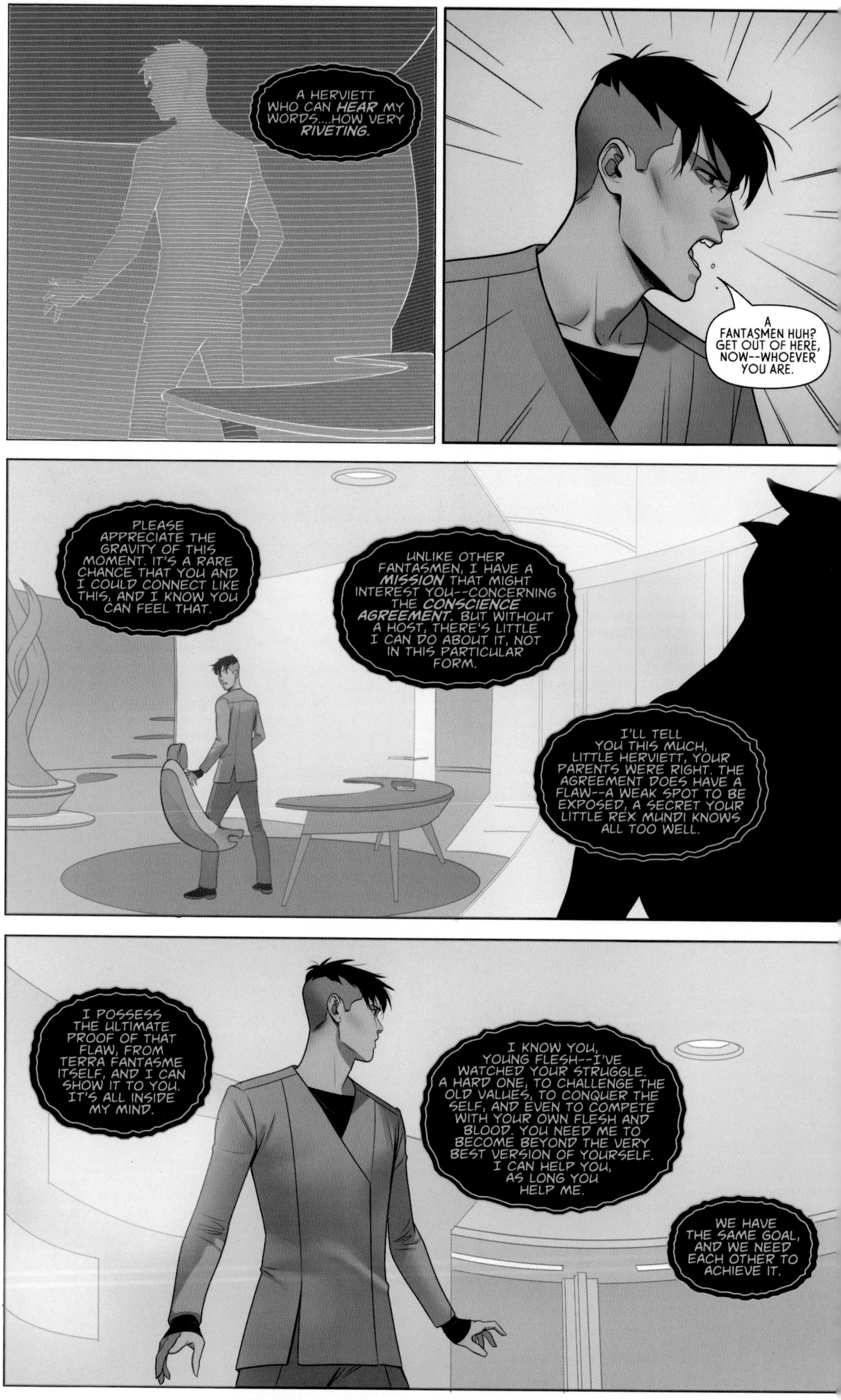
A HERVIETT WHO CAN HEAR MY WORDS....HOW VERY RIVETING.
A FANTASMEN HUH? GET OUT OF HERE, NOW--WHOEVER YOU ARE.
PLEASE APPRECIATE THE GRAVITY OF THIS MOMENT. IT'S A RARE CHANCE THAT YOU AND I COULD CONNECT LIKE THIS, AND I KNOW YOU CAN FEEL THAT.
UNLIKE OTHER FANTASMEN, I HAVE A MISSION THAT MIGHT INTEREST YOU--CONCERNING THE CONSCIENCE AGREEMENT. BUT WITHOUT A HOST, THERE'S LITTLE I CAN DO ABOUT IT, NOT IN THIS PARTICULAR FORM.
I'LL TELL YOU THIS MUCH, LITTLE HERVIETT, YOUR PARENTS WERE RIGHT. THE AGREEMENT DOES HAVE A FLAW--A WEAK SPOT TO BE EXPOSED, A SECRET YOUR LITTLE REX MUNDI KNOWS ALL TOO WELL.
I POSSESS THE ULTIMATE PROOF OF THAT FLAW, FROM TERRA FANTASME ITSELF, AND I CAN SHOW IT TO YOU. IT'S ALL INSIDE MY MIND.
I KNOW YOU, YOUNG FLESH--I'VE WATCHED YOUR STRUGGLE. A HARD ONE, TO CHALLENGE THE OLD VALUES, TO CONQUER THE SELF, AND EVEN TO COMPETE WITH YOUR OWN FLESH AND BLOOD. YOU NEED ME TO BECOME BEYOND THE VERY BEST VERSION OF YOURSELF. I CAN HELP YOU, AS LONG YOU HELP ME.
WE HAVE THE SAME GOAL, AND WE NEED EACH OTHER TO ACHIEVE IT.

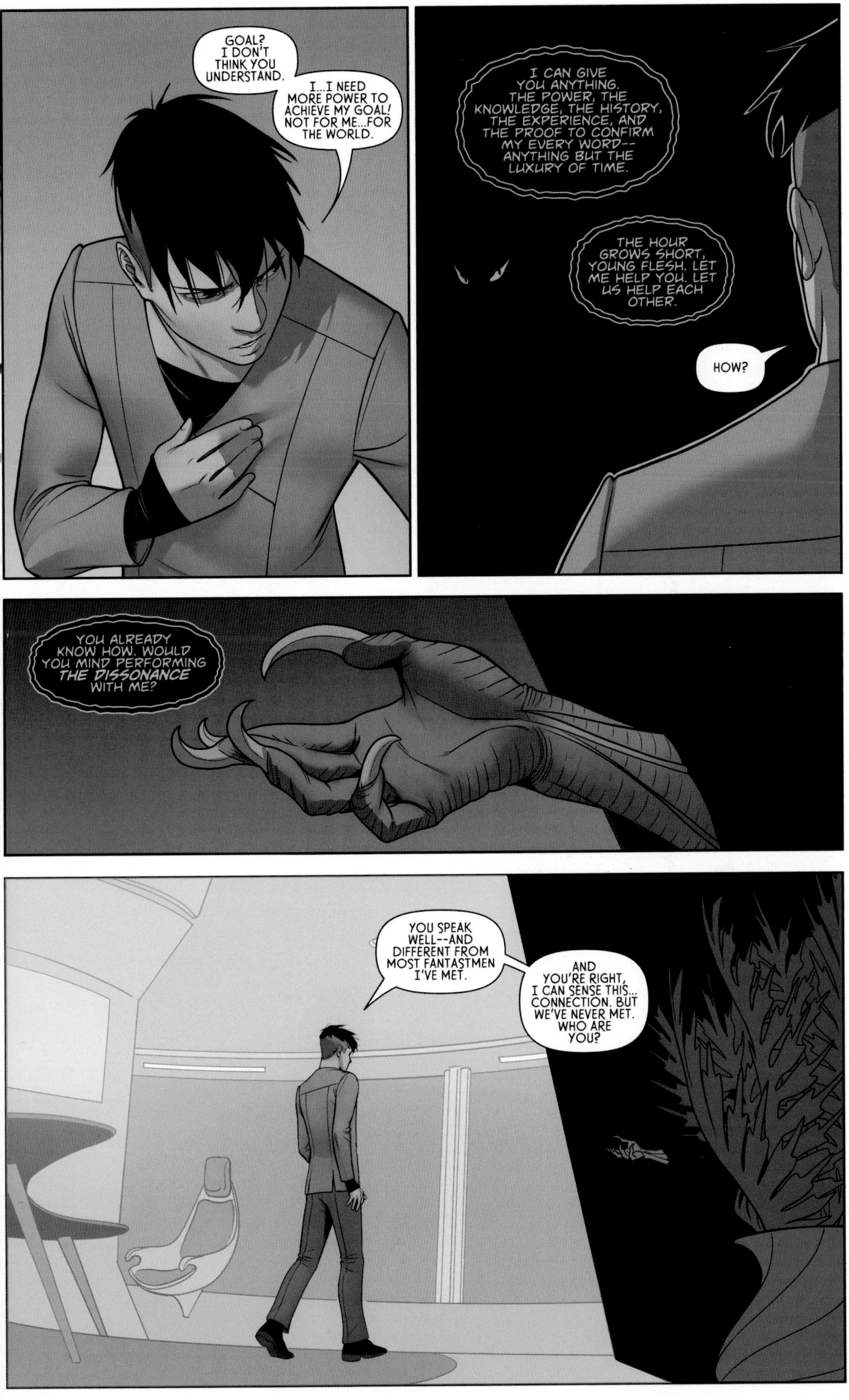
GOAL? I DON'T THINK YOU UNDERSTAND.
I...I NEED MORE POWER TO ACHIEVE MY GOAL! NOT FOR ME...FOR THE WORLD.
I CAN GIVE YOU ANYTHING. THE POWER, THE KNOWLEDGE, THE HISTORY, THE EXPERIENCE, AND THE PROOF TO CONFIRM MY EVERY WORD-- ANYTHING BUT THE LUXURY OF TIME.
THE HOUR GROWS SHORT, YOUNG FLESH. LET ME HELP YOU. LET US HELP EACH OTHER.
HOW?
YOU ALREADY KNOW HOW. WOULD YOU MIND PERFORMING THE DISSONANCE WITH ME?
YOU SPEAK WELL--AND DIFFERENT FROM MOST FANTASTMEN I'VE MET.
AND YOU'RE RIGHT, I CAN SENSE THIS... CONNECTION. BUT WE'VE NEVER MET. WHO ARE YOU?

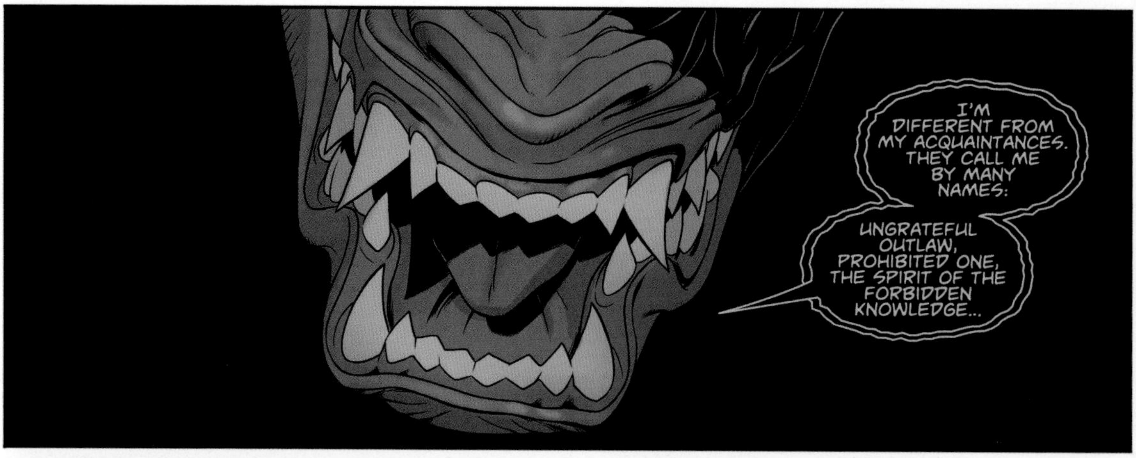
I'M DIFFERENT FROM MY ACQUAINTANCES. THEY CALL ME BY MANY NAMES:
UNGRATEFUL OUTLAW, PROHIBITED ONE, THE SPIRIT OF THE FORBIDDEN KNOWLEDGE...

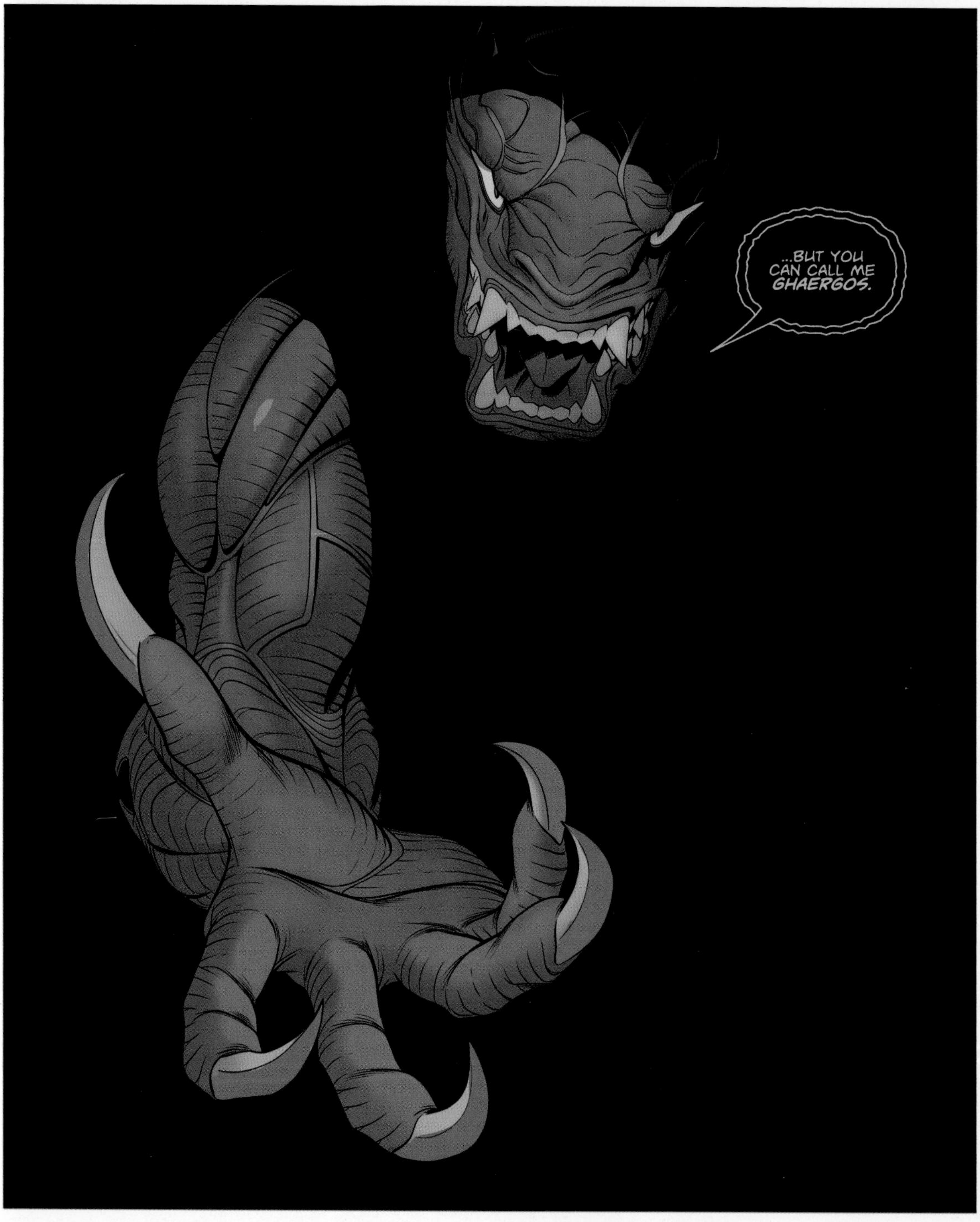
...BUT YOU CAN CALL ME GHAERGOS.

CHAPTER 3

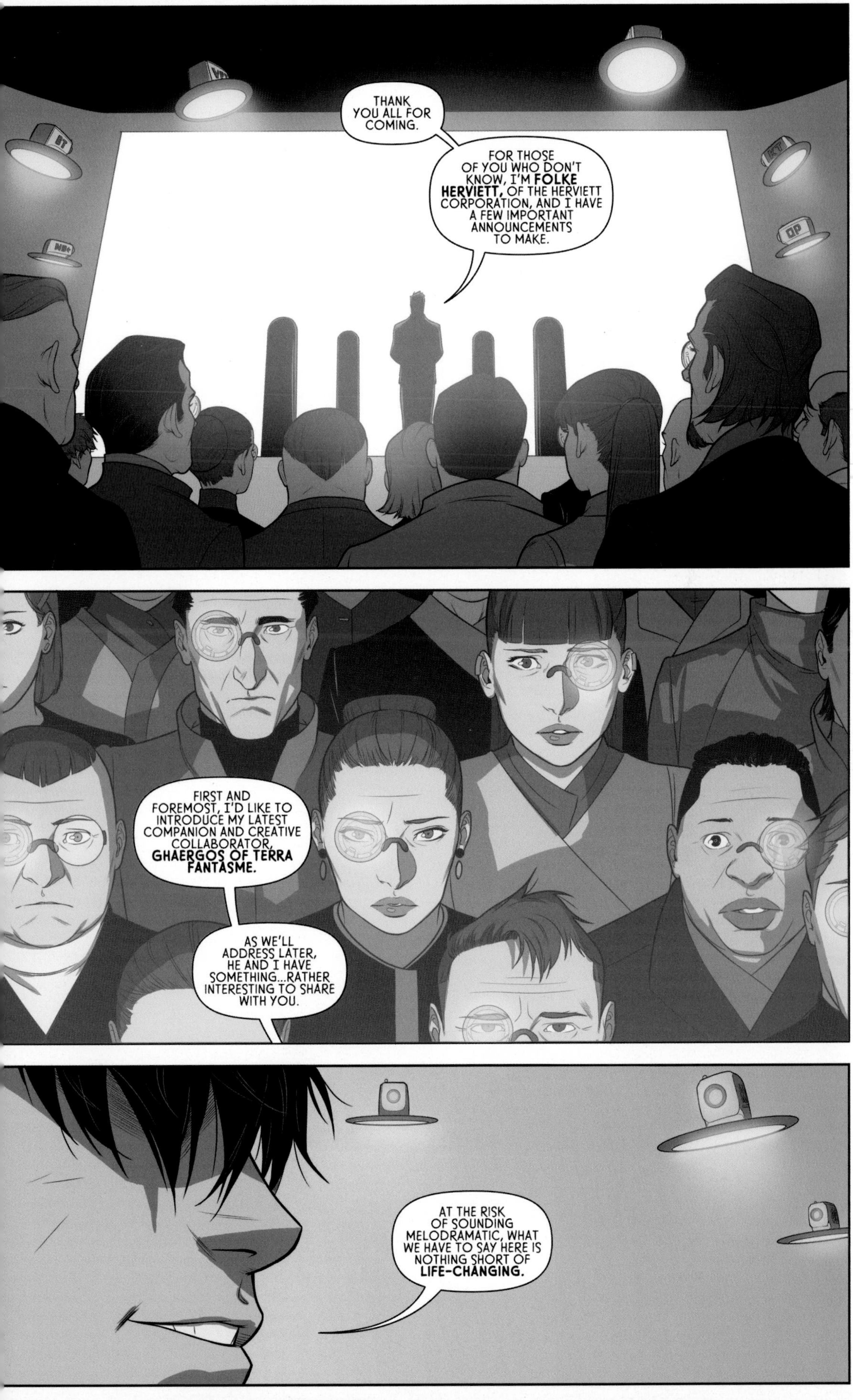
THANK YOU ALL FOR COMING.
FOR THOSE OF YOU WHO DON'T KNOW, I'M **FOLKE HERVIETT,** OF THE HERVIETT CORPORATION, AND I HAVE A FEW IMPORTANT ANNOUNCEMENTS TO MAKE.
FIRST AND FOREMOST, I'D LIKE TO INTRODUCE MY LATEST COMPANION AND CREATIVE COLLABORATOR, **GHAERGOS OF TERRA FANTASME.**
AS WE'LL ADDRESS LATER, HE AND I HAVE SOMETHING...RATHER INTERESTING TO SHARE WITH YOU.
AT THE RISK OF SOUNDING MELODRAMATIC, WHAT WE HAVE TO SAY HERE IS NOTHING SHORT OF **LIFE-CHANGING.**

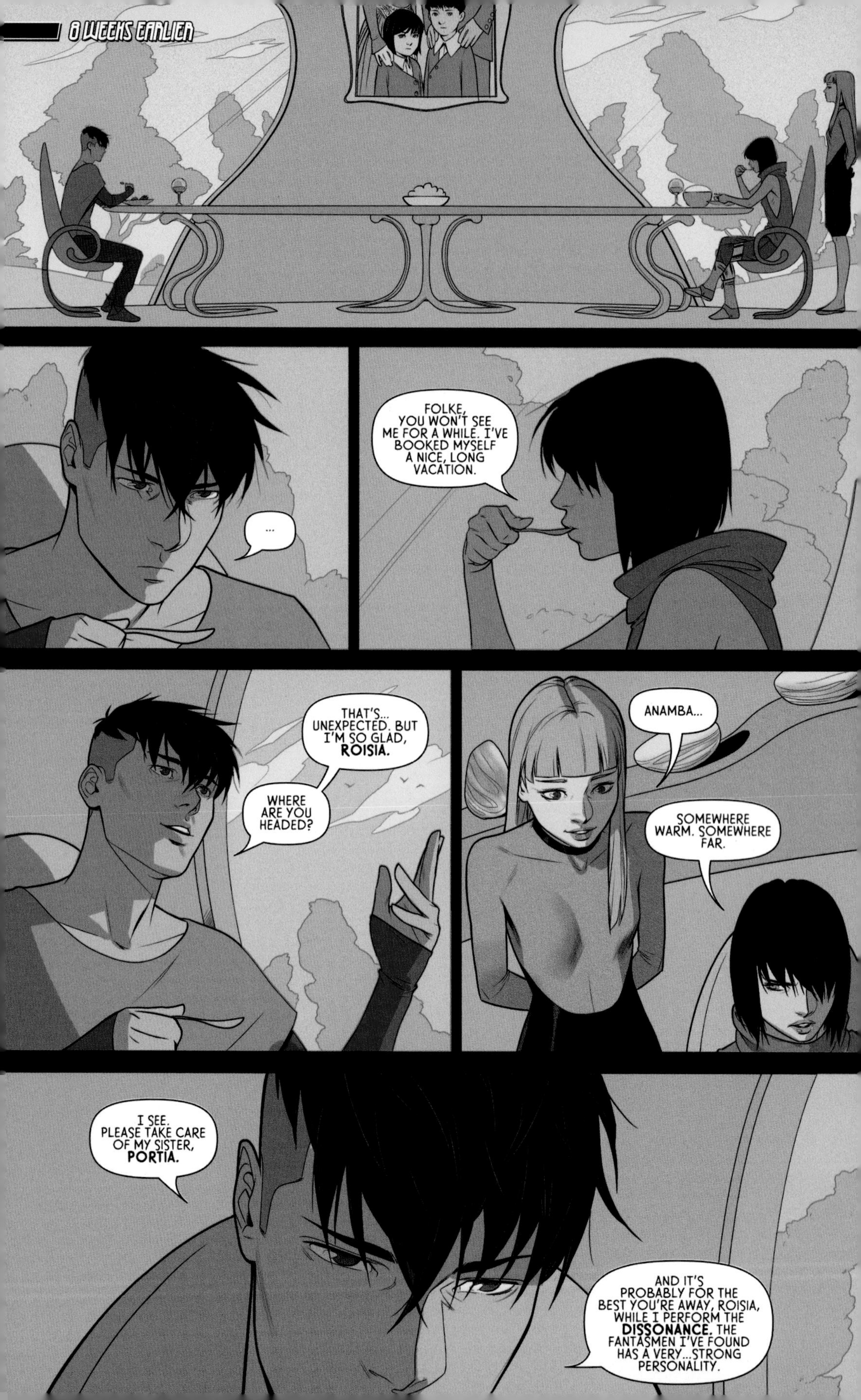
8 WEEKS EARLIER
FOLKE, YOU WON'T SEE ME FOR A WHILE. I'VE BOOKED MYSELF A NICE, LONG VACATION.
...
THAT'S... UNEXPECTED. BUT I'M SO GLAD, ROISIA.
WHERE ARE YOU HEADED?
ANAMBA...
SOMEWHERE WARM. SOMEWHERE FAR.
I SEE. PLEASE TAKE CARE OF MY SISTER, PORTIA.
AND IT'S PROBABLY FOR THE BEST YOU'RE AWAY, ROISIA, WHILE I PERFORM THE DISSONANCE. THE FANTASMEN I'VE FOUND HAS A VERY...STRONG PERSONALITY.

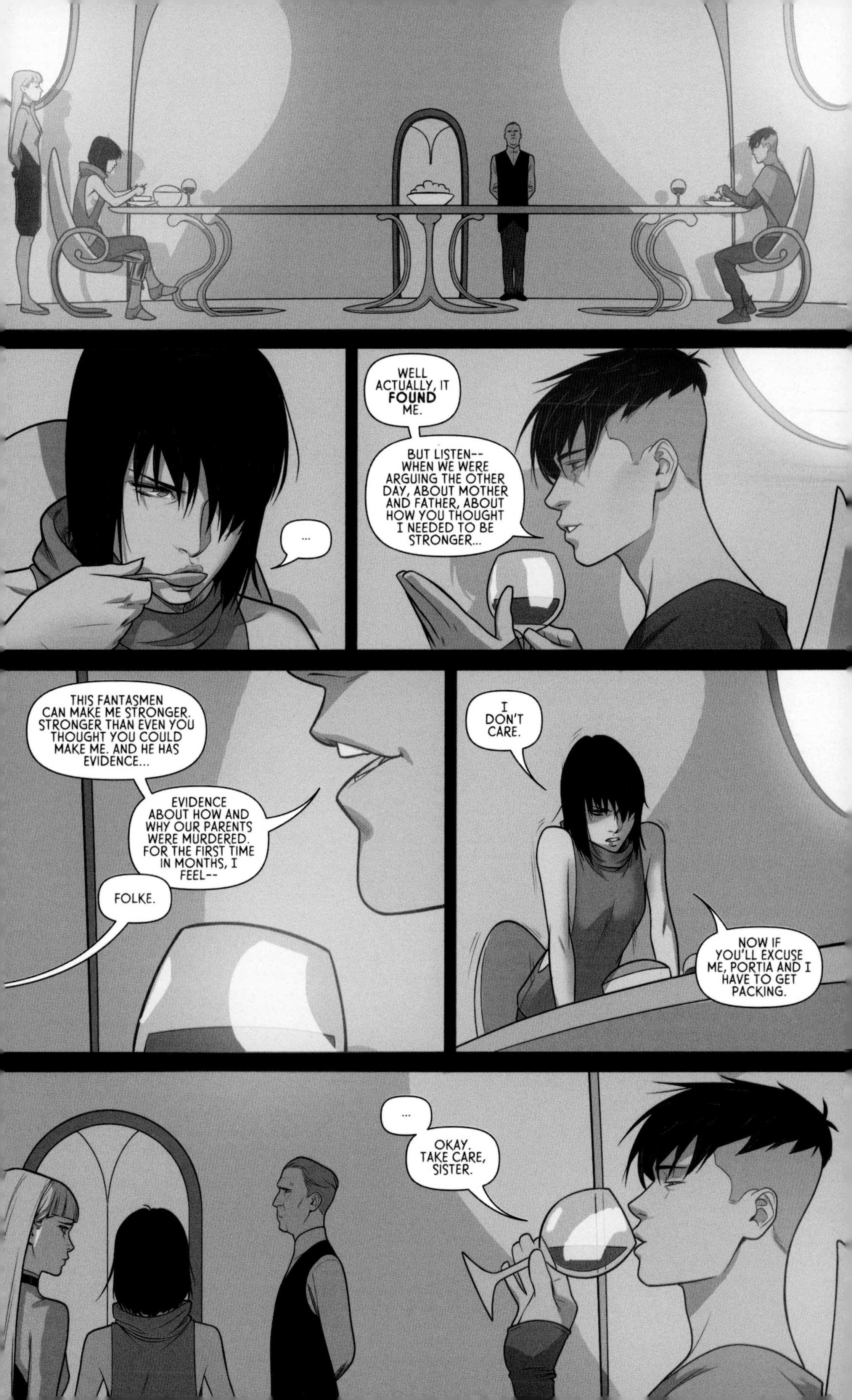
WELL ACTUALLY, IT FOUND ME.
BUT LISTEN-- WHEN WE WERE ARGUING THE OTHER DAY, ABOUT MOTHER AND FATHER, ABOUT HOW YOU THOUGHT I NEEDED TO BE STRONGER...
...
THIS FANTASMEN CAN MAKE ME STRONGER. STRONGER THAN EVEN YOU THOUGHT YOU COULD MAKE ME. AND HE HAS EVIDENCE...
EVIDENCE ABOUT HOW AND WHY OUR PARENTS WERE MURDERED. FOR THE FIRST TIME IN MONTHS, I FEEL--
FOLKE.
I DON'T CARE.
NOW IF YOU'LL EXCUSE ME, PORTIA AND I HAVE TO GET PACKING.
...
OKAY. TAKE CARE, SISTER.

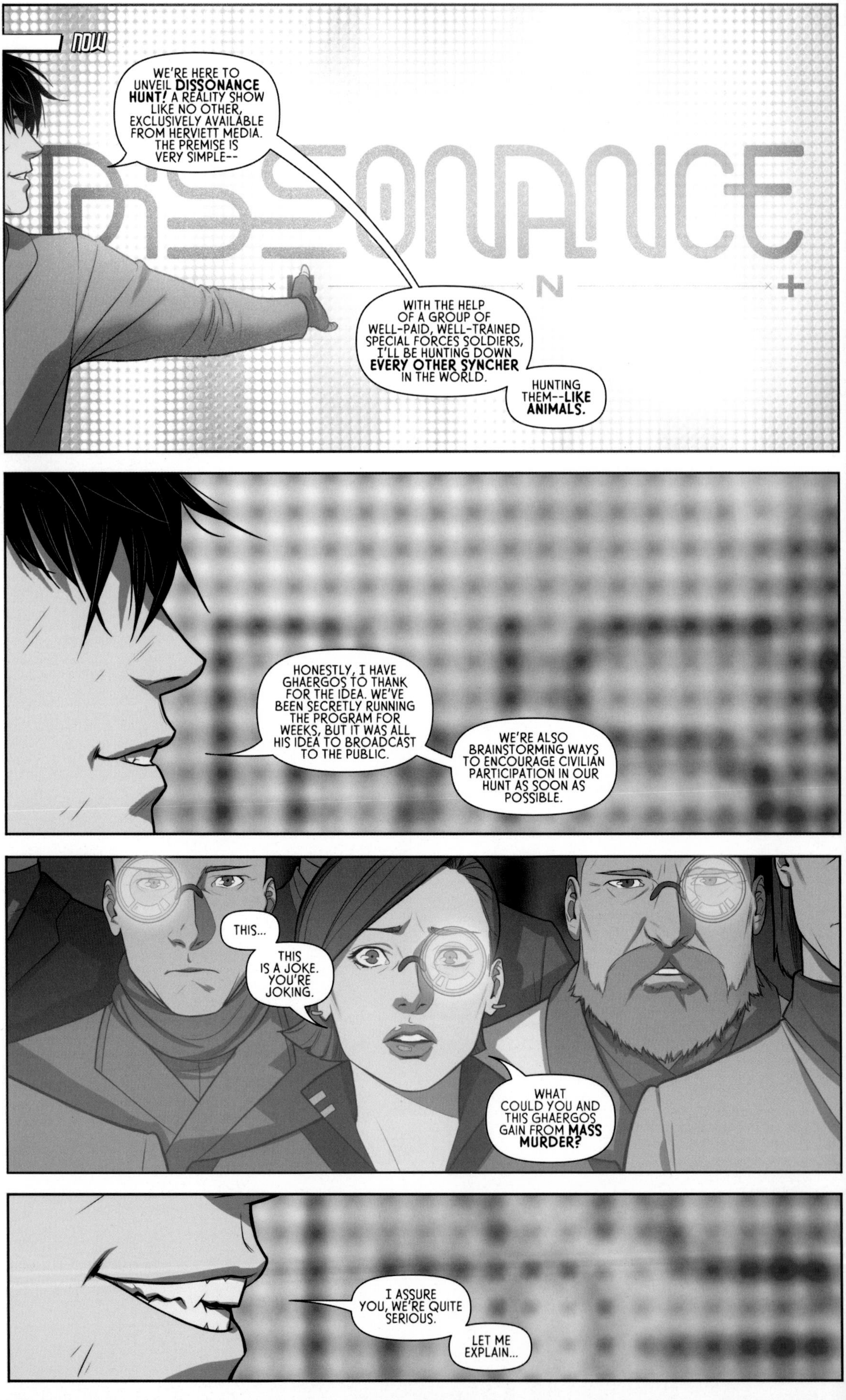
NOW
WE'RE HERE TO UNVEIL DISSONANCE HUNT! A REALITY SHOW LIKE NO OTHER, EXCLUSIVELY AVAILABLE FROM HERVIETT MEDIA. THE PREMISE IS VERY SIMPLE--
DISSONANCE
N
WITH THE HELP OF A GROUP OF WELL-PAID, WELL-TRAINED SPECIAL FORCES SOLDIERS, I'LL BE HUNTING DOWN EVERY OTHER SYNCHER IN THE WORLD.
HUNTING THEM--LIKE ANIMALS.
HONESTLY, I HAVE GHAERGOS TO THANK FOR THE IDEA. WE'VE BEEN SECRETLY RUNNING THE PROGRAM FOR WEEKS, BUT IT WAS ALL HIS IDEA TO BROADCAST TO THE PUBLIC.
WE'RE ALSO BRAINSTORMING WAYS TO ENCOURAGE CIVILIAN PARTICIPATION IN OUR HUNT AS SOON AS POSSIBLE.
THIS...
THIS IS A JOKE. YOU'RE JOKING.
WHAT COULD YOU AND THIS GHAERGOS GAIN FROM MASS MURDER?
I ASSURE YOU, WE'RE QUITE SERIOUS.
LET ME EXPLAIN...

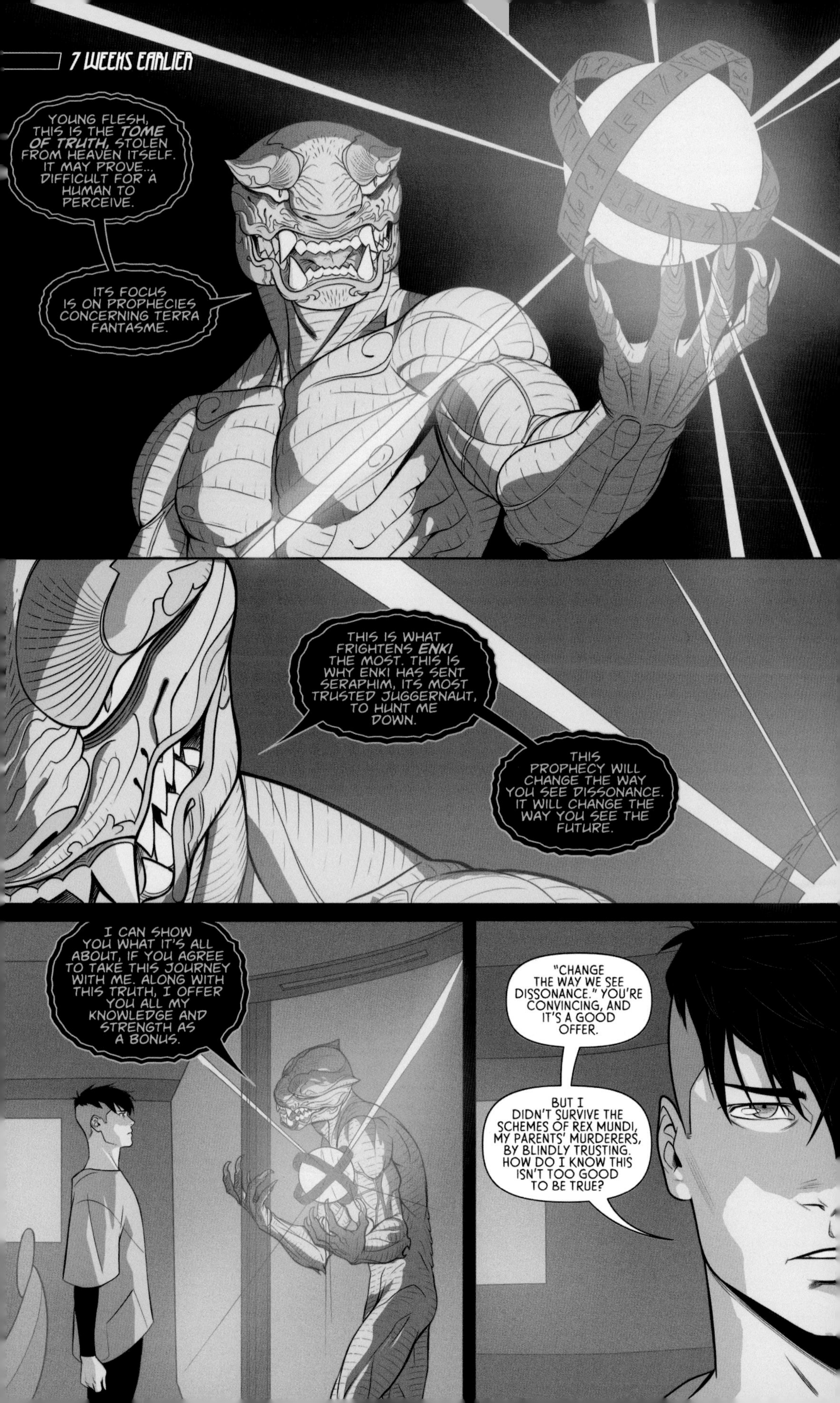
7 WEEKS EARLIER
YOUNG FLESH, THIS IS THE TOME OF TRUTH, STOLEN FROM HEAVEN ITSELF. IT MAY PROVE... DIFFICULT FOR A HUMAN TO PERCEIVE.
ITS FOCUS IS ON PROPHECIES CONCERNING TERRA FANTASME.
THIS IS WHAT FRIGHTENS ENKI THE MOST. THIS IS WHY ENKI HAS SENT SERAPHIM, ITS MOST TRUSTED JUGGERNAUT, TO HUNT ME DOWN.
THIS PROPHECY WILL CHANGE THE WAY YOU SEE DISSONANCE. IT WILL CHANGE THE WAY YOU SEE THE FUTURE.
I CAN SHOW YOU WHAT IT'S ALL ABOUT, IF YOU AGREE TO TAKE THIS JOURNEY WITH ME. ALONG WITH THIS TRUTH, I OFFER YOU ALL MY KNOWLEDGE AND STRENGTH AS A BONUS.
"CHANGE THE WAY WE SEE DISSONANCE." YOU'RE CONVINCING, AND IT'S A GOOD OFFER.
BUT I DIDN'T SURVIVE THE SCHEMES OF REX MUNDI, MY PARENTS' MURDERERS, BY BLINDLY TRUSTING. HOW DO I KNOW THIS ISN'T TOO GOOD TO BE TRUE?

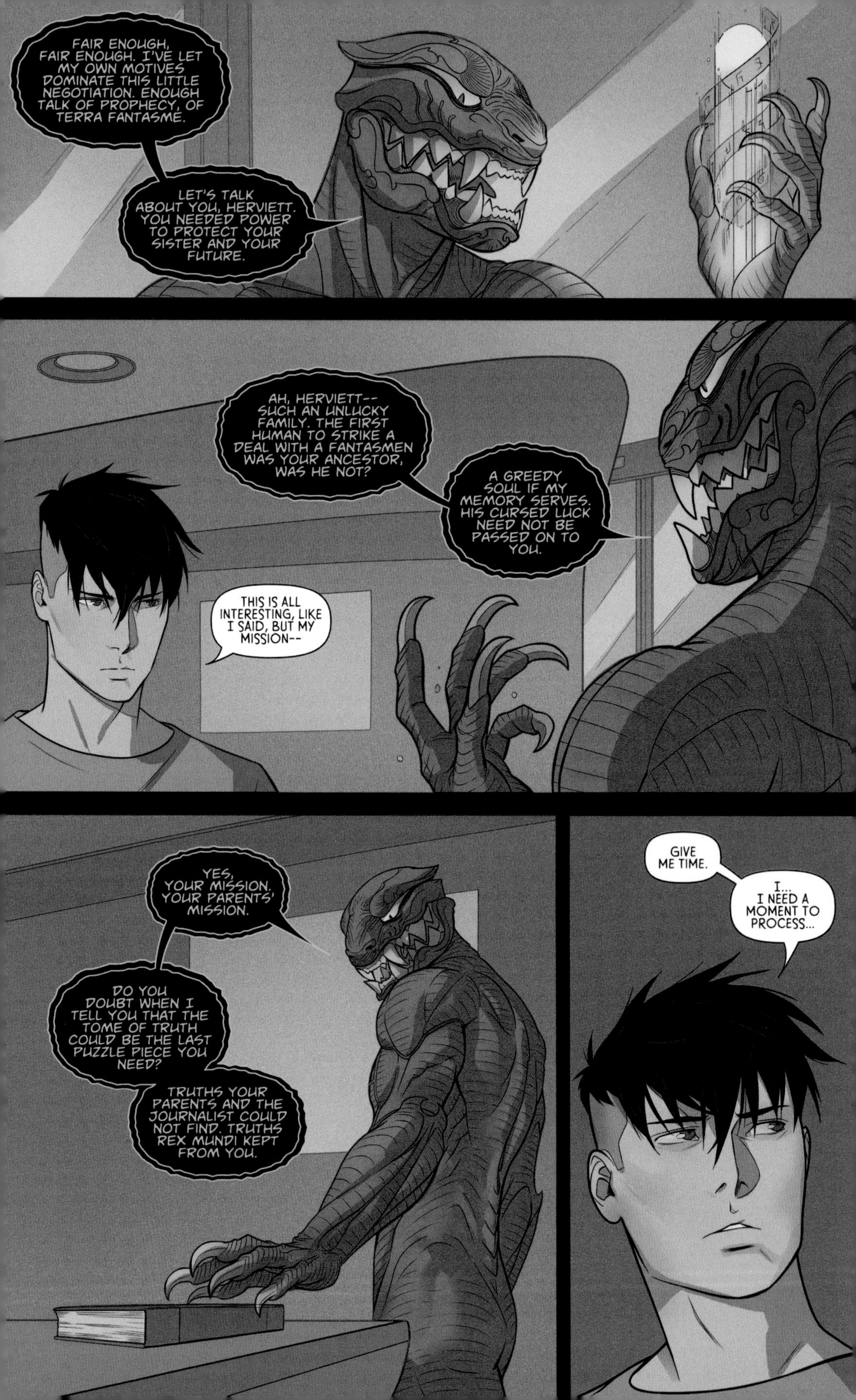
FAIR ENOUGH, FAIR ENOUGH. I'VE LET MY OWN MOTIVES DOMINATE THIS LITTLE NEGOTIATION. ENOUGH TALK OF PROPHECY, OF TERRA FANTASME.
LET'S TALK ABOUT YOU, HERVIETT. YOU NEEDED POWER TO PROTECT YOUR SISTER AND YOUR FUTURE.
AH, HERVIETT-- SUCH AN UNLUCKY FAMILY. THE FIRST HUMAN TO STRIKE A DEAL WITH A FANTASMEN WAS YOUR ANCESTOR, WAS HE NOT?
A GREEDY SOUL IF MY MEMORY SERVES. HIS CURSED LUCK NEED NOT BE PASSED ON TO YOU.
THIS IS ALL INTERESTING, LIKE I SAID, BUT MY MISSION--
YES, YOUR MISSION. YOUR PARENTS' MISSION.
DO YOU DOUBT WHEN I TELL YOU THAT THE TOME OF TRUTH COULD BE THE LAST PUZZLE PIECE YOU NEED?
TRUTHS YOUR PARENTS AND THE JOURNALIST COULD NOT FIND. TRUTHS REX MUNDI KEPT FROM YOU.
GIVE ME TIME.
I... I NEED A MOMENT TO PROCESS...

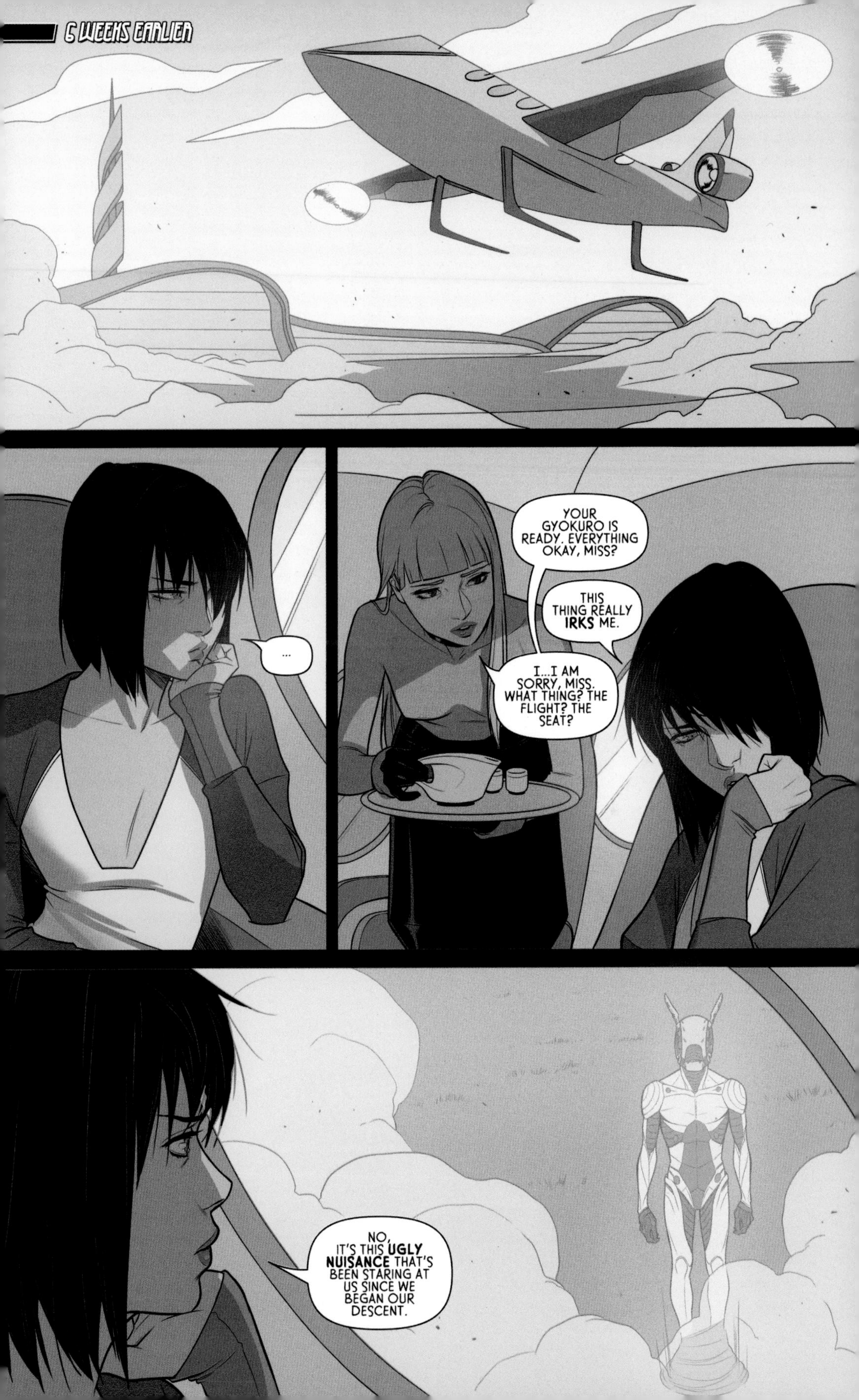
6 WEEKS EARLIER
...
YOUR GYOKURO IS READY. EVERYTHING OKAY, MISS?
THIS THING REALLY **IRKS** ME.
I...I AM SORRY, MISS. WHAT THING? THE FLIGHT? THE SEAT?
NO, IT'S THIS **UGLY NUISANCE** THAT'S BEEN STARING AT US SINCE WE BEGAN OUR DESCENT.

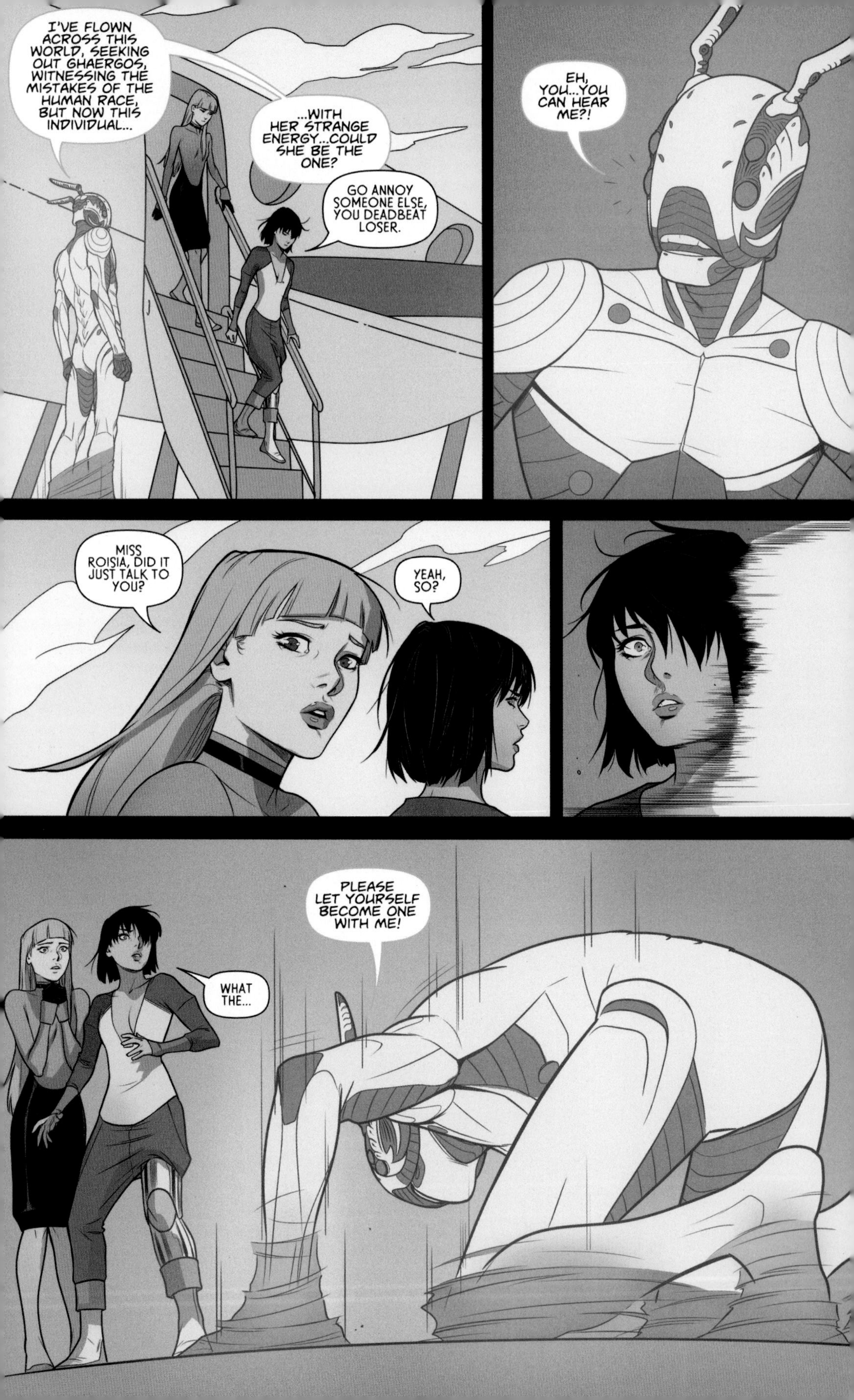
I'VE FLOWN ACROSS THIS WORLD, SEEKING OUT GHAERGOS, WITNESSING THE MISTAKES OF THE HUMAN RACE, BUT NOW THIS INDIVIDUAL...
...WITH HER STRANGE ENERGY...COULD SHE BE THE ONE?
GO ANNOY SOMEONE ELSE, YOU DEADBEAT LOSER.
EH, YOU...YOU CAN HEAR ME?!
MISS ROISIA, DID IT JUST TALK TO YOU?
YEAH, SO?
PLEASE LET YOURSELF BECOME ONE WITH ME!
WHAT THE...

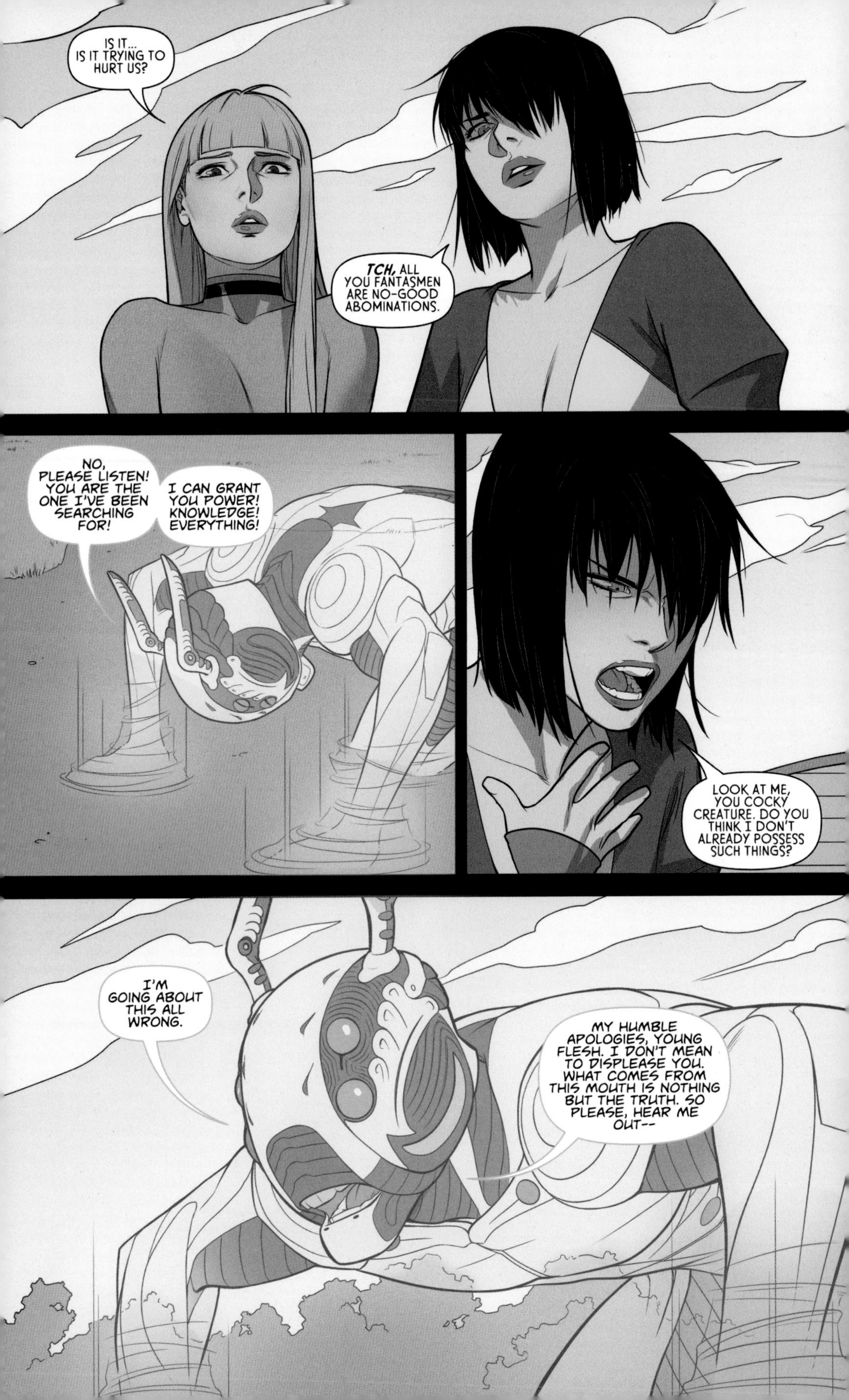

IS IT... IS IT TRYING TO HURT US?
TCH, ALL YOU FANTASMEN ARE NO-GOOD ABOMINATIONS.
NO, PLEASE LISTEN! YOU ARE THE ONE I'VE BEEN SEARCHING FOR!
I CAN GRANT YOU POWER! KNOWLEDGE! EVERYTHING!
LOOK AT ME, YOU COCKY CREATURE. DO YOU THINK I DON'T ALREADY POSSESS SUCH THINGS?
I'M GOING ABOUT THIS ALL WRONG.
MY HUMBLE APOLOGIES, YOUNG FLESH. I DON'T MEAN TO DISPLEASE YOU. WHAT COMES FROM THIS MOUTH IS NOTHING BUT THE TRUTH. SO PLEASE, HEAR ME OUT--

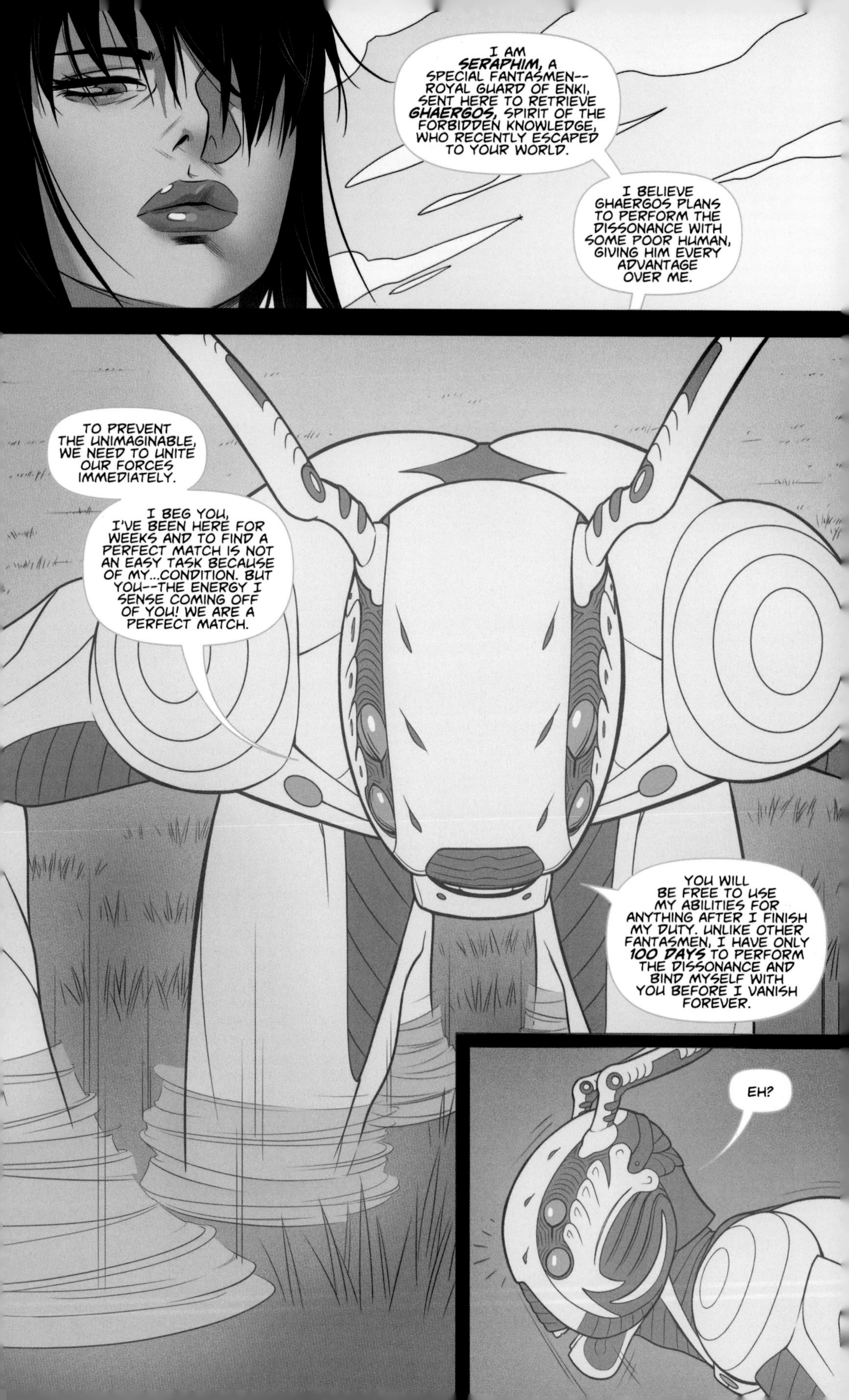
I AM **SERAPHIM,** A SPECIAL FANTASMEN--ROYAL GUARD OF ENKI, SENT HERE TO RETRIEVE **GHAERGOS,** SPIRIT OF THE FORBIDDEN KNOWLEDGE, WHO RECENTLY ESCAPED TO YOUR WORLD.
I BELIEVE GHAERGOS PLANS TO PERFORM THE DISSONANCE WITH SOME POOR HUMAN, GIVING HIM EVERY ADVANTAGE OVER ME.
TO PREVENT THE UNIMAGINABLE, WE NEED TO UNITE OUR FORCES IMMEDIATELY.
I BEG YOU, I'VE BEEN HERE FOR WEEKS AND TO FIND A PERFECT MATCH IS NOT AN EASY TASK BECAUSE OF MY...CONDITION. BUT YOU--THE ENERGY I SENSE COMING OFF OF YOU! WE ARE A PERFECT MATCH.
YOU WILL BE FREE TO USE MY ABILITIES FOR ANYTHING AFTER I FINISH MY DUTY. UNLIKE OTHER FANTASMEN, I HAVE ONLY **100 DAYS** TO PERFORM THE DISSONANCE AND BIND MYSELF WITH YOU BEFORE I VANISH FOREVER.
EH?

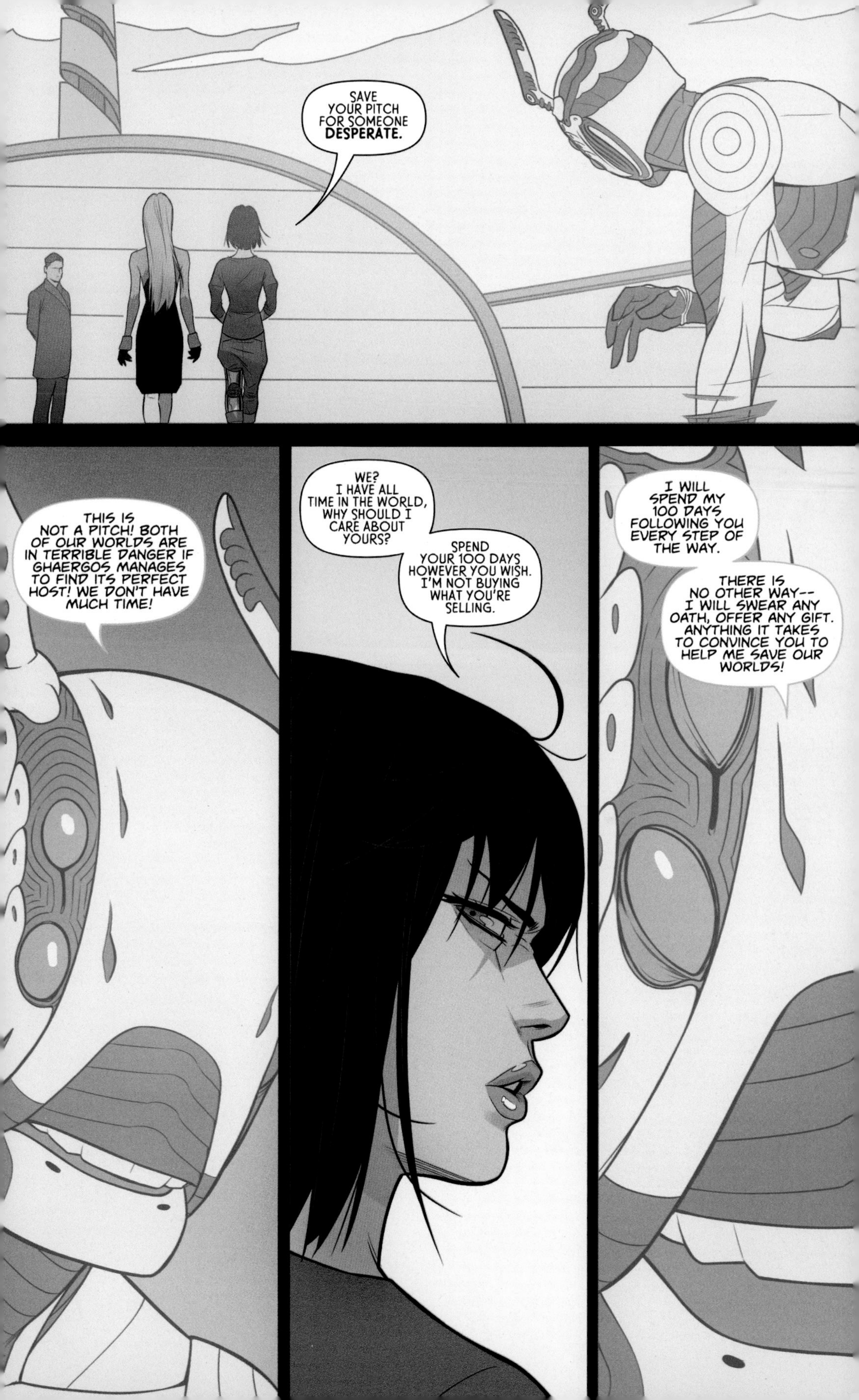
SAVE YOUR PITCH FOR SOMEONE **DESPERATE.**
THIS IS NOT A PITCH! BOTH OF OUR WORLDS ARE IN TERRIBLE DANGER IF GHAERGOS MANAGES TO FIND ITS PERFECT HOST! WE DON'T HAVE MUCH TIME!
WE? I HAVE ALL TIME IN THE WORLD, WHY SHOULD I CARE ABOUT YOURS?
SPEND YOUR 100 DAYS HOWEVER YOU WISH. I'M NOT BUYING WHAT YOU'RE SELLING.
I WILL SPEND MY 100 DAYS FOLLOWING YOU EVERY STEP OF THE WAY.
THERE IS NO OTHER WAY-- I WILL SWEAR ANY OATH, OFFER ANY GIFT. ANYTHING IT TAKES TO CONVINCE YOU TO HELP ME SAVE OUR WORLDS!

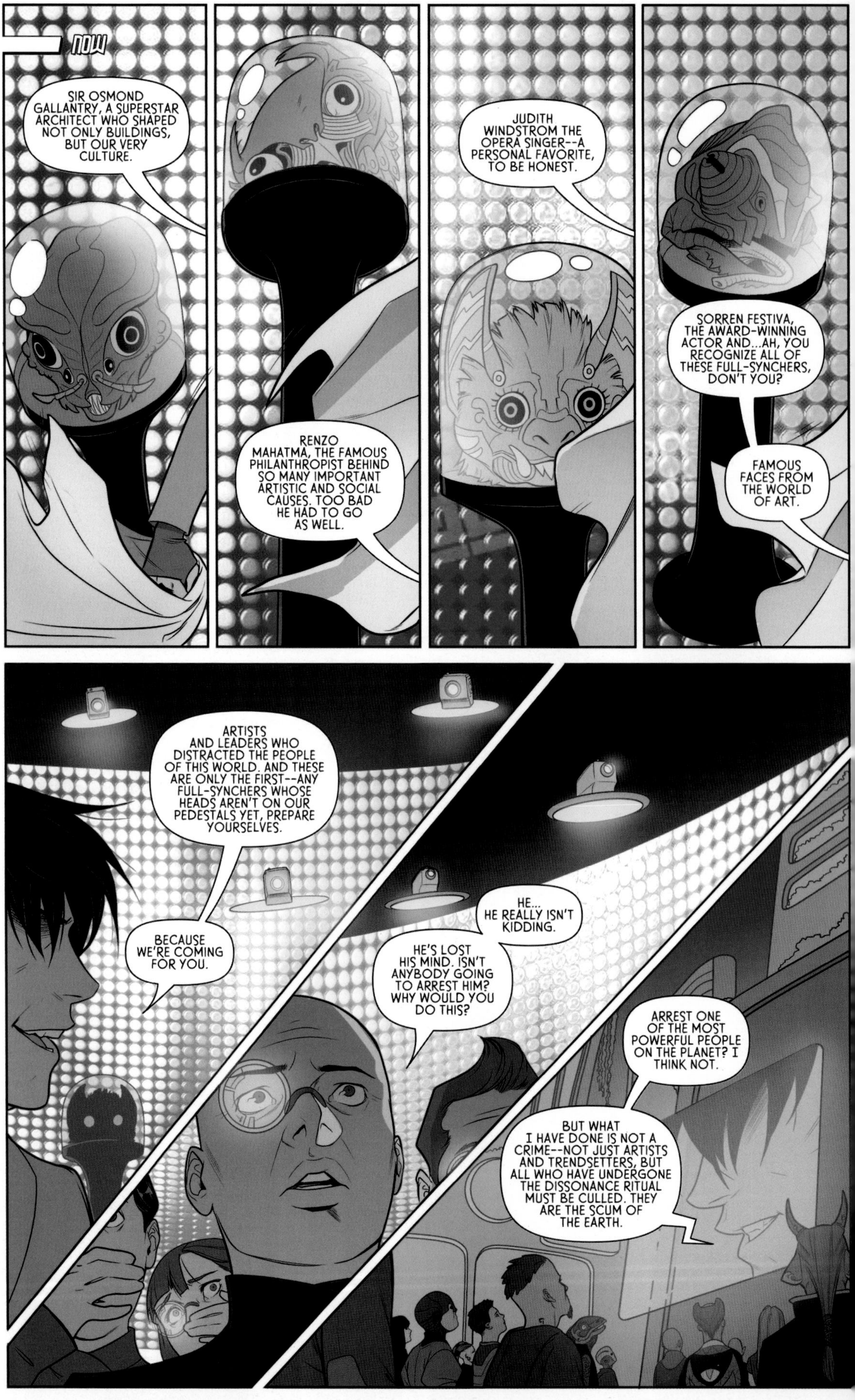
NOW
SIR OSMOND GALLANTRY, A SUPERSTAR ARCHITECT WHO SHAPED NOT ONLY BUILDINGS, BUT OUR VERY CULTURE.
RENZO MAHATMA, THE FAMOUS PHILANTHROPIST BEHIND SO MANY IMPORTANT ARTISTIC AND SOCIAL CAUSES. TOO BAD HE HAD TO GO AS WELL.
JUDITH WINDSTROM THE OPERA SINGER--A PERSONAL FAVORITE, TO BE HONEST.
SORREN FESTIVA, THE AWARD-WINNING ACTOR AND...AH, YOU RECOGNIZE ALL OF THESE FULL-SYNCHERS, DON'T YOU?
FAMOUS FACES FROM THE WORLD OF ART.
ARTISTS AND LEADERS WHO DISTRACTED THE PEOPLE OF THIS WORLD. AND THESE ARE ONLY THE FIRST--ANY FULL-SYNCHERS WHOSE HEADS AREN'T ON OUR PEDESTALS YET, PREPARE YOURSELVES.
BECAUSE WE'RE COMING FOR YOU.
HE... HE REALLY ISN'T KIDDING.
HE'S LOST HIS MIND. ISN'T ANYBODY GOING TO ARREST HIM? WHY WOULD YOU DO THIS?
ARREST ONE OF THE MOST POWERFUL PEOPLE ON THE PLANET? I THINK NOT.
BUT WHAT I HAVE DONE IS NOT A CRIME--NOT JUST ARTISTS AND TRENDSETTERS, BUT ALL WHO HAVE UNDERGONE THE DISSONANCE RITUAL MUST BE CULLED. THEY ARE THE SCUM OF THE EARTH.

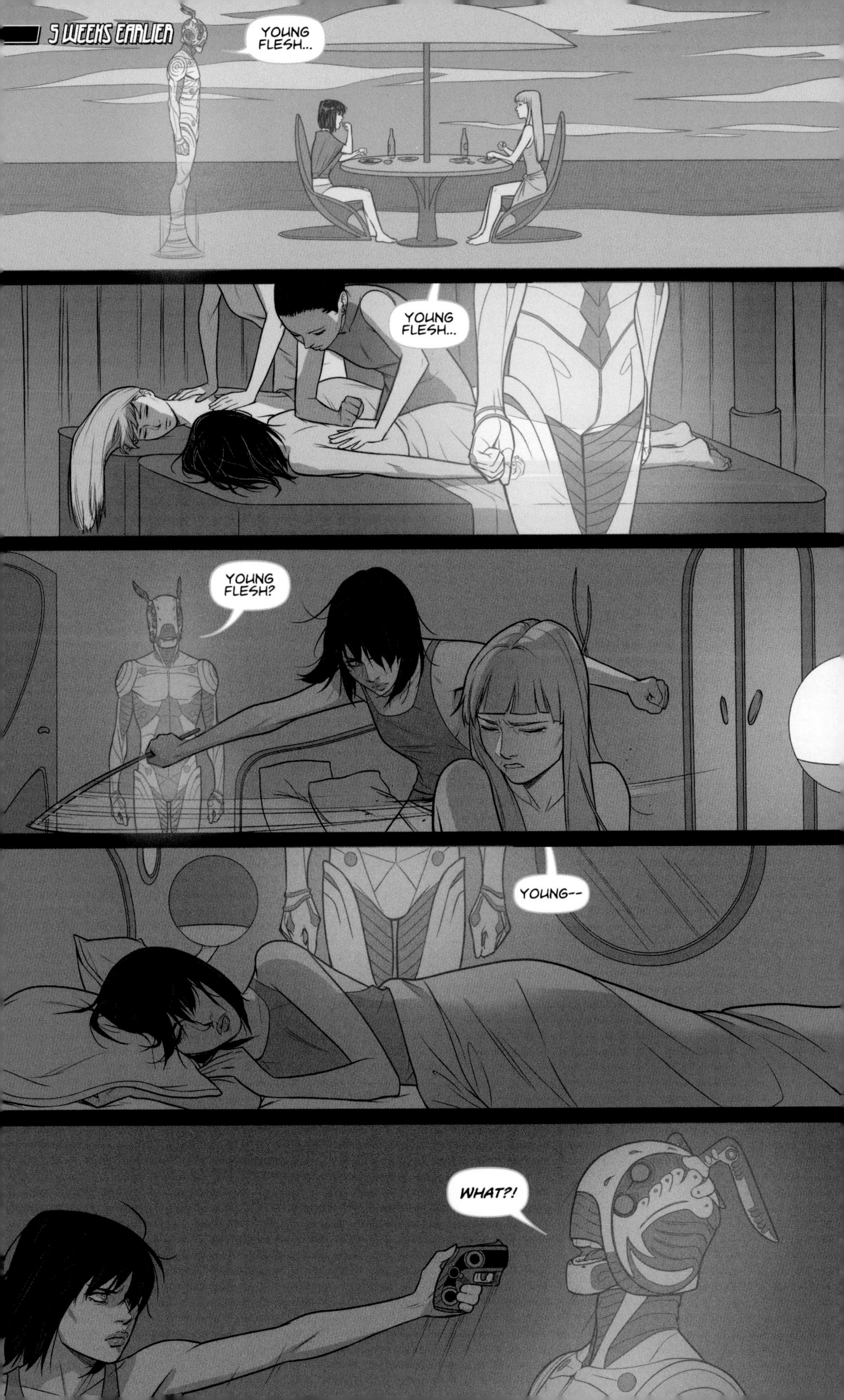
5 WEEKS EARLIER
YOUNG FLESH...
YOUNG FLESH...
YOUNG FLESH?
YOUNG--
WHAT?!

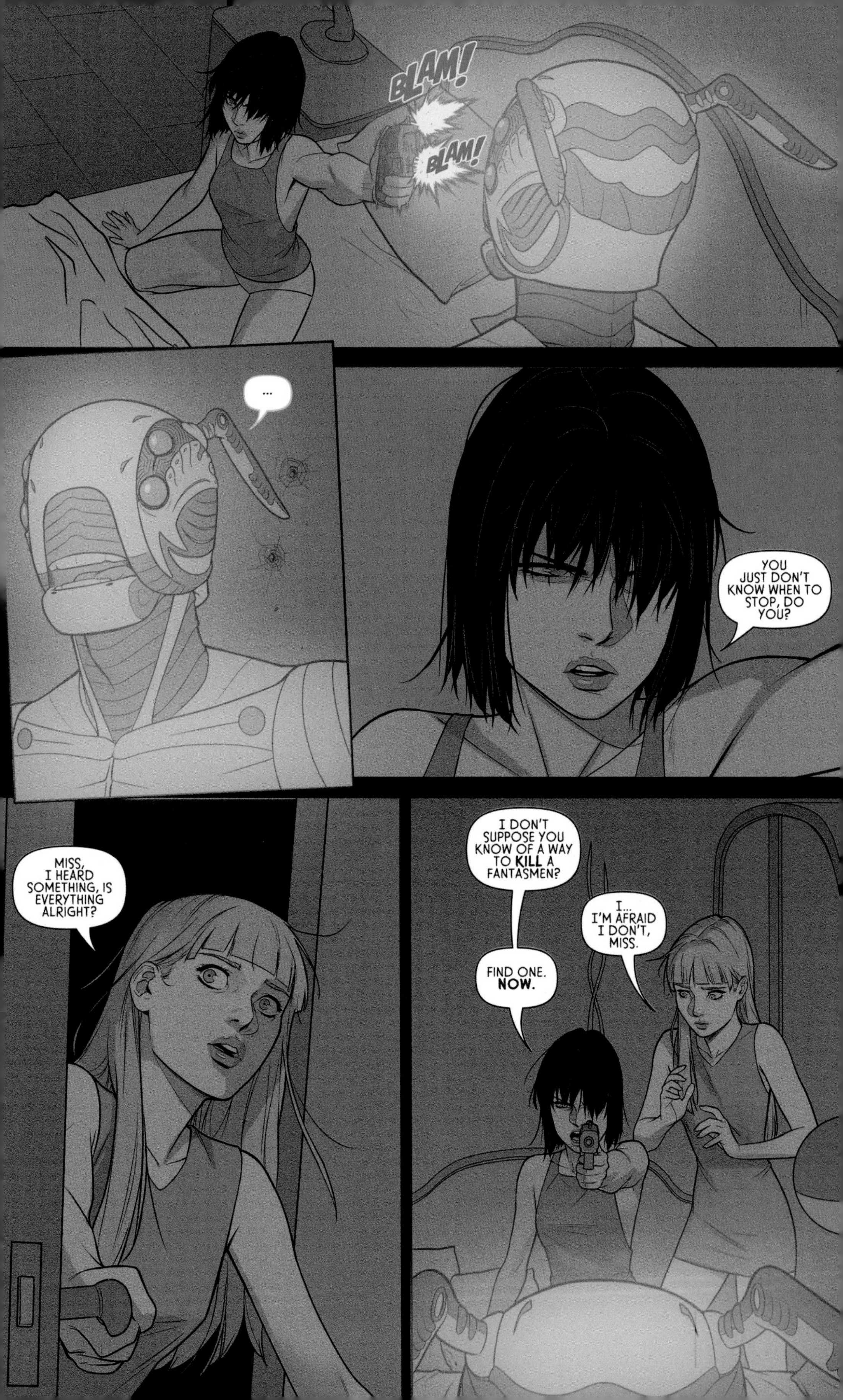
BLAM!
BLAM!
...
YOU JUST DON'T KNOW WHEN TO STOP, DO YOU?
MISS, I HEARD SOMETHING, IS EVERYTHING ALRIGHT?
I DON'T SUPPOSE YOU KNOW OF A WAY TO **KILL** A FANTASMEN?
I... I'M AFRAID I DON'T, MISS.
FIND ONE. **NOW.**

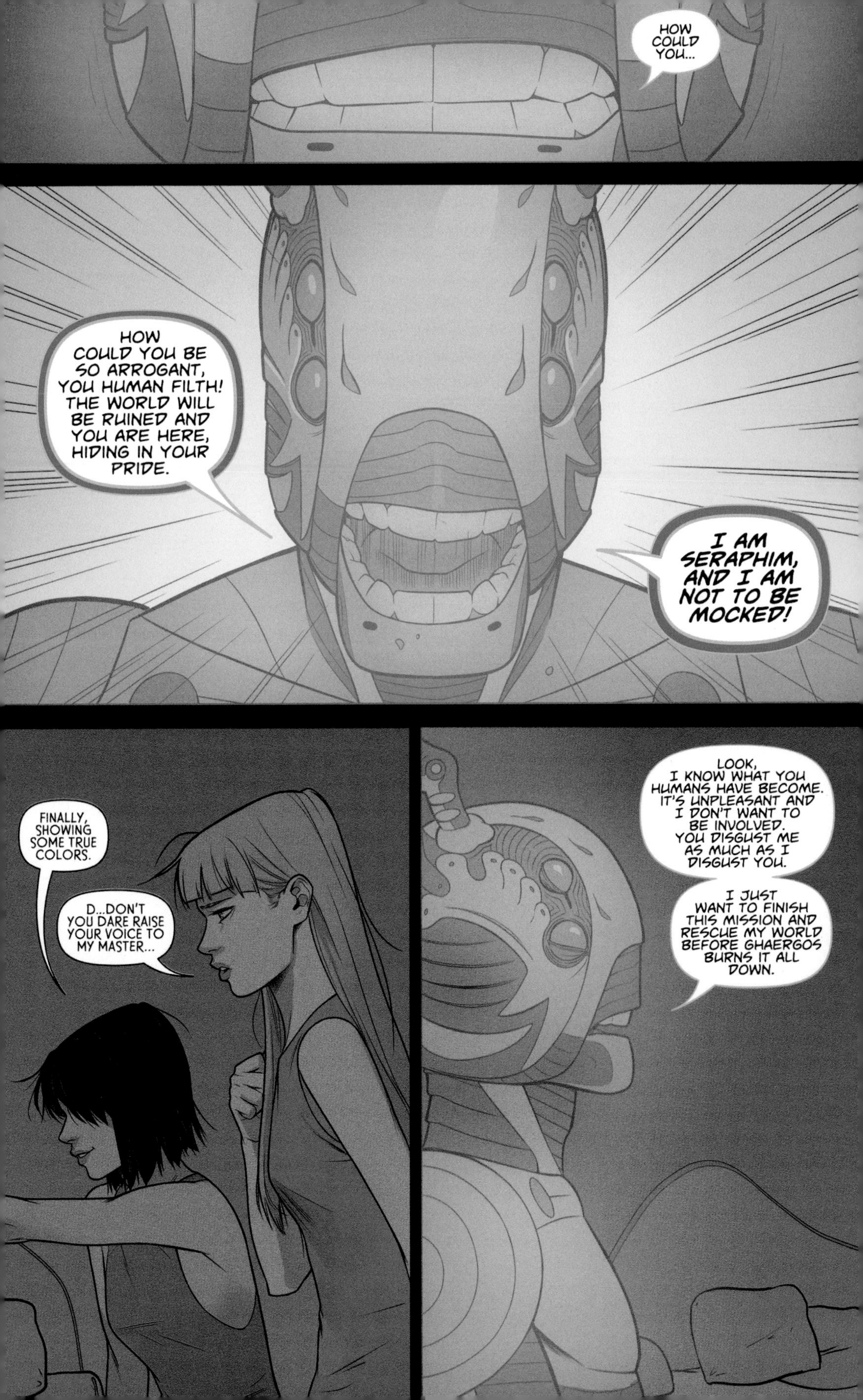
HOW COULD YOU...
HOW COULD YOU BE SO ARROGANT, YOU HUMAN FILTH! THE WORLD WILL BE RUINED AND YOU ARE HERE, HIDING IN YOUR PRIDE.
I AM SERAPHIM, AND I AM NOT TO BE MOCKED!
FINALLY, SHOWING SOME TRUE COLORS.
D...DON'T YOU DARE RAISE YOUR VOICE TO MY MASTER...
LOOK, I KNOW WHAT YOU HUMANS HAVE BECOME. IT'S UNPLEASANT AND I DON'T WANT TO BE INVOLVED. YOU DISGUST ME AS MUCH AS I DISGUST YOU.
I JUST WANT TO FINISH THIS MISSION AND RESCUE MY WORLD BEFORE GHAERGOS BURNS IT ALL DOWN.

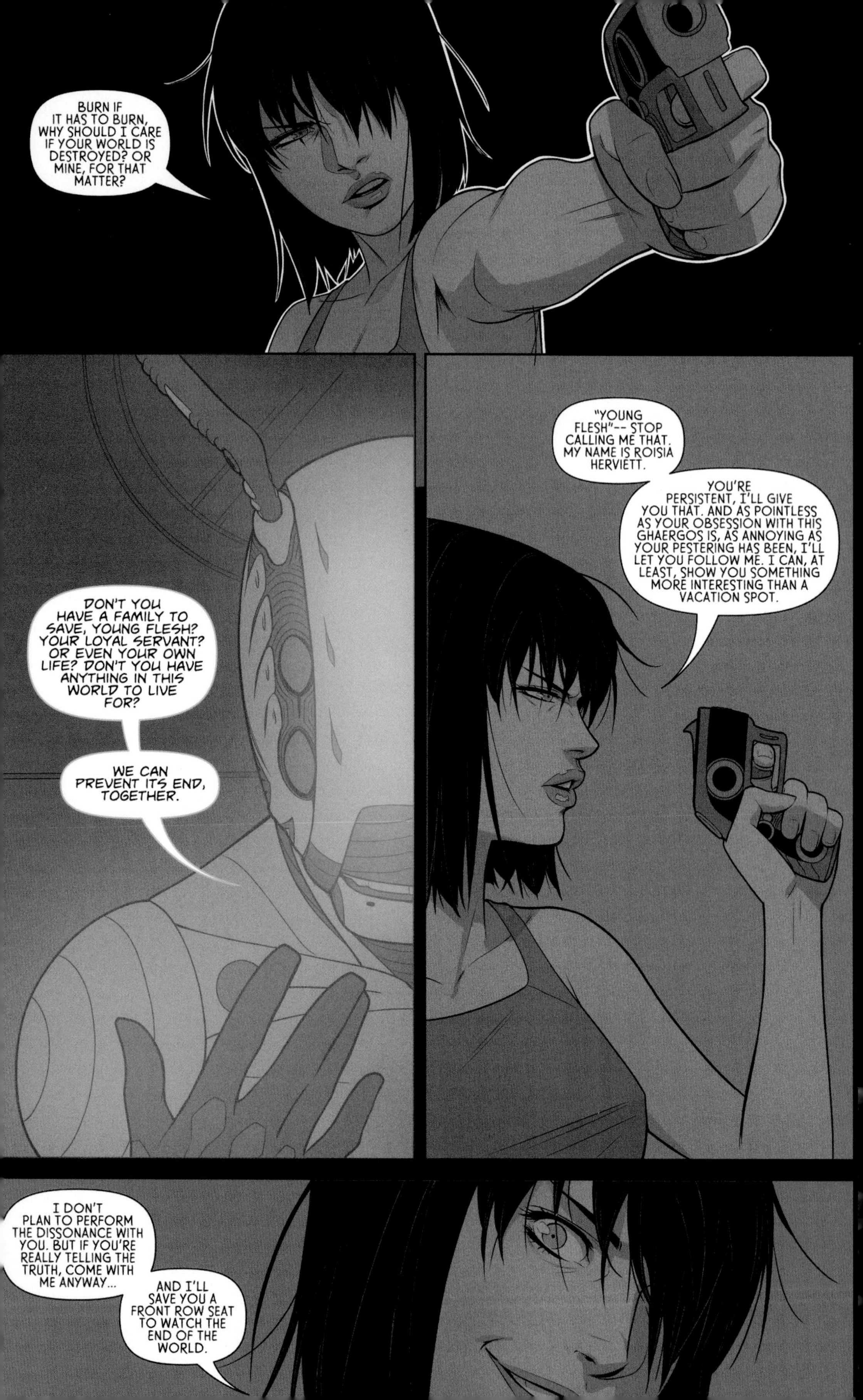
BURN IF IT HAS TO BURN, WHY SHOULD I CARE IF YOUR WORLD IS DESTROYED? OR MINE, FOR THAT MATTER?
DON'T YOU HAVE A FAMILY TO SAVE, YOUNG FLESH? YOUR LOYAL SERVANT? OR EVEN YOUR OWN LIFE? DON'T YOU HAVE ANYTHING IN THIS WORLD TO LIVE FOR?
WE CAN PREVENT ITS END, TOGETHER.
"YOUNG FLESH"-- STOP CALLING ME THAT. MY NAME IS ROISIA HERVIETT.
YOU'RE PERSISTENT, I'LL GIVE YOU THAT. AND AS POINTLESS AS YOUR OBSESSION WITH THIS GHAERGOS IS, AS ANNOYING AS YOUR PESTERING HAS BEEN, I'LL LET YOU FOLLOW ME. I CAN, AT LEAST, SHOW YOU SOMETHING MORE INTERESTING THAN A VACATION SPOT.
I DON'T PLAN TO PERFORM THE DISSONANCE WITH YOU. BUT IF YOU'RE REALLY TELLING THE TRUTH, COME WITH ME ANYWAY...
AND I'LL SAVE YOU A FRONT ROW SEAT TO WATCH THE END OF THE WORLD.

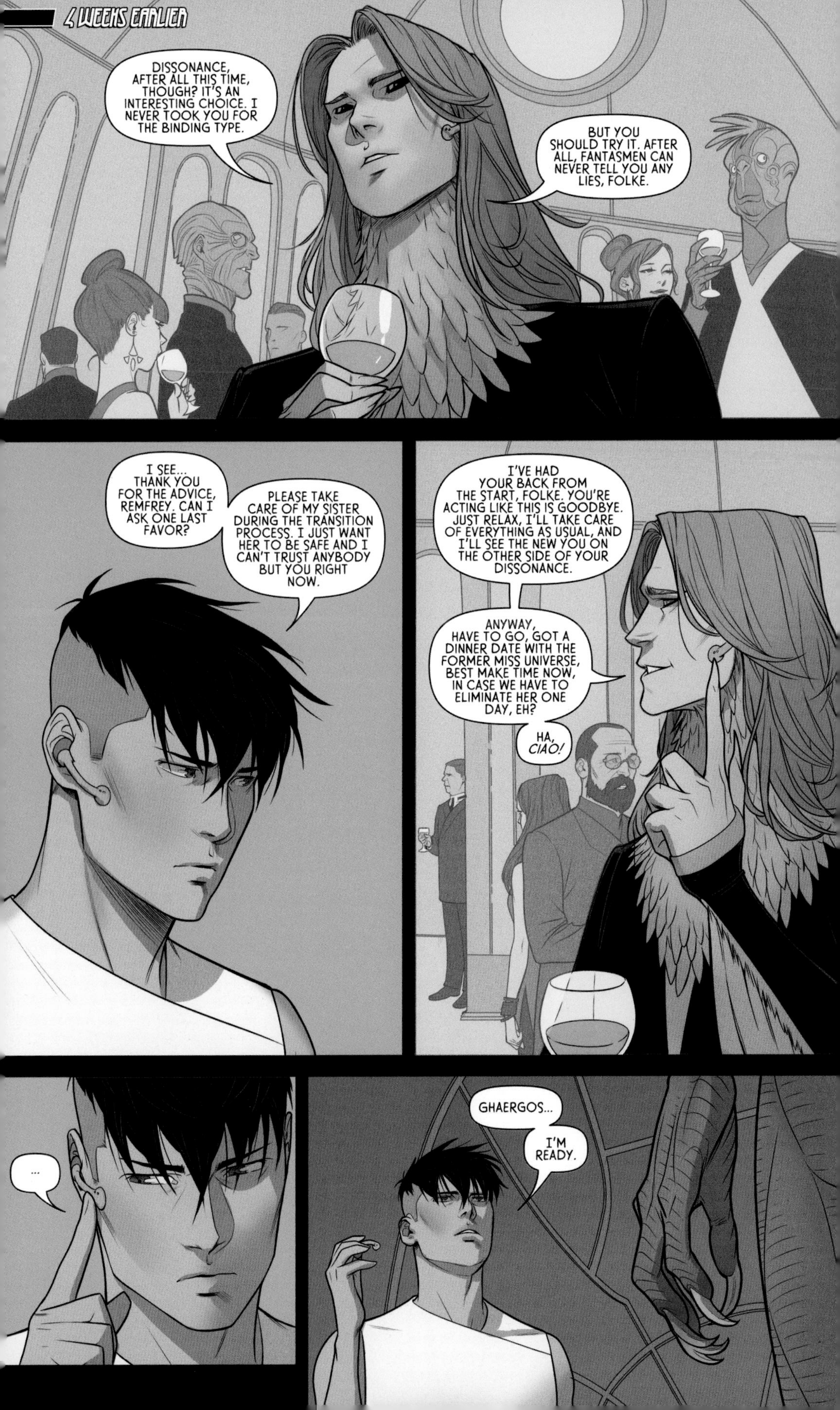
4 WEEKS EARLIER
DISSONANCE, AFTER ALL THIS TIME, THOUGH? IT'S AN INTERESTING CHOICE. I NEVER TOOK YOU FOR THE BINDING TYPE.
BUT YOU SHOULD TRY IT. AFTER ALL, FANTASMEN CAN NEVER TELL YOU ANY LIES, FOLKE.
I SEE... THANK YOU FOR THE ADVICE, REMFREY. CAN I ASK ONE LAST FAVOR?
PLEASE TAKE CARE OF MY SISTER DURING THE TRANSITION PROCESS. I JUST WANT HER TO BE SAFE AND I CAN'T TRUST ANYBODY BUT YOU RIGHT NOW.
I'VE HAD YOUR BACK FROM THE START, FOLKE. YOU'RE ACTING LIKE THIS IS GOODBYE. JUST RELAX, I'LL TAKE CARE OF EVERYTHING AS USUAL, AND I'LL SEE THE NEW YOU ON THE OTHER SIDE OF YOUR DISSONANCE.
ANYWAY, HAVE TO GO, GOT A DINNER DATE WITH THE FORMER MISS UNIVERSE, BEST MAKE TIME NOW, IN CASE WE HAVE TO ELIMINATE HER ONE DAY, EH?
HA, *CIAO!*
...
GHAERGOS...
I'M READY.

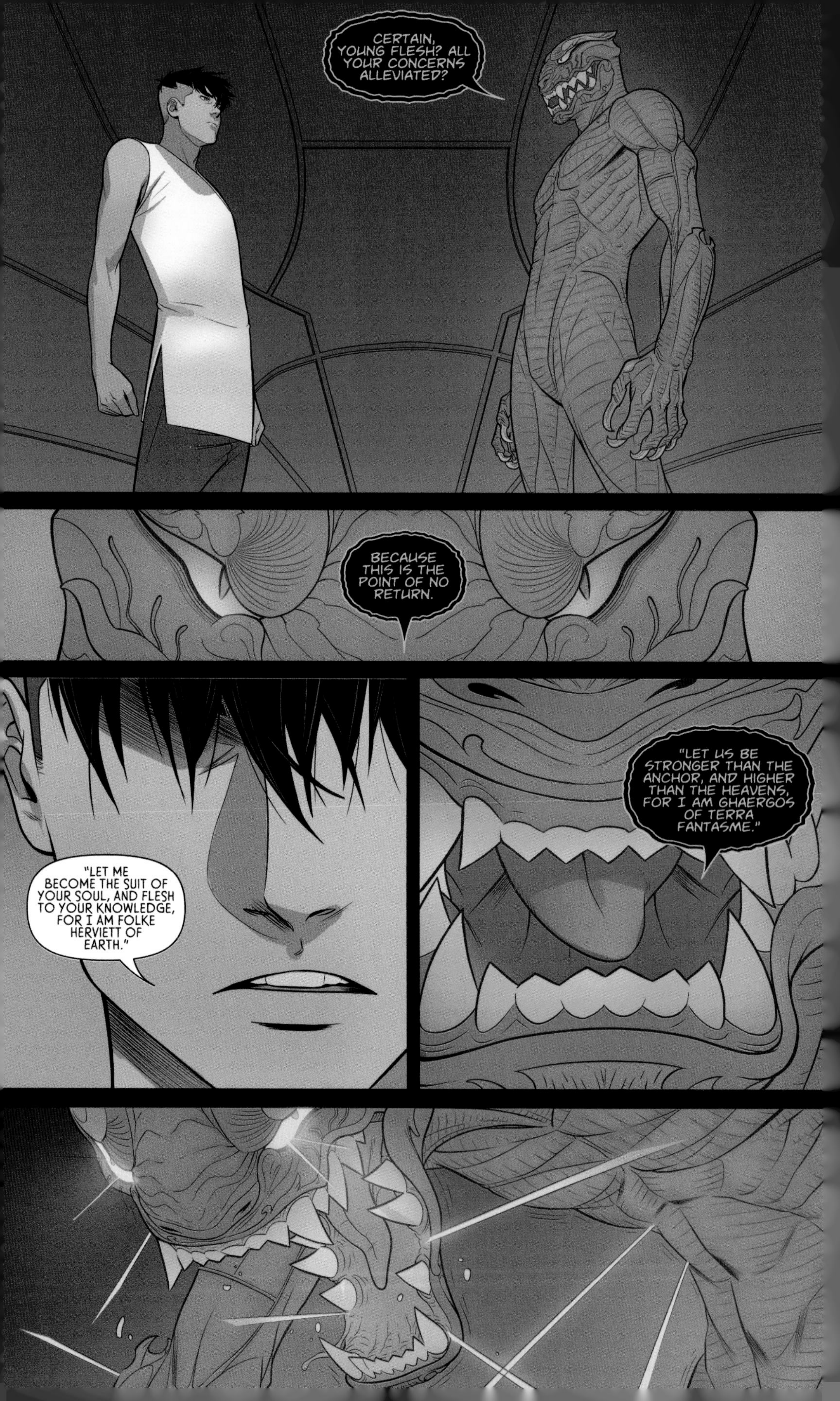
CERTAIN, YOUNG FLESH? ALL YOUR CONCERNS ALLEVIATED?
BECAUSE THIS IS THE POINT OF NO RETURN.
"LET ME BECOME THE SUIT OF YOUR SOUL, AND FLESH TO YOUR KNOWLEDGE, FOR I AM FOLKE HERVIETT OF EARTH."
"LET US BE STRONGER THAN THE ANCHOR, AND HIGHER THAN THE HEAVENS, FOR I AM GHAERGOS OF TERRA FANTASME."

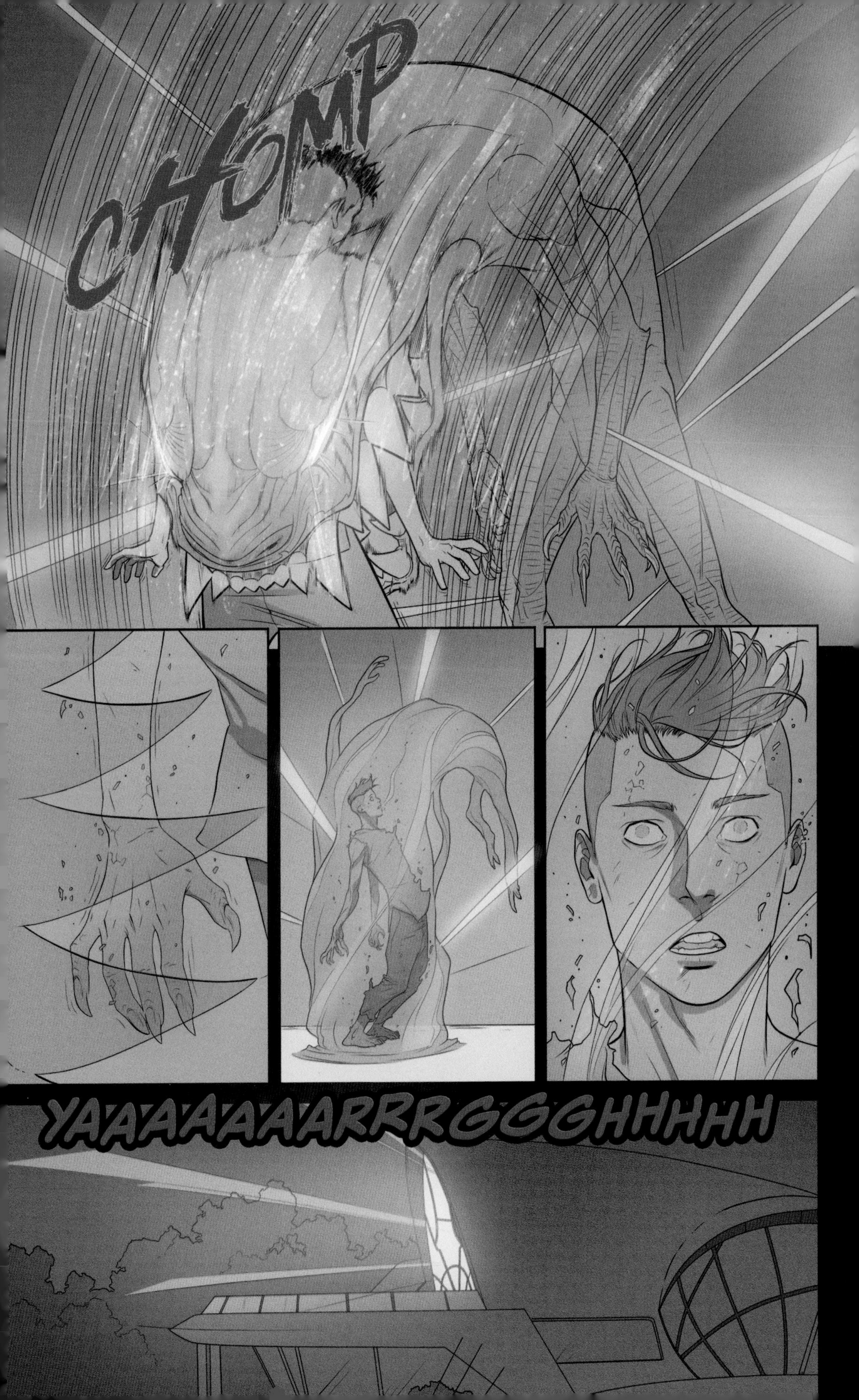
CHOMP
YAAAAAAARRRGGGHHHHH

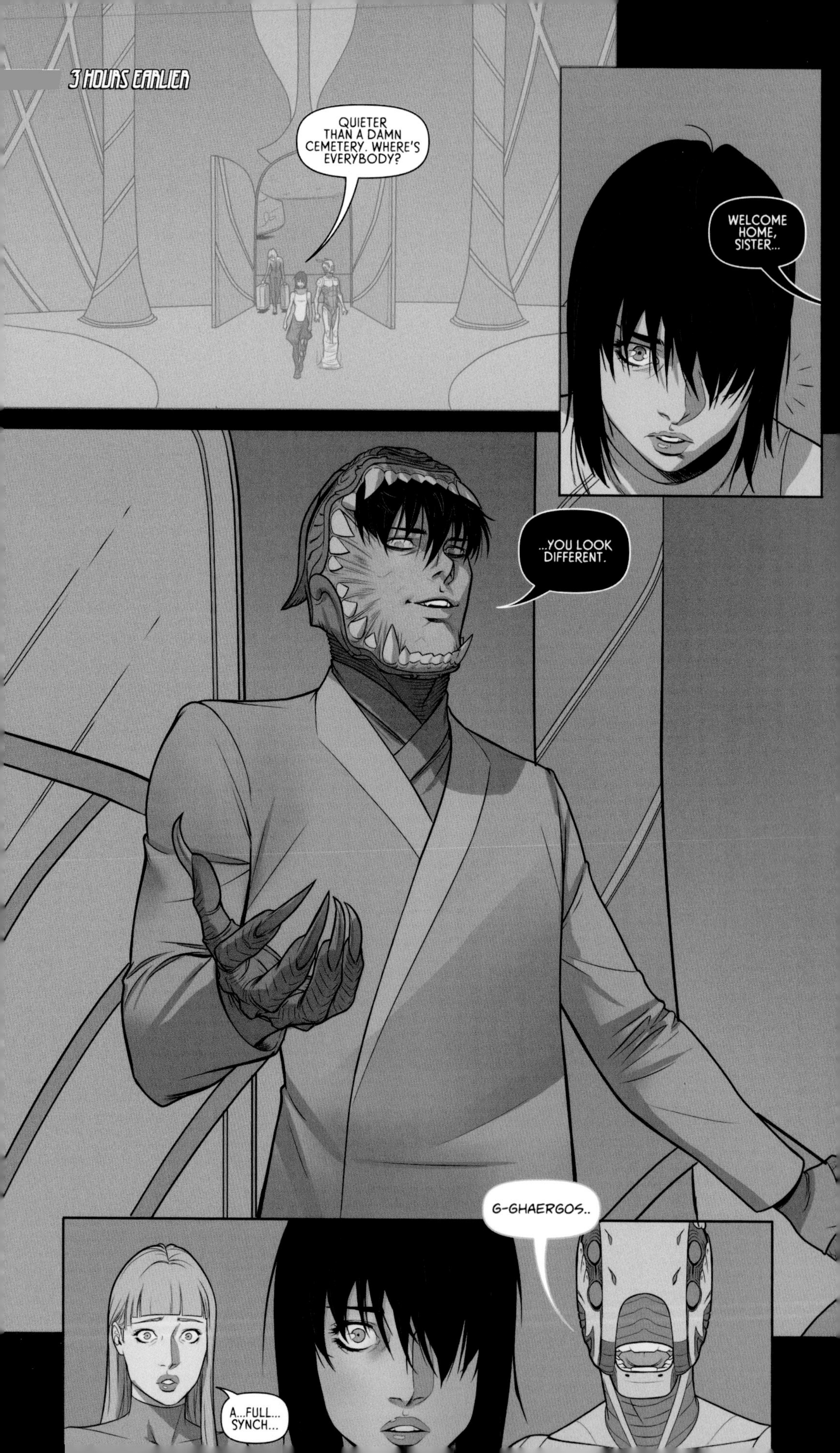
3 HOURS EARLIER
QUIETER THAN A DAMN CEMETERY. WHERE'S EVERYBODY?
WELCOME HOME, SISTER...
...YOU LOOK DIFFERENT.
G-GHAERGOS..
A...FULL... SYNCH...

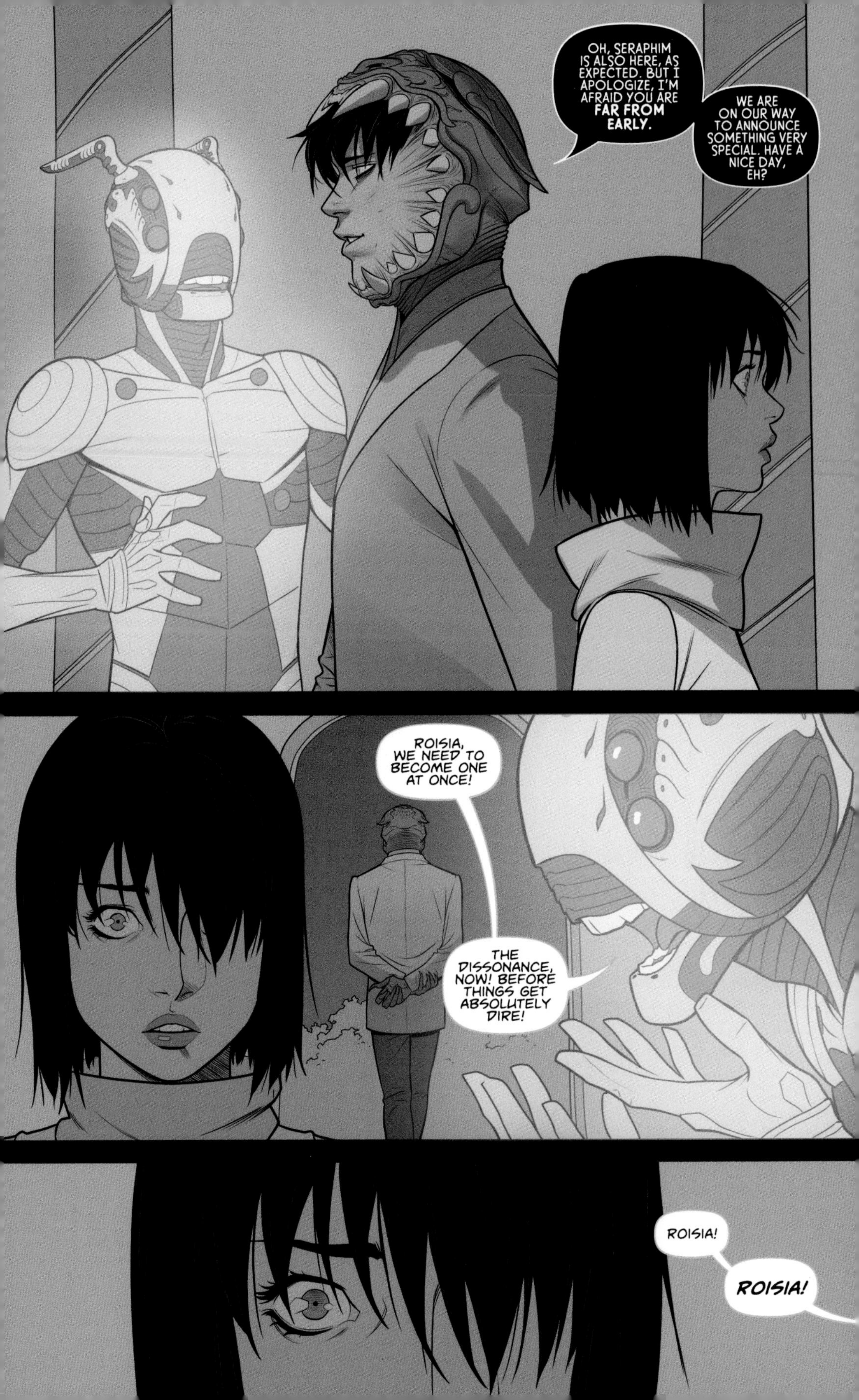
OH, SERAPHIM IS ALSO HERE, AS EXPECTED. BUT I APOLOGIZE, I'M AFRAID YOU ARE **FAR FROM EARLY.**
WE ARE ON OUR WAY TO ANNOUNCE SOMETHING VERY SPECIAL. HAVE A NICE DAY, EH?
ROISIA, WE NEED TO BECOME ONE AT ONCE!
THE DISSONANCE, NOW! BEFORE THINGS GET ABSOLUTELY DIRE!
ROISIA!
ROISIA!

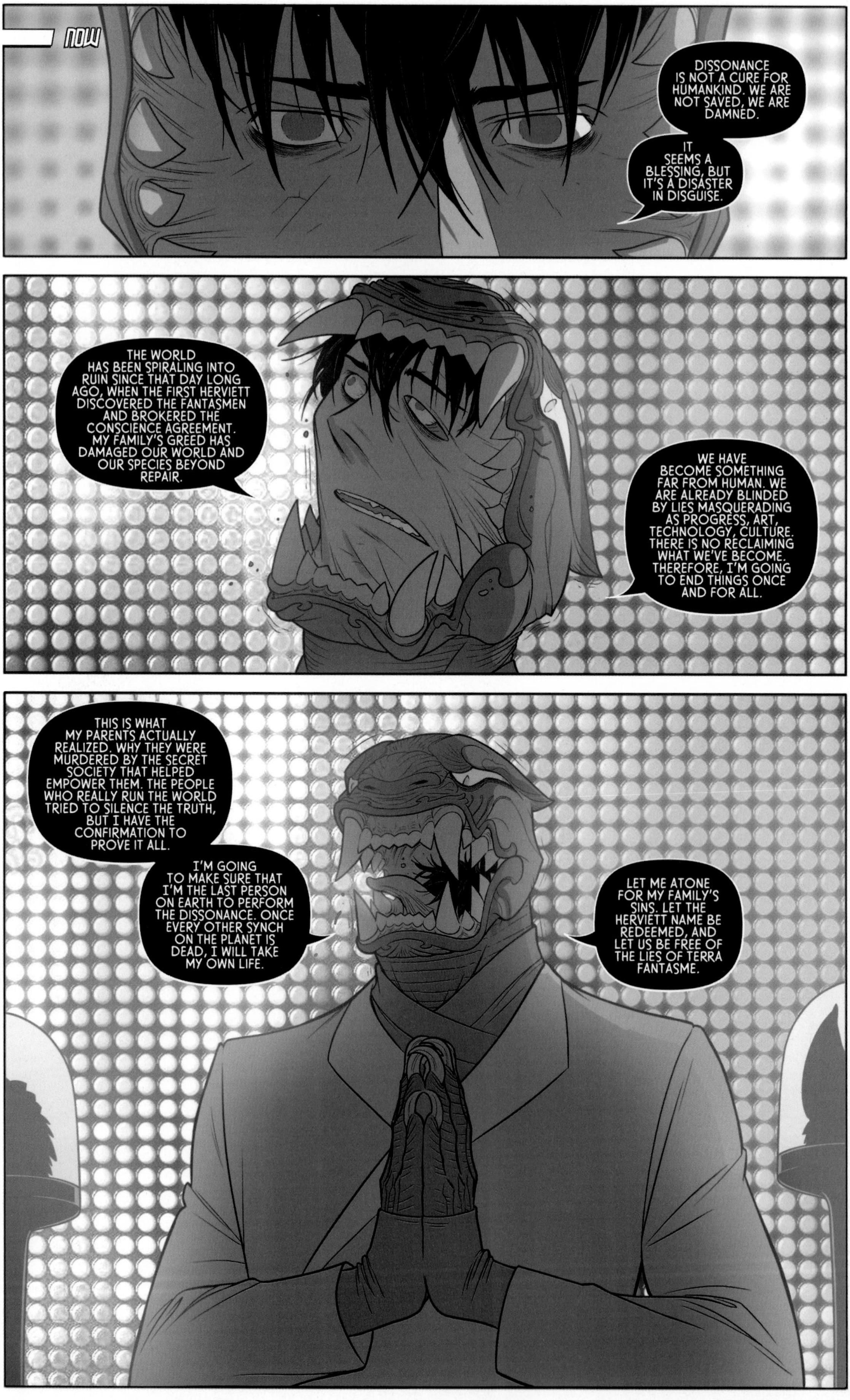
NOW
DISSONANCE IS NOT A CURE FOR HUMANKIND. WE ARE NOT SAVED, WE ARE DAMNED.
IT SEEMS A BLESSING, BUT IT'S A DISASTER IN DISGUISE.
THE WORLD HAS BEEN SPIRALING INTO RUIN SINCE THAT DAY LONG AGO, WHEN THE FIRST HERVIETT DISCOVERED THE FANTASMEN AND BROKERED THE CONSCIENCE AGREEMENT. MY FAMILY'S GREED HAS DAMAGED OUR WORLD AND OUR SPECIES BEYOND REPAIR.
WE HAVE BECOME SOMETHING FAR FROM HUMAN. WE ARE ALREADY BLINDED BY LIES MASQUERADING AS PROGRESS, ART, TECHNOLOGY, CULTURE. THERE IS NO RECLAIMING WHAT WE'VE BECOME. THEREFORE, I'M GOING TO END THINGS ONCE AND FOR ALL.
THIS IS WHAT MY PARENTS ACTUALLY REALIZED. WHY THEY WERE MURDERED BY THE SECRET SOCIETY THAT HELPED EMPOWER THEM. THE PEOPLE WHO REALLY RUN THE WORLD TRIED TO SILENCE THE TRUTH, BUT I HAVE THE CONFIRMATION TO PROVE IT ALL.
I'M GOING TO MAKE SURE THAT I'M THE LAST PERSON ON EARTH TO PERFORM THE DISSONANCE. ONCE EVERY OTHER SYNCH ON THE PLANET IS DEAD, I WILL TAKE MY OWN LIFE.
LET ME ATONE FOR MY FAMILY'S SINS. LET THE HERVIETT NAME BE REDEEMED, AND LET US BE FREE OF THE LIES OF TERRA FANTASME.

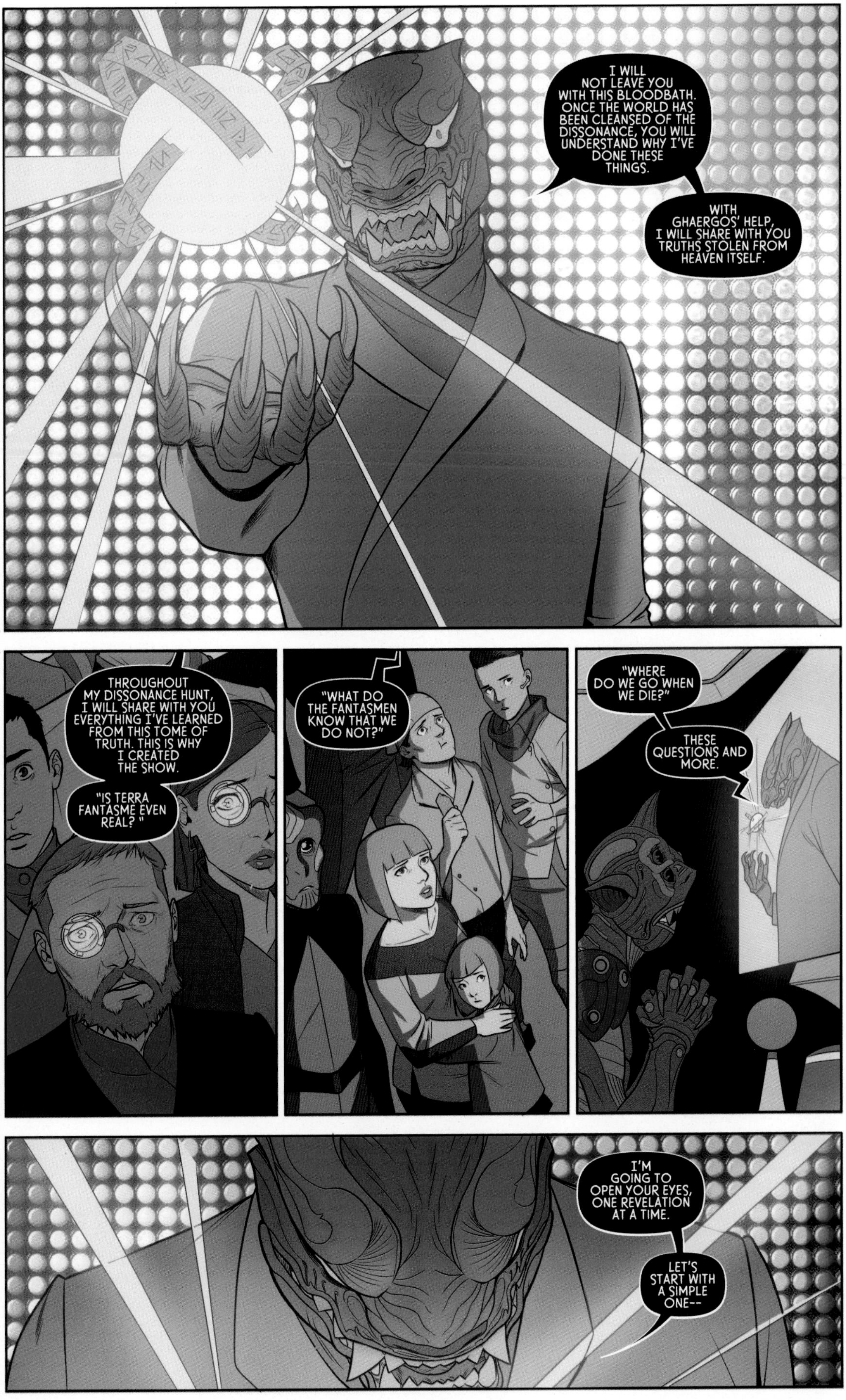
I WILL NOT LEAVE YOU WITH THIS BLOODBATH. ONCE THE WORLD HAS BEEN CLEANSED OF THE DISSONANCE, YOU WILL UNDERSTAND WHY I'VE DONE THESE THINGS.
WITH GHAERGOS' HELP, I WILL SHARE WITH YOU TRUTHS STOLEN FROM HEAVEN ITSELF.
THROUGHOUT MY DISSONANCE HUNT, I WILL SHARE WITH YOU EVERYTHING I'VE LEARNED FROM THIS TOME OF TRUTH. THIS IS WHY I CREATED THE SHOW.
"IS TERRA FANTASME EVEN REAL?"
"WHAT DO THE FANTASMEN KNOW THAT WE DO NOT?"
"WHERE DO WE GO WHEN WE DIE?"
THESE QUESTIONS AND MORE.
I'M GOING TO OPEN YOUR EYES, ONE REVELATION AT A TIME.
LET'S START WITH A SIMPLE ONE--

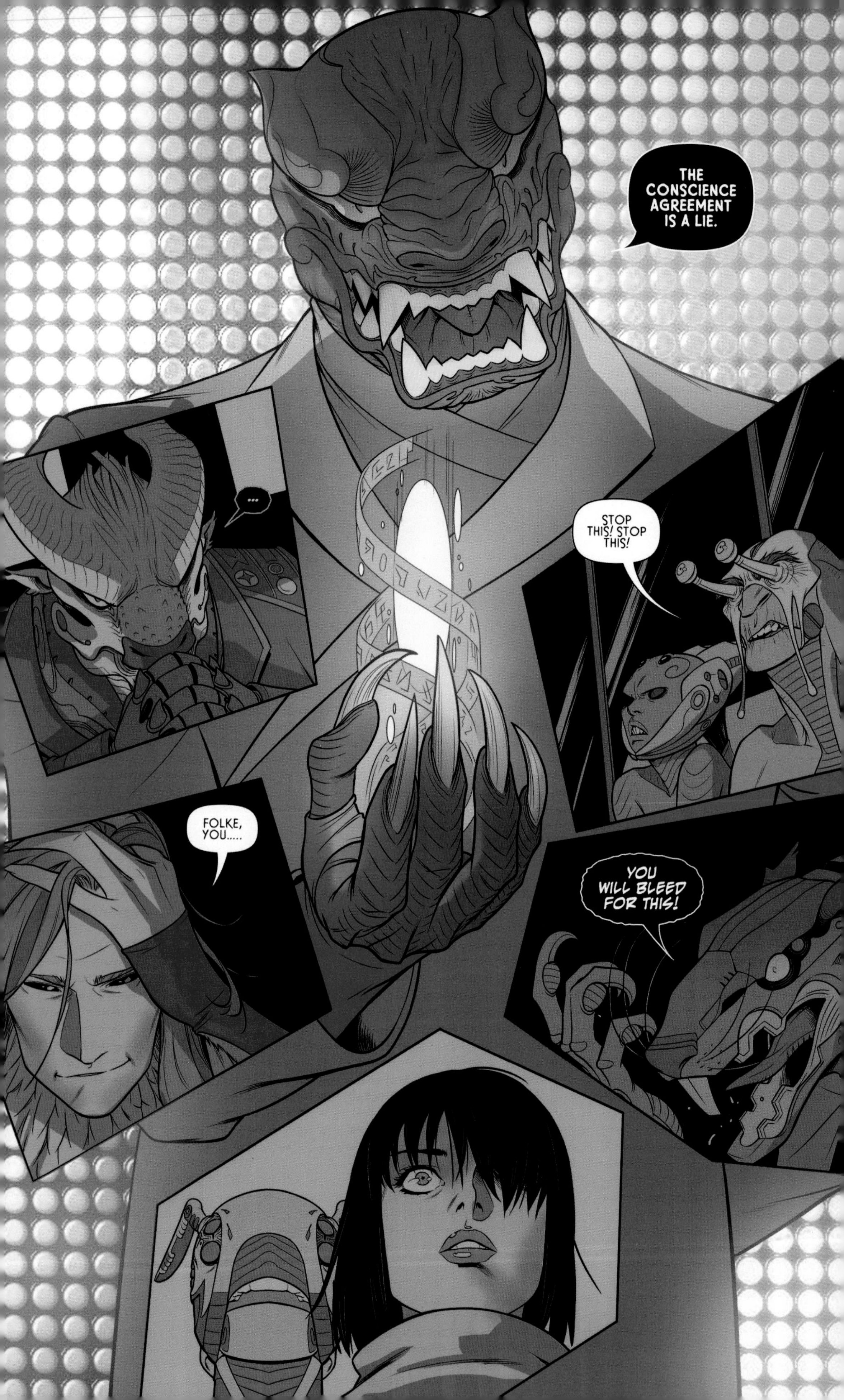
THE CONSCIENCE AGREEMENT IS A LIE.
...
STOP THIS! STOP THIS!
FOLKE, YOU.....
YOU WILL BLEED FOR THIS!

CHAPTER 4

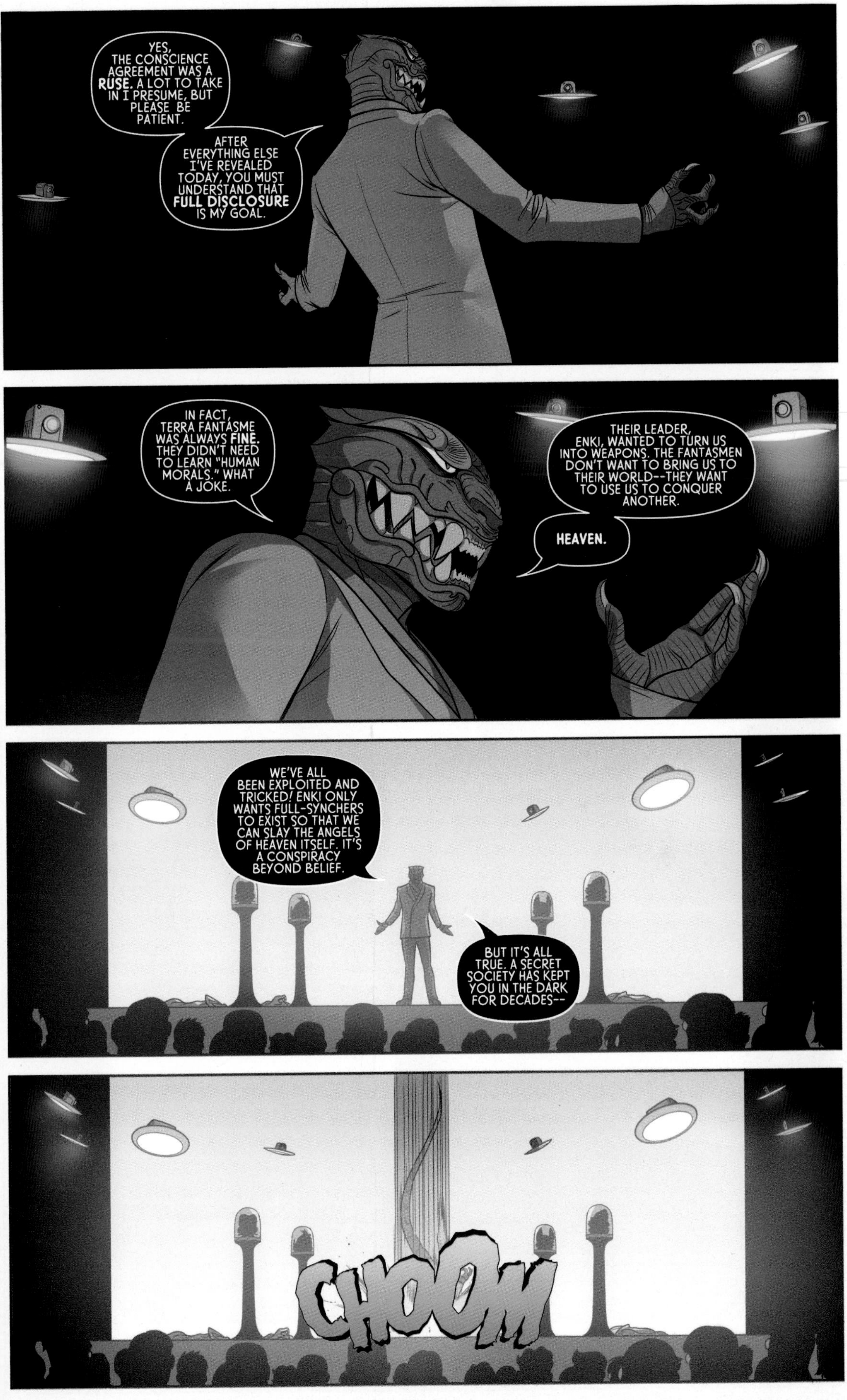
YES, THE CONSCIENCE AGREEMENT WAS A **RUSE.** A LOT TO TAKE IN I PRESUME, BUT PLEASE BE PATIENT.
AFTER EVERYTHING ELSE I'VE REVEALED TODAY, YOU MUST UNDERSTAND THAT **FULL DISCLOSURE** IS MY GOAL.
IN FACT, TERRA FANTASME WAS ALWAYS **FINE.** THEY DIDN'T NEED TO LEARN "HUMAN MORALS." WHAT A JOKE.
THEIR LEADER, ENKI, WANTED TO TURN US INTO WEAPONS. THE FANTASMEN DON'T WANT TO BRING US TO THEIR WORLD--THEY WANT TO USE US TO CONQUER ANOTHER.
HEAVEN.
WE'VE ALL BEEN EXPLOITED AND TRICKED! ENKI ONLY WANTS FULL-SYNCHERS TO EXIST SO THAT WE CAN SLAY THE ANGELS OF HEAVEN ITSELF. IT'S A CONSPIRACY BEYOND BELIEF.
BUT IT'S ALL TRUE. A SECRET SOCIETY HAS KEPT YOU IN THE DARK FOR DECADES--
CHOOM

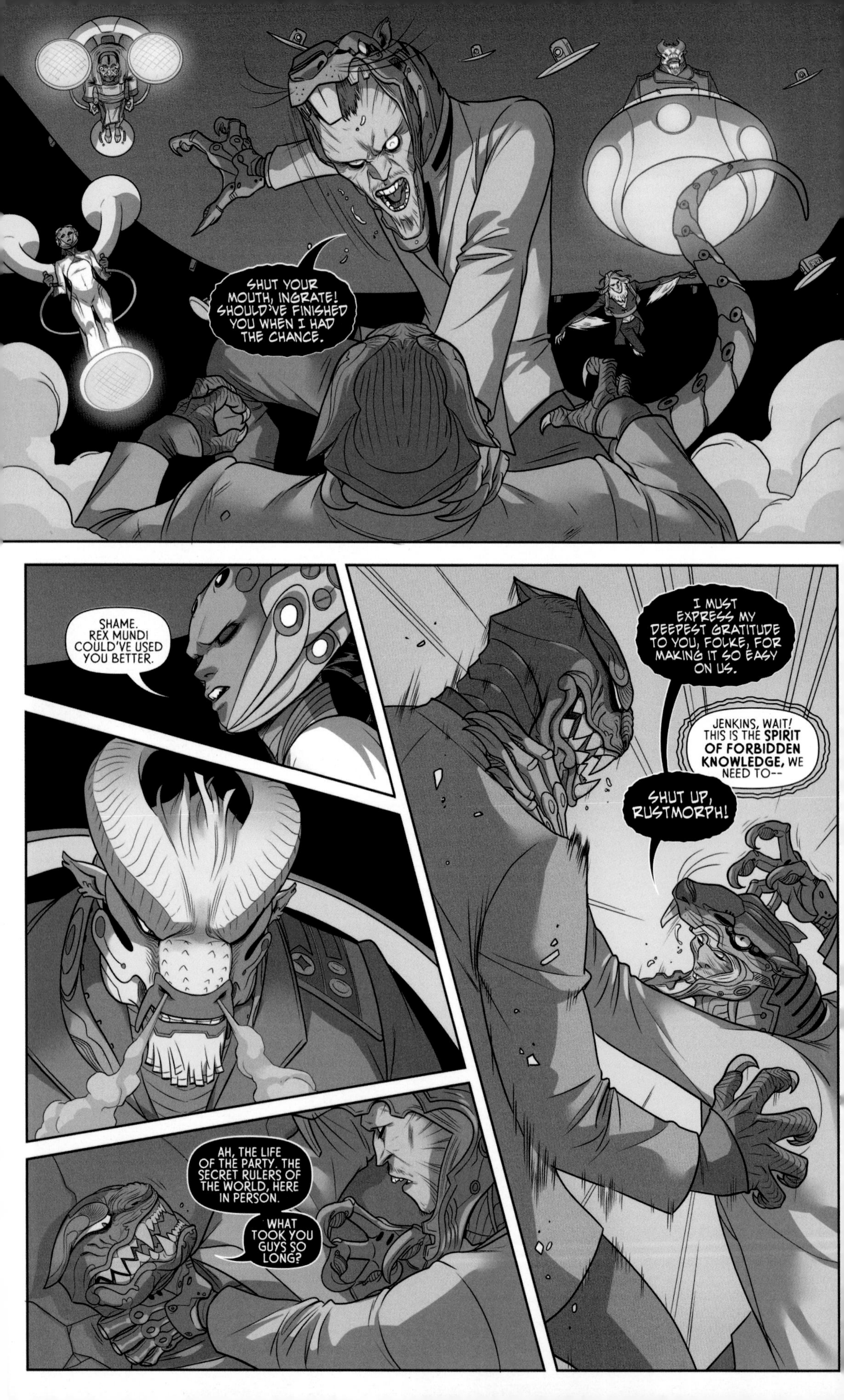
SHUT YOUR MOUTH, INGRATE! SHOULD'VE FINISHED YOU WHEN I HAD THE CHANCE.
SHAME. REX MUNDI COULD'VE USED YOU BETTER.
I MUST EXPRESS MY DEEPEST GRATITUDE TO YOU, FOLKE, FOR MAKING IT SO EASY ON US.
JENKINS, WAIT! THIS IS THE SPIRIT OF FORBIDDEN KNOWLEDGE, WE NEED TO--
SHUT UP, RUSTMORPH!
AH, THE LIFE OF THE PARTY. THE SECRET RULERS OF THE WORLD, HERE IN PERSON.
WHAT TOOK YOU GUYS SO LONG?

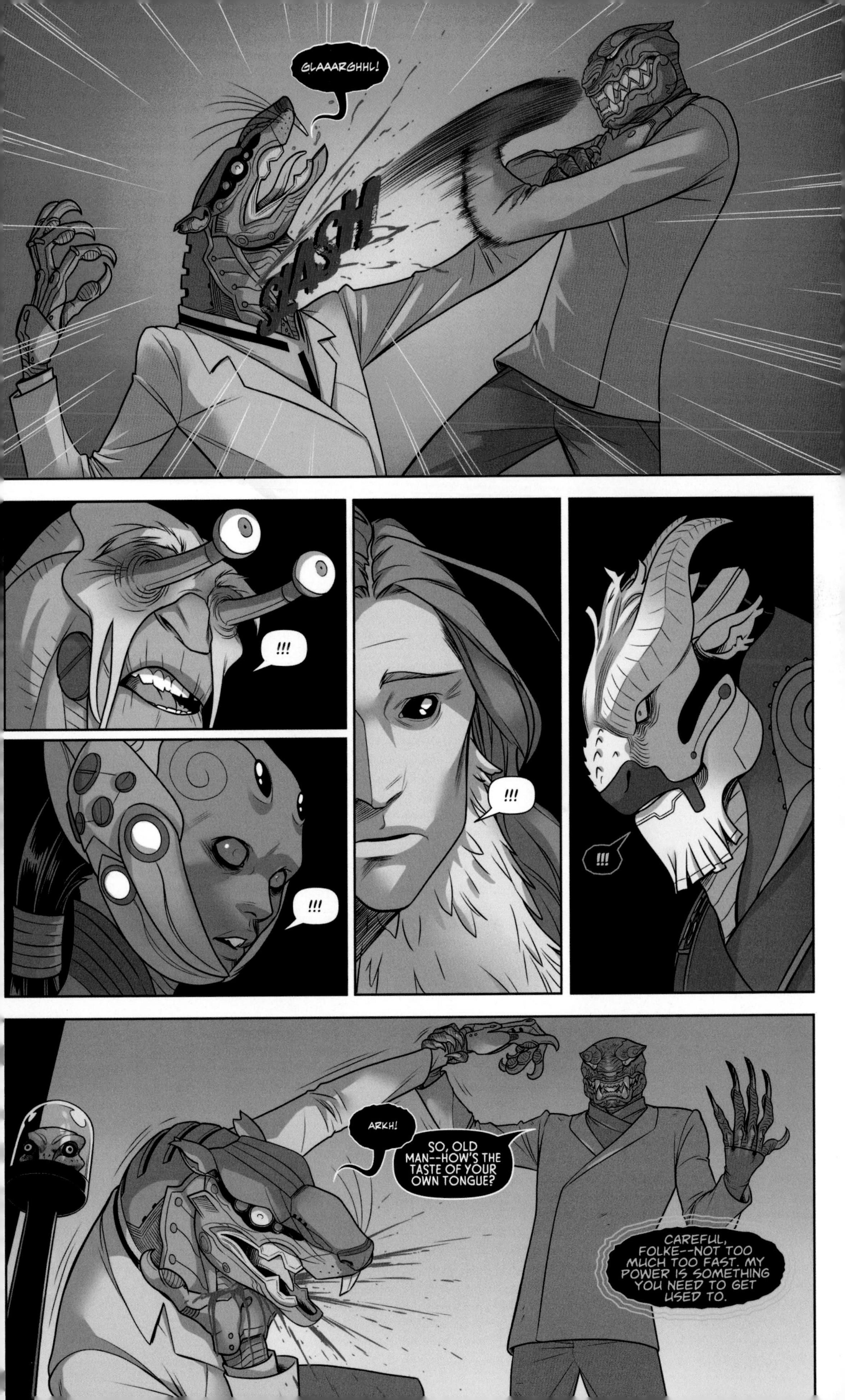
GLAAARGHHL!
SLASH
!!!
!!!
!!!
!!!
ARKH!
SO, OLD MAN--HOW'S THE TASTE OF YOUR OWN TONGUE?
CAREFUL, FOLKE--NOT TOO MUCH TOO FAST. MY POWER IS SOMETHING YOU NEED TO GET USED TO.

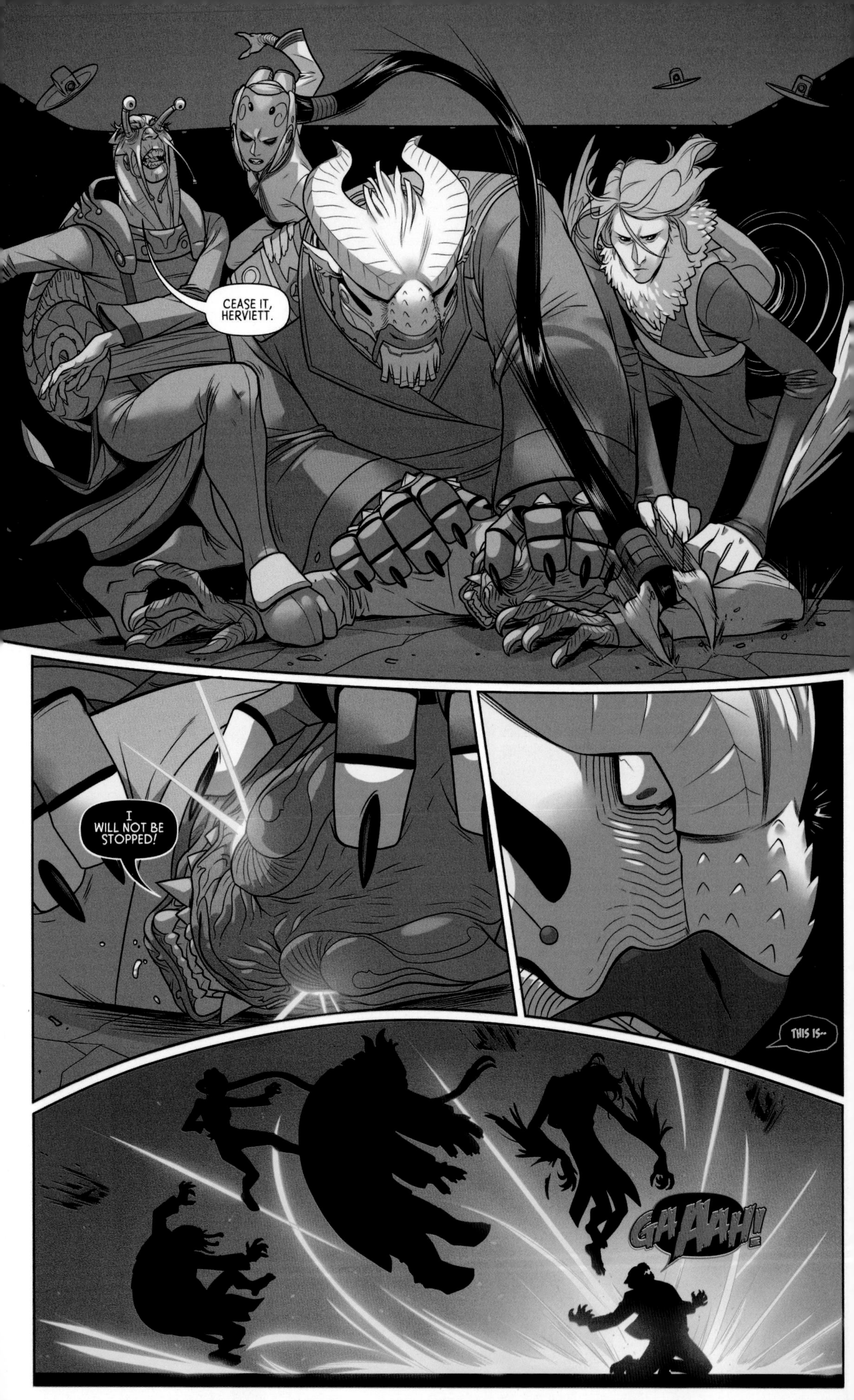
CEASE IT, HERVIETT.
I WILL NOT BE STOPPED!
THIS IS--
GAAAH!

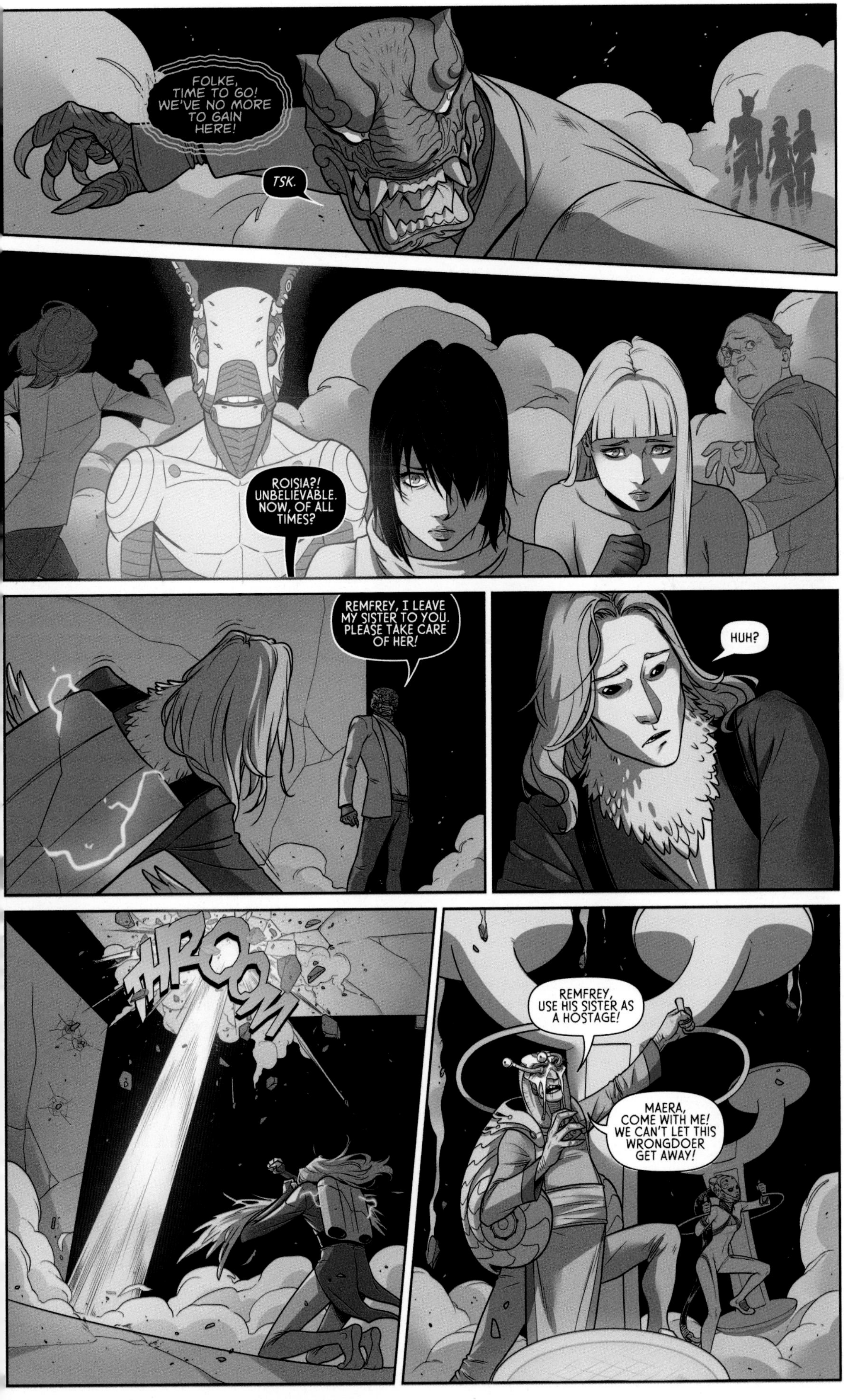
FOLKE, TIME TO GO! WE'VE NO MORE TO GAIN HERE!
TSK.
ROISIA?! UNBELIEVABLE. NOW, OF ALL TIMES?
REMFREY, I LEAVE MY SISTER TO YOU. PLEASE TAKE CARE OF HER!
HUH?
THROOM
REMFREY, USE HIS SISTER AS A HOSTAGE!
MAERA, COME WITH ME! WE CAN'T LET THIS WRONGDOER GET AWAY!

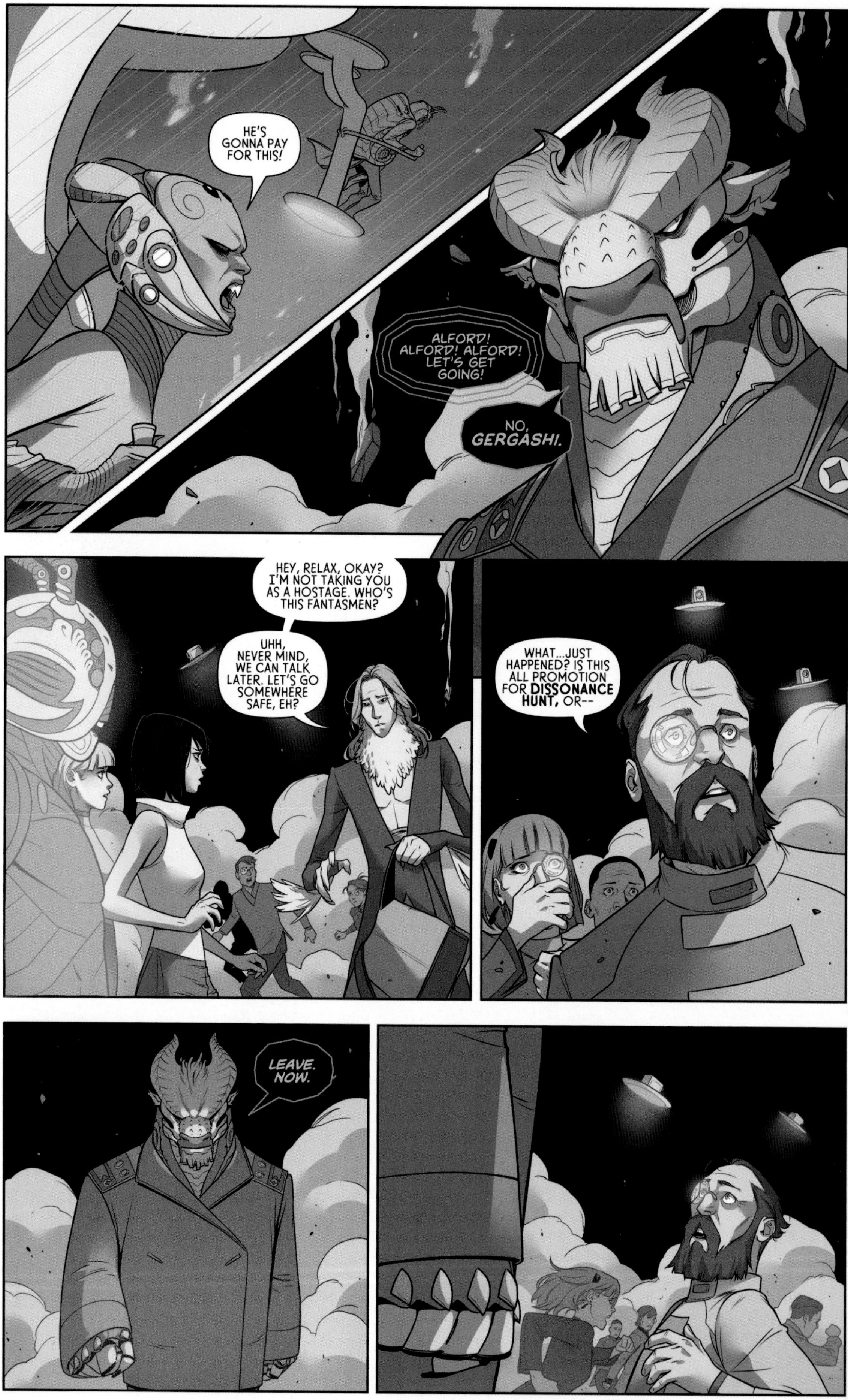
HE'S GONNA PAY FOR THIS!
ALFORD! ALFORD! ALFORD! LET'S GET GOING!
NO, GERGASHI.
HEY, RELAX, OKAY? I'M NOT TAKING YOU AS A HOSTAGE. WHO'S THIS FANTASMEN?
UHH, NEVER MIND, WE CAN TALK LATER. LET'S GO SOMEWHERE SAFE, EH?
WHAT...JUST HAPPENED? IS THIS ALL PROMOTION FOR DISSONANCE HUNT, OR--
LEAVE. NOW.

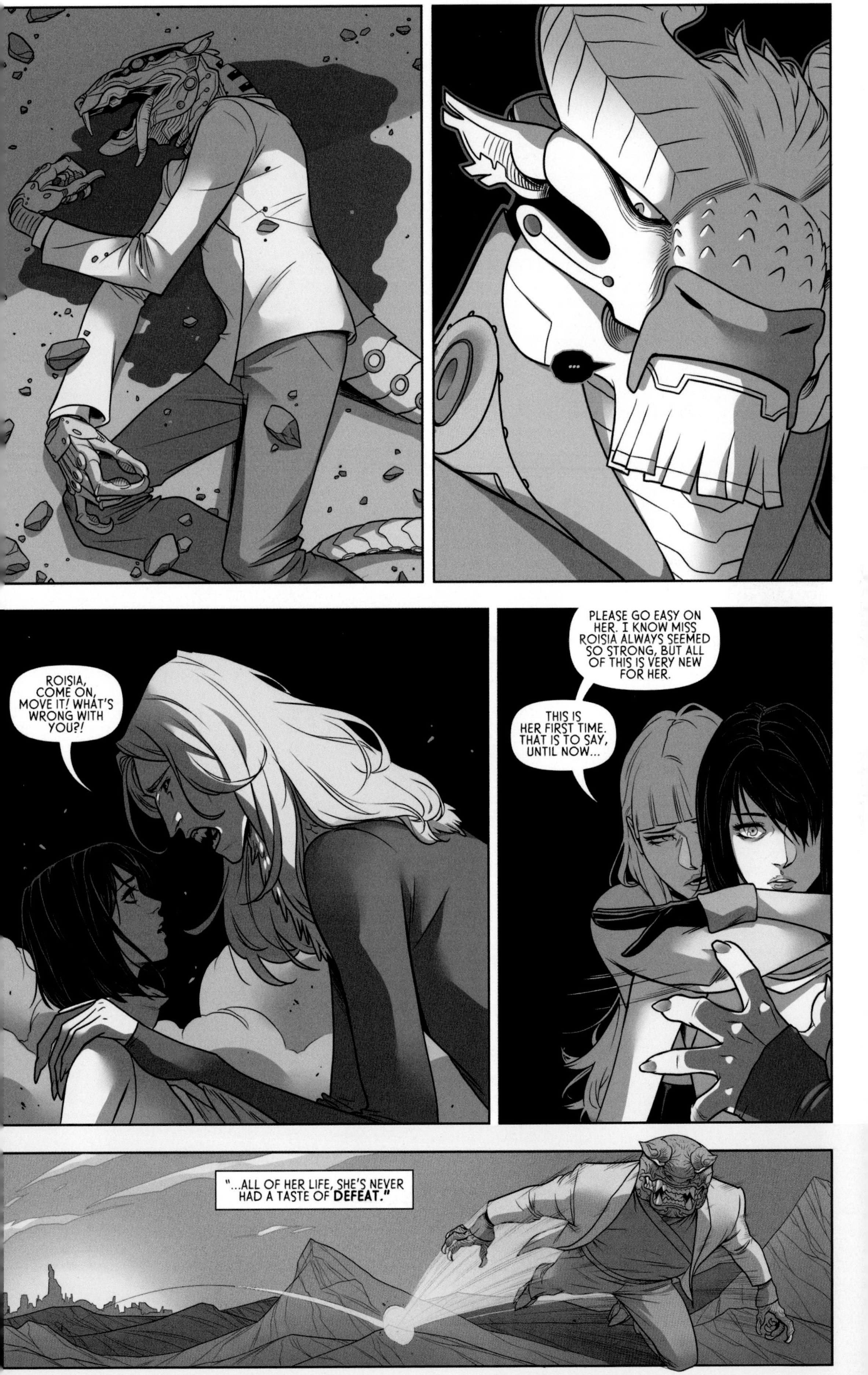
...
ROISIA, COME ON, MOVE IT! WHAT'S WRONG WITH YOU?!
PLEASE GO EASY ON HER. I KNOW MISS ROISIA ALWAYS SEEMED SO STRONG, BUT ALL OF THIS IS VERY NEW FOR HER.
THIS IS HER FIRST TIME. THAT IS TO SAY, UNTIL NOW...
"...ALL OF HER LIFE, SHE'S NEVER HAD A TASTE OF DEFEAT."

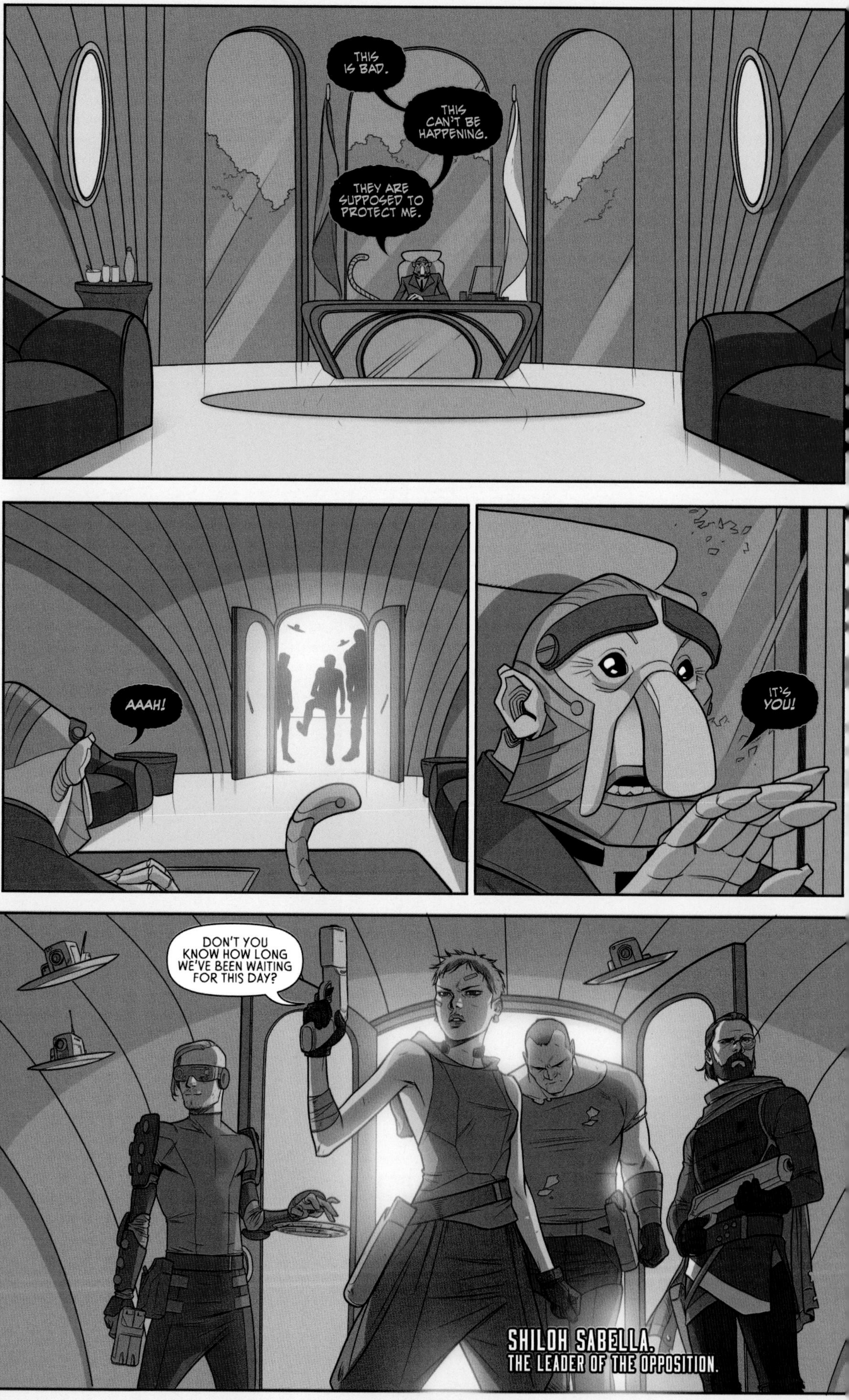
THIS IS BAD.
THIS CAN'T BE HAPPENING.
THEY ARE SUPPOSED TO PROTECT ME.
AAAH!
IT'S YOU!
DON'T YOU KNOW HOW LONG WE'VE BEEN WAITING FOR THIS DAY?
SHILOH SABELLA.
THE LEADER OF THE OPPOSITION.

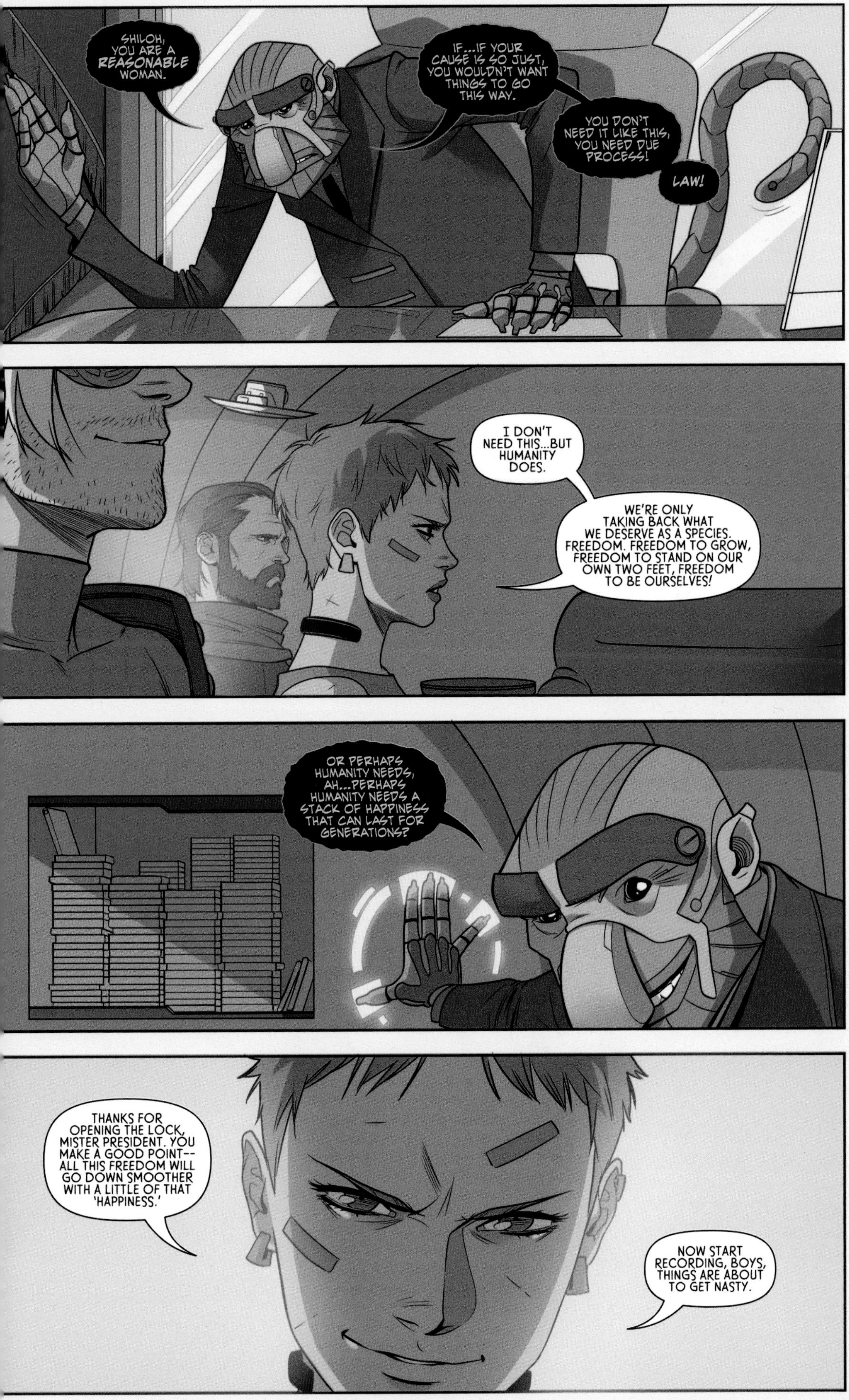
SHILOH, YOU ARE A REASONABLE WOMAN.
IF...IF YOUR CAUSE IS SO JUST, YOU WOULDN'T WANT THINGS TO GO THIS WAY.
YOU DON'T NEED IT LIKE THIS, YOU NEED DUE PROCESS!
LAW!
I DON'T NEED THIS...BUT HUMANITY DOES.
WE'RE ONLY TAKING BACK WHAT WE DESERVE AS A SPECIES. FREEDOM. FREEDOM TO GROW, FREEDOM TO STAND ON OUR OWN TWO FEET, FREEDOM TO BE OURSELVES!
OR PERHAPS HUMANITY NEEDS, AH...PERHAPS HUMANITY NEEDS A STACK OF HAPPINESS THAT CAN LAST FOR GENERATIONS?
THANKS FOR OPENING THE LOCK, MISTER PRESIDENT. YOU MAKE A GOOD POINT-- ALL THIS FREEDOM WILL GO DOWN SMOOTHER WITH A LITTLE OF THAT 'HAPPINESS.'
NOW START RECORDING, BOYS, THINGS ARE ABOUT TO GET NASTY.

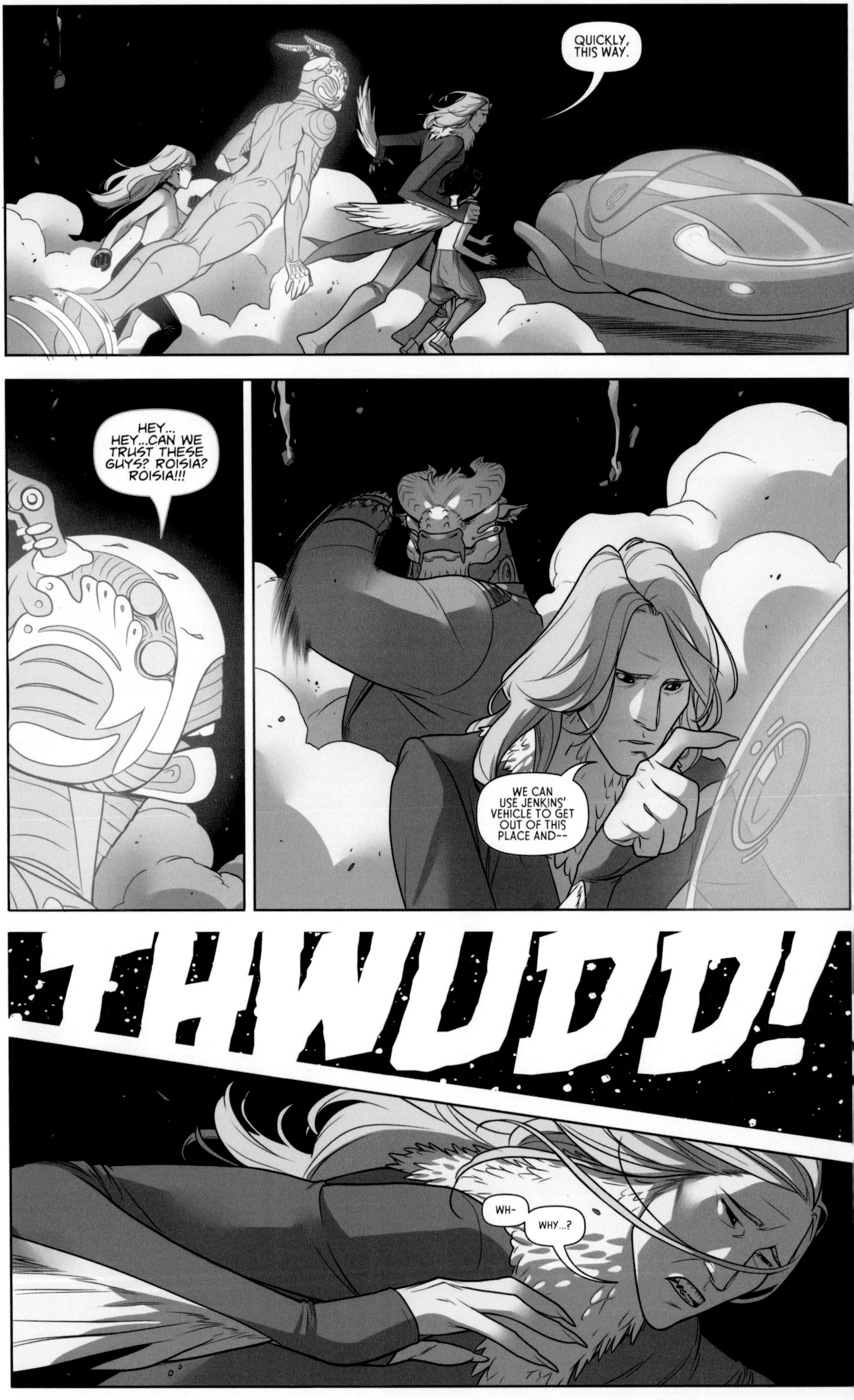
QUICKLY, THIS WAY.
HEY... HEY...CAN WE TRUST THESE GUYS? ROISIA? ROISIA!!!
WE CAN USE JENKINS' VEHICLE TO GET OUT OF THIS PLACE AND--
THWUDD!
WH-
WHY...?

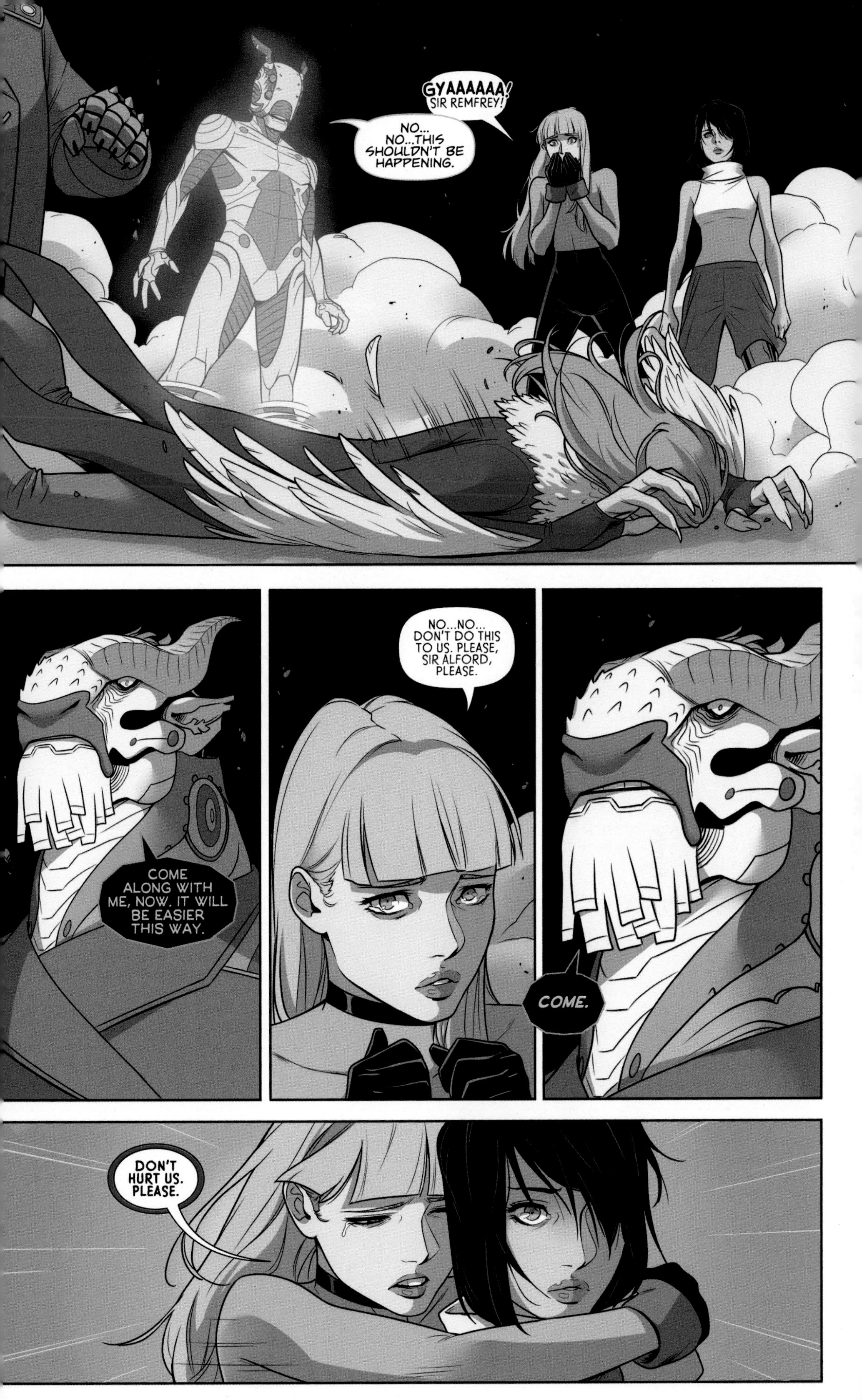
GYAAAAAA! SIR REMFREY!
NO... NO...THIS SHOULDN'T BE HAPPENING.
COME ALONG WITH ME, NOW. IT WILL BE EASIER THIS WAY.
NO...NO... DON'T DO THIS TO US. PLEASE, SIR ALFORD, PLEASE.
COME.
DON'T HURT US. PLEASE.

AFTER ALL HIS TALK OF KILLING EVERY FULL-SYNCHER IN THE WORLD, HE RUNS AT THE FIRST SIGHT OF US? I SWEAR THE COWARD WENT THIS WAY.
YOU AREN'T WRONG, MY DEAR.
WHAT'S YOUR EXCUSE FOR RUNNING AWAY THIS TIME, BOY?
A SIMPLE ACT OF COWARDICE, "AVOIDING UNNECESSARY CASUALTIES," OR PICKING OUT YOUR OWN GRAVE?

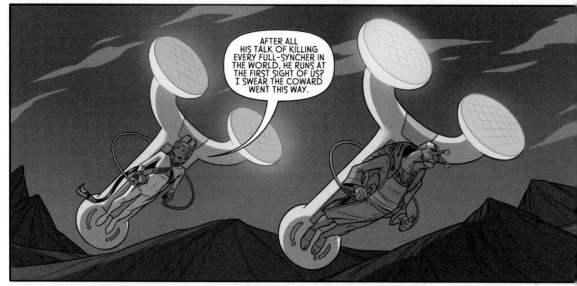

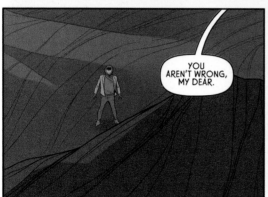

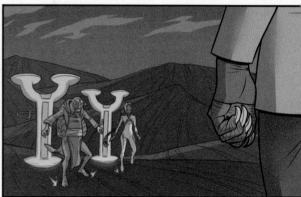

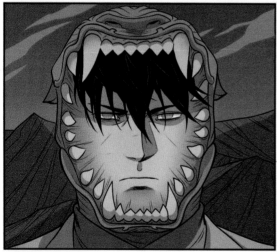

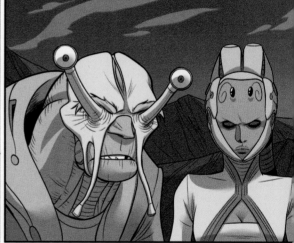

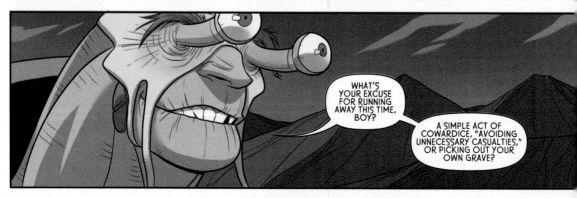

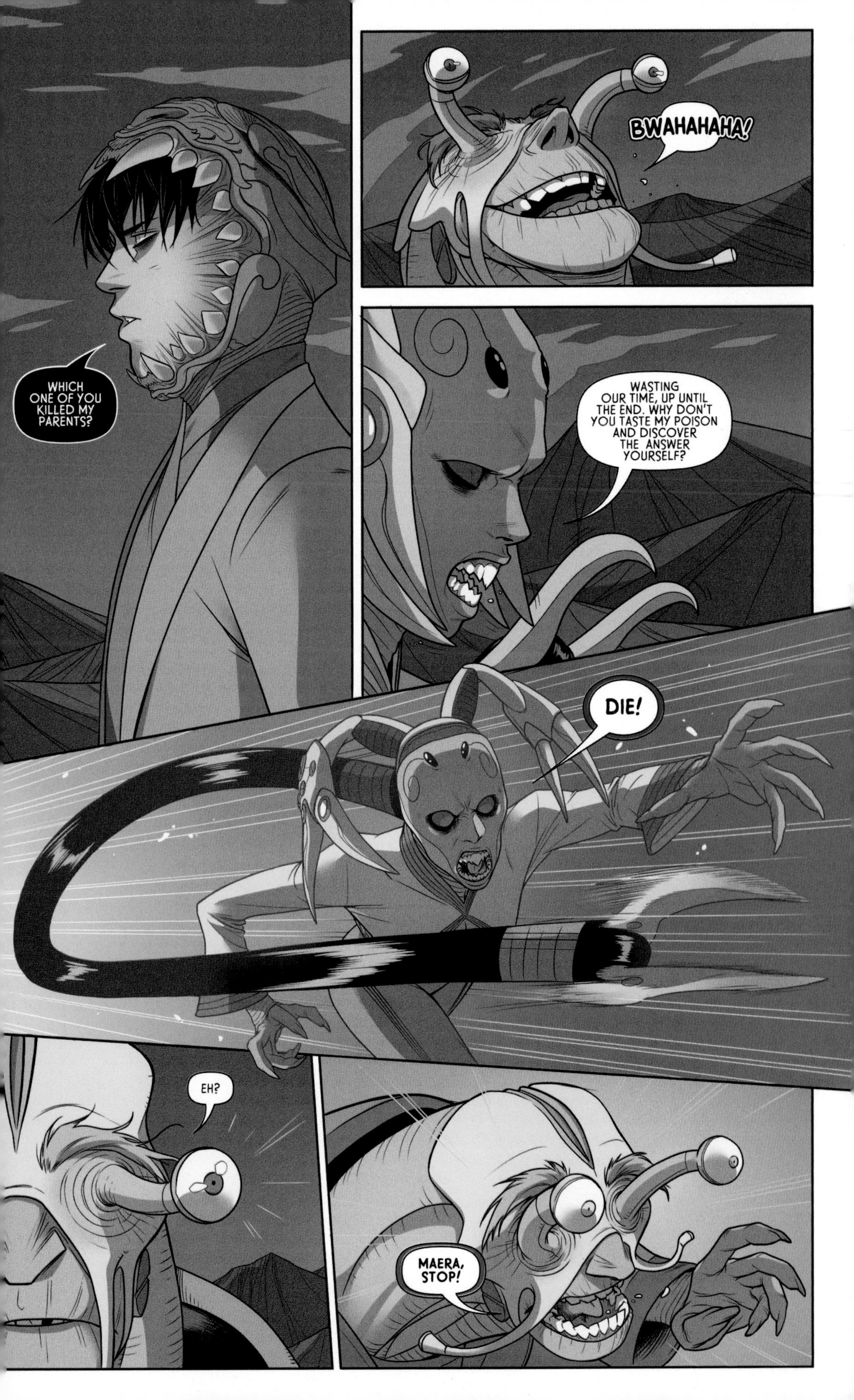

WHICH ONE OF YOU KILLED MY PARENTS?
BWAHAHAHA!
WASTING OUR TIME, UP UNTIL THE END. WHY DON'T YOU TASTE MY POISON AND DISCOVER THE ANSWER YOURSELF?
DIE!
EH?
MAERA, STOP!

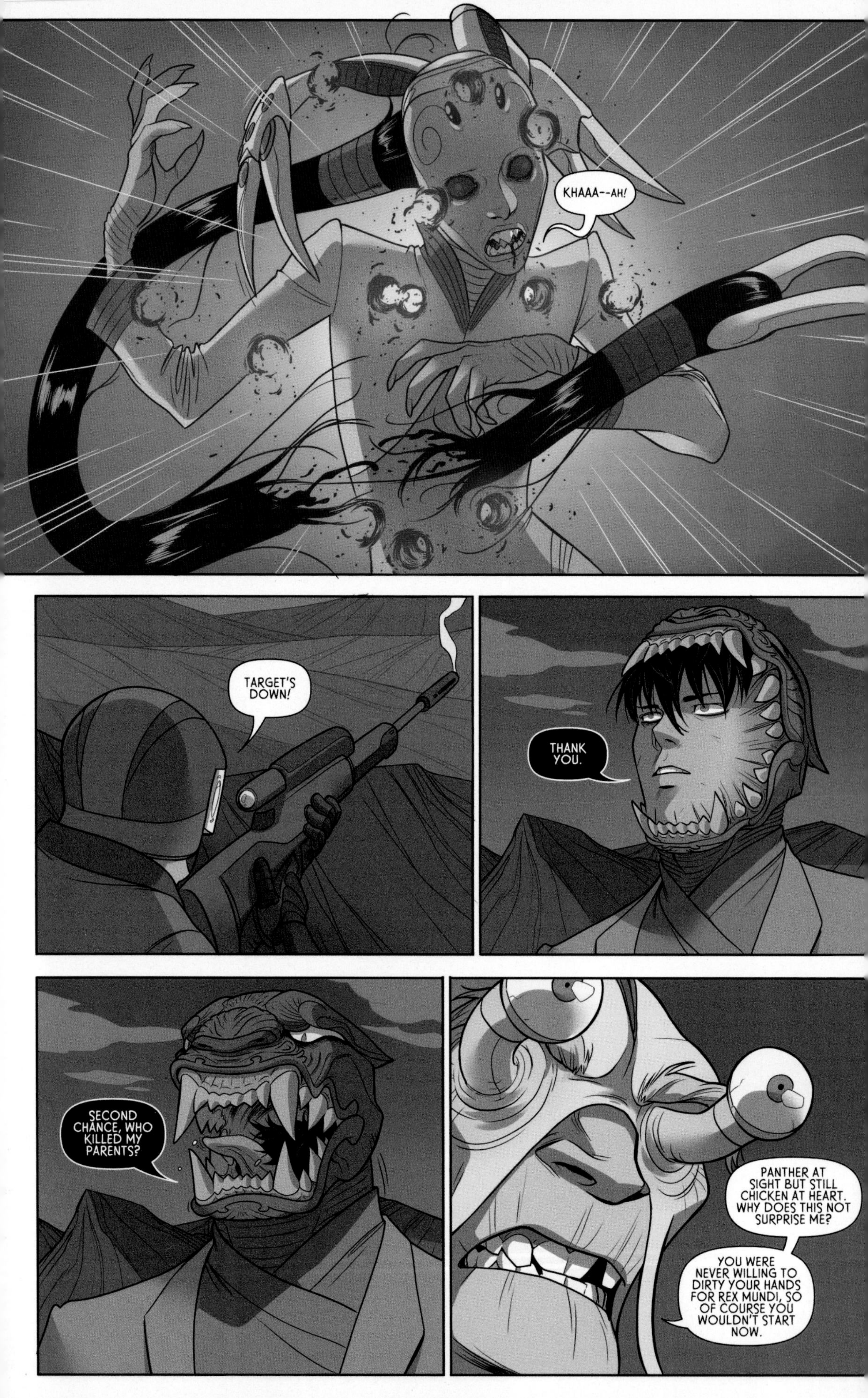
KHAAA--AH!
TARGET'S DOWN!
THANK YOU.
SECOND CHANCE, WHO KILLED MY PARENTS?
PANTHER AT SIGHT BUT STILL CHICKEN AT HEART. WHY DOES THIS NOT SURPRISE ME?
YOU WERE NEVER WILLING TO DIRTY YOUR HANDS FOR REX MUNDI, SO OF COURSE YOU WOULDN'T START NOW.

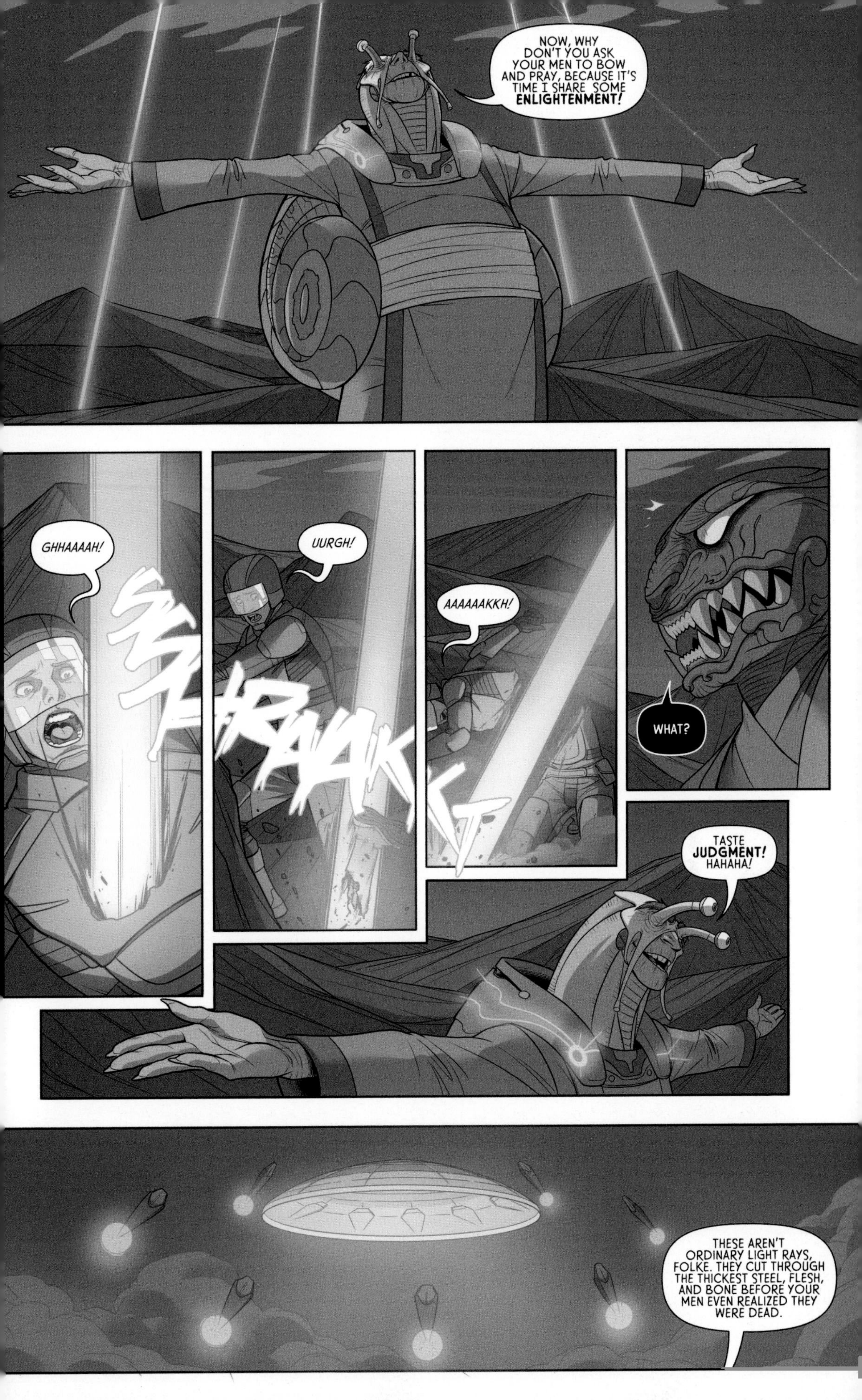
NOW, WHY DON'T YOU ASK YOUR MEN TO BOW AND PRAY, BECAUSE IT'S TIME I SHARE SOME ENLIGHTENMENT!
GHHAAAAH!
UURGH!
AAAAAAKKH!
WHAT?
TASTE JUDGMENT! HAHAHA!
THESE AREN'T ORDINARY LIGHT RAYS, FOLKE. THEY CUT THROUGH THE THICKEST STEEL, FLESH, AND BONE BEFORE YOUR MEN EVEN REALIZED THEY WERE DEAD.

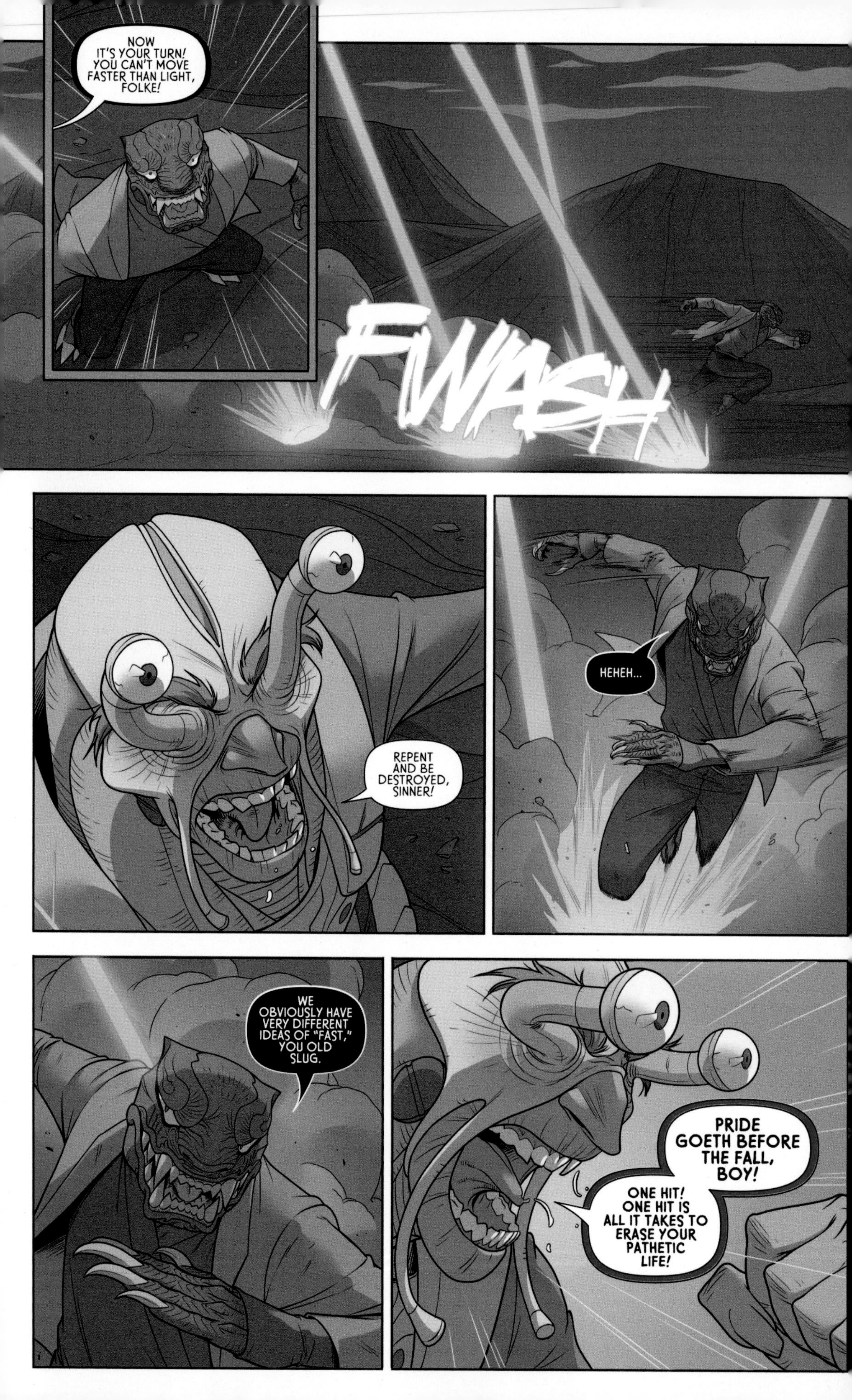
NOW IT'S YOUR TURN! YOU CAN'T MOVE FASTER THAN LIGHT, FOLKE!
FWASH
REPENT AND BE DESTROYED, SINNER!
HEHEH...
WE OBVIOUSLY HAVE VERY DIFFERENT IDEAS OF "FAST," YOU OLD SLUG.
PRIDE GOETH BEFORE THE FALL, BOY!
ONE HIT! ONE HIT IS ALL IT TAKES TO ERASE YOUR PATHETIC LIFE!

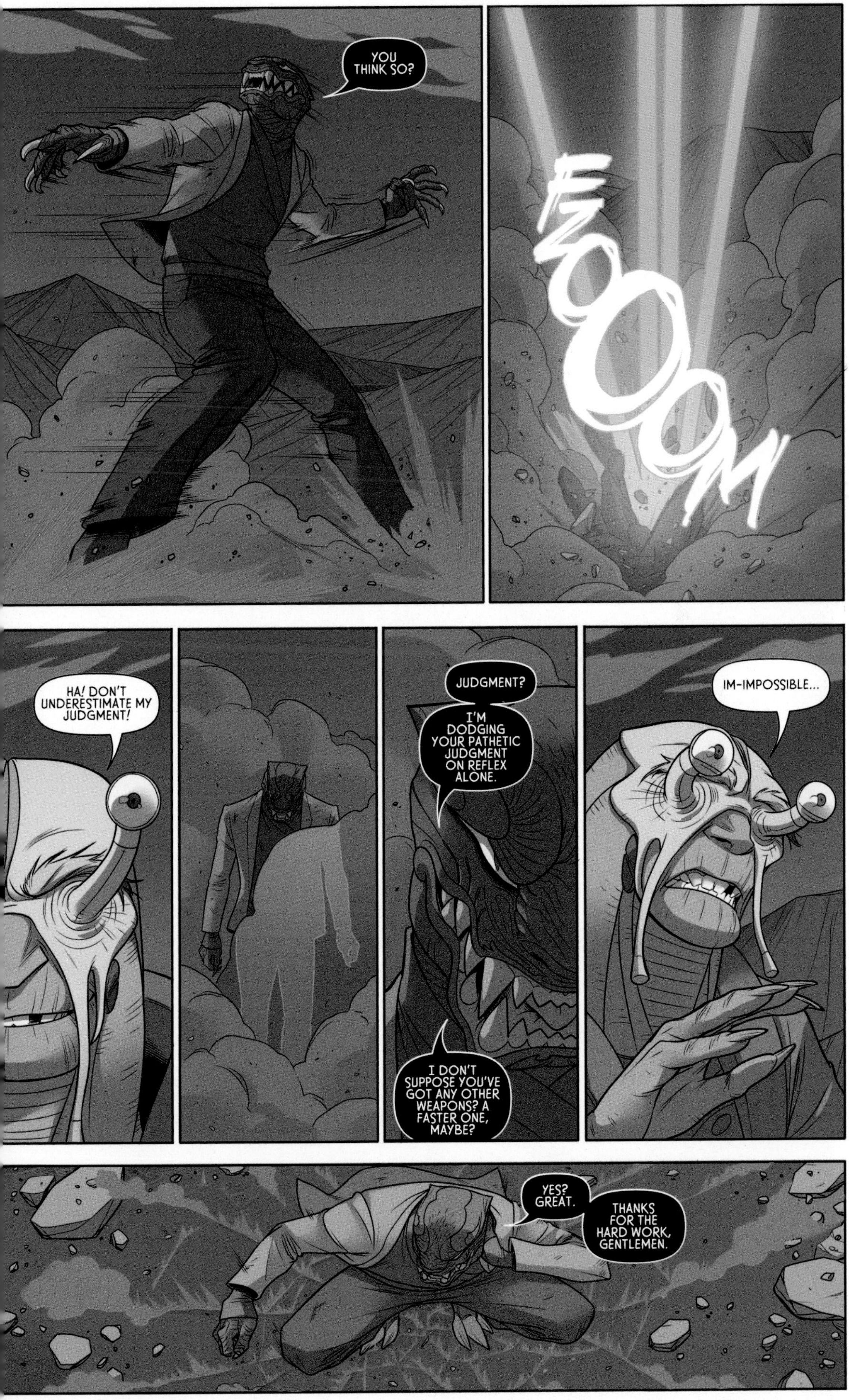
YOU THINK SO?
FZOOOOM
HA! DON'T UNDERESTIMATE MY JUDGMENT!
JUDGMENT?
I'M DODGING YOUR PATHETIC JUDGMENT ON REFLEX ALONE.
I DON'T SUPPOSE YOU'VE GOT ANY OTHER WEAPONS? A FASTER ONE, MAYBE?
IM-IMPOSSIBLE...
YES? GREAT.
THANKS FOR THE HARD WORK, GENTLEMEN.

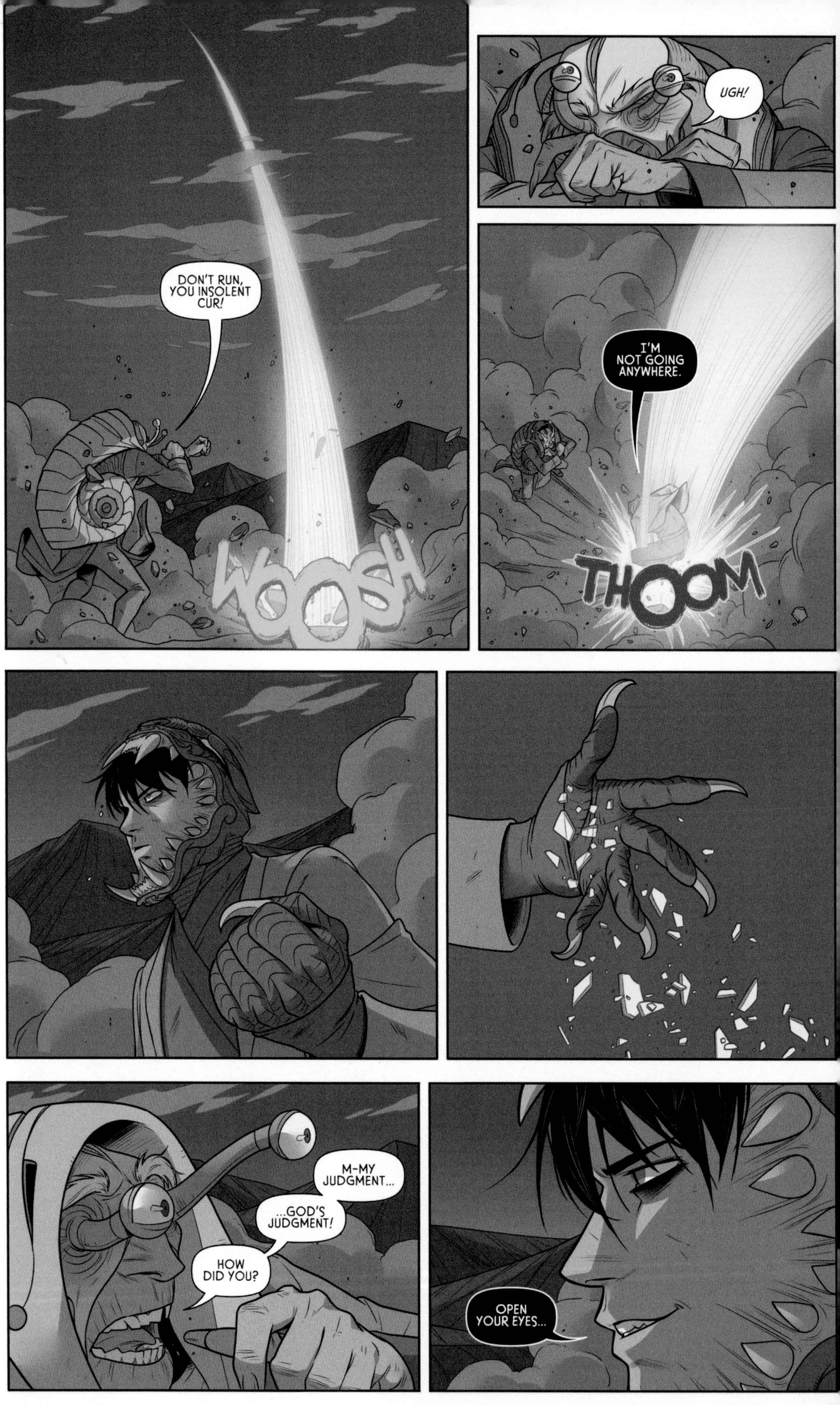
DON'T RUN, YOU INSOLENT CUR!
WOOSH
UGH!
I'M NOT GOING ANYWHERE.
THOOM
M-MY JUDGMENT...
...GOD'S JUDGMENT!
HOW DID YOU?
OPEN YOUR EYES...

"THERE'S ALWAYS SOMETHING GREATER THAN GOD."

HERVIETT

I AM STILL A HERVIETT, WIKTOR. MY MOUTH, EARS, AND EYES ARE EVERYWHERE. DON'T FORGET THAT.

WITH GHAERGOS HELPING ME, ONLY ONE FANTASMEN CAN MATCH MY SPEED AND STRENGTH, AND IT'S DEFINITELY NOT YOU. NOT EVEN CLOSE.

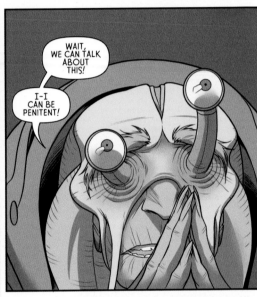

WAIT, WE CAN TALK ABOUT THIS!

I-I CAN BE PENITENT!

YOU DIDN'T OFFER ME GOD'S FORGIVENESS.

I WON'T BE GIVING YOU MINE.

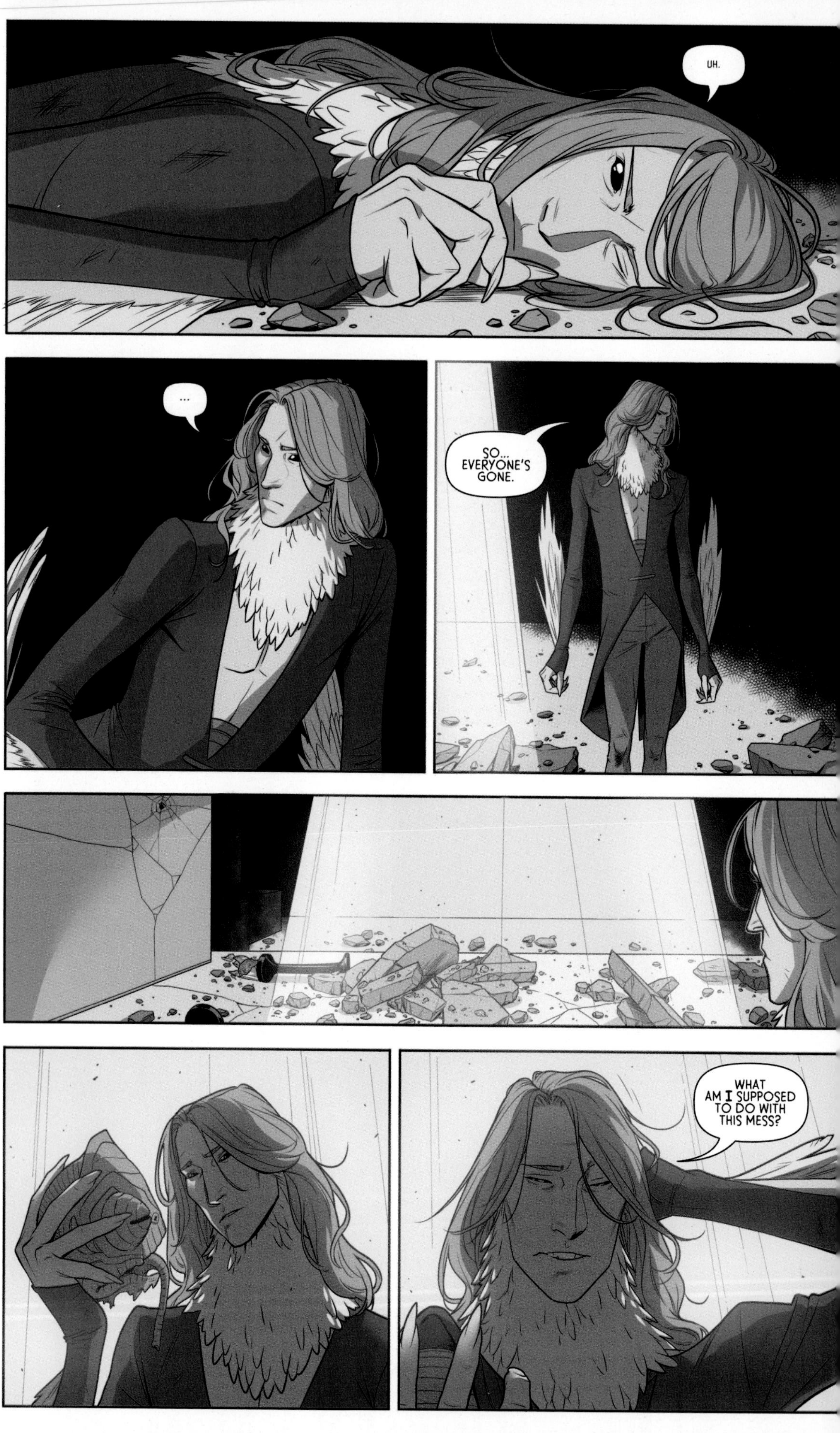
UH.
...
SO... EVERYONE'S GONE.
WHAT AM I SUPPOSED TO DO WITH THIS MESS?

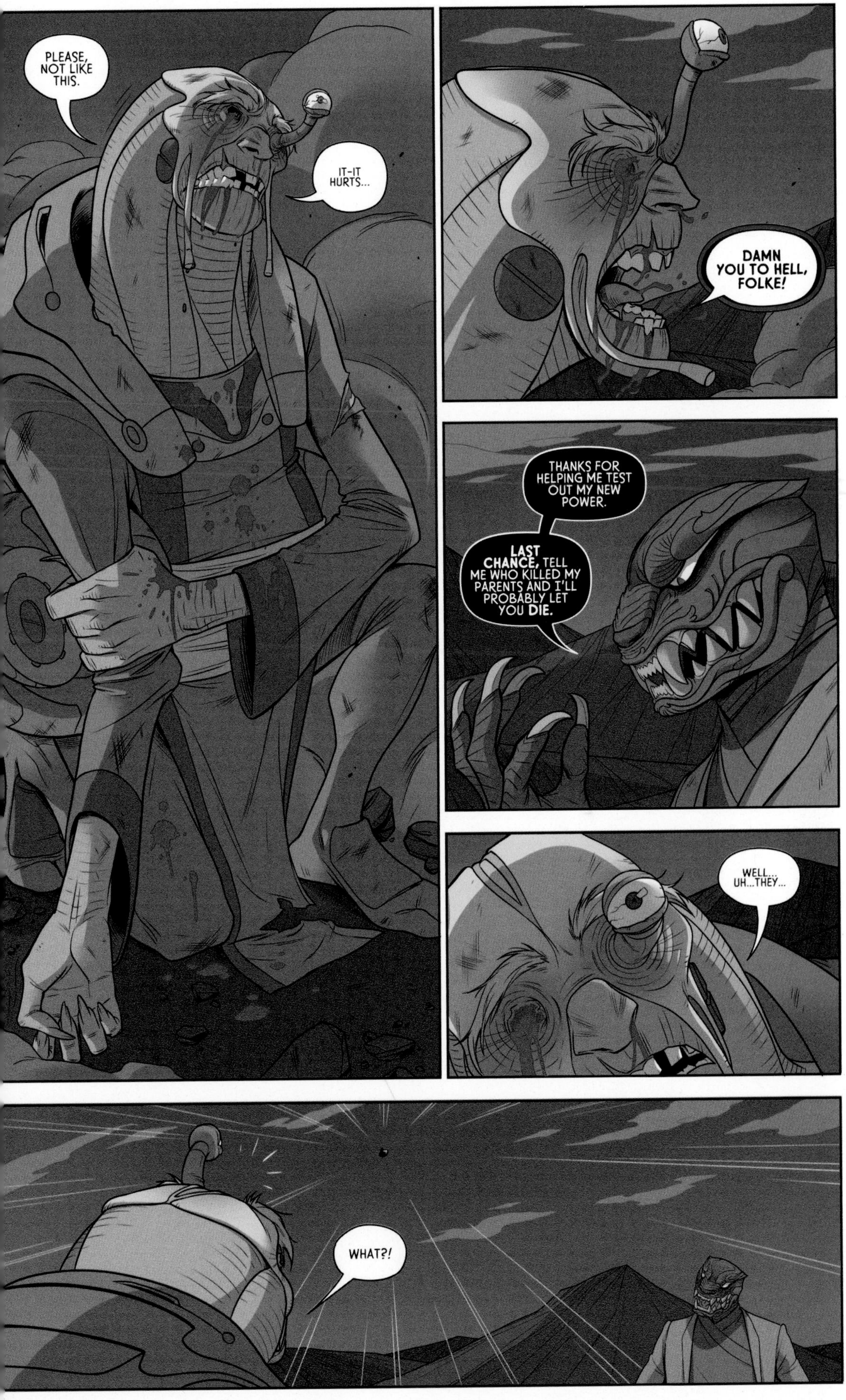
PLEASE, NOT LIKE THIS.
IT-IT HURTS...
DAMN YOU TO HELL, FOLKE!
THANKS FOR HELPING ME TEST OUT MY NEW POWER.
LAST CHANCE, TELL ME WHO KILLED MY PARENTS AND I'LL PROBABLY LET YOU DIE.
WELL... UH...THEY...
WHAT?!

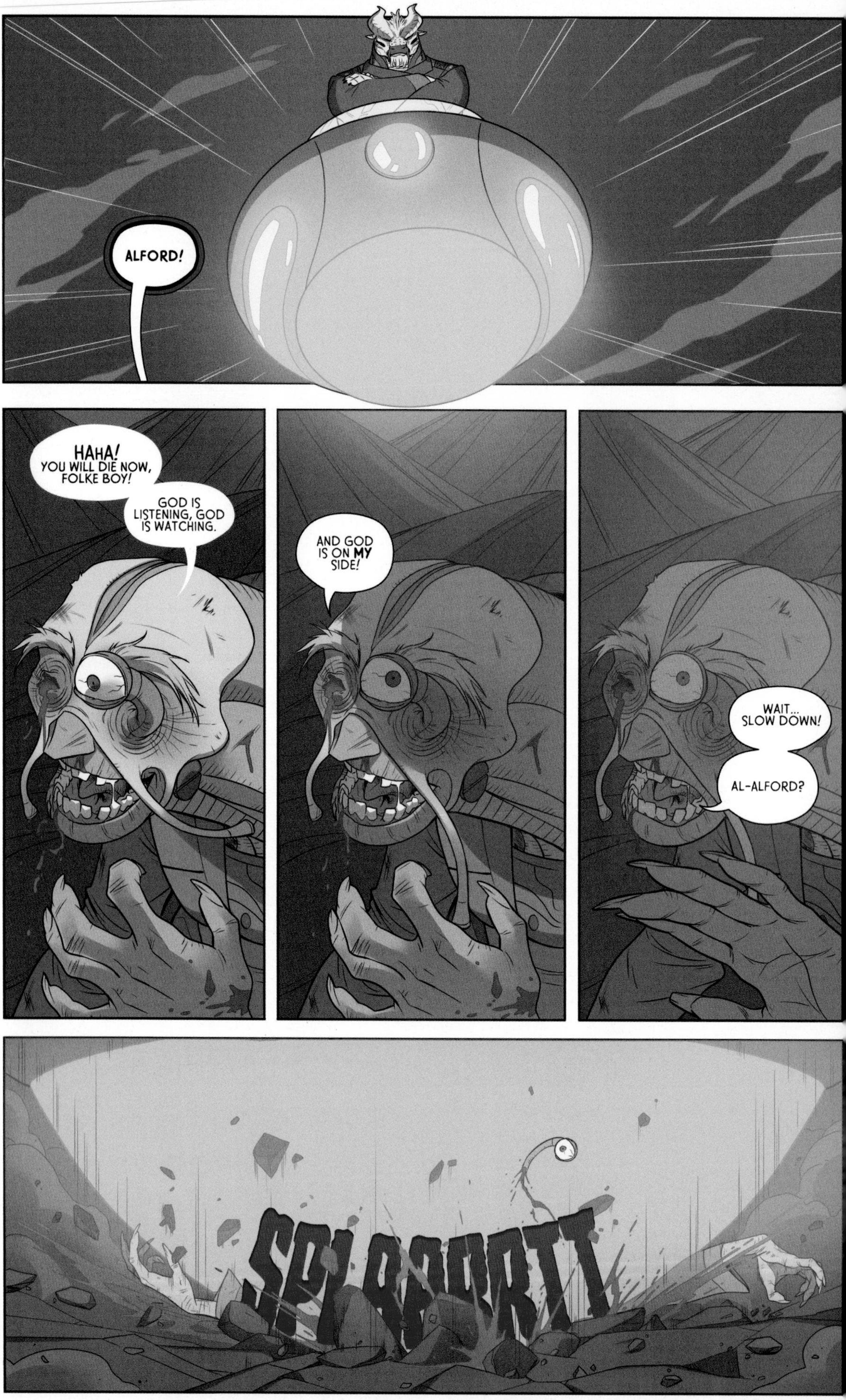
ALFORD!
HAHA! YOU WILL DIE NOW, FOLKE BOY!
GOD IS LISTENING, GOD IS WATCHING.
AND GOD IS ON MY SIDE!
WAIT... SLOW DOWN!
AL-ALFORD?

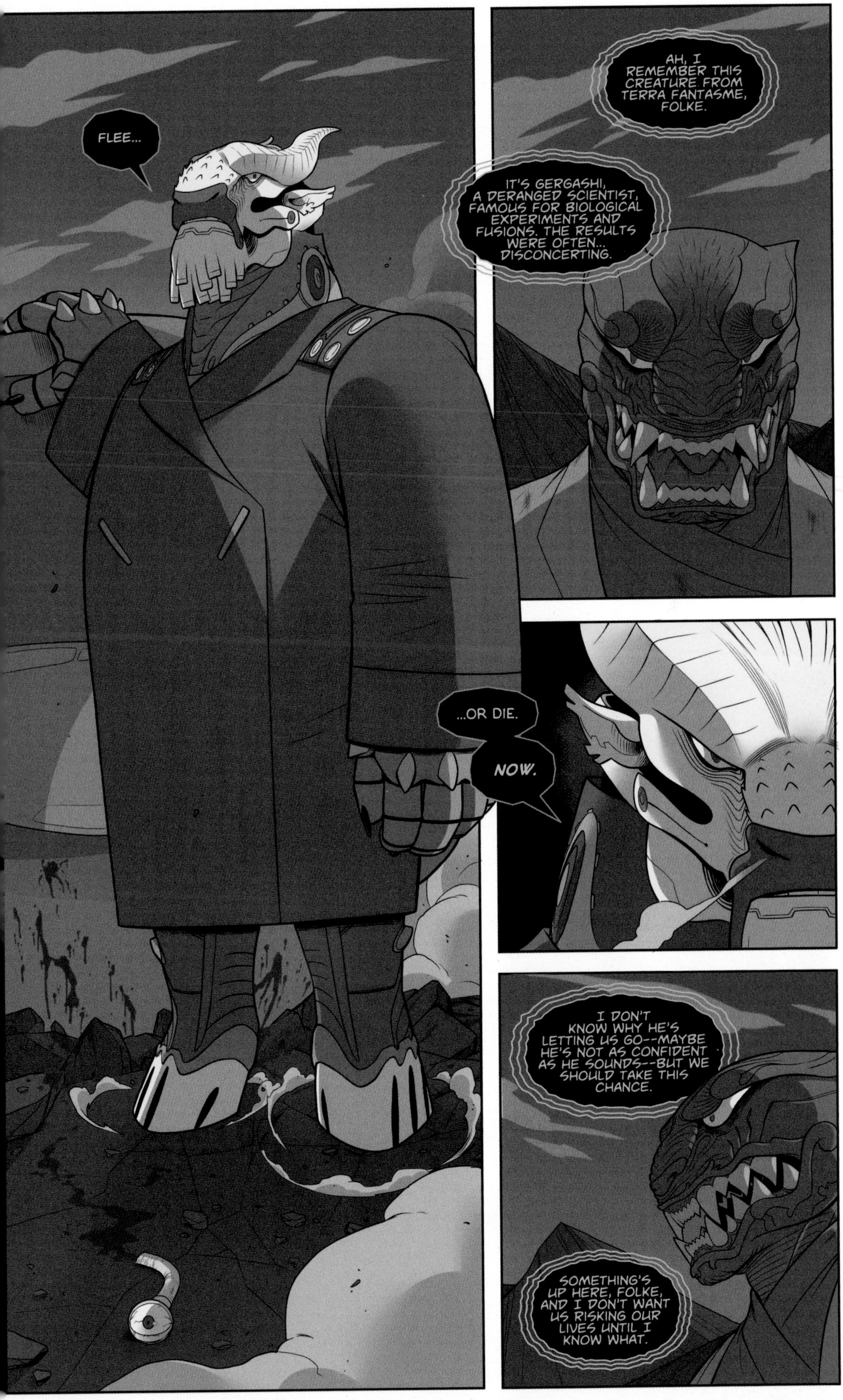
FLEE...
AH, I REMEMBER THIS CREATURE FROM TERRA FANTASME, FOLKE.
IT'S GERGASHI, A DERANGED SCIENTIST, FAMOUS FOR BIOLOGICAL EXPERIMENTS AND FUSIONS. THE RESULTS WERE OFTEN... DISCONCERTING.
...OR DIE.
NOW.
I DON'T KNOW WHY HE'S LETTING US GO--MAYBE HE'S NOT AS CONFIDENT AS HE SOUNDS--BUT WE SHOULD TAKE THIS CHANCE.
SOMETHING'S UP HERE, FOLKE, AND I DON'T WANT US RISKING OUR LIVES UNTIL I KNOW WHAT.

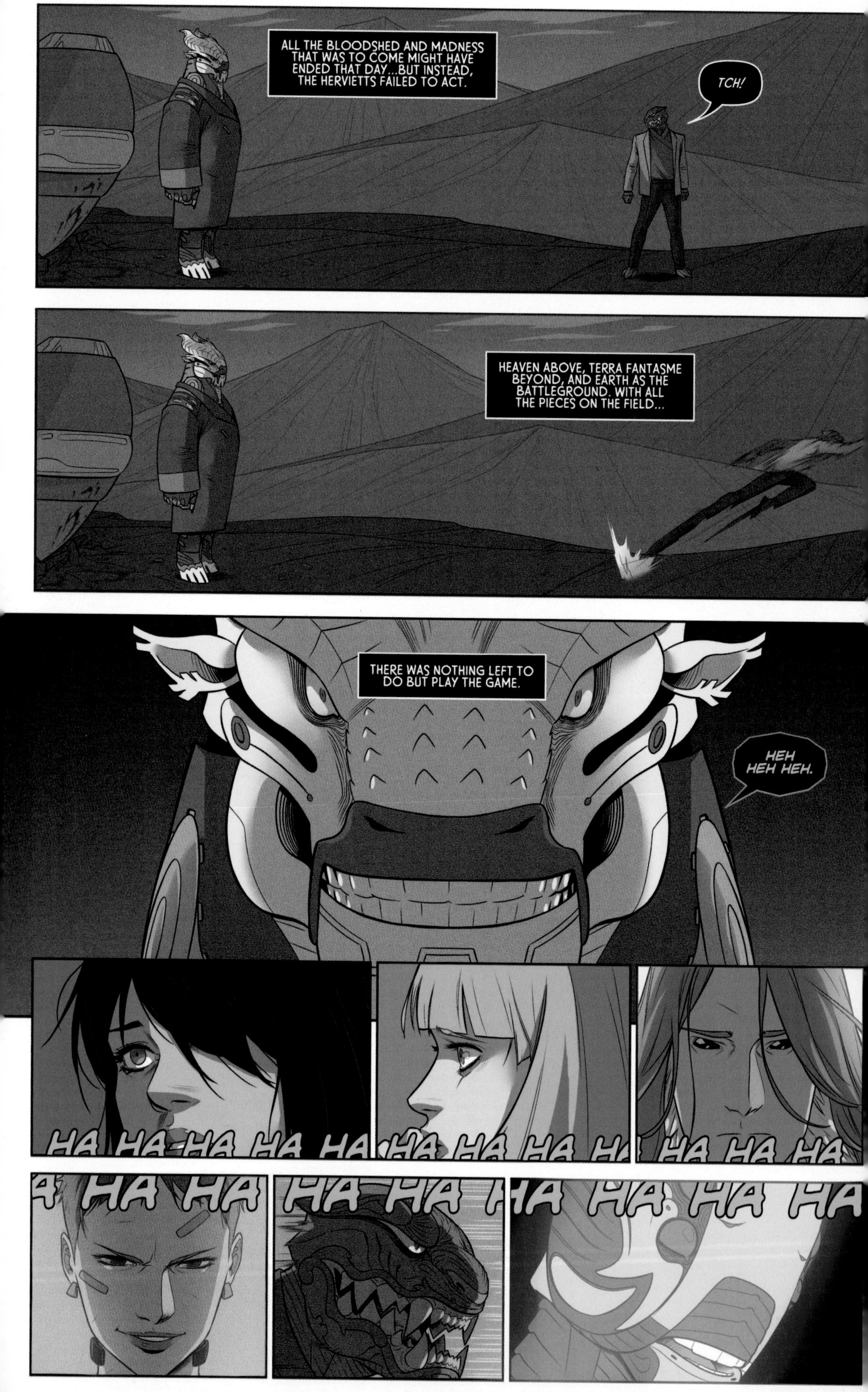
ALL THE BLOODSHED AND MADNESS THAT WAS TO COME MIGHT HAVE ENDED THAT DAY...BUT INSTEAD, THE HERVIETTS FAILED TO ACT.
TCH!
HEAVEN ABOVE, TERRA FANTASME BEYOND, AND EARTH AS THE BATTLEGROUND. WITH ALL THE PIECES ON THE FIELD...
THERE WAS NOTHING LEFT TO DO BUT PLAY THE GAME.
HEH HEH HEH.
HA HA HA HA HA
HA HA HA HA
HA HA HA
HA HA
HA HA
HA HA HA HA

COVER
GALLERY
ART BY :

VARSAM KURNIA

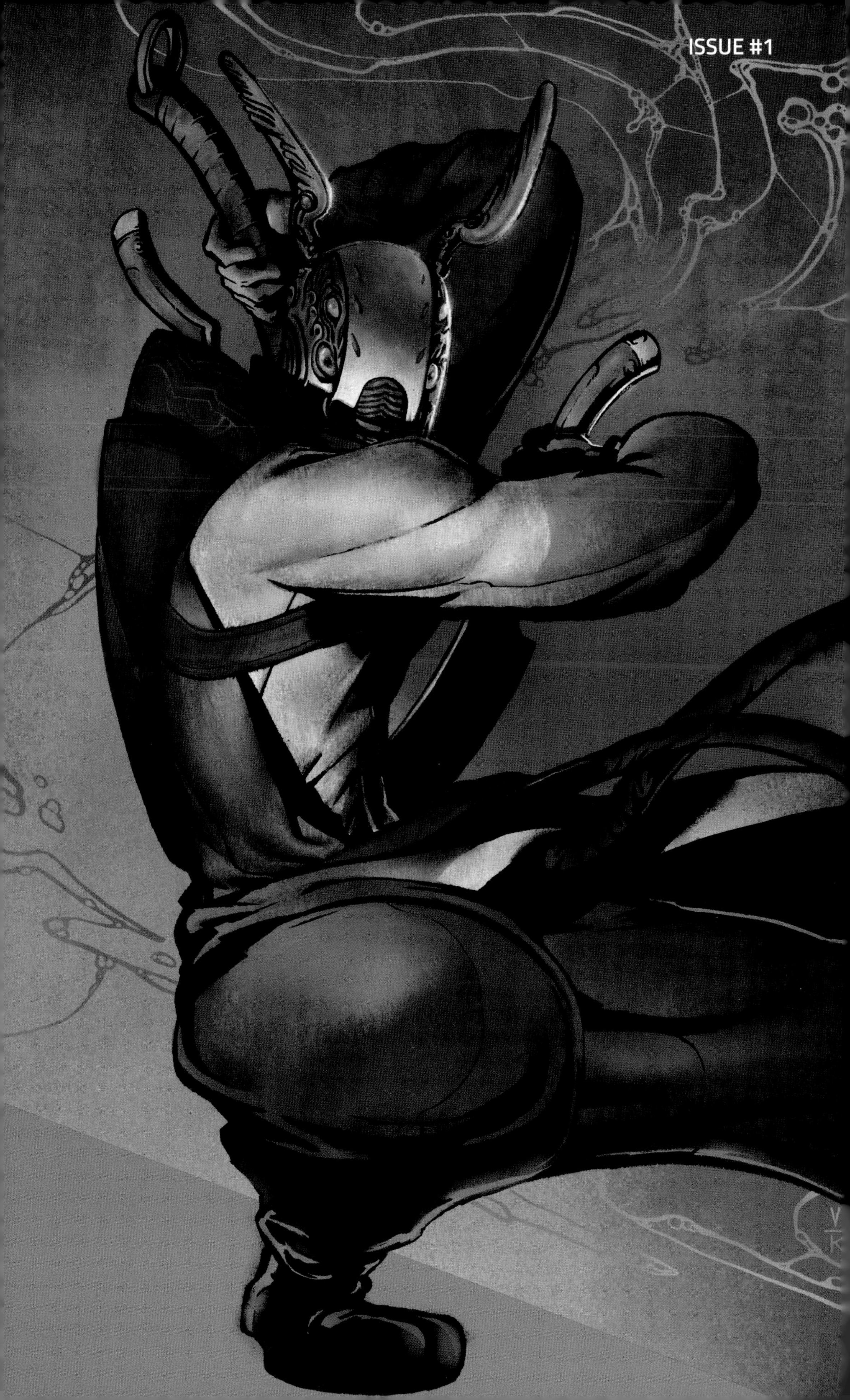
ISSUE #1

ISSUE #2

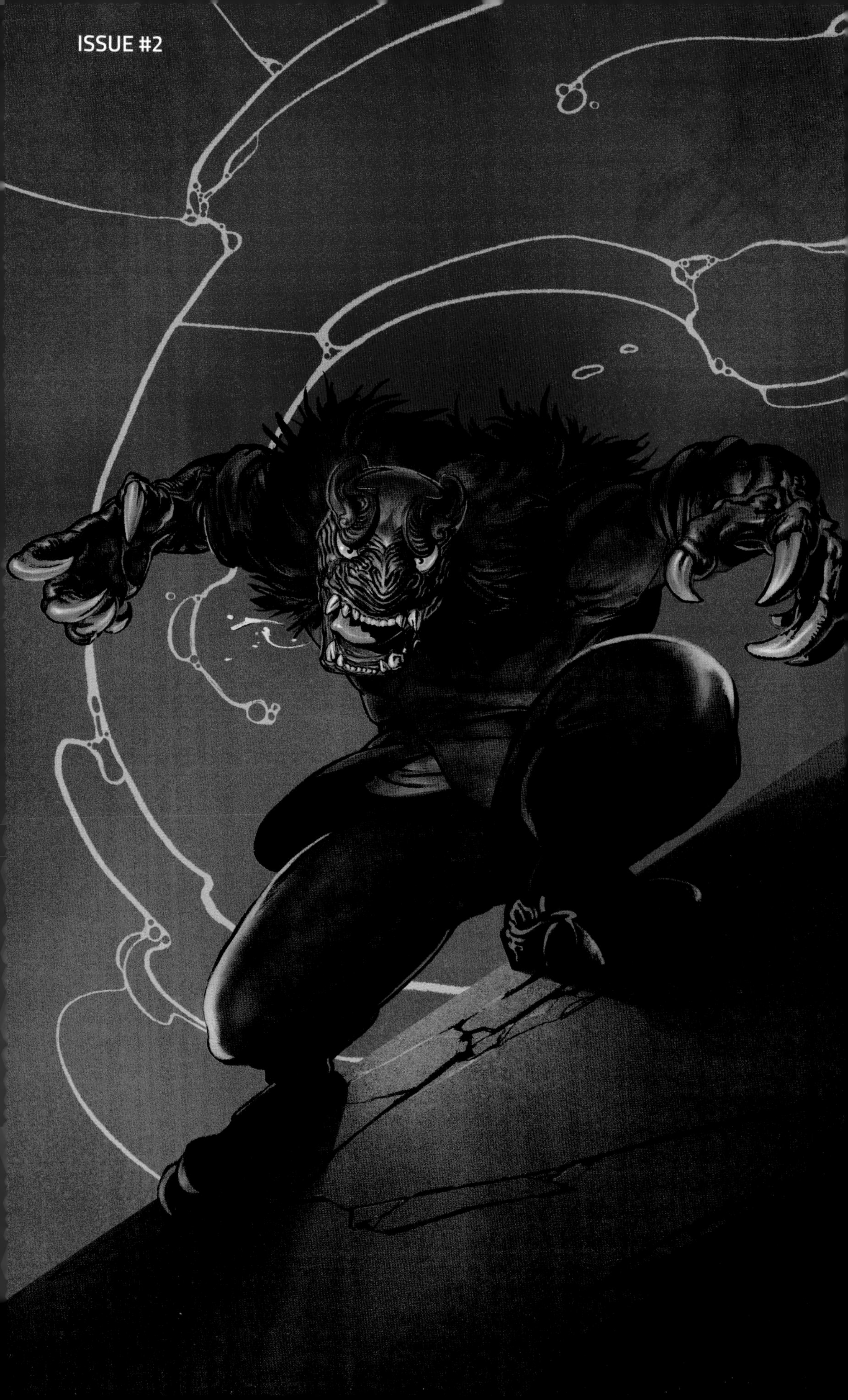

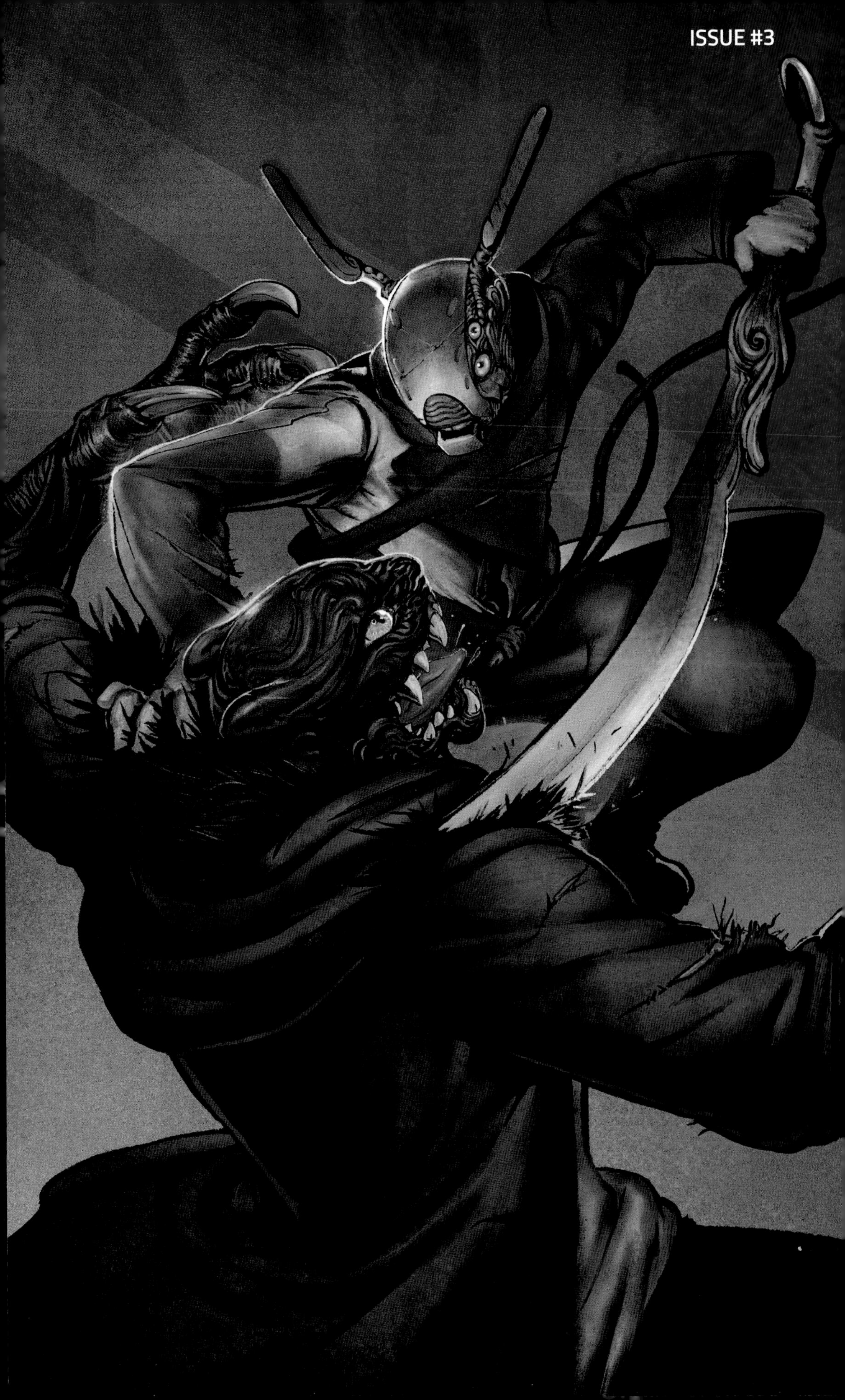
ISSUE #3

ISSUE #4

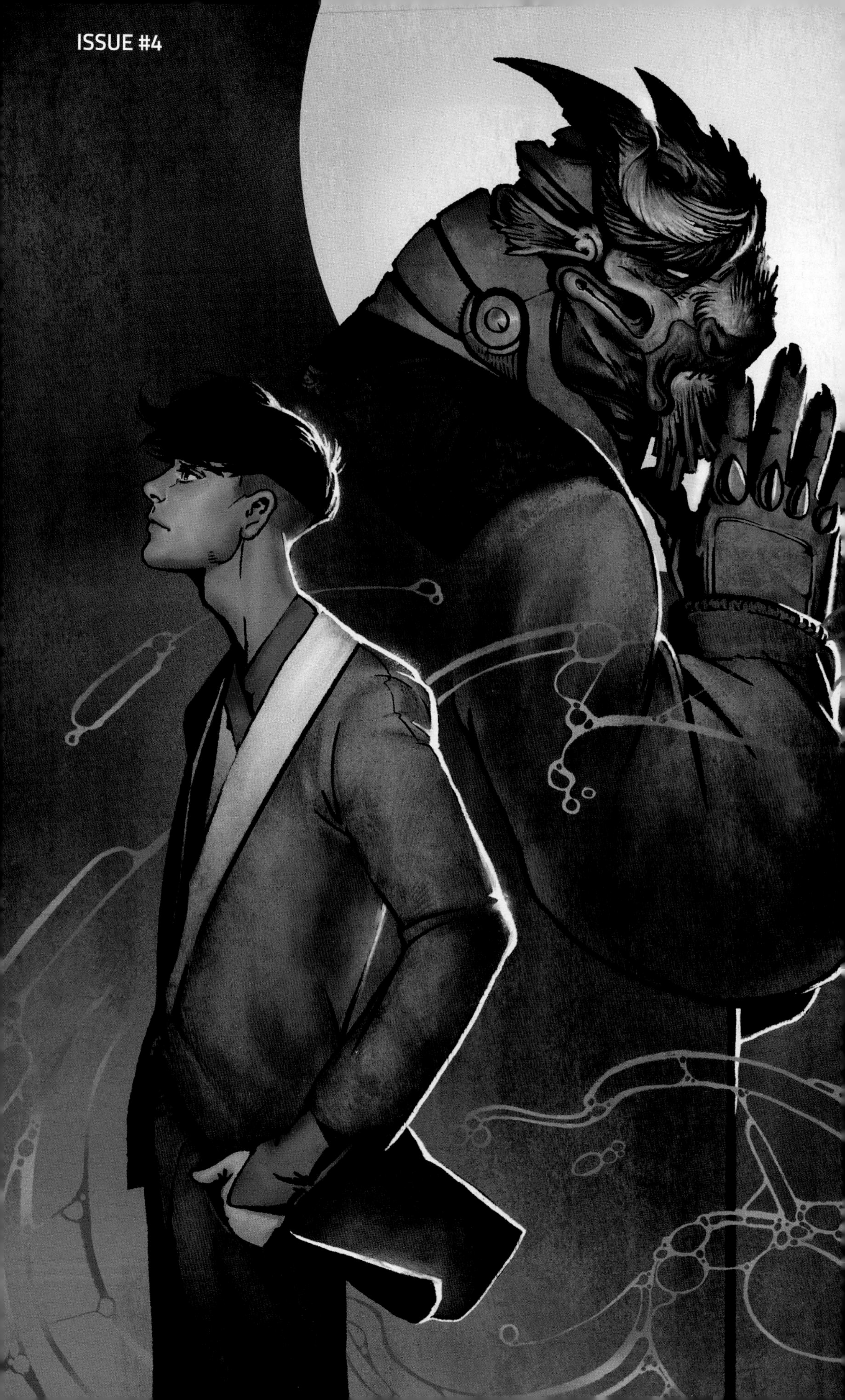

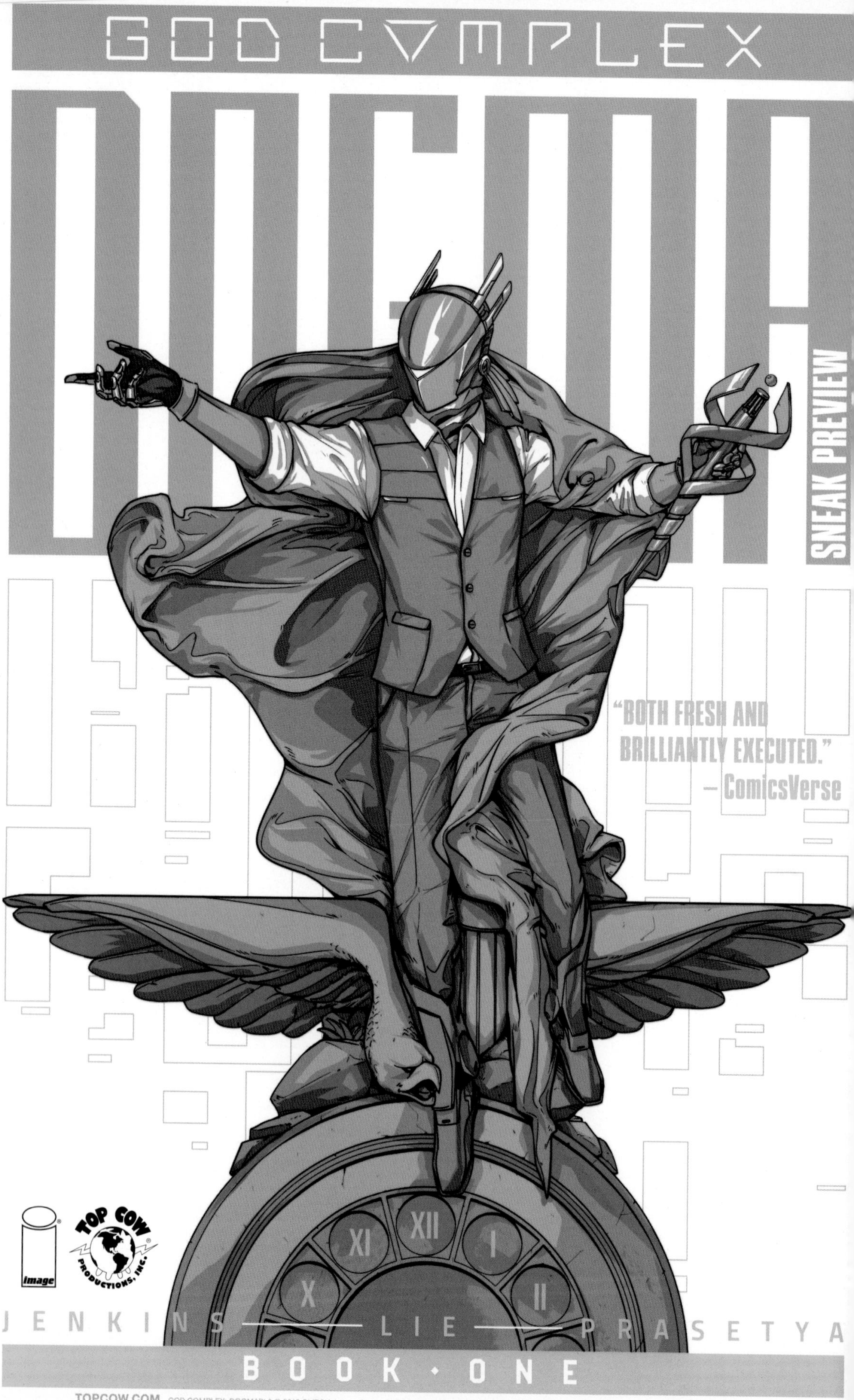

GOD COMPLEX
DOGMA
SNEAK PREVIEW
"BOTH FRESH AND BRILLIANTLY EXECUTED."
– ComicsVerse
XI XII I
X II
image
TOP COW PRODUCTIONS, INC.
JENKINS — LIE — PRASETYA
BOOK • ONE

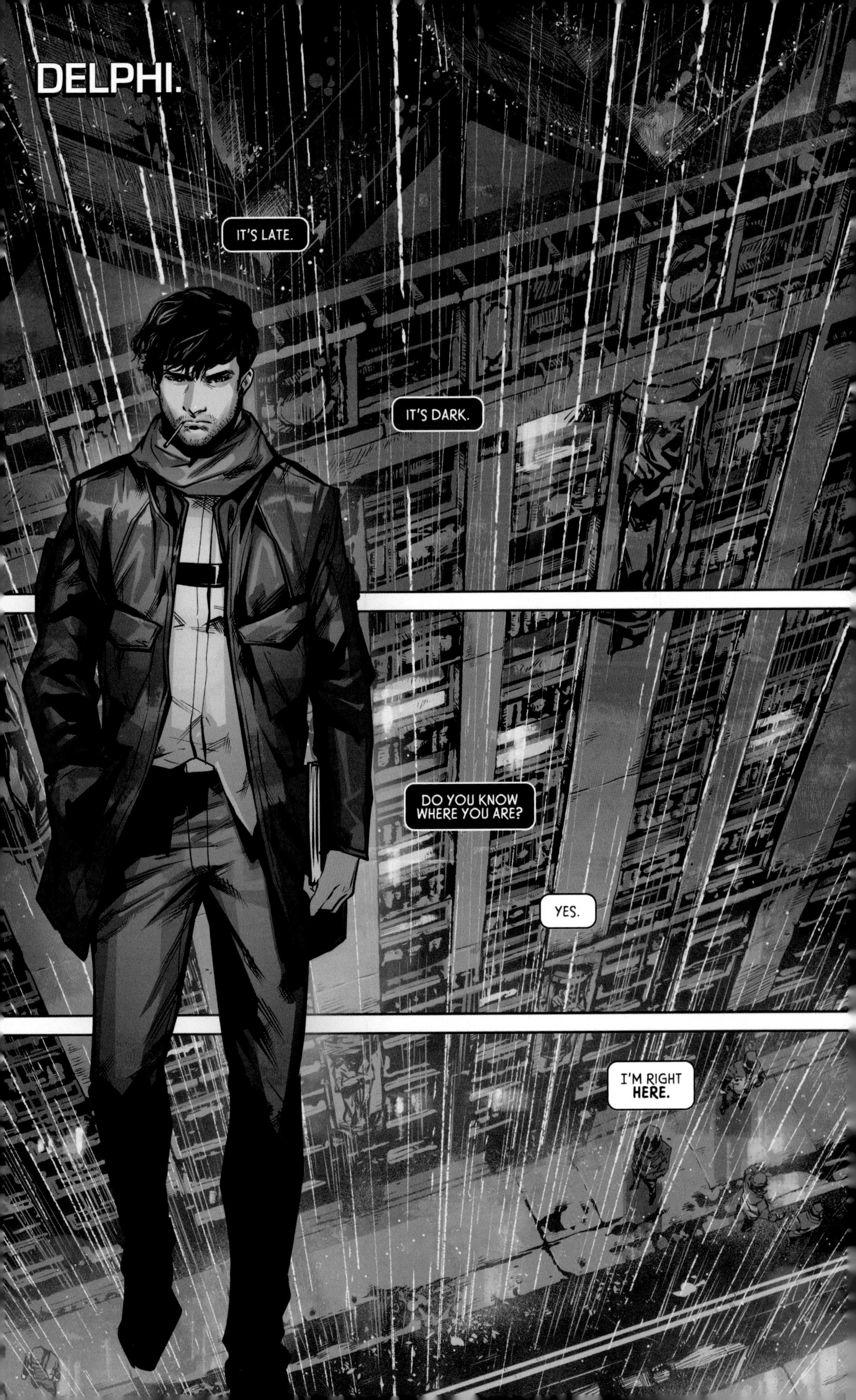
DELPHI.
IT'S LATE.
IT'S DARK.
DO YOU KNOW WHERE YOU ARE?
YES.
I'M RIGHT HERE.

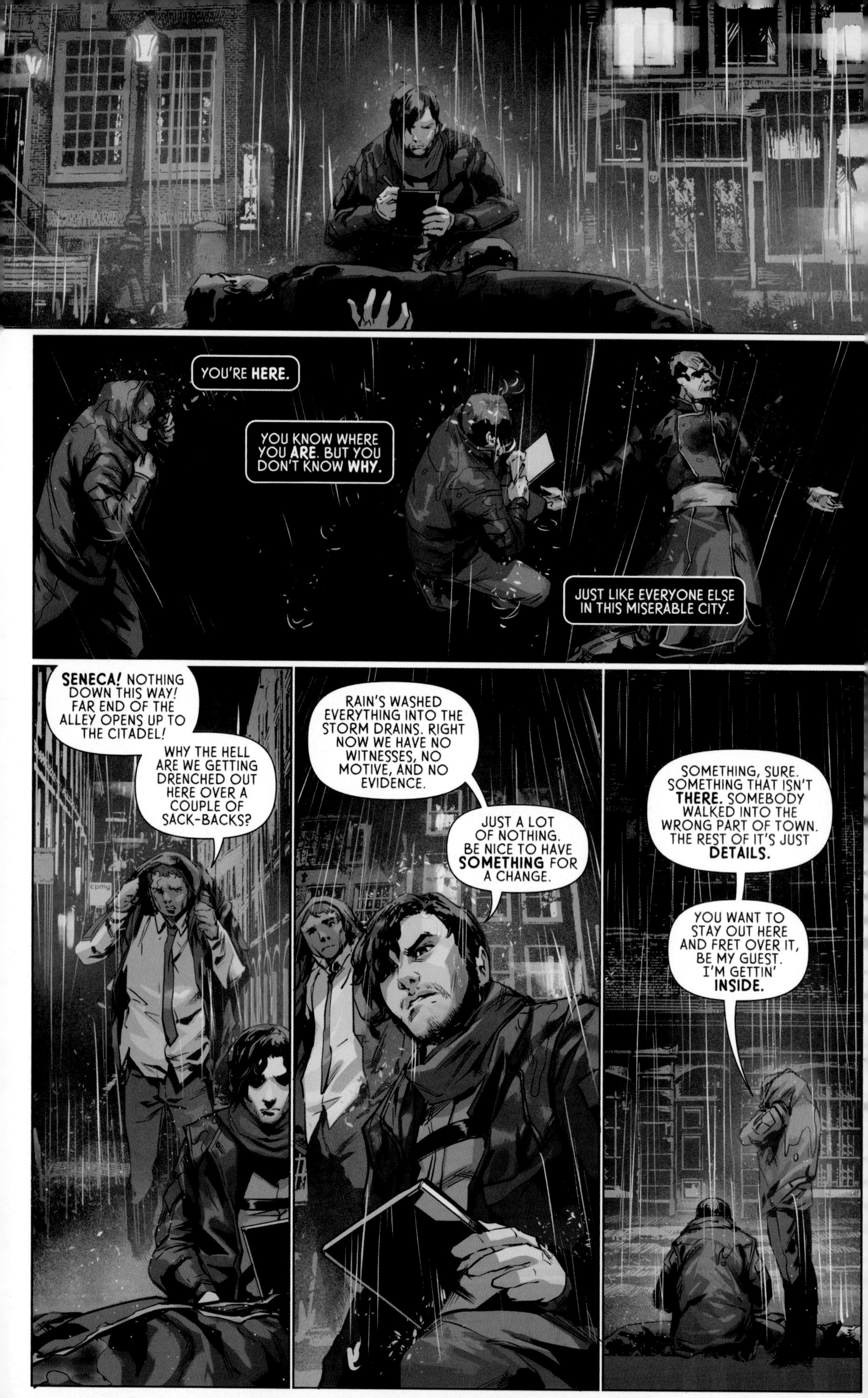

YOU'RE **HERE.**
YOU KNOW WHERE YOU **ARE**. BUT YOU DON'T KNOW **WHY.**
JUST LIKE EVERYONE ELSE IN THIS MISERABLE CITY.
SENECA! NOTHING DOWN THIS WAY! FAR END OF THE ALLEY OPENS UP TO THE CITADEL!
WHY THE HELL ARE WE GETTING DRENCHED OUT HERE OVER A COUPLE OF SACK-BACKS?
RAIN'S WASHED EVERYTHING INTO THE STORM DRAINS. RIGHT NOW WE HAVE NO WITNESSES, NO MOTIVE, AND NO EVIDENCE.
JUST A LOT OF NOTHING. BE NICE TO HAVE **SOMETHING** FOR A CHANGE.
SOMETHING, SURE. SOMETHING THAT ISN'T **THERE.** SOMEBODY WALKED INTO THE WRONG PART OF TOWN. THE REST OF IT'S JUST **DETAILS.**
YOU WANT TO STAY OUT HERE AND FRET OVER IT, BE MY GUEST. I'M GETTIN' **INSIDE.**

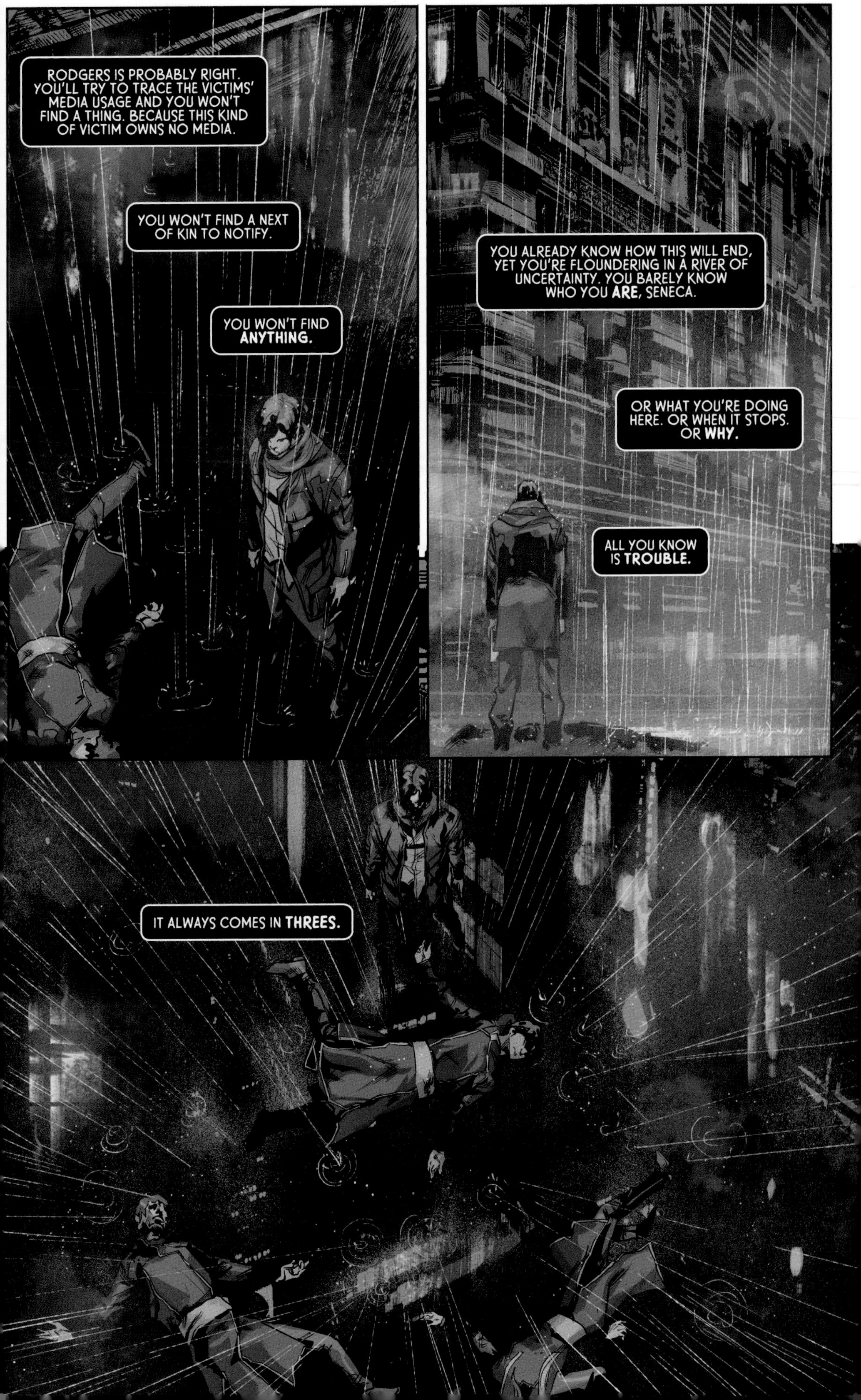
RODGERS IS PROBABLY RIGHT. YOU'LL TRY TO TRACE THE VICTIMS' MEDIA USAGE AND YOU WON'T FIND A THING. BECAUSE THIS KIND OF VICTIM OWNS NO MEDIA.
YOU WON'T FIND A NEXT OF KIN TO NOTIFY.
YOU WON'T FIND **ANYTHING.**
YOU ALREADY KNOW HOW THIS WILL END, YET YOU'RE FLOUNDERING IN A RIVER OF UNCERTAINTY. YOU BARELY KNOW WHO YOU **ARE,** SENECA.
OR WHAT YOU'RE DOING HERE. OR WHEN IT STOPS. OR **WHY.**
ALL YOU KNOW IS **TROUBLE.**
IT ALWAYS COMES IN **THREES.**

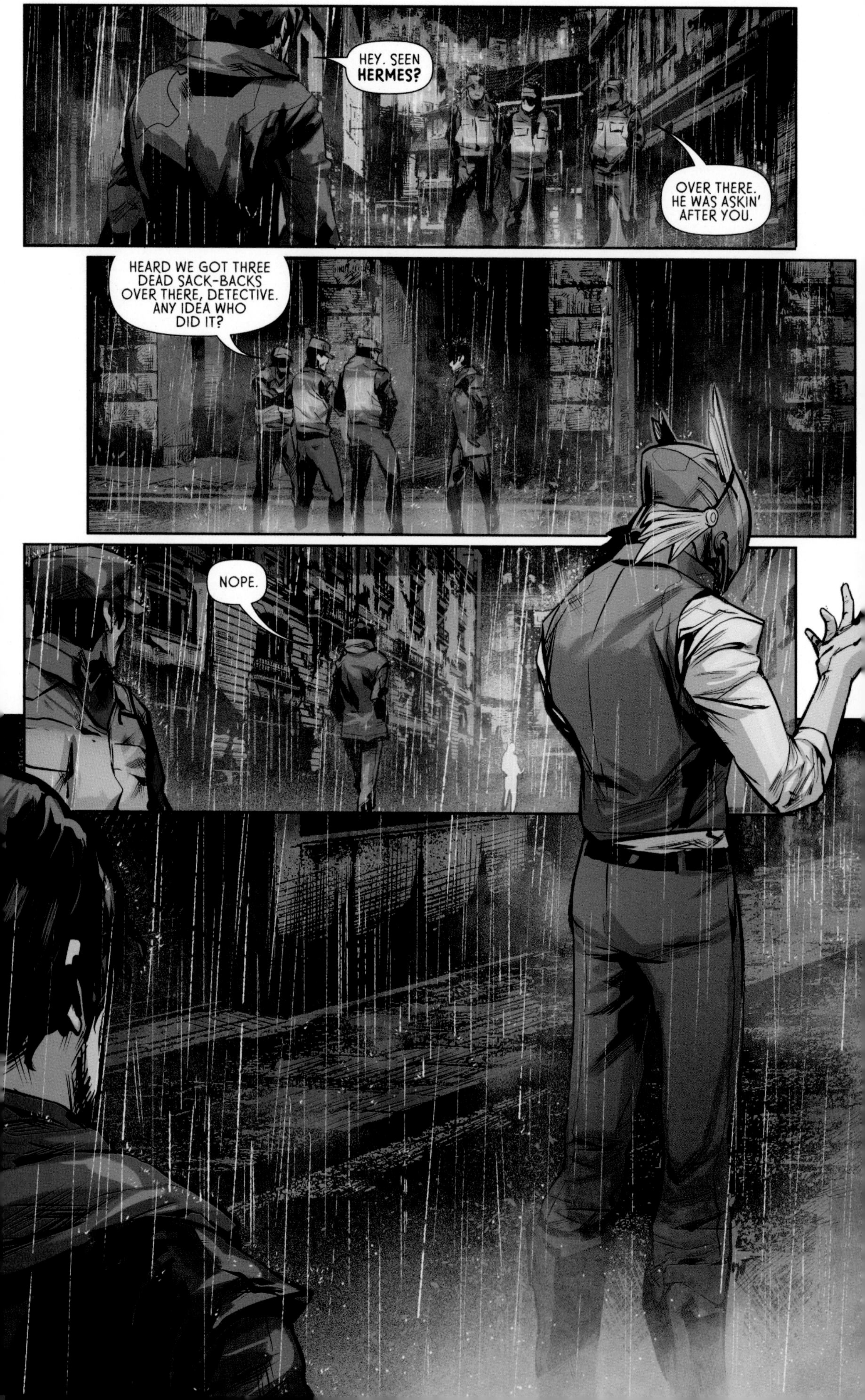
HEY. SEEN HERMES?
OVER THERE. HE WAS ASKIN' AFTER YOU.
HEARD WE GOT THREE DEAD SACK-BACKS OVER THERE, DETECTIVE. ANY IDEA WHO DID IT?
NOPE.

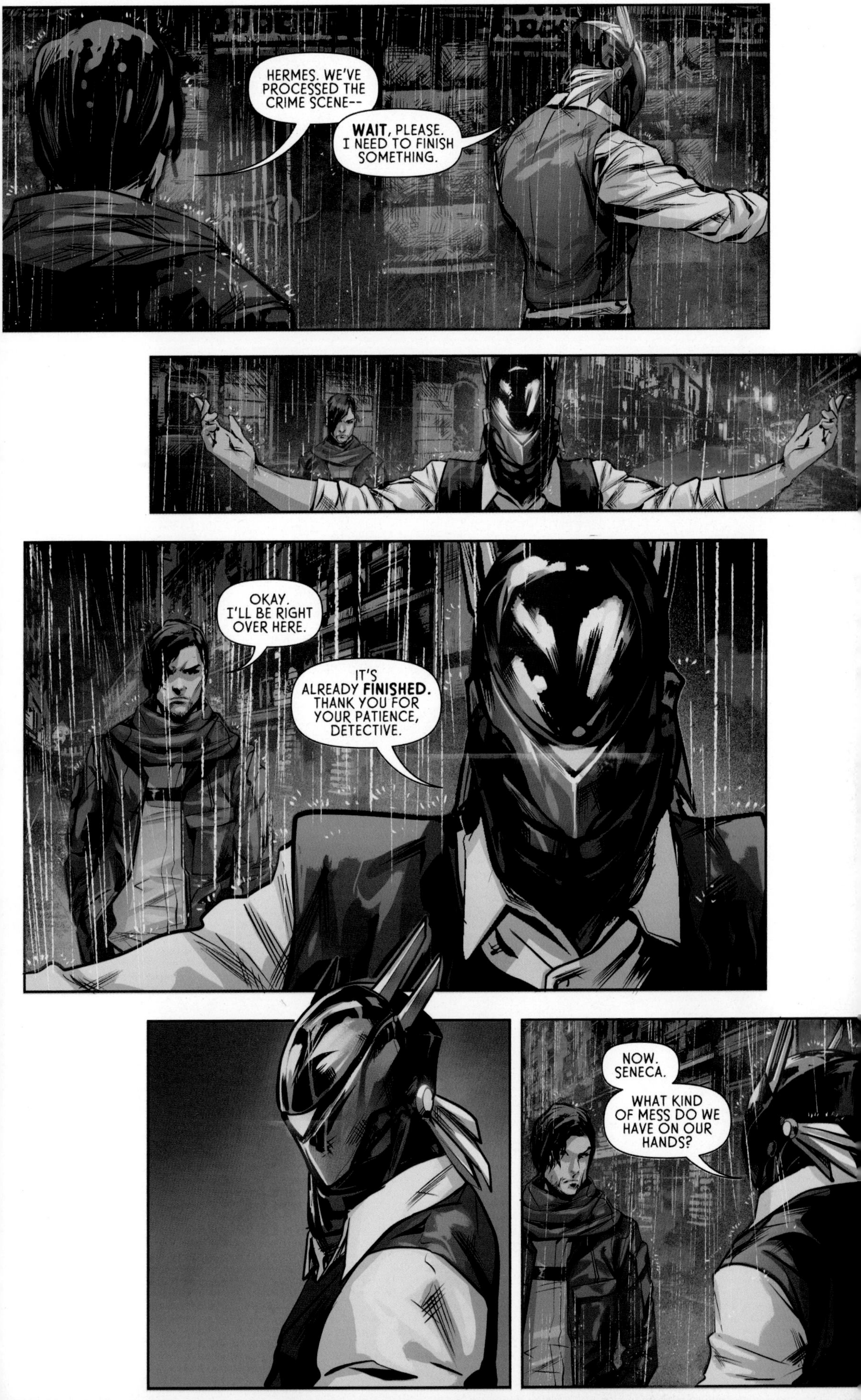
HERMES. WE'VE PROCESSED THE CRIME SCENE--
WAIT, PLEASE. I NEED TO FINISH SOMETHING.
OKAY. I'LL BE RIGHT OVER HERE.
IT'S ALREADY FINISHED. THANK YOU FOR YOUR PATIENCE, DETECTIVE.
NOW. SENECA.
WHAT KIND OF MESS DO WE HAVE ON OUR HANDS?

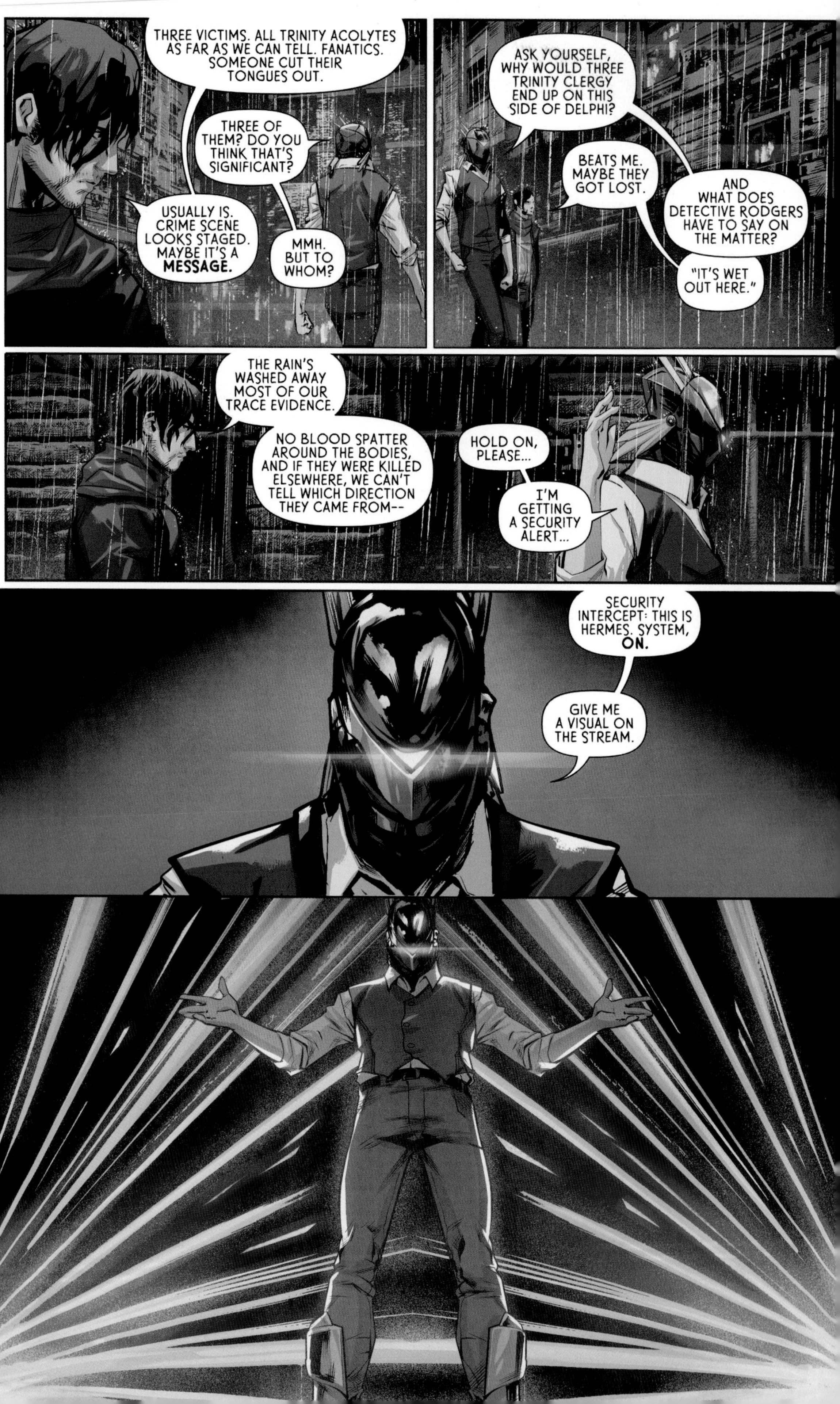

THREE VICTIMS. ALL TRINITY ACOLYTES AS FAR AS WE CAN TELL. FANATICS. SOMEONE CUT THEIR TONGUES OUT.
THREE OF THEM? DO YOU THINK THAT'S SIGNIFICANT?
USUALLY IS. CRIME SCENE LOOKS STAGED. MAYBE IT'S A **MESSAGE.**
MMH. BUT TO WHOM?
ASK YOURSELF, WHY WOULD THREE TRINITY CLERGY END UP ON THIS SIDE OF DELPHI?
BEATS ME. MAYBE THEY GOT LOST.
AND WHAT DOES DETECTIVE RODGERS HAVE TO SAY ON THE MATTER?
"IT'S WET OUT HERE."
THE RAIN'S WASHED AWAY MOST OF OUR TRACE EVIDENCE.
NO BLOOD SPATTER AROUND THE BODIES, AND IF THEY WERE KILLED ELSEWHERE, WE CAN'T TELL WHICH DIRECTION THEY CAME FROM--
HOLD ON, PLEASE...
I'M GETTING A SECURITY ALERT...
SECURITY INTERCEPT: THIS IS HERMES. SYSTEM, **ON.**
GIVE ME A VISUAL ON THE STREAM.

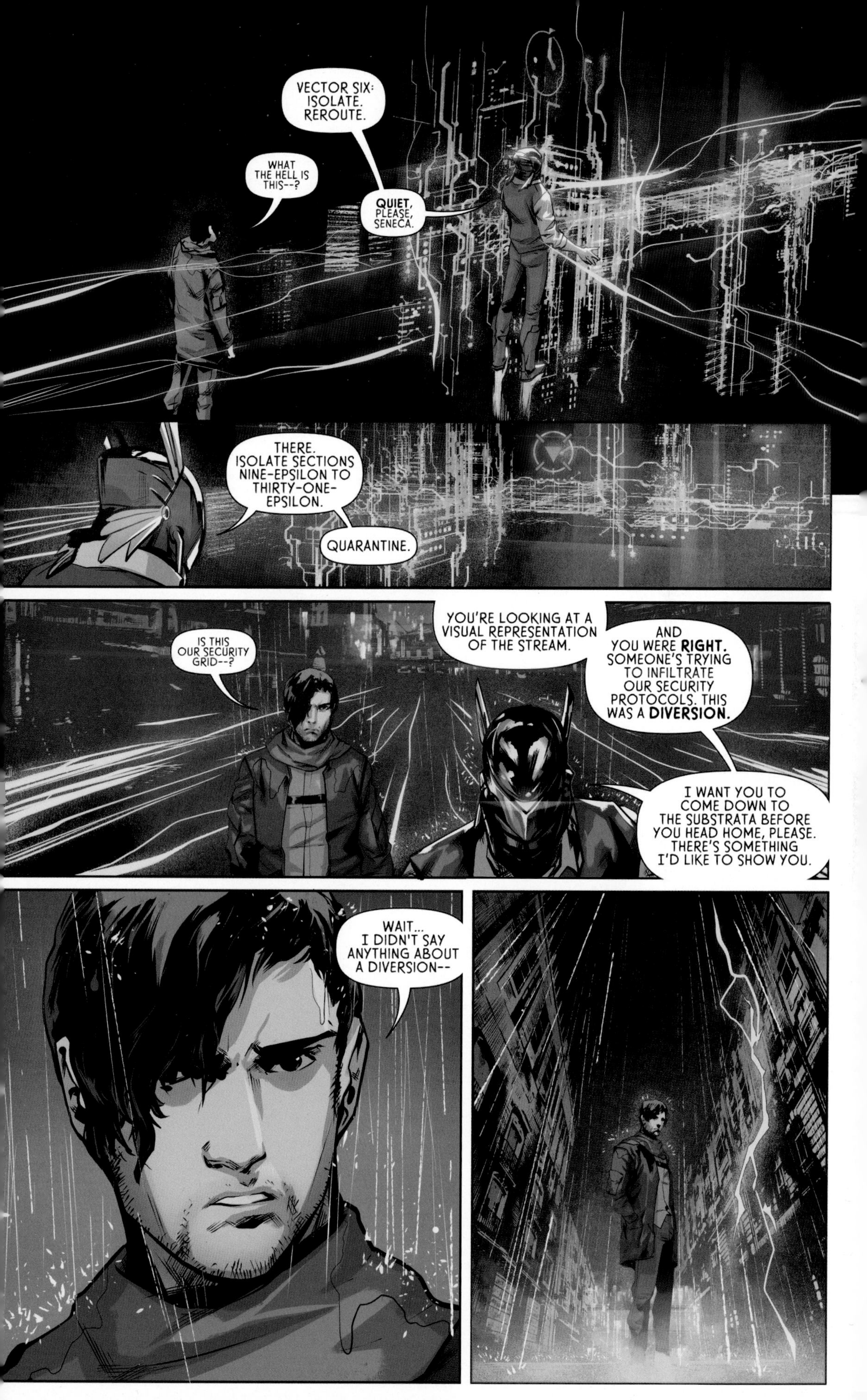
VECTOR SIX: ISOLATE. REROUTE.
WHAT THE HELL IS THIS--?
QUIET, PLEASE, SENECA.
THERE. ISOLATE SECTIONS NINE-EPSILON TO THIRTY-ONE-EPSILON.
QUARANTINE.
IS THIS OUR SECURITY GRID--?
YOU'RE LOOKING AT A VISUAL REPRESENTATION OF THE STREAM.
AND YOU WERE **RIGHT.** SOMEONE'S TRYING TO INFILTRATE OUR SECURITY PROTOCOLS. THIS WAS A **DIVERSION.**
I WANT YOU TO COME DOWN TO THE SUBSTRATA BEFORE YOU HEAD HOME, PLEASE. THERE'S SOMETHING I'D LIKE TO SHOW YOU.
WAIT... I DIDN'T SAY ANYTHING ABOUT A DIVERSION--

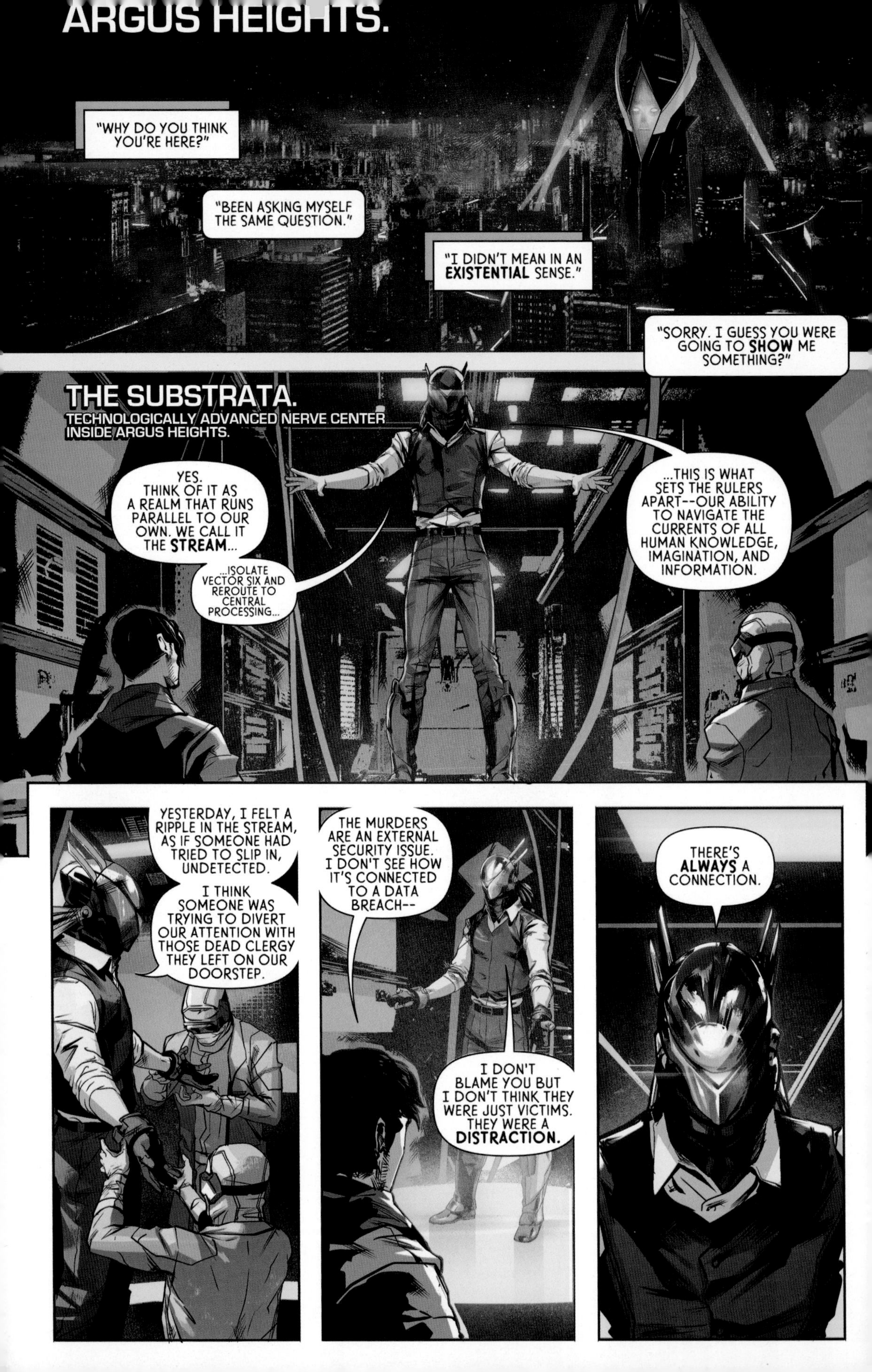
ARGUS HEIGHTS.
"WHY DO YOU THINK YOU'RE HERE?"
"BEEN ASKING MYSELF THE SAME QUESTION."
"I DIDN'T MEAN IN AN EXISTENTIAL SENSE."
"SORRY. I GUESS YOU WERE GOING TO SHOW ME SOMETHING?"
THE SUBSTRATA.
TECHNOLOGICALLY ADVANCED NERVE CENTER INSIDE ARGUS HEIGHTS.
YES. THINK OF IT AS A REALM THAT RUNS PARALLEL TO OUR OWN. WE CALL IT THE STREAM...
...ISOLATE VECTOR SIX AND REROUTE TO CENTRAL PROCESSING...
...THIS IS WHAT SETS THE RULERS APART--OUR ABILITY TO NAVIGATE THE CURRENTS OF ALL HUMAN KNOWLEDGE, IMAGINATION, AND INFORMATION.
YESTERDAY, I FELT A RIPPLE IN THE STREAM, AS IF SOMEONE HAD TRIED TO SLIP IN, UNDETECTED.
I THINK SOMEONE WAS TRYING TO DIVERT OUR ATTENTION WITH THOSE DEAD CLERGY THEY LEFT ON OUR DOORSTEP.
THE MURDERS ARE AN EXTERNAL SECURITY ISSUE. I DON'T SEE HOW IT'S CONNECTED TO A DATA BREACH--
I DON'T BLAME YOU BUT I DON'T THINK THEY WERE JUST VICTIMS. THEY WERE A DISTRACTION.
THERE'S ALWAYS A CONNECTION.

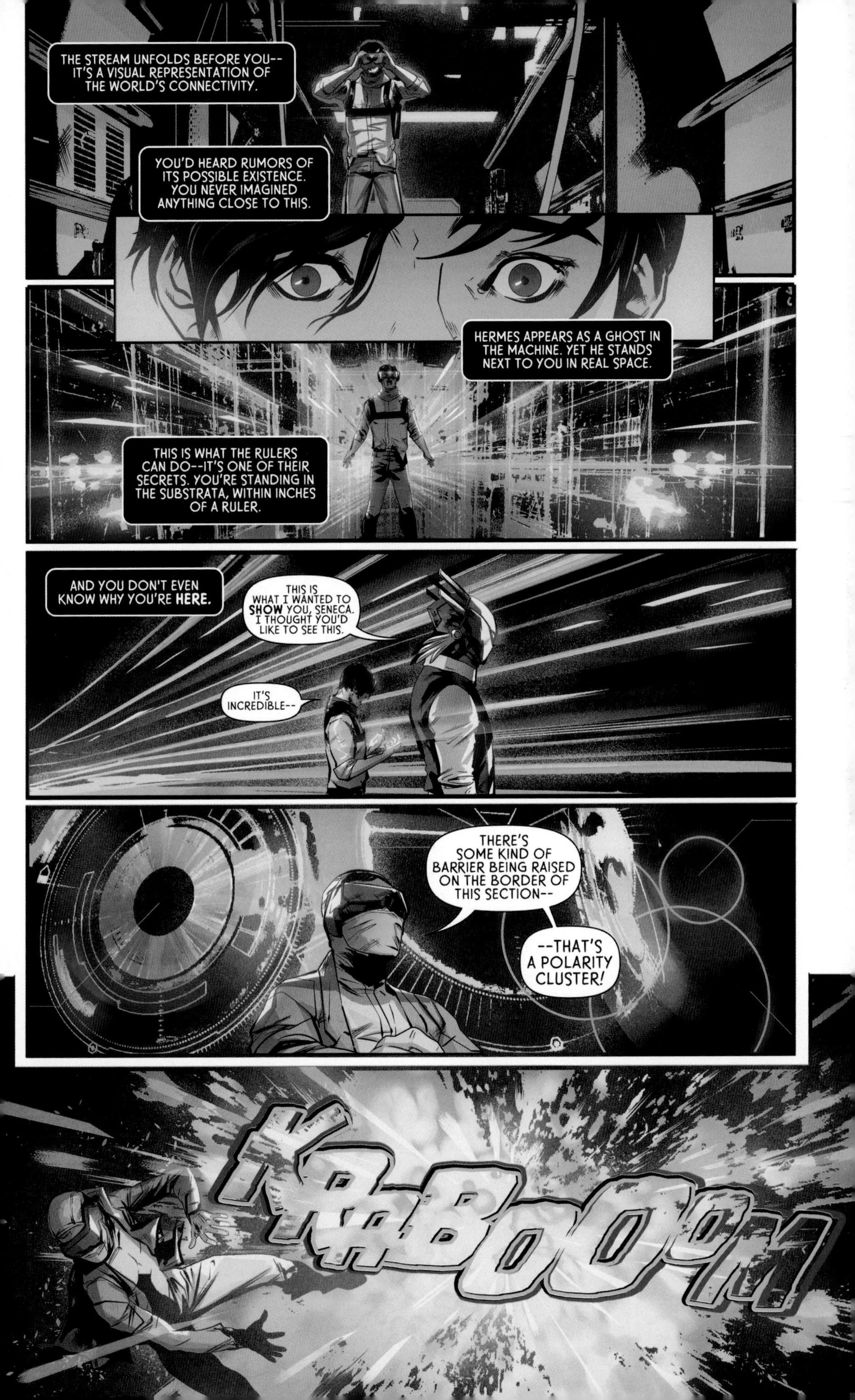
THE STREAM UNFOLDS BEFORE YOU-- IT'S A VISUAL REPRESENTATION OF THE WORLD'S CONNECTIVITY.
YOU'D HEARD RUMORS OF ITS POSSIBLE EXISTENCE. YOU NEVER IMAGINED ANYTHING CLOSE TO THIS.
HERMES APPEARS AS A GHOST IN THE MACHINE. YET HE STANDS NEXT TO YOU IN REAL SPACE.
THIS IS WHAT THE RULERS CAN DO--IT'S ONE OF THEIR SECRETS. YOU'RE STANDING IN THE SUBSTRATA, WITHIN INCHES OF A RULER.
AND YOU DON'T EVEN KNOW WHY YOU'RE **HERE.**
THIS IS WHAT I WANTED TO **SHOW** YOU, SENECA. I THOUGHT YOU'D LIKE TO SEE THIS.
IT'S INCREDIBLE--
THERE'S SOME KIND OF BARRIER BEING RAISED ON THE BORDER OF THIS SECTION--
--THAT'S A POLARITY CLUSTER!
KRABOOM

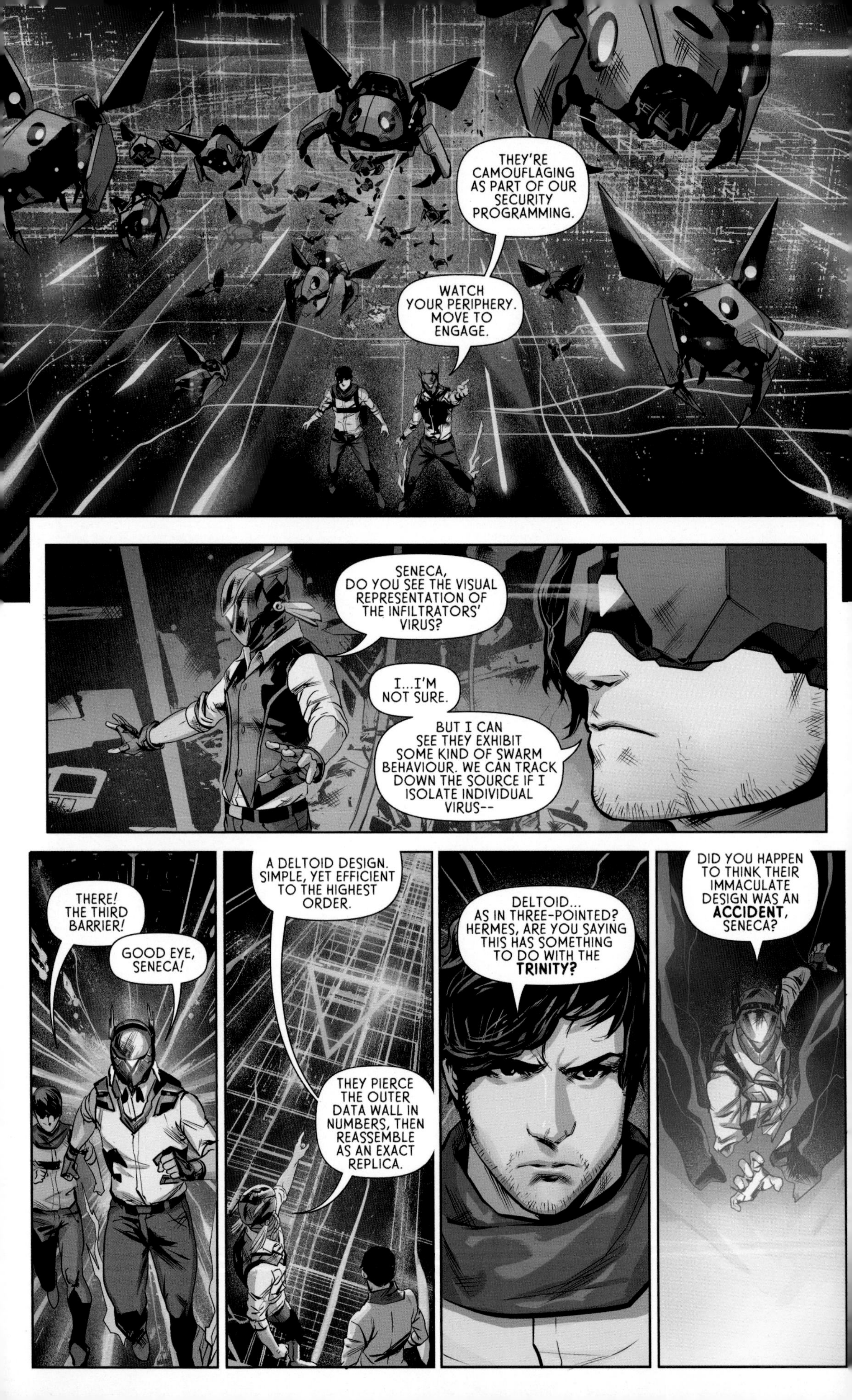
THEY'RE CAMOUFLAGING AS PART OF OUR SECURITY PROGRAMMING.
WATCH YOUR PERIPHERY. MOVE TO ENGAGE.
SENECA, DO YOU SEE THE VISUAL REPRESENTATION OF THE INFILTRATORS' VIRUS?
I...I'M NOT SURE.
BUT I CAN SEE THEY EXHIBIT SOME KIND OF SWARM BEHAVIOUR. WE CAN TRACK DOWN THE SOURCE IF I ISOLATE INDIVIDUAL VIRUS--
THERE! THE THIRD BARRIER!
GOOD EYE, SENECA!
A DELTOID DESIGN. SIMPLE, YET EFFICIENT TO THE HIGHEST ORDER.
THEY PIERCE THE OUTER DATA WALL IN NUMBERS, THEN REASSEMBLE AS AN EXACT REPLICA.
DELTOID... AS IN THREE-POINTED? HERMES, ARE YOU SAYING THIS HAS SOMETHING TO DO WITH THE **TRINITY?**
DID YOU HAPPEN TO THINK THEIR IMMACULATE DESIGN WAS AN **ACCIDENT**, SENECA?

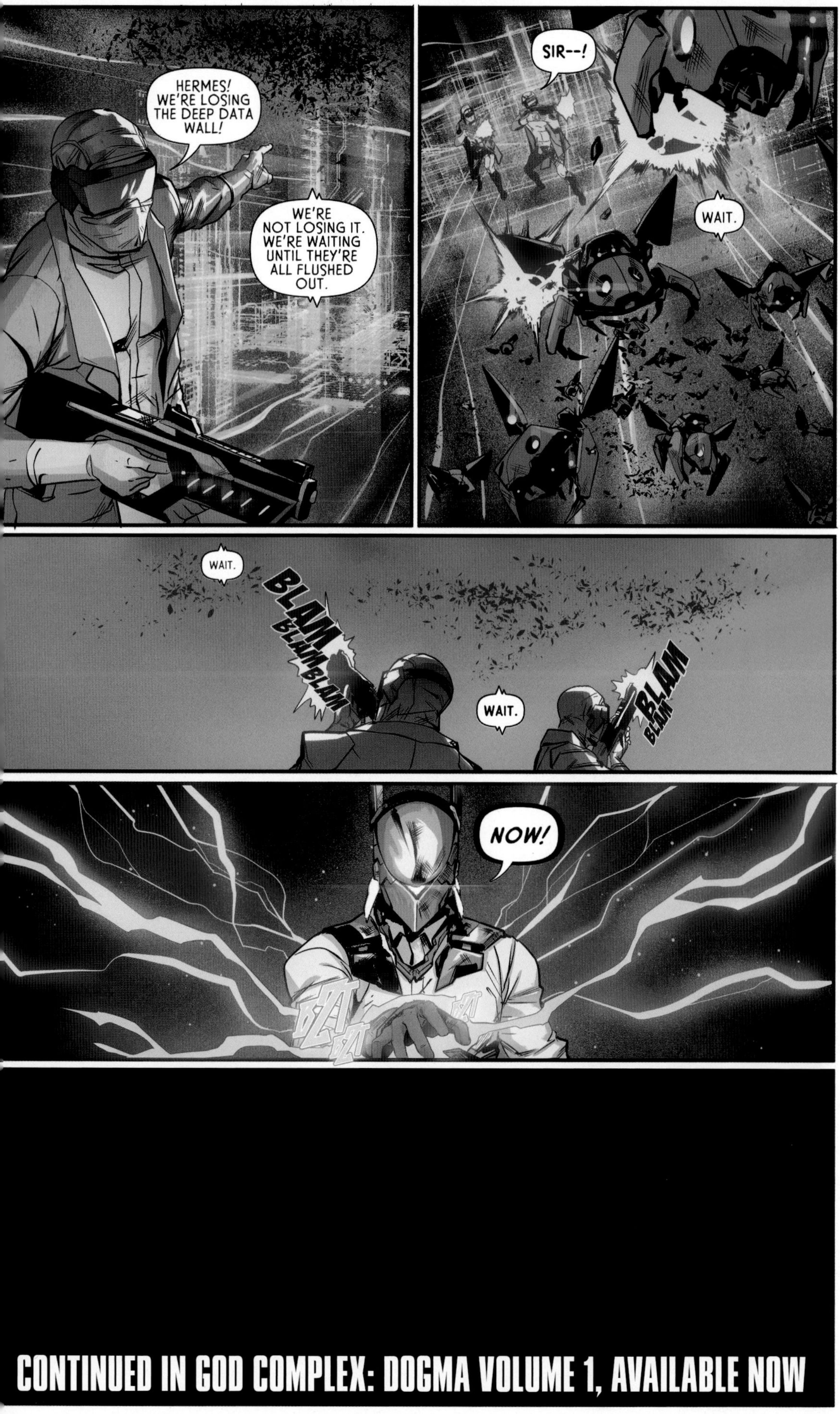
HERMES! WE'RE LOSING THE DEEP DATA WALL!
WE'RE NOT LOSING IT. WE'RE WAITING UNTIL THEY'RE ALL FLUSHED OUT.
SIR--!
WAIT.
WAIT.
BLAM BLAM BLAM
WAIT.
BLAM BLAM
NOW!

CONTINUED IN GOD COMPLEX: DOGMA VOLUME 1, AVAILABLE NOW

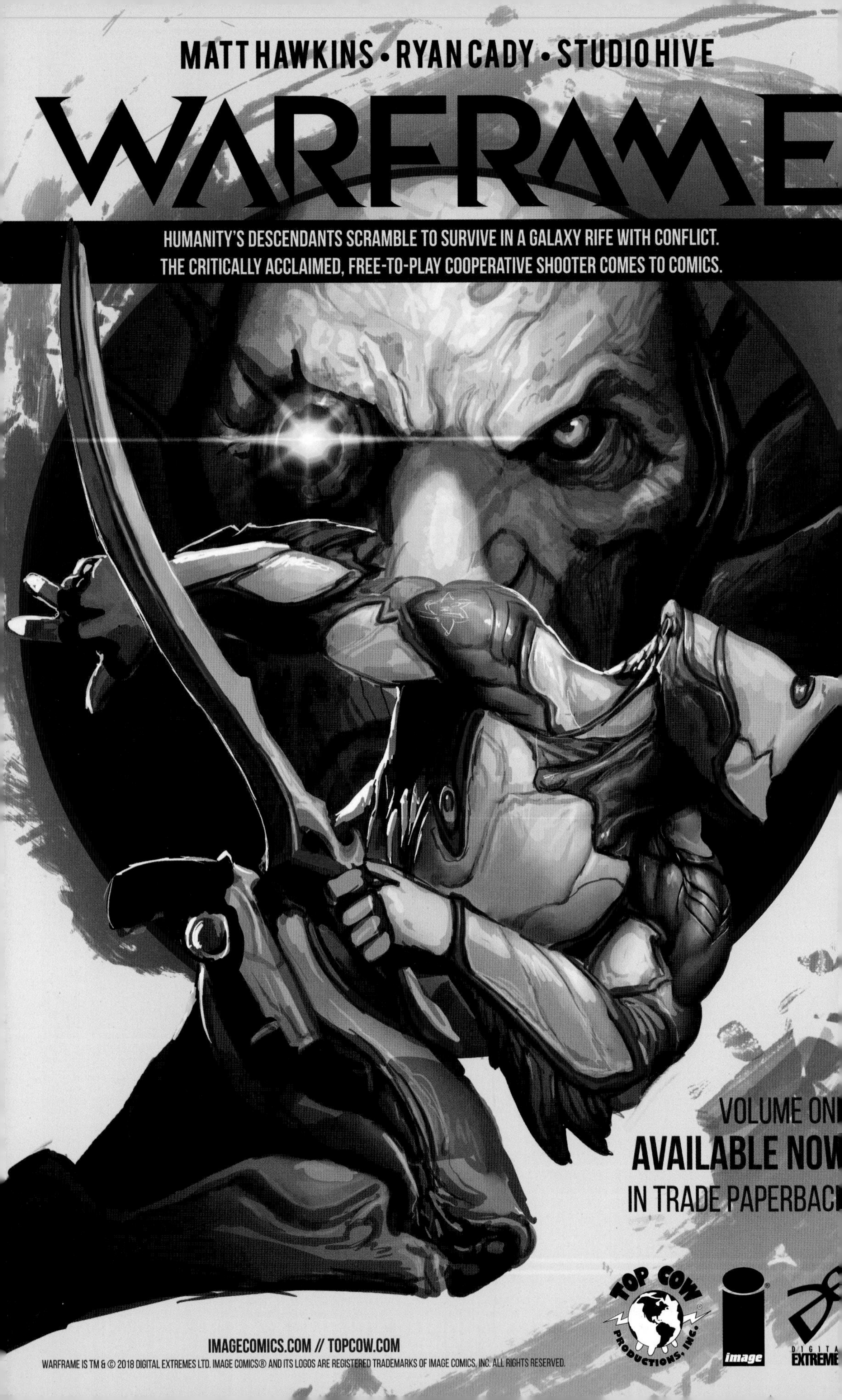

MATT HAWKINS • RYAN CADY • STUDIO HIVE
WARFRAME
HUMANITY'S DESCENDANTS SCRAMBLE TO SURVIVE IN A GALAXY RIFE WITH CONFLICT.
THE CRITICALLY ACCLAIMED, FREE-TO-PLAY COOPERATIVE SHOOTER COMES TO COMICS.
VOLUME ONE
AVAILABLE NOW
IN TRADE PAPERBACK
IMAGECOMICS.COM // TOPCOW.COM
WARFRAME IS TM & © 2018 DIGITAL EXTREMES LTD. IMAGE COMICS® AND ITS LOGOS ARE REGISTERED TRADEMARKS OF IMAGE COMICS, INC. ALL RIGHTS RESERVED.

The Top Cow essentials checklist:

IXth Generation, Volume 1
(ISBN: 978-1-63215-323-4)

Aphrodite IX: Rebirth Volume 1
(ISBN: 978-1-60706-828-0)

Artifacts Origins: First Born
(ISBN: 978-1-60706-506-7)

Blood Stain, Volume 1
(ISBN: 978-1-63215-544-3)

Cyber Force: Rebirth, Volume 1
(ISBN: 978-1-60706-671-2)

The Darkness: Origins, Volume 1
(ISBN: 978-1-60706-097-0)

Death Vigil, Volume 1
(ISBN: 978-1-63215-278-7)

Eclipse, Volume 1
(ISBN: 978-1-5343-0038-5)

Eden's Fall, Volume 1
(ISBN: 978-1-5343-0065-1)

Genius, Volume 1
(ISBN: 978-1-63215-223-7)

God Complex, Volume 1
(ISBN: 978-1-5343-0657-8)

Magdalena: Reformation
(ISBN: 978-1-5343-0238-9)

Port of Earth, Volume 1
(ISBN: 978-1-5343-0646-2)

Postal, Volume 1
(ISBN: 978-1-63215-342-5)

Rising Stars Compendium
(ISBN: 978-1-63215-246-6)

Romulus, Volume 1
(ISBN: 978-1-5343-0101-6)

Sunstone, Volume 1
(ISBN: 978-1-63215-212-1)

Symmetry, Volume 1
(ISBN: 978-1-63215-699-0)

The Tithe, Volume 1
(ISBN: 978-1-63215-324-1)

Think Tank, Volume 1
(ISBN: 978-1-60706-660-6)

Witchblade 2017, Volume 1
(ISBN: 978-1-5343-0685-1)

Witchblade: Borne Again, Volume 1
(ISBN: 978-1-63215-025-7)

For more ISBN and ordering information on our latest collections go to:
www.topcow.com
Ask your retailer about our catalogue of collected editions,
digests, and hard covers or check the listings at:
Barnes and Noble, Amazon.com,
and other fine retailers.

To find your nearest comic shop go to:
www.comicshoplocator.com